What We Need to Survive

ELENA JOHANSEN

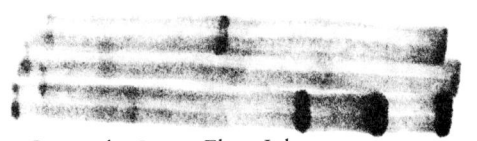

Copyright © 2015 Elena Johansen

All rights reserved.

Cover art by JD&J.

ISBN: 1517523729
ISBN-13: 978-1517523725

This is a work of fiction. Names, characters, places and incidents either are products of the author's imagination or are used fictitiously. Any resemblance to actual events or locales or persons, living or dead, is entirely coincidental.

For my husband

You're not Paul, and I'm not Nina, but if we ever have to face the end of the world together, you know I'm not leaving your side. I could never have done this without you.

CONTENTS

1	Cigarette Lighters	1
2	A Flashlight	9
3	A Blanket	14
4	Engines	19
5	Granola Bars	28
6	A Sliver of Soap	34
7	A Wristwatch	39
8	A Barrette	44
9	A Coil of Rope	50
10	Toothbrushes	60
11	A Knife	66
12	A Needle and Thread	72
13	Grave Markers	79
14	Bandages	86
15	Bed Sheets	92
16	Tweezers	99
17	A Sweater	103
18	A Fireplace	111
19	Whiskey	118
20	A Deck of Cards	127
21	A Pair of Scissors	131

CONTENTS

22	An Outhouse	139
23	Canned Peaches	143
24	Kitchen Chairs	152
25	A Silk Nightgown	158
26	Hiking Boots	164
27	A Piano	170
28	A Pair of Socks	175
29	Books	183
30	Glasses	187
31	Curtains	192
32	A Bench	198
33	Pillows	204
34	A Bed	211
35	Dirt	216
36	Candles	220
37	A Backpack	226
38	A Maple Tree	233
39	Shovels	238
40	Pens and Paper	243
41	A Truck	248

ACKNOWLEDGMENTS

As much as it feels like it sometimes, I did not do this alone, slaving away over a notebook in some dusty garret room, isolated from the world.

So I'd like to thank Rabecca, Christine, Ian, Tara, Matt, and Alice for reading the various stages of this beast and poking holes in the plot, shipping character combinations I didn't expect, and telling me what I did wrong (very important) and what I did right (very satisfying).

Publishing this would not have been possible without their help, and while I've thanked them all many times already, they deserve that and more. Seeing your name in print is neat, isn't it?

CHAPTER ONE
CIGARETTE LIGHTERS

August 23rd, 4:23 pm – Somewhere along US-36, Central Ohio

Paul kicked a rock out of his path, watching it bounce and skitter down the highway.

He saw no point in wasting breath on cursing the weather. One squall of rain caught him earlier in the day, forcing him into the cramped shelter of one of the abandoned cars dotting the road. But the boom of thunder in the distance worried him. He'd spent plenty of nights out in the open. Sleeping in the rain was miserable enough, but he imagined sleeping through a storm would be next to impossible.

He looked up, but thick forest on both sides of the highway hid all but the narrowest strip of sky. Blank, unbroken gray hovered above him. There was no way to judge how close the storm was, except for the unreliable system of counting Mississippis.

The closest building he remembered passing was at least half an hour behind him, maybe an hour. The closest town he'd left behind yesterday afternoon. Turning back might get him to shelter before the storm struck, if he hurried.

Or it might not. The road ahead curved away from him, and the trees could hide anything.

Paul kept moving forward, faster under the threat of rain.

Ten minutes later, he spied a gas station and picked up his pace even more.

As he got closer, the station didn't seem promising. Most of the windows gaped empty, broken down to their frames, and the front door hung askew on a broken hinge. The first fallen leaves of the season littered the parking lot. Shards of glass from the broken windows and random bits of trash lay scattered among them.

The rain started as Paul reached the edge of the parking lot. He sprinted for the cover of the roof protecting the pumps.

Hard-won caution kept him from dashing the rest of the way inside. Instead he approached the building with slow, deliberate steps, holding up his empty hands. "Hello in there!" he called. "Anybody home?"

There was no answer, but Paul remained wary. When he was a few yards from the open door, he stopped and called again. "Is anyone there? I ain't lookin' for trouble, just a place to get out of the rain."

A shuffling sound came from his right, and a movement that flickered in the corner of his eye. He turned toward it and saw a gun pointed in his direction. The gunman himself hid in the shadow of the empty window frame.

"Stay where you are!" the man shouted. His voice was deep and authoritative, the kind of voice that focused the attention of anyone who heard it. Paul didn't doubt it belonged to a man willing to shoot him, if necessary.

"No trouble," Paul repeated. "I was hopin' this place was empty, 'cause I'd rather be inside than out with a storm overhead. But if I ain't welcome, I'll move on."

"Stay right there, and give me a minute!"

Paul did as the man ordered, watching the gun in the window, which didn't move. He guessed the man was talking to someone inside, but he couldn't hear anything. While he waited, the rain grew heavier, pinging on the corrugated metal of the roofing like the highest notes played on a huge steel drum.

"You got any weapons?" the deep-voiced man called out.

"Just the knife on my belt," Paul answered. "No guns."

"You can wait out the storm with us in here, then be on your way. Sound reasonable?"

Paul lowered his hands. "Yeah, that's good." The gun disappeared from the window, and the knot of tension in Paul's chest loosened. He hadn't believed he was going to get shot, but he was relieved to be right.

Unless they were going to rob him the minute he walked in the door. But it was too late to run now. If they meant to take his supplies, then the man with the gun could shoot him in the back when he fled.

Best to play along.

A man with dark brown skin and chin-length dreadlocks appeared in the doorway. He was shorter than Paul, but that didn't mean he could be dismissed as a threat, since he was much more heavily muscled. His straight-backed posture and firm gaze shouted *military* to Paul. Or maybe *cop*. And he sported a holster on his belt. The man with the gun.

Unless there's more than one of 'em.

When Paul didn't move, he flashed a grin, wide and startlingly white. "Come on in," he said, beckoning with one hand. He stood aside to let Paul through.

The inside of the station wasn't in any better shape than the outside. The metal shelving units were empty, all the chocolate bars and potato chips gone. Glass-fronted refrigerators lined the back wall, but those were empty, too. At the counter, the cash register lay on its side, the drawer popped loose. Paul guessed that had happened in the first few days, when looters thought money still meant something. It hadn't taken long before that wasn't true anymore. Dark patches stained the white linoleum floor. Paul hoped they weren't blood. Though they probably were.

"I'm John," the man said. His voice sounded almost friendly, and Paul lifted his hand in automatic reaction to meet John's for a shake. He dropped it when he saw there was no hand offered.

"Paul." He settled for giving John a nod instead.

John turned and headed for an open space beyond the counter. Paul meant to follow, but he stopped short at the sight of a girl crouched under the window. She was small, her thin limbs folded in on themselves to take up as little space as possible. Her black hair was oddly uneven in length, not quite reaching her shoulders. Paul guessed it was growing out from whatever shorter style she'd had, before. Her wide eyes watched him with silent tension, like a fawn ready to bolt to safety.

Paul hadn't met many kids on the road, but most of them looked a lot like her. Frail and frightened, not ready to face what the world had become since the plague had ruined everything.

Before Paul could decide what to say to her—or even if he should say anything at all—she shot to her feet and followed John across the room. Her ill-fitting clothes didn't completely hide the curves of her body, and the swing of her hips was shocking and compelling at the same time. She wasn't a young girl at all. Her head wouldn't even reach Paul's shoulder, but she was a grown woman, right down to the angry toss of her hair.

But still frightened.

Paul let her have her distance from him. With any luck, the storm would pass before nightfall, leaving him time to move on and make camp somewhere else for the night. He'd shared makeshift shelter with strangers before, talked, and traded, but he never slept well. And it was no great leap to guess the woman didn't want him there.

Though she had let him in, at least. That was why she'd been at the window, Paul guessed—John had checked with her before giving Paul permission.

Lightning flashed outside. Paul counted four-Mississippi before the thunder rolled over the building. After the next strike, he counted three.

If the light were better, he could pass the time scribbling in his notebook. A half-formed song had haunted his thoughts for days, and he'd welcome a chance to jot down the lyrics. But it would be a waste of ink and paper trying to write by lightning flashes.

If the company were better, he could talk and see about some trading. He was running lower than he liked on food, though he had enough to see him through the next day or two. The towns on this stretch of the highway all seemed to be one or two days apart, so he expected to hit another one tomorrow. He could spend a day searching houses for supplies.

Glancing around the interior of the station, he wondered if there was a rack of local road maps. So far, he'd been navigating by the ones posted on the walls at rest stations. But it was too dark to see much of anything, except a weak glow from the far corner. Someone had lit a candle. He heard low voices talking. John's, he recognized. Another one, lighter and higher-pitched, he assumed was the woman's. But there was a third, too, higher still and squeaky.

Another flash of lightning drew Paul's attention back to the window. No need to introduce himself to the others if they were only company while the storm lasted. With nothing else to do, he cleared a space on the counter, sat on it, and watched the storm.

There was a light patter of footsteps. Paul turned just as someone reached out to touch his arm. "Hi."

"Hi," Paul replied.

The boy looked about nine or ten. His skin was almost the same deep brown shade as John's. The glow of the candlelight behind him traced the edges of his short corkscrew curls, giving them a faint golden sheen.

"Do you want to trade with us before we eat dinner?" he asked, half-polite and half-shy. "Maybe we have something different, if you're tired of what you got."

"Sure." Paul slid off the counter top and followed the boy over to the others.

John sat cross-legged with his back to one wall. "Aaron, I told you not to bother him."

Aaron shrugged as he settled beside John. "I just wanted to see if he had any different food we could trade for. I'm tired of peanut butter crackers."

In the corner, the woman sat with her knees drawn up before her. She flicked a glance at Paul but said nothing as he pulled off his pack and sat down several feet away.

"You might be in luck, then, Aaron," Paul said. "I've got some granola bars. The s'mores kind, I think."

Aaron gave him a big smile that was nearly identical to John's. Paul didn't want to leap to any conclusions based on the fact that they were both black, but they looked enough alike to be father and son. So far, they were acting like it.

Paul stole another glance at the woman as she stared into the candle flame, ignoring everything else. Her skin was a lighter golden brown, under the smudges of dirt. And despite the realization that she wasn't a child, she didn't look anywhere near old enough to be Aaron's mother. So who was she, and how did she end up with them?

The sound of a zipper snapped his thoughts back into focus—Aaron had a battered red backpack on the floor in front of him. He reached in and pulled out two packets of crackers.

Paul rifled through his own supplies and turned up two granola bars in exchange. He was about to ask what else they might want, open-ended, to see if he could draw the woman out at all. Before he could, he heard wet, squelching footsteps from the front of the building. He leaped to his feet, whirling to face the newcomers. Three of them, two women and a man, all middle-aged, all splattered with rain.

"Easy, Paul." John's voice was firm. "They're with us."

"If we'd known the rain would start so soon," the man said, "we could've just set these outside and let the storm fill them up." He had a large metal water bottle in each hand. One he passed to John, the other he set on the floor beside him as he sat down. "So you made a new friend while we were gone?"

A soft snort came from the corner, but John answered them without acknowledging it. "Just sharing the roof until the storm passes."

The man pulled off his baseball cap, ran a tanned hand through his salt-and-pepper hair, and smiled. "I don't blame you for not wanting to get rained on." He stuck out his other hand, which Paul shook briefly. "Mark."

"Paul."

"And this is my wife, Sarah," he went on as one of the women sat down on his other side. The rain plastered her short blond hair to her forehead, but she smiled too and passed the extra bottle she carried to Aaron.

"Nice to meet you, Paul," she said.

The final newcomer was still standing, looking down at Paul with a curious intensity. "Hello there." *Handsome,* Paul mentally tacked on, because that was the exact tone she used. Since she was staring, he did too.

She was tall, or maybe she only seemed tall because she was lean and angular. Her hair was a riot of messy red curls in dire need of a wash, but she was pretty, in a faded, tired sort of way. Before the plague hit, she must have been beautiful. Before her eyes grew ringed with dark circles and her cheeks hollowed out from lack of food. "I'm Alison."

Paul nodded. Alison tilted her head to the side for a moment, clearly waiting for more. When she didn't get it, she strode past him. Behind him, which made his shoulder blades itch before he realized she was going to the small woman's side.

Who still hadn't given her name. Someone would, though. Paul could be patient.

Alison leaned against the wall and tapped it twice with the extra bottle in her hand. The sound reminded Paul of a food dish being set on the floor for a pet. Without looking, the woman reached her hand up, palm flat, and Alison set the bottle on it. Neither of them said a word.

When Alison sat down between her and Paul, closer to him than he would have liked, he had to resist the urge to pull away. No sense in being rude if he was only here until the storm let up.

"So, Paul," Mark said with forced cheerfulness, "which way you headed?"

"East."

Mark's lips twisted behind his dark scruff of a beard, which hadn't gone as white as his hair yet. "Damn, us too. I was hoping you were coming from there, so we could get an idea what the road ahead was like."

Shaking his head, Paul said, "Sorry I can't be more help."

"Maybe you can," Sarah said. "Do you have anything to trade?"

With an easy smile, Paul asked, "What d'you need?"

Sarah pursed her lips as she thought, and the cuteness of the expression took years off her face. "Extra socks?" she asked, hopeful enough that Paul knew she needed them, but resigned enough that she didn't expect to get them.

Paul shook his head and turned to Mark.

"Smokes." Which earned him a light slap on the shoulder from his wife. "What, it's been weeks now!" But Paul's answer was another shake of his head.

John had Aaron seated in his lap and was finger-combing the boy's hair. "I'm not holding my breath that you've got any natural-hair care products. I'm more likely to get struck by lightning. Inside."

The dry, deadpan tone startled a laugh out of Paul. "I ain't even got anything for myself right now," he said, scratching at his dark blond hair. "I'm way overdue for a wash, and dunkin' my head in a river ain't the same. I'd shave it all off if electric razors were still a thing."

Mark gestured at him. "You've got a knife."

"I'd cut myself to ribbons. I think I'll keep bein' shaggy for now."

Aaron, sensing his turn, piped up. "Any books? I've read the one I have about a dozen times by now."

"Not much of a reader," Paul answered. "What book you got?"

"*Treasure Island*," Aaron said. "I like adventure stories."

Alison snorted. "You're living in one."

John gave her a narrow-eyed look over Aaron's head, but he didn't say anything.

"Pain killers."

The sharp and sudden request focused Paul's attention on its source, the unnamed woman. Gone was the frightened doe of a girl—now her eyes were hard and flat. "Half a bottle of aspirin," he offered. "What'll you give me for it?"

"All I've got to spare is food. Cheese crackers, chocolate bars, take your pick. Or a can of Red Bull, if you're afraid to sleep in here with us tonight and want to stay awake instead."

"Nina..." John said with more than a hint of warning in his voice.

So she's got a name after all.

"It's thunderstorm season," she said. "We've been lucky so far they haven't been worse, but this one's not going to pass over in an hour like you hope. We're going to be here overnight."

Alison hunched forward, elbows on her knees. "How do you know?"

"The weather here isn't much different from where I grew up," she answered with a slight shrug. "I lived with this every summer as a kid." She turned back to Paul. "Anyway, does that work for you?"

Medicine of any kind was valuable, even the common stuff like aspirin. Food was never a bad trade, but he doubted she had enough to spare. "You hurt?" he asked, stalling.

"Cramps," she answered shortly, and Paul suppressed a grin.

Any urge he'd felt to smile, though, disappeared when Alison spoke. "I'd think you'd be glad you're having them."

Paul found the bottle in his pack and rolled it across the floor toward Nina. It stopped at the toe of her boot, and she stared at it without speaking.

"Don't need any food," Paul said, though it wasn't strictly true. "I've got enough for myself for now. But since y'all were here first, I figure anything left in this place is yours, and I saw some lighters in the display on the counter. I'd be happy with a few of those. Seems like a good thing to have, and they might come in handy for trades down the line."

Off to his other side, John and Mark traded a stunned look—Paul guessed they hadn't noticed the lighters. Mark got up to retrieve them. "Let's see . . ." he said, counting. "If we each keep one for ourselves, that leaves six for you. Sound good?"

"Sure," Paul said. Mark brought them over to him, and out of the corner of his eye Paul watched Nina. She didn't reach out to take the aspirin until the lighters were in his hands. Mark distributed the rest of them while Nina swallowed a few pills with a swig from her water bottle. She noticed Paul watching and nodded at him.

He figured that was the closest she would come to thanking him, so he gave her a smile. Not the huge, dazzling grin that his mother had once told him would break hearts someday. Instead it was the small curve at the corners that his girlfriends, over the years, had all told him was sweet. He used the first one on women he wanted to impress—the second was usually reserved for the ones he was already close to. But the last thing he wanted to do was make Nina think he was attracted to her.

Even though he was. Illuminated by the candlelight, Paul could see she had beautiful eyes, big, vividly blue, and fringed with thick lashes. He had a pronounced weakness for women with gorgeous eyes.

But Paul could see Nina wasn't like some of the other women he'd met on the road in the aftermath of the plague. The ones just as lonely as he was, who were willing to trust him for the length of one night before they parted ways in the morning. He never looked back, and neither did they. There hadn't been many, and it had been weeks since the last time, so it was only natural he'd find himself falling in lust with someone.

Even if prying words out of that someone was a challenge.

Before the silence between them stretched on too long, Paul forced himself to look away. "Alison, you want anything?"

CHAPTER TWO
A FLASHLIGHT

August 23rd, 4:17 pm – The gas station

In the wake of that loaded question, Nina swallowed another snort. As if it weren't obvious what Alison wanted. If she scooted any closer to the stranger, she'd be in his lap.

Not that he wasn't handsome in an outdoorsy, Nordic kind of way, all cheekbones and lankiness wrapped up in blue plaid flannel. But he'd called himself shaggy, which was an accurate description. In the last ten minutes, he'd pushed his hair out of his eyes at least four times, with an unconscious grace that meant he didn't even realize he did it anymore. And his beard was patchy at best and needed a trim.

He probably hadn't had one, before.

Alison's voice brought her out of her sour musings. "Any spare clothing? I could use a new shirt."

Nina resisted the urge to hug herself like she was defending her own shirt from theft. Alison hadn't wanted to let her have it when they'd stumbled across the thrift shop three days ago. The shirt was too big for Nina and they shouldn't waste it on her, she'd said.

But Nina had nothing else to wear but a tight, thin t-shirt that was starting to go holey. The green canvas button-down was in the best condition of everything they turned up. John was adamant that the group give the best things to the person who needed them most, so Alison lost the debate. She'd ended up with two spare bras instead, which she'd shoved into her pack with a scowl.

Nina was happy not to have to deal with that particular item of clothing at all. How any woman could sleep in a bra was beyond her understanding.

"Best I can do is an undershirt," Paul was saying. "My spare. It's clean, I haven't worn it yet. Can't promise it will fit well. What'll you give me for it?"

But Alison shook her head. "I'll pass, I was hoping for something heavier. Thanks, anyway."

A crack of thunder sounded, so deafening the lightning strike might have been in the room with them. It emphasized the silence that fell after the unsuccessful trading session. It didn't escape Nina's notice that Paul hadn't asked for anything for himself, just in trade for what they wanted.

Though he was right about needing some shampoo. She just didn't have any to spare. Even if she did, he might not want to smell like strawberries. Or he might be practical enough not to care.

His silence on his own behalf, though, made her wonder what he carried that he felt so rich he didn't need to ask for anything.

"So," Mark began awkwardly. "You headed somewhere? Trying to find someone?"

Nina closed her eyes and leaned her head back against the wall. This stranger wouldn't be the first to pour out his troubles to this group, and she doubted he'd be the last, either. But she had no interest in listening.

With the storm raging around them, there wasn't anywhere she could go.

"Ain't got anyone left." He said it simply, not puppy-dog sad like he was angling for pity.

But Sarah would give it to him anyway, of course. "I'm sorry to hear that, Paul. We've all lost loved ones. I'm so grateful I still have Mark."

Though Nina kept her eyes shut, she could picture Sarah leaning into her husband, maybe giving his upper arm a squeeze. Because she'd seen it plenty of times over the last week. And turned away from it to give them their moments of privacy.

And to hide her envy.

Not that she wanted Mark himself, not in the slightest. Pot-bellied and gruff and awkward was not a combination Nina found appealing. But Sarah was the sweetest, happiest woman Nina had met in the months since the plague. Some of her happiness, at least, must be because she still had a husband to lean on and fuss over. They made such a perfect pair Nina couldn't imagine what either of them would be like without the other.

"And Alison," Sarah added a moment later.

There was a long pause. "Sisters?" Paul asked. Nina thought she could hear the raised eyebrow in his tone, which almost made her giggle.

"Old friends," Alison told him. "And neighbors. Three houses down for what, twenty years?"

"Twenty-one," Mark corrected. "You and Brett moved in just a few months after we did."

Nina felt a stab of pity for Alison then, in the glaring silence that followed. Sarah had let it slip once that Alison had been married, but Nina hadn't known her husband's name—she never talked about him.

Alison was probably the person in their strange little family who talked about herself the least. Except Nina herself. Mark told funny stories about his old friends, without displaying the slightest outward twinge of awareness that they were all gone. Sarah had a few of those stories, too, and plenty of hilarious tales about Mark himself. Even John told tales of Aaron as a kid, though usually not in his hearing. Aaron didn't like to be reminded he was ever younger and less capable than he was now.

Alison said little, and Nina even less.

No one rushed to fill the void in the conversation, which went on so long even Nina got uncomfortable. She pushed herself off the wall and stood. "I'm going to take a look around."

"In the dark?" Alison's voice was laced with sarcasm.

Nina responded by holding up her new lighter and wiggling it like she was teasing the other woman in a game of keep-away. Alison grunted.

Before Nina was two steps away from the group, she stopped short at the sound of Paul's voice. "I can do better, if you like." She turned back to see him pull a flashlight out of his backpack.

No wonder he hadn't asked for anything.

"Come on, then," she said. She wasn't about to ask to borrow it only to suffer the embarrassment of him saying no. Because who would trust something so valuable to someone he'd just met? If she wanted the light, she'd have to put up with his company to get it.

A cursory search of the shelves turned up the same result as earlier, when the group first found the place—empty. There hadn't been time before Paul showed up to investigate anything else. Now, in the back of the building she and Paul found a short hallway with one door at the end and one on either side.

"Emergency exit," Paul said, shining his light over the darkened sign. "Sometimes those things will run on battery power for weeks. For a while it was creepy, seein' red lights somewhere when everything else was out."

Nina was glad she hadn't run into that, but didn't bother to say so. "Speaking of batteries, how long are you willing to run that flashlight? Do you have any spares?"

"Nope, last set."

"Then let's find out what's behind door number one," she said, opening the door to their right.

The smell drifting out was faint but unpleasant. Paul leaned in and ran the beam around the room. "The bathroom. No bodies," he observed.

"But it looks like the toilet backed up a while ago." There were stains all over the seat and the floor around it, trailing down to the drain in the center of the room. "The most that's probably in there is some cheap toilet paper. I say skip it."

Paul shut the door. "Agreed."

The other door turned out to be a supply closet. Not much remained. Paul aimed the light over her shoulder so she could sort through the items on the shelves.

Most of the cleaning products she would have expected to find were gone. What was left was an odd mixture. A scrub brush for the toilet. A spray bottle half-full of something that smelled like bleach mixed with a cloying floral perfume. A few soft cloths, clean and dry, which were a good find—she passed them back to Paul. A shoe box with random pieces of metal and plastic. Some of them were unidentifiable, but Nina recognized a few things. Extra brackets for the shelves, spare nozzles for the self-serve drink station, and half a package of zip ties. She handed Paul the ties, too, and left the rest.

On the bottom shelf, there was a tool box. "Jackpot," Paul said.

"You got a thing for tools?"

"Bound to be useful stuff in there." He didn't seem bothered by her crack at him. "If that's all, we should take the box over and sort it out with everyone."

She swiveled to look up at him and got half-blinded by the flashlight. When she squinted, he pointed it away from her. "I thought you said everything here was ours since we were here first. What makes you think you get anything?"

The light clicked off, leaving them both in blackness that seemed darker than before they started. "You got any batteries?"

She tried to stifle a sigh and only half-succeeded. "Point taken."

Before Paul could reply, lightning blazed through the sky outside, outlining his body in a flare of incandescence. Nina flinched. Thunderstorms didn't spook her, but strangers standing too close to her in the dark did.

He switched the beam back on and pointed it at the floor, leading her back through the shelving units to the others. If he'd noticed her unease, he made no comment. In fact, through the whole sorting and dividing process, he said little, and nothing at all to her for the rest of the night. Nina's prediction about the storm turned out to be true. After a meager dinner, John assigned the watch rotation, and everyone spread out their blankets.

Nina curled up on top of hers with her pack for a pillow, as she did every night. Paul didn't have a blanket, but he stretched out away from the rest of them, lying between two sets of shelves.

All Nina could see of him were the worn soles of his giant hiking boots. A tear was starting across the middle of the left one. He should have asked for boots, but he hadn't, because it must have been obvious no one would have those to spare. Not for themselves, even, let alone in his size, whatever it must be with those massive feet. Looking up at him earlier, when he was standing so close, was like trying to see the top floor of a skyscraper from the sidewalk below it. With the flashlight on, she might as well have been staring at the sun.

Watching his boots, she kept waiting for them to move, for him to stand up, to do something. What, she didn't know. He was a fool or an idiot to trust them. He had food and a flashlight and meds and who knew what all else in his pack. He was such an easy target, even with a knife. Nina had a knife, too. So did everyone else but Aaron. John had a gun. Why wasn't Paul afraid they were going to rob him?

If she kept looking at him, she'd keep thinking about him, so she turned away. Instead she watched Sarah watch the storm through the broken windows until she finally fell asleep.

CHAPTER THREE
A BLANKET

August 24th, 5:15 am – The gas station

A hand came down on Paul's shoulder, and he struggled out of the depths of his dream. He couldn't remember any details, only the feeling of warm skin against his. Then the insistent stirring of his body made him realize what kind of dream he'd been having, and he groaned.

There was a soft giggle near his ear. A woman's voice. A woman's hand. She was kneeling or crouching over him from behind. There was no light—the candle had burned down, or someone blew it out. The giggle didn't identify her, because Paul hadn't heard any of the women laugh.

Her other hand touched one side of his face, brushing his hair back, caressing his cheek. "I could see that you wanted me," she whispered.

For a single heartbeat, Paul pictured blue eyes and soft, dark hair hanging loose. He imagined it coming down to curtain his face as she kissed him. The kiss was both satisfying and strange, each of them upside-down to the other. He sucked and nipped at her bottom lip, and she did the same to his. Encouraged by her response, he lifted both hands to hold her head.

But he groaned again when his fingers wound through tangled curls instead of the fine, straight hair he'd been hoping for.

Alison.

She misinterpreted the sound, though, and broke off the kiss with another soft laugh. "Hungry, are you? Me too. Come on, I've got my blanket set up outside." There was a rustle of clothing as she stood and headed for the door.

Paul wrestled with the decision as he listened to the faint night sounds of the woods. No thunder, no rain—the storm was finally over.

It wasn't Alison he wanted. It wasn't fair to either of them to pretend otherwise. Paul always tried to be an honest man, and this was far from honest.

But he was leaving in the morning, and he'd never see Alison again. Nina, either. What harm could it do? Comfort of any kind was in short supply these days. It seemed foolish to turn down any he was offered.

And his last passing encounter with a woman had been almost two months ago. In the first days of the aftermath, he'd seen more people, so there had been more chances. This one was the first in what felt like a long time.

He got to his feet and followed her out.

In the wake of the storm, the air was cool and damp. The moon cast enough light to show Alison heading to the edge of the trees. She had spread her blanket out in a tiny clearing, free of bits of twig and fallen branches. The breeze shivered the leaves above them, sending straggling raindrops into Paul's hair.

Part of him recoiled at the preparations she'd made. He felt like an animal letting itself be led into the trap.

The rest of him just wanted another kiss, and another, and everything that followed.

Alison sank to her knees on the blanket. The moonlight reflected in her eyes, turning them silver, before Paul's shadow fell over her. She reached for his hand and pulled him to her side.

Usually for Paul, there was an awkward moment when he first took a new lover. The moment when he wasn't sure what he should do, what she wanted from him. He'd smile his sweet smile and ask a shy, disarming question or two. He'd skim his fingertips down her arm and wait for her to answer.

Alison skipped all that by grabbing his ass with both hands, grinding her hips against him, and devouring his mouth with an aggressive kiss.

Well, it was clear she wasn't looking for romance, at least, and probably not even any real tenderness. Paul lowered his expectations, figuring this was going to be nothing more than a hurried, impersonal romp that got him relief and nothing more. He wasn't looking for love, he knew better than that. But sometimes, he found a woman who was willing to take it a little slower, a little sweeter.

Not Alison, though. Before he could do more than frame her face in his hands, she was tugging at his clothing. She had his shirt unbuttoned and off his shoulders before he even started to think of undressing her. His undershirt was over his head a few heartbeats later. She bent her head to lave one of his nipples with her tongue. It felt surprisingly good, drawing a moan from him. She laughed and pushed him flat onto his back on the blanket, settling herself astride his hips.

He didn't mind when a woman wanted to be in control, but something about that laugh set his teeth on edge.

She leaned down to lick his chest and suck on his nipple again, wriggling her body against his trapped erection. He reached up to start in on her clothes, but she batted his hands away with another laugh.

Fine.

She lifted her hips and reached with one hand for the fly of his jeans. He had a moment to admire her dexterity at getting it undone with such speed before her hand wrapped around him, stroking as much as his clothing allowed. The pleasure of her touch flowed through him, relaxing muscles he hadn't even realized were tense, easing the worries he had about whether he should be doing this.

But then her hand moved lower, squeezing his balls tightly, and at the same time, she bit his nipple, hard.

Not fine.

He bolted upright, collecting both her wrists in a solid grip and trapping her hands between their bodies. She let out a gasp, but in the shadows he couldn't read her expression—he couldn't tell if she was excited by his sudden display of strength, or afraid of it. "No," he said. "That's not what I want."

"You're not going to be my good boy, Paul?" she whispered. "I promise you won't regret it."

"I don't like it rough, and I ain't nobody's plaything," he answered as she tested his hold on her. "If this is how it's gonna be, then it's over right now."

"Come on, pretty boy, you're too lonely to say no to me," she crooned, giving up her token struggle. "You'll let me do whatever I want, and you'll thank me for it when I'm through."

He shoved her off him, not caring that she landed hard on her side with a little cry. "No, I won't," he insisted, standing up and setting his clothes back to rights. "We're done."

As he strode away, she called out to him. "Fine, I don't need you anyway!" But the defiance in her tone didn't completely mask the frustration, or the bitterness.

Paul was tempted to grab his pack and leave right away—there was moonlight enough to see the road, to walk safely, if he was careful. But he didn't want to worry the others when they woke in the morning. He didn't want them to think something had happened to him, even though something had. He didn't want them to think he was a thief, either, and had somehow made off with their stuff in the night. He could imagine each of them checking their packs, making an inventory, and didn't want to cause them the trouble. Alison wouldn't make a scene, not inside, not in front of the others. He'd be safe from her spite if he stayed with the group.

He lay back down in the spot he'd chosen, far enough from the others to seem unthreatening. He wanted to get back to sleep. But between his frustrated desire and the nagging regret over having gone with Alison in the first place, his thoughts wouldn't settle.

Alison waited more than a half hour before she came back. She laid her blanket out, then checked on each of the sleepers. Paul closed his eyes and mimicked their deep, even breathing to fool her. When she'd finished her round, she hopped up to sit on the counter, staring out the broken windows.

Paul had wondered, listening for her return, if she was giving him time to fall asleep so she wouldn't have to face him immediately. The other possibility was that she was out there getting herself off instead. Either, or both. Didn't really matter.

It occurred to Paul, before she came back, that he could do the same—but despite his body's insistence, he wasn't in the mood. Alison's aggressive lust had soured him. He didn't want that kind of poison touching his fantasies. After a while, Alison left again, maybe to circle the building to check for dangers, maybe to relieve herself. While she was gone, Paul sat up and tried to reshape his pack into a better pillow. He lay back down, wishing he'd never tried to take shelter here at all.

But he thought of Aaron's smile when he traded the boy new food.

He thought of Nina, her face grave as she nodded, thanking him for the aspirin.

Then he remembered the brief look of terror on Nina's face before they'd rejoined the others after their search. He hadn't meant to frighten her, but he had, just by being there.

He'd been stupid to think, even for a second, that she could have been the one to kiss him in the darkness.

Maybe his luck would be better the next time he met up with anybody. Maybe he'd find the comfort and companionship he craved, someone he could trust, someone who trusted him.

Someone he could stay with.

As bad as the night had been, by dawn, he was feeling almost optimistic again. He'd say a quick goodbye and be on his way. Find some food in the next town tomorrow, maybe a new pair of boots, and keep going until he ran across more people.

Paul reached back to prod his pack again, settling his head more comfortably, and closed his eyes to shut out the first faint traces of light from the windows. He was used to getting up with the sun, but maybe the others weren't. Maybe he could sleep in a little today.

Then he heard the engines in the distance.

CHAPTER FOUR
ENGINES

August 24th, 6:12 am – The gas station

Nina woke up disoriented and tense, not sure if she was still dreaming.

She struggled to slow her panicked breathing, trying to listen for the sound she wasn't sure if she had heard, or only dreamed. She sat up and looked for the others. The shadows were deep in their corner, tucked away in the back of the station, but she saw the dim shapes of them lying on their blankets, still asleep.

Except for one. Alison. Nina tried to recall last night's conversation about dividing the watches, but all she remembered was Sarah had taken the first one. The last one could have been Alison's, but if it was, where was she?

Then Nina remembered Paul. She looked over to find him sitting up, leaning forward to see past the shelves he had slept between. She followed his gaze out the windows to the uniform, blank grayness of a foggy morning.

"Where's Alison?" she asked in a whisper.

"Don't know," he answered in kind. "Call of nature, maybe."

"What woke you?"

"Same thing as you, I expect. You hear the engines, too?"

Nina wanted to curse. "I was hoping I only dreamed that."

"Time to go, then," he said, standing up. She expected to see him shrug his pack on and head out the door within seconds. Instead, he looked down at her. "Wake the others, will you? They don't know me yet, I don't want to startle 'em. Be quick, though. I'll see if I can find Alison."

Nina gaped at him as he started for the door, his pack left behind. She couldn't think of anything he could have said that would have shocked her more. "Wait!"

He turned back and crouched near her. "What?"

Now that she had his attention, there didn't seem to be a way to express her confusion, at least not all of it. She settled on the simplest piece. "Why aren't you running? You don't owe us anything. You could be half a mile from here before the rest of us are all up and moving in the same direction."

Paul shook his head. "Now's not the best time, Nina. Wake them up, and I'll find Alison," he repeated. Then he was gone.

She stared after him for few heartbeats before Mark stirred in his sleep. The movement pulled Nina out of her reverie. She gripped his shoulder and shook him awake. "Engines," she whispered as he groaned and rolled over.

"Shit!" he hissed, but he was already reaching out to wake up his wife.

Nina crept past them toward John and Aaron. "John!" she said, taking hold of his leg. She knew better than to wake him up from any closer, where he could reach her with his hands. His eternal combat readiness made him dangerous when he was surprised. "John, wake up, now!"

John bolted upright and raised his arms in a defensive pose, scanning for the threat. When he saw Nina, he relaxed a fraction. "What is it?"

"Listen," she whispered. "Engines."

"Shit," John spat out, sounding so much like Mark had a moment ago that she almost giggled. He glanced down to see Aaron still asleep beside him, then to his other side where Mark and Sarah were gathering their blankets together. "Alison? Paul?"

"Alison wasn't here when I woke up," Nina answered. "Paul was already awake, though, and he told me to wake everyone while he went looking for her. Let's hope she just ducked outside to pee."

John listened to her report, then to the not-quite-silence outside. If he was surprised Paul had stuck around to help, he didn't waste time commenting on it. "They don't sound too close yet, probably going slow because of the fog. If we're quick, we can make it out the back before they get here. Go up front and be our lookout for a minute, see if you can spot Paul or Alison. If you do, wave them around to the back of the building. I'll get everyone together at the back door."

Nina crossed to the windows and crouched underneath one of the them, as she had the night before when John called her over. This morning, though, she wasn't weighing in on a new arrival. Now she searched for signs of life in the fog, whether it was Alison or Paul, or the headlights of an approaching vehicle.

There was a chance whoever headed their way was friendly. A chance. But in Nina's experience, anyone who still had a car that ran and enough gas to drive it this long after everything fell apart also had enough firepower to defend it. And to take whatever else they might want. Nina shivered at the thought.

As she listened to John giving quiet instructions, she scanned the tree line for Alison and Paul. There was no good reason for Alison to have gone far from the station. Nina wondered why she wasn't back yet on her own, even if Paul hadn't found her. She hoped they'd appear before the owners of the engines did, and worried about what would happen if they didn't.

Just before Nina was about to give up her lookout position, Paul came striding through the fog on her left. Alison followed a step behind. In the dim gray light, Nina couldn't be sure, but Alison seemed flushed, and Paul's expression was grim. Nina leaned out of the window, careful of the broken glass, and waved one arm to get their attention. They both froze. Nina pointed at them, then swept her hand around, trying to show them they should meet up with the group at the back door. Paul nodded once and turned to follow her instructions. Alison hesitated before doing the same.

Her job done, Nina was about to join the others, but she saw movement on the road. First one set of headlights came into view, then a second. "They're here," she called out softly. "Just pulling in."

"We're ready," John answered. "Let's go."

Nina darted away from the window, as fast as she could while staying low, and retrieved her things. John had Mark, Sarah, and Aaron gathered next to the restroom. John held an extra pack Nina recognized as Alison's. Mark had another one, Paul's.

"They're headed around back," Nina told John, nodding at the pack.

"Good. Out we go."

They moved to the fire exit. "It's got an alarm," Mark said. "That won't still go off without power, right?"

"I don't think so," John answered. "Even if it does, it's too late to get out the front. Just be ready to run."

"Can we hide?" Sarah asked. "If they're here checking for gas, maybe they won't bother coming inside."

Mark shook his head. "No, honey, even if they don't expect to find much, they'll come in. This place is pretty well looted, but Paul noticed the lighters, right? They'll want to be sure there's nothing here before they move on."

"We're going to have to risk it." John's expression was grave, but it softened as he wrapped his free arm around his son's shoulders. "You ready, little man?"

Aaron smiled, but his voice shook when he answered. "Yeah, but I don't know how fast I can go."

"That's okay. We're going to try sneaking out the fire exit, but if the alarm goes off, Mark is going to pick you up and carry you while he runs." John glanced at Mark, who nodded. Nina held her hands out to take Paul's pack, since Mark couldn't manage both it and Aaron, if he needed to. "Mark's legs are a lot longer than yours, so we'll be faster that way. I'm going to be right behind you, making sure nobody follows. If we get separated, Mark's going to keep you safe until I find you, so behave yourself and do what he says just like you would for me. You got that, son?"

"Yeah, Dad," Aaron answered. "I can do that."

Nina understood Aaron needed the coaching to keep him calm, but she couldn't help feeling like this was taking time they didn't have to spare. How long would it take to check if the pumps still worked? Whether they did or not, it wouldn't be long before they'd come inside to scavenge whatever wasn't already gone. "Ready?" she asked, before anyone could say anything else. Everyone nodded at her, so she stood up and pressed on the security bar to open the door.

Silence.

They all slipped through one at a time, John going last and easing the door shut behind them. Paul and Alison were waiting on the other side. Nina shrugged Paul's pack off her shoulder and handed it to him while John set out the escape plan.

"All right." His tone was clipped but quiet. "Single file, except Mark and Aaron together at the front. I'll cover us at the rear. Stay low and keep the person ahead of you in sight."

There was no fence around the back of the building, which was more luck than Nina expected. There was only a small strip of asphalt where the dumpsters sat. After a few yards it gave way to a waving field of tall grass, overgrown from going all summer without being mowed. Mark moved forward, holding Aaron's hand. Once they crossed into the field, the grass was higher than the boy's head, almost to Mark's shoulder. Alison followed a moment later.

Watching them disappear into the fog, Nina felt a trace of the same panic she'd felt when she woke up. The grass was tall enough to hide her from any pursuers, but it would also make keeping track of each other difficult. If Mark and Aaron got separated, Aaron could easily get lost, and Nina wasn't much so much bigger that she wasn't worried for herself.

Paul went next. Tall as he was, he crouched low enough that Nina could only see the top of his head. She sprang forward, taking her place in line. She had the best chance of not getting lost if she followed the person who was easiest to see.

When she crossed into the grass, she barely had to duck at all. It was damp with dew, but it made no noise as she passed through it, pushing handfuls out of her way to keep Paul's blue shirt in sight.

The field hadn't seemed big looking out from the gas station, but crossing it seemed to take forever. Nina kept calm, but she dreaded someone coming around the corner of the building and spotting one of them. There was nothing she could do but keep moving forward. Or what she hoped was forward. toward the trees, at least.

She steadied her breathing, kept pushing grass stalks out of the way, and concentrated on putting one foot in front of the other. Before her anxiety had time to ratchet up again, she reached the trees and saw Paul a few yards away, under the shadow of the branches.

He turned and saw her. "Good," he said. "Now we wait."

"Where are the others?"

"Don't know," he said, shifting his weight from one foot to the other. "I lost Alison partway across."

"I was following you, and you weren't following them?"

Before Paul could reply to her quietly furious accusation, John appeared, threading his way through the trees toward them. "Just the two of you?"

Nina fixed Paul with a glare as he nodded at John. "I lost Alison."

"Where's Sarah, though? She was behind you, Nina."

"We've only been here a minute," Nina said. "Did you pass her, somehow?"

"I must have. Dammit!"

Nina flinched at John's sudden anger. She moved closer to the edge of the field, chose a tree with a convenient low-hanging branch, and pulled herself up into it.

"Nina!" Paul hissed as she clambered from branch to branch, gaining height. "What are you doing?"

"Trying to see who's still out there." She found a branch about twelve feet up that was solid, relatively straight, and pointed in the right direction. Once she settled herself on it, she inched forward until she was just behind the outer screen of leaves. She could push one offshoot branch to the side for an unobstructed view, and let it snap back if she needed cover. It was an ideal spot, and for the second time that morning, Nina felt like she'd had some luck tossed her way.

"You're gonna fall and break your neck!" Paul said.

"Shh!" Nina answered. "I'll be fine."

The eastern sky was starting to lighten from leaden gray to the clear, pale yellow of morning sunlight. The fog seemed thinner already, patchy in spots.

Like Paul's beard. Nina stifled a sudden urge to giggle.

"Well, d'you see anything?" Paul demanded.

Nina scanned the field. There was one section of grass waving out of sync with the breeze, and it was creeping forward. "There's someone still out there. I can't see who it is, just where the grass is moving. But it's close, they'll be right on top of us soon."

"It must be Sarah," John said. "When she gets here, we'll go find the others. They can't be far."

A sliver of sun peeked out from the clouds and set the last tendrils of fog aglow for a moment before they vanished completely. Nina blinked a few times to clear her eyes of the afterimages. When she focused again, there was a man coming around the back corner of the building. She bit her lip to hold in a curse. It was a race, now, for Sarah to reach them before the man spotted her.

Or Nina.

She eased the bent branch back into place. "Stay quiet," she called down as softly as she thought she could while still being heard. "There's a man checking the back of the station."

"Did he see you?" John asked.

"I don't think so. He wasn't looking this way. But I'm coming down."

Nina swung down to hang from her branch, then used the others like monkey bars until she reached the lowest one again. She noticed Paul watching her with a critical eye. Remembering his comment earlier about breaking her neck, she expected him to make another, but he didn't. He took half a step forward as she dropped the last few feet to land safely on the ground, his hands outstretched to steady her if she fell. She didn't need him to, because she didn't fall, but she could admit to herself the gesture was kind.

Which only made her wonder again why he was still here. He could circle back to the road and be on his way inside of ten minutes. He didn't need them.

Before she could voice any of those thoughts, Sarah crossed into the trees, stumbling and crying. Nina moved toward her, but John was there first, setting his big hands on her shoulders.

Sarah reached up to grip his arms, her words tumbling out in a nervous babble. "I got lost, I couldn't see Nina, I couldn't see anyone, I couldn't see..."

"Shh, Sarah," John said. "It's okay, we're here."

"Mark?"

John dropped his hands and took a step back. "Now that you're here, we can go find the others." He looked to Paul while Sarah wiped her eyes dry. "When you lost sight of Alison, was she drifting right, or left?"

"Left, maybe," he said after a moment's hesitation. "It happened so fast."

"It's all right. We'll try that way first." John turned and started picking his way through the trees.

The others followed him along the tree line, just far enough in to keep under cover of the forest. None of them were particularly quiet as they moved. The sounds of snapping twigs and rustling fallen leaves didn't carry far enough to matter. What no one did, though Nina would have bet they were all tempted to do, was shout for their missing companions. The three of them couldn't have been far away, so they would hear it, but then, so might the man on the other side of the field.

After five minutes of quiet, careful searching, Nina spotted Aaron's red backpack. At least, she hoped that was the flash of color she saw off to her right. "Over here," she said.

John joined her, then looked down at her with a wide grin. "That's my boy, all right. Let's go."

Sarah broke rank first, dashing past John to throw herself at Mark, though she at least managed not to shout his name. Mark let go of Aaron's hand to hug his wife, and Aaron gave them all a huge smile as he dashed forward. John sank down on one knee and embraced his son.

Nina watched the happy reunion for a moment before glancing at the others. Alison drifted a few paces away and stood with her back to the group, arms crossed, guarding them on the gas station side. Paul was hanging back with a wistful look on his face.

When John finally let go of his son, he faced Paul. "Thank you," he said, holding out his hand. "Nina told me how you helped us. You could have left without us."

Paul came forward and took it, returning John's firm shake. "No, don't think I could have," he answered. Then he stepped back. "Nice to meet you," he said, addressing everyone. "Good luck on the road ahead."

He turned to go, but before he took three steps, Sarah called out to him. "Wait!"

John shushed her, but Paul twisted to look over his shoulder. His wistful look was back, stronger, almost like longing.

Sarah offered him a warm smile. "You can come with us, if you like," she said.

Nina felt a cold hand squeeze her heart. She wanted to object, but no one spoke, and she couldn't find the words.

"Y'all don't want to talk this over before you offer?" Paul asked, coming back to them.

"You could have left without us," John repeated. "We might not have gotten away at all."

Paul shook his head. "Nina heard them, too. She would've gotten you out in time."

"But you came and found me, when you didn't have to," Alison said, though it came out through gritted teeth.

"You would've run, and been fine," he replied.

"Why *didn't* you leave?" Nina demanded. He hadn't answered her the first time, and the question had been circling through her mind ever since.

He scratched at the back of his head with one hand. "Didn't seem right to abandon the people who shared their fire with you."

Alison snorted. "Not much of a fire," she said over her shoulder

"You gave what you had."

"No, you traded for it," Nina protested. "We didn't give you anything."

"The company, then. It's been awhile since I had anyone to talk to."

"Then stay with us," Sarah said in a firm tone.

He opened his mouth to speak, to give his answer, his eyes flicking back and forth between them—but then he looked squarely at Nina and seemed to change his mind. "They didn't ask you first this time," he said, and a wash of heat ran over her face. "But I will. I'm inclined to say yes, but if you can't abide me here, then I'm gone. No argument and no hard feelings."

Nina met his eyes, and he didn't look away. Before, she hadn't been close enough, or the light hadn't been good enough, to tell what color they were. Now he stood in a patch of sunlight, looking down at her. She could see his eyes were a striking shade of green, deep as moss around the edges but flecked with gold in the center. The intensity of his expression told her he knew she was uncomfortable with him. And he was offering her a way out.

She wanted to tell him to go, but that was stupid and selfish. In less than a day, he'd shown he was observant, quick-witted, and helpful. He'd been willing to risk his own safety by throwing his lot in with the group instead of striking out alone again. And if that weren't enough in his favor, he was capable of giving orders when he had to—there had been no hesitation when he told Nina what to do—but perfectly willing to follow them, too. Nina had no reason to turn him away. No good reason, at least.

All she had to say was no. She didn't even have to explain herself. She wouldn't have to admit how intimidating his size was when she was so small. She didn't think she could explain how she couldn't imagine learning to trust him, even though he hadn't given her a single reason why she shouldn't. She couldn't shake the feeling that he was going to be the one who wouldn't let her hide in the corner when she needed to. From the intent way he watched her, she knew he would never ignore her, which wasn't reassuring.

But it wasn't a good reason to send him off on his own again, not when it was obvious he'd be an asset to the group. Nina didn't doubt for a second that Paul would pull his weight.

"You can stay," she said, her voice little more than a whisper.

He smiled at her, a tiny upward curve at the corners of his mouth. He didn't need it to make him handsome, but it did make him seem trustworthy. "Thank you."

CHAPTER FIVE
GRANOLA BARS

August 24th, 11:53 am – Traveling east along US-36, Central Ohio

The first few hours on the road with his new companions taught Paul a fair bit about what he could expect from them.

First he walked alongside Aaron, who chattered happily about any number of things. He started with the toad he'd seen in a pond three days before and somehow ended up with how much he liked seeing the leaves start to change.

Paul listened, asked gentle but leading questions whenever the boy stopped to take a breath, and didn't learn anything. Aaron never mentioned his mother, so Paul guessed she had passed before the mysterious illness had struck the country. He thought the kid might be more subdued if she'd died in the plague, or since then in the aftermath. Aaron had been scared a few hours ago when they'd been in danger, but now he was as buoyant as a balloon. He treated the day as a grand adventure with a new friend. There were worse ways to react to what the world had become, though, so Paul resolved never to be too grim around him.

When Aaron dashed ahead to catch up with his father, walking at the head of the line with Mark, Paul slowed down to fall into step with Sarah and Alison.

"You're awfully sweet to that boy," Sarah said by way of greeting, flashing him a smile. Alison's mouth tightened into a hard line, and she kept her eyes focused on the road.

"Well, it's nice to see a kid happy," Paul replied. "I ain't seen many people who still have family with 'em after this long."

There were a few moments of silence when none of them seemed to know what to say next. Paul's curiosity about everyone made him want to pelt Sarah with questions. She'd been the most welcoming, which he hoped would translate into the most forthcoming. But Alison's presence made that awkward, given what had happened between them the night before.

But there was one important question he thought he should ask. "So where are we headed?"

"John's sister's house," Sarah said. "It's . . . oh, I forget the name of the town, right now. But it's on this highway, east of here."

"Coshocton," Alison said shortly.

"Does he know if she survived?"

Sarah shook her head. "He said he got a call from her in the first few days, before everything went out. Her daughter had gotten sick, but she and her husband were still okay. After that . . ."

Paul watched John as he walked out in the lead, holding his son's hand. "So now he's gotta find out."

"Yeah," Alison said. "Losing your family is one kind of hell, and having to search for them is another."

Paul stole a glance at the two of them, and he was stunned by the desolation on Alison's face. But Sarah threaded her arm through Alison's and took her hand, and Alison responded with a faint smile.

"How did y'all end up with John and Aaron?" Paul asked, half out of honest curiosity and half to change the subject.

"John's car broke down on our street," Sarah said. "He'd come down to Indianapolis from Chicago, then headed east. We're from Richmond, near the Ohio border. It was . . . three days after the first plague deaths were reported on the news?"

Alison nodded a silent confirmation. "Our power grid hadn't failed yet, so most of the neighborhood was staying put. We'd lost a few people by then, but things hadn't fallen apart completely. I was staying with Mark and Sarah, because . . ."

When she trailed off, Sarah rushed to pick up the thread of the story. "So John and Aaron start going from door to door, asking for a place to stay the night. John said he was going to try to fix the car in the morning. We took them in. But by the time we woke the next day, the power had gone out, and the phones. So there was no calling a tow truck or a mechanic when John couldn't get the car running again."

"He and Aaron stayed another night with us," Alison continued. "We ate up the food that would spoil—that's the last time I had ice cream."

"It seemed pretty obvious the power wasn't coming back," Sarah said. "John decided the second morning he and Aaron were going to keep going on foot. We were already seeing people passing through, traveling like we are now."

"So we went with them," Alison said. "There wasn't much reason to stay."

Paul looked to Sarah. "Nowhere to go on your own?" he asked, his tone gentle.

"Before the phones went out," Sarah replied, "Mark heard from his mother. She called to say goodbye. She'd gotten sick." She paused again, clearing her throat. "I didn't have any family left. My parents passed away years ago, and my sister and I had a falling out. I haven't seen her or heard from her since. She might still be out there, but I don't know where she was living, so I wouldn't know where to start looking." Sarah sniffled and reached up to wipe her eyes. Paul pretended not to notice. "And you said you didn't have anyone. Who did you lose?"

"My father and my younger brother," Paul answered. He hadn't spoken much to anyone about those first chaotic days of the plague, but Sarah was turning out to be easy to talk to. "Steve was still at home with Dad, he just about to graduate high school. But I'd moved out ages ago, practically the second I turned eighteen. The day after the news came out about the first cases, Steve called me, told me Dad was sick. I didn't get on all that well with him, but when family calls, you come runnin'. I needed to be there with them. I drove straight through for almost two days, but I wasn't in time. Dad died about an hour before I got there, and by then, Steve was sick, too. I stayed with him till the end."

"Your mother?" Alison asked.

"Cancer, when I was thirteen."

"Friends?" Sarah prompted. "Girlfriend?" She paused, then added, "Boyfriend?"

Paul let out a laugh that was half snort. "None of the above. Haven't had anyone like that in my life for quite a while. And none of the friends I had before were the kind of friends you could count on after the end of the world."

"How terrible for you, Paul," Sarah said with a sigh. "I know there's so many people out there with no one left, and it breaks my heart." Then her tone brightened some, like she was making an effort to be cheerful. "So where was home, before? I know a Southern accent when I hear one, so you're a bit far north."

"Well, not that far, really. Louisville. Once you cross the Ohio River, you Midwesterners think it's the South, but the Deep Southerners down in Georgia and Alabama would disagree." He smiled down at her. "Besides, my accent is charming, and farther south they all sound like they walked off the set of *Gone with the Wind*."

Alison laughed, and Paul didn't know whether to feel encouraged or worried that she didn't seem angry anymore. "Where were you, though? That you had to drive two days to get there?"

"New York City, if you can believe that. I was just as happy to get out of there. Things started falling apart real quick those first days, and I didn't have much reason to stay."

Ahead, Mark stopped and turned, motioning his wife forward. "Excuse me," she said to Paul, and hurried to catch up to her husband. He seemed to ask her something, and they fell into step behind John and Aaron.

Alison gave him a sidelong glance and took a deep breath. "I'm sorry about earlier," she said. Paul hadn't expected an apology, so he wasn't ready with a reply in time. "If I'd known you'd be staying . . ." she added.

"You wouldn't have led me outside," he finished for her.

"Yeah."

"It's all right, Alison. If I'd known myself, I wouldn't have gone with you. But it seemed like a bad reason not to stay. Unless this mess makes you so uncomfortable you don't want me around . . ." Not that Paul wanted to leave, or expected her to ask him to, but the offer seemed like an olive branch.

"You didn't seem concerned with my opinion before," she remarked dryly, casting a glance over her shoulder. Paul didn't need to follow it to know she'd looked back at Nina.

"She have to approve everybody?" he asked, low enough he hoped he wouldn't be overheard. "How did that happen?"

Alison laughed, but it wasn't a pleasant sound. "Oh, no, pretty boy, you want to know her secrets, you won't get them out of me. Ask her, if you're brave enough. Just don't expect her to tell you anything." Something ahead caught her attention, and she started to speed up. "Glad we talked," she called out as she pulled away from Paul. She jogged forward to catch up with Mark, who was walking alone. Sarah had joined John and Aaron out in front, each taking one of the boy's hands so they could swing him between them.

Which just left Nina free. She'd been last in line all morning—Paul guessed she wanted to be there to keep an eye on him. She'd let him come along, but didn't seem to like him, or to trust him. Now, with no one to talk to, he imagined he could feel her eyes boring into his back. He thought about slowing down to let her catch up. But if she were determined to remain last, he'd only be forcing the two of them further away from the rest of the group. Keeping an even pace, he waited to see if she decided to talk to him on her own.

She didn't.

After an hour of his own company, the others ahead of him stopped next to a fallen log by the side of the road. By the time he reached them, they were sitting on it and digging into their packs. Aaron pulled out a granola bar, and Paul's stomach gave a timely rumble. The others produced similar food—energy bars, packets of cheese crackers. Sarah broke one piece off a chocolate bar and popped it into her mouth before replacing it in her bag and drawing out a bag of peanuts. Convenience-store food, just like the night before.

"Nice place to stop for lunch, don't you think?" Sarah said.

Paul settled beside her on the log and pulled off his own backpack. He sorted through his food, then pulled out a vacuum-sealed package and tore off the top.

Mark glanced over at it, then did a double-take. "Paul, is that . . . salami?"

Everyone was watching him now, even Nina. She had caught up to them and settled cross-legged a few feet away on the stump of the tree the rest of them were using as a bench. "Yep," he answered. Everyone was silent for a moment, and he knew they were all thinking the same thing. Everyone wanted some, but no one wanted to ask first.

With slow, deliberate movements, though he could feel them all watching him like hawks, Paul pulled the entire stack of salami out. He lay it on the back of the package over his knee and begin to divide it up. He stretched out a hand to offer the first portion to Nina. "Want some?"

She stared at him for a moment before reaching into her bag for an energy bar and holding it out.

"Nope," he said. "I'm guessing y'all haven't had any meat for a while. This one's a gift. For takin' me in."

Nina wrinkled her nose at him, clearly about to object.

Paul didn't let her. "I insist," he said.

She took the salami from him, dropped the energy bar into her backpack, and began to eat. He didn't doubt she could have wolfed the whole thing down in a few seconds, but she took her time, making the unexpected treat last.

Paul fought down a smile that threatened to break free. Since they'd seen Nina accept it, no one else would refuse. He divided the rest into six portions, Aaron's slightly smaller, John's and his own slightly larger. John didn't have his height, but Paul didn't have John's bulk. Those balanced out, leaving them both larger than either Sarah, Mark, or Alison.

He passed out the portions silently. Everyone replaced their unopened food, or in Aaron's case, folded the wrapper down over his half-eaten granola bar, saving the rest for later. Paul admired the kid's discipline, which put John another notch up in his estimation.

After lunch, Paul fell into step beside Nina. Well, sort of. He only took two strides for every three of hers, but she made no effort to move away, which he felt was progress.

She was silent.

He waited.

"I just met you yesterday," she said after maybe half an hour without a word. "I'm not telling you my life story."

Paul chuckled. "Didn't expect you to."

"Even after all the others did?"

"Nah," he said easily. "Haven't talked to John yet. Though Aaron told me some. Mark, neither, but Sarah talks plenty about him."

"That's certainly true," she agreed with a hint of wryness.

With a glance down at his watch, Paul decided he would time how long it took Nina to break the silence between them again. He could be patient.

"So if you're not trying to get me to tell you how I ended up here, what's your plan for our little chat?"

Seventeen minutes. I thought it'd be at least half an hour. "Don't have one."

She looked up at him, the exasperation clear on her face. "I find that hard to believe."

"I don't mind if you don't wanna talk," he said, returning the look with the most guileless expression he could muster. "Not everyone's a talker. I am, but if you're not, that's fine. We'll just walk. It's a nice day. We can just walk in the sunshine."

She let out her breath in huff. While she didn't say another word to him all afternoon, she also stayed beside him, instead of falling behind to the end of the line where she'd been all morning.

Progress.

CHAPTER SIX
A SLIVER OF SOAP

August 27th, 5:15 pm—A stream north of US-36, Central Ohio

Nina squared her shoulders, planted her feet, and waited for John to attack her.

This training could only help her some, since she would never have this much warning if someone was actually trying to hurt her. But anything she could learn to defend herself was better than doing nothing. John had suggested he train her with surprise attacks at random times to sharpen her reflexes, but she declined. She didn't think her nerves could tolerate the strain. Maybe when her fledgling skills had improved. Maybe.

So she was content to confine her lessons to the evening. Whenever the weather was good, whenever they had an open stretch of ground, whenever they weren't too tired or hungry. John would have liked to workout at least every other day; Nina admired his ambition, but conditions weren't in their favor. This was their fourth session since Nina had joined them two weeks ago.

John charged.

Nina dodged the hands reaching for her throat with an easy sidestep, but she wasn't quick enough to avoid the attack completely. John got a hold on her arm, and he used his grip to pivot, his momentum swinging him behind her. Before she could break free, he slid his other arm around her neck in a choke hold. A loose one, since he didn't want to hurt her accidentally, but the spike of adrenaline it produced was real enough.

She grabbed his arm with both hands and tried to pull it away, but John's limbs were as solid and immovable as tree trunks. She had no leverage. He hadn't taught her yet how to break this hold, so for a few moments she struggled, trying to work out what to do. By then she thought she would have passed out if the fight were real, so she tapped his arm twice with one hand, their signal for defeat.

They broke apart. John stretched his arm to work out a kink while Nina rubbed at her throat. "What could you have done differently?" John asked.

Nina liked that he made her think through her mistakes before he corrected them. Given time to reflect, Nina came up with a partial answer. "I was attacking a strong point instead of a weak one," she said. "On some level, I knew your arm wasn't going to give, so I shouldn't have wasted so much time trying."

"Good," he said with quiet approval. "What else?"

"My legs were free," she went on. "I don't know exactly what I should have done, but I bet it involved kicking you."

John nodded, the faintest hint of a smile on his face. "You're never going to win a fight on strength, not with your build. Focus on getting your attacker off his feet, and his hands off you. Disable his legs so he won't be able to chase you at full speed."

He moved close again, demonstrating a few simple moves in slow motion, then had Nina try them against him. She was as careful not to use full force as he was. When he showed her a kick almost guaranteed to break a person's knee, she definitely didn't want to break his. But by the end of the session, she had learned three different ways to break a choke hold, and used them all successfully at least twice.

"Good work tonight," John said, giving her a solid pat on the shoulder. "We'll practice this again next time."

Nina nodded and turned to head back to camp. The spot they'd chosen was a short distance downstream from the others. It wasn't far enough away to be out of sight, but it gave them at least the illusion of privacy.

As she got closer, she saw it hadn't worked. Paul lounged with his back against a convenient rock. He held a battered notebook against his drawn-up knee and was writing in it.

While they trained, John insisted on total focus, and he was quick to catch any signs of distraction. Nina always shut out her surroundings as much as possible. She hadn't given a thought to any of their companions, and she hadn't noticed Paul observing their session. She couldn't be certain he'd been watching the whole time, but she wouldn't have bet against it.

She hoped whatever he was writing—*and what could he possibly be writing?*—had nothing to do with watching her fight. Or anything to do with her at all.

She intended to ignore him as she walked by, but as hard as she tried to focus on the trees or the ground or the clouds, he had this way of catching her eye. He nodded, and she nodded back, grateful he made no comment.

Alison did, though. "All done playing kung fu?" she asked with a mocking sweetness.

Nina didn't bother to answer, knowing whatever she said, there would be more, and worse, to come. She swung her pack onto her shoulder and said, to no one in particular, "I'm going to get cleaned up." Instead of heading for the nearest stretch of the stream, though, she turned back the way she came. She was sweaty enough to want to strip down and give herself a good scrub, not just splash her face and hands.

Sarah called out as Nina reached the edge of the camp. "Wait a minute, and I'll come with you. I've got a few things that could stand washing."

Nina would have preferred to be alone, but at least it was Sarah. She waited for her to gather her dirty clothes, then walked beside her some distance from the others, this time far enough to be out of sight. There was clump of trees on the bank of the stream that would provide cover if someone startled them.

As Nina began to undress, Sarah gave her a concerned look and seemed to want to say something, but didn't.

Nina had no answer for something that wasn't said, so she ignored the look and removed her boots and socks, then rolled the hems of her jeans halfway up her shins. She turned away, unbuttoning her shirt, making a face at how it was starting to fray at the cuffs. The sleeves were too long and constantly caught on things—she should start rolling them up.

Underneath, her t-shirt was damp with sweat. Whatever Sarah intended to say, she kept it to herself while Nina took off that shirt off too, then the tissue-thin camisole underneath. She would have liked to strip completely and dunk herself in the water, but the stream was little more than a trickle. Even as small as she was, she didn't think there was enough water to bother. It didn't look deeper than her shins, so there would be no proper bath, not without a bucket or two.

A bucket would be a good thing to have. But annoying to carry. Nina shrugged to herself and rummaged through her pack for her bar of soap, which was fading to a mere sliver. She fished it out of its plastic bag—the sturdy kind with the zipper top, salvaged from an abandoned house on one of their foraging trips—and wet it in the stream to lather up.

Sarah chose that exact moment to speak. "Paul seems nice, doesn't he?"

The soap slipped out of Nina's hands and fell into the stream with a tiny plunk. If it had been bigger, it might have sunk immediately, which would have made it easier to retrieve. But the little sliver was light and drifted like a tiny canoe, carried downstream by the current. Nina cursed and splashed after it. The soap was the last she had, and worth getting her jeans wet for. Though she knew she'd be cold tonight while they dried.

When she waded back to Sarah, half-naked and furiously embarrassed, the other woman was watching her with a hint of a smile. "So that's how it is?"

Nina scowled at her. "No." But even as she said it, she knew Sarah wouldn't believe her. Sarah was sweet and trusting and softhearted. She would probably love nothing more than shepherding a budding romance along. She seemed to think Paul's constant attention and observation were signs of attraction.

And they could be, because if they weren't, then Nina didn't have any idea what they were. But she didn't want them to be anything.

Sarah apparently did.

Nina soaped and scrubbed herself in silence. She had a faded dish towel she used in place of a more proper one. She dipped one end into the stream to wet it and wipe herself down, then used the other end to dry off. Sarah, a few yards upstream, hummed to herself while she rinsed and wrung out a few articles of clothing. She and Mark had one spare shirt a piece, so every few days they switched from one to the other and Sarah washed the dirty ones. Nina would have traded several days' food for any new clothing—especially socks. She was on her third pair now, and they were getting ragged, sporting several holes in both heels.

But she doubted she'd run into anyone carrying spare socks they'd be willing to trade. Paul hadn't had any when Sarah asked, and his pack was apparently a bottomless pit of wonders, as far as Nina could tell. She sighed and struggled into her clothing. The soap went back into its plastic bag, and the dishtowel she threaded through the strapping on the outside of her pack, where it could hang to dry without getting anything else wet.

"You done?" she asked Sarah.

The older woman nodded, still humming, and wrung out the shirts one last time before draping them over her arm. She glanced down at Nina's jeans, noting the darker fabric where she'd splashed herself. "Let's ask John for a fire tonight. Those will dry faster, and the last thing we need is for anyone to take a chill, sleeping in wet clothes."

Nina wasn't sure John would want to bother, since the evening was warm, but she nodded, and tried to smile, even though she was still irritated with Sarah. "All right. Let's head back."

She was hoping Paul wouldn't be watching for her return, as he had been earlier, and she was pleased to be right. When she and Sarah got back, he was sitting cross-legged on the ground facing Aaron, and they were . . . playing cards?

She hadn't known anyone had found a deck. Without much other entertainment available, card games were one of the best ways to pass the time. Decks of cards had become a pretty valuable commodity. Someone asked after them at every trading session Nina had been in, except for the night they met Paul.

After a moment, though, the answer was obvious. They were Paul's, and he'd had them the whole time, probably waiting to use them for a trade later.

Aaron pursed his lips, consulting the cards in his hand, and then said, "Go fish." Paul drew a card from the pile on the ground between them, smiled, and nodded at the boy.

Sarah's voice at her shoulder startled Nina, who'd forgotten the other woman was there. "I guess he means to stay, then." She threw Nina another significant glance as she passed, going to speak to John. A few minutes later, the watches for the night were settled, and Sarah and Mark headed into the trees to gather wood for a fire.

Nina chose her spot, dropped her pack, and settled herself beside it, leaning back and watching the sky overhead change color as the sunset began. She couldn't help but hear the others moving about the camp, building the fire, talking, playing games. But she let it all pass around her as the sky faded from oranges and pinks to the dark blue of twilight, then finally to star-sprinkled black.

CHAPTER SEVEN
A WRISTWATCH

August 30th, 12:00 am – A forested hill south of US-36, Central Ohio

The alarm on Paul's watch went off. The soft but irritating beep cut through the sounds of the woods at night. It was his turn to keep watch. He yawned and stretched, sitting up.

Mark, who had been on duty for the first part of the night, was nowhere in sight.

Paul stood and moved around the campfire quietly, checking the identity of the blanket-wrapped forms surrounding it. John was closest, his feet just a few inches from Paul's pack, which served as his pillow. Aaron was right beside him. Nina came next, on the far side of the fire from where Paul had slept. Then Sarah, with Mark's empty blanket laid out beside her, waiting for him.

Paul came around to the last space before he reached his own again, where Alison should have been. Her pack was there, but she wasn't.

His first instinct was to wake up John and tell him they were missing. His second, which he heeded, was to wait, because it could be nothing. Alison could be answering nature's call, and Mark walking around to keep himself awake.

Paul sat down next to his pack and pulled out his water bottle, taking a drink and thinking. It could be that simple, but something felt off, and he was having trouble pinning it down. He glanced over at Alison's empty patch of ground again, and it hit him—her blanket was missing, too.

"Oh, hell," he muttered. He knew exactly what a missing blanket meant.

This was only the fourth night since Paul joined the group that they had posted any kind of watch. They had at the gas station, when they were under shelter, and for good reason.

When they camped out, though, things were different. If the evening was warm enough and they went without a fire, they also went without a watch. Since they never camped less than half a mile from the road, John figured no one would stumble across them without a fire to announce their location. When the weather was cold enough to need a fire, then they kept watch.

They'd passed over Paul the first time they camped out, and he hadn't minded. Last time, he'd been given the final watch, and tonight, the middle one. He wasn't sure he remembered the watch assignments from the first night, but he thought Alison might have had one. He wondered if she and Mark had snuck off together then, too.

And he wondered if any of the others knew. Sarah obviously didn't. Paul couldn't imagine her letting it go on. But if he had discovered it, someone else might have too.

If someone had, then they'd kept silent about it.

Paul checked the time. Ten past midnight. They could be back any minute—Mark should have woken him for his turn, but Paul had set the alarm in case Mark had fallen asleep. They wouldn't expect him to be awake when they returned.

He lay back down and closed his eyes, pretending to sleep, waiting. Alison came back first. Paul heard the rustle of her clothing as she lay down, the faint crackling of food wrappers in her pack as she set her head atop it. A few minutes later, he heard Mark return, circle the sleepers around the fire once, checking on them as Paul had done. Then he felt a hand on his shoulder. "Paul," he said in a low voice. "It's time."

He opened his eyes, yawned, and stretched, just as he had when his alarm had woken him. For now, at least, he didn't want to let on that he knew of their tryst. "Everything good?" he asked, faking another yawn as he sat up.

"Yeah, fine," Mark answered. "Wake up Nina in a few hours, remember. Just..."

When Mark trailed off, Paul raised his eyebrow at him, watching a sudden look of worry cross his face in the firelight. "What?"

Mark sighed. "Try to wake her without getting too close." He looked across the fire to Nina. "She startles easy."

"Good to know," Paul replied. He already knew, but no need to tell Mark about how he knew. "Go on, then, get some sleep. You look like you could use it."

He hadn't meant it as a dig, but Mark looked back at Paul with a hint of panic. It vanished as soon as Paul smiled at him. He pulled off his baseball cap, nodded to Paul, and went to his blanket, laying down beside his wife and draping his arm over her.

Paul watched them, considering. He'd never been in this situation before and wanted to weigh his options.

The easiest was to keep quiet and let things go on as they were. He didn't like being dishonest, but it had only been a week since joining them at the gas station. They liked him well enough, accepted him, and seemed to trust him some—enough to give him a watch, at least. But he doubted their trust extended far enough to believe him if he accused Mark of cheating on his wife, which was his other option. He tried to imagine any scenario stemming from that decision which would end well, but he couldn't. If they believed him, then at best it would be tension and hurt feelings, and at worst, a shattered marriage. If they didn't believe him, Paul could see himself getting turned out on his own.

He didn't know it would happen, but it seemed a real possibility, and not one he wanted to face. Now that he had the safety of numbers, he didn't relish the idea of being on his own again so soon.

For most of the next three hours, he watched the others sleeping around the fire, listening for anything out of place. His thoughts ran in circles, chasing down an answer which never appeared. It was nearly time to wake Nina when Aaron started to toss and turn and mumble in his sleep.

Paul waited to see if John would wake up, but Aaron's nightmare—if that's what it was—didn't make him cry out. John only shifted onto his side and settled back into deep sleep. So Paul crossed over to Aaron and laid his hand on the boy's shoulder.

"Bad dream?" Paul asked when Aaron opened his eyes.

After a long pause, he nodded.

"Wanna talk about it?"

Aaron answered immediately with a shake of his head.

"That's fine," Paul told him. "Morning's still a long way off, though. Think you can get back to sleep?"

Aaron sat up and rubbed his eyes. "I don't know. Sometimes if I try right away, I just have the same nightmare over again."

"Definitely don't want that." Paul tilted his head to the side, considering his next question. "Does singing you back to sleep help at all?"

Aaron wrinkled his nose. "Lullabies are for babies."

"Yeah, babies get a lot of them, that's true. But they're not *just* for babies.

They're for everybody. My little brother had trouble sleepin' for a while, and I'd sit with him and sing to him, and he said it helped."

"Why couldn't he sleep?" Aaron asked.

"It was after our mom died," Paul said. "He was only six, and he didn't really understand. He was afraid if he fell asleep, he might not wake up."

"I didn't think that when my mom died," Aaron said. "I dream about—" He stopped, took a deep breath, and tried again. "I dream about all those dead people we see. And the ones we don't, the ones that are inside the houses we go by. But in the dream, they're not dead. They're trying to get out and find us."

Paul wasn't sure if he meant the people were alive and trapped, or zombies. He decided not to ask for clarification. "That ain't gonna happen."

Aaron made a face again. "I *know*," he insisted. "I know it's not real."

Paul sighed. "But that don't mean it ain't scary. I get it, Aaron, I'm sorry. Do you get tired of people treating you stupid 'cause you're a kid?"

That won Paul a smile from the boy. "All the time! Mark and Sarah are nice, but they're almost as bad as Dad about letting me have any fun. And Alison doesn't think I understand *anything*. She treats me like I'm five years old."

There was a name missing from the list, but Paul stopped himself before he asked. It seemed wrong to try to weasel information out of Aaron. "So, you want to see if you can get back to sleep now? I'll sing if you want."

Aaron lay back down and closed his eyes. "Okay. But nothing for babies."

Paul laughed softly and began to sing "Swing Low, Sweet Chariot" as quietly as he could. Since Aaron didn't stop him by the end of the first verse, he kept going, until the boy rolled onto his side and curled up against his father's back. Paul smiled as he stood, then walked around the camp to stretch his legs.

The new alarm he'd set on his watch beeped. He made his way around the fire, placing his feet with care to make as little noise as possible. When he was a few feet from Nina, he changed tactics and deliberately stepped on a small fallen branch, snapping it in half beneath his foot.

Nina sat up, scraping her tousled hair back from her face and looking around for the sound. He crouched down beside her and whispered, "Sorry. Big feet, kinda clumsy."

"It's okay," she told him as she unwound herself from her blanket. "You can't help being a skyscraper. It must be hard to see the ground at all from that far up."

The teasing, so unexpected, nearly knocked Paul right over. But since she sounded grumpy, not angry, he played along. "Yeah, y'all look like ants down there." She turned to him and gave him a look, but her face was in shadow, so he had to guess at what it was. Some sort of narrow-eyed, withering glare. He wanted to laugh, but held it in, not wanting to wake anyone with the sudden noise.

"Anything interesting happen?" Nina asked.

"No," Paul answered without hesitation. "Nothing but quiet."

CHAPTER EIGHT
A BARRETTE

August 30th, 3:00 am – A forested hill south of US-36, Central Ohio

Nina watched Paul stretch out in his spot by the fire, settling in for sleep.

She replayed their conversation in her head, and it stunned her to realize how easily she had fallen into teasing. Paul had been with them a week, and without her even noticing, her attitude toward him was starting to thaw out.

Three nights ago, John gave him the last watch, saying it was time he started helping out with that—and everyone had woken up in the morning alive, safe, and slightly grumpy. As usual. Tonight he'd had the middle watch and woken Nina up on time for her turn.

Maintaining her wariness was getting harder with every passing day, because he never did anything wrong.

Paul crossed his arms over his chest and tucked his hands under them to keep warm. The only scavenging they'd managed to do since he joined the group was for more food. Though Sarah managed to turn up a yo-yo for Aaron, which had kept him entertained for the past three days. But no one had found a blanket for Paul.

Nina bundled up her own blanket, brushed off a few clinging bits of bark and leaf, and went over to him. "Here," she whispered, holding it out. "Since I won't need it again tonight."

He opened his eyes and propped himself up on one elbow. When he didn't reach out to take it, she realized how foolish she looked. Her blanket was pink fleece printed with cartoon ponies, a little girl's blanket, not even close to big enough for him. She ended up with a lot of kids' stuff because of her height, which even in thick-soled boots didn't top five feet. She hadn't stopped to think about that, though, when she'd decided to offer it to him. She just didn't want him to be cold.

But the awkwardness didn't last. "Thank you," Paul said as he took it and wrapped it around his shoulders like a shawl. He held it in place with one hand at his neck as he lay back down. "G'night, Nina."

She mumbled a goodnight back as she held in a laugh which would have startled everyone awake. He looked ridiculous, but he'd taken the whole thing seriously. She almost wished she hadn't done it, seeing how silly he looked. If he wasn't the first one awake in the morning, someone would see she'd lent him her blanket. Nina didn't want anyone to know she'd been kind to him—she didn't have much of a reputation for it.

Not like Paul. Nina had known nice guys with a capital N before—men little better than doormats waiting for women to notice how sweet and wonderful they were and fall madly in love. Or the kind who paraded how nice they were because they expected credit for it. Paul was neither.

When had Nina ever known a man who would sing a lullaby to a frightened boy, not to impress anyone, but just because he wanted to help? When Paul moved to check on Aaron, Nina had woken up from a nightmare of her own. As the pounding of her heart slowed, she'd listened in on the whole thing, which was utterly beyond her experience. She couldn't even remember her own parents singing to her as a child.

And she'd never felt the lack until now.

The warm, soft ache in her chest got Nina thinking as she moved around the campfire, checking on each sleeping person. Maybe she was starting to thaw out with everyone. The day before, she'd wished she knew any tricks with a yo-yo so she could teach them to Aaron. He was figuring plenty out on his own, but she thought it would be fun to help. It was definitely funny to watch when he messed up and the thing tried to run away from him. But he always wound it back up and tried again until he got it right.

She found the whole thing inexplicably charming, and it was getting under her skin.

Just like Paul.

With at least three hours until sunrise and nothing much to do except think, Nina decided it was time to let herself think about him. She'd been trying hard not to, at least, not more than necessary for the practical, day-to-day stuff. *If Paul's going for water, I need to give him my bottle.* She thought about him the same way she thought about everyone in their strange family —*who is where, who do I need to tell what, who needs my help with something*.

But in the snapping, leaping firelight, she settled herself cross-legged near the blaze and relaxed her guard for a while.

Paul's eyes sprang to mind first. Nina had never met anyone with eyes like his. And it wasn't only the strange sunlight-in-the-forest coloring, but the way he seemed to notice the smallest details about everything. Paul pointed out to Mark that his bootlace was fraying through before he noticed himself, so he could repair it before it split in two. Paul had been the one to see Sarah left the needle in her jeans, where she'd stuck it after mending a tear in her blanket. Since Sarah had the only sewing kit, and it only had three needles, losing even one would have been bad.

Nina wasn't comfortable feeling like Paul was always watching her. On a rational level, it wasn't true, because he was watching the others too. After some consideration, though, she realized his outward attention wasn't the root of the problem. What made her heart shiver and stutter was Paul's constant awareness of her—he always knew precisely where she was in relation to him. She wouldn't have been surprised if he could be blindfolded, spun around in a circle until he was dizzy, and still point directly at her, if he were asked to.

Which made her the donkey to pin the tail on. Nina wrinkled her nose at the unflattering comparison. But she didn't want to be his north star, either.

She wondered if any of the others felt the same way. Maybe she was giving in to her imagination and seeing, or sensing, something that wasn't there. Either way, she could admit to herself she was getting used to the feeling. Somehow, whenever she did need Paul for something practical, he was nearby, only a few feet away, already turning toward her. It was handy, even if it was uncanny at the same time.

And he always knew when to shut up.

He was a talker, he'd said so himself, and Nina couldn't object to it as a label. Paul spoke comfortably with everyone about anything. He was solemn when the subject was serious, but he showed more than a little humor whenever there was opportunity. And his knack for gentle teasing won Sarah over the first day he was with them. Maybe, Nina reflected, that was why she'd teased him a few minutes before. He was rubbing off on her.

But he never seemed to out-talk his welcome with anyone, even Nina. She knew she was the prickliest of the bunch, excepting Alison, maybe, in her worst moods. The others sometimes approached her like she was a porcupine ready to shoot its spines at them. Not that porcupines actually could, but once she thought of it that way it became lodged in her head.

Paul, though, treated her more like a house cat. Whatever mood she was in, he was content to go along with it, because there wouldn't be any use fighting it. You can't make a cat want to curl up in your lap when you want it to—you have to wait until it does. If you pick up even the friendliest cat when it's in the wrong mood, it might hiss at you, jump down, and stalk away.

Nina decided she was better off as a cat than a porcupine.

The rare times she wanted to talk, Paul was happy to provide conversation. As soon as the impulse started to fade, he seemed content with sitting or walking beside her in silence, or even leaving her alone completely. But when he left, it always seemed natural. He never said, "Well, you're cranky now, I'd better go talk to someone else." He just found someplace else to be for a while, doing something else that needed doing. Like volunteering to fetch water, or wood for the fire. Even when she had been determined not to like him, she had to admire his tact.

Hard on the heels of that thought came the realization that she didn't remember deciding not to be determined not to like him. She wasn't sure when she'd stopped.

Which was exactly why she didn't usually indulge in these sessions of introspection.

But that lullaby...

Paul's speaking voice was pleasant. Nothing amazing. His soft, drawling accent was what drew you in and made you want to spill every thought in your head—not his voice itself.

But his singing voice was honey drizzled over sandpaper. Nina couldn't remember the last time she'd heard that song, but now it was like she'd never forgotten the words. She had it stuck in her head, playing on infinite repeat, but only in his voice. Warm and sweet and just a little rough.

She wanted to hear him sing again.

Which could be a problem, because she didn't want to want him to do anything at all.

But she had at least figured out why she'd teased him and offered him her blanket. Mystery solved.

The thought of sharing anything of her history with him, though, made her cringe. She couldn't imagine telling him anything about what had happened to her during the plague and after it, like she'd heard Sarah and Alison do...

Nina threw the brakes on that train of thought, shivering. Time to get up and walk the perimeter, get herself moving for a while.

She was only doing it to shake off the chill. She didn't think she'd find anything out of the ordinary, but John had drilled the habit into everyone. Circle the camp and look for signs of anything unusual. John had the only gun, but everyone had knives—except for Aaron, but he wasn't assigned watches, either. John always said he didn't expect them to stumble across someone trying to sneak into the camp at night—but when you stop checking, that's when someone will.

Nina knew that herself, firsthand, though she wouldn't have called her entrance "sneaking."

So she made a wide circle around the camp every hour or so during her watches. She used them to gather more wood for the fire, bending to pick up the big twigs and small branches before she could snap them like Paul had.

She knew he wasn't clumsy. He never dropped anything, never once fumbled an object from those long, graceful fingers. Paul stepped on the branch on purpose so he could wake her without touching her. He couldn't have known she was only pretending to be asleep, so she could pretend she hadn't heard him singing.

He hadn't touched her once, not even in passing, since he'd grabbed her wrist the first morning. His fingers didn't even brush her hand when he returned her water bottle after he filled it, or when he'd given her the salami.

Deciding to stop making an effort to dislike him wasn't the same as deciding to trust him, though. He was just close to impossible not to like.

Something caught Nina's eye, the tiniest glint of light where there shouldn't be any. The firelight was dim this far away, so she couldn't tell what it was. She reached down to pick it up, and her fingers closed over something small and metal. A barrette.

She studied the ground around her feet, searching for anything else odd nearby. It would have been easier with a flashlight, but she wasn't about to wake Paul to borrow his—only if it were an emergency. Which it wasn't.

So she did her best without extra light. When she set down the bundle of twigs so she could use both hands, she realized the oddest thing was what wasn't there. This patch of ground was clear of dead fall.

Everyone did that to spread their blankets out. No one wanted a twig poking them in the side.

She went back to the fire and studied the barrette. She thought it looked familiar, but she wasn't sure. Paul could have told her, she was certain, but she wasn't going to ask him, because she thought it might be Alison's. Sarah kept her fair hair short so she didn't need to bother with barrettes or hair bands. But Alison was forever pushing her auburn curls off her face, tying them back into ponytails or securing them with pins and clips.

It could belong to someone else, someone who had passed this way before.

If it were Alison's, though, why would she have lost a barrette out there on her watch?

But Alison didn't have a watch tonight. Mark was first, then Paul, then Nina herself.

It wasn't hard for Nina to fill in the rest of the story. Either Mark or Paul had woken Alison during his watch and led her out into the forest with her blanket. Then they'd had a quiet little romp when no one else would know about it.

If it had been Paul...

Nina didn't care much for the idea, which left her with a twisting, sour feeling in her stomach. But there was no real harm in it, beyond the fact that he should have been keeping watch and not having a good time with Alison instead. There was so little privacy, though, living as they did—so if that's how things stood, she could hardly blame them.

But picturing the two of them together was difficult. Alison made eyes at him when it seemed like he wasn't looking, though Nina was certain he knew anyway. She flirted with him from time to time, but her tone was more predatory than playful. Paul had this way of deflecting it without flirting back, but without being rude either. Another expression of his tact, and not an easy one to accomplish.

And if it was Mark... poor Sarah. Nina hoped she was wrong about the whole thing, because it would be better than Mark cheating on his wife with their friend.

But she didn't have any proof of anything. It might not be Alison's barrette at all, which meant everything was in her imagination. She looked at it again, studying it in the firelight, and tried to be sure.

By morning, she hadn't come to any sort of conclusion. She'd thought about what to do with it. Keeping it was a bad idea, because if someone found it on her, she'd have to explain how she'd come by it. Trying to return it to Alison was even worse. If it was hers, and she realized where she'd lost it, then she would know Nina knew something was going on.

Just before sunrise, she did another sweep around the perimeter, trying to take the same path and find the same cleared spot again. When she thought she had, she dropped the barrette.

Paul was awake when she got back. "Anything interesting happen?" he asked. She wondered if he realized that's exactly what she'd said to him.

"Nope," she answered, just as he had. "Nothing but quiet."

CHAPTER NINE
A COIL OF ROPE

September 9th, 3:47 pm – US-36, just outside Mount Vernon, Ohio

Nina washed out and refilled her water bottle in the shallows of the river. It was a proper river, wide and dark and swift, not one of the little streams they'd been finding here and there when they camped.

John had led them off the road, down a shallow slope which deposited them at the river's edge. This would make an excellent campsite, a broad, flat space next to a huge source of fresh water for drinking and cleaning. But it was too early to stop for the day, and John never let them camp any closer to a major road than half a mile.

Nina wondered, then, why John had called a halt early. At least until he pulled out the map, spread it on a conveniently large and flat rock, and dove headfirst into an argument with Mark and Sarah.

The three of them were taking turns tracing routes on the paper with their forefingers, then turning to each other and voicing an opinion. The conversational volume was escalating from *normal* to *I'm trying not to shout, but I want to*. Alison sat by herself on a different rock, watching the clouds and ignoring the argument, just as Nina was trying to.

She'd seen this play out once before. She hadn't wanted to step in the first time, and she didn't see a reason to this time either.

Alison's reasons for not getting involved could only be guessed at, but Nina had decided she went where the group went. She didn't have anyone to look for or anywhere in particular she wanted to go.

Which was something she had in common with Paul. He seemed content to follow the herd as well, which puzzled her, because every indication was he'd been doing fine on his own.

Maybe he did enjoy the company, like he'd said. Paul seemed energized by his own kindness, and he had been kind to them, consistently, unfailingly. Paul could be counted on to do what was needed with no argument or complaining. And he'd still have enough to spare at the end of the day for game of cards, or telling stories, or just a smile.

Nina had never thought of herself as unkind, but comparing herself to him, she thought she could try harder to help. No one had ever said she didn't pull her weight. But if she was banking her survival on safety in numbers, she needed to be a more active part of the group instead of a passenger.

It felt odd to have this train of thought lead her to a minor epiphany in the middle of an argument she still wanted nothing to do with. But she looked around, wondering what else she could contribute instead.

Paul was lounging against the withered stump of a tree a few yards away, and for once, he wasn't watching her. Instead he kept an eye on Aaron, who had taken off his shoes and socks and rolled up his pants so he could play in the shallows of the river. So Paul had babysitting duty covered while John was busy. No one could accuse Paul of not pulling his weight, either.

Remembering the bottle in her hand, Nina decided to clean and fill everyone's bottles. They'd all dumped their packs in a central location where the campfire would likely be if the group stayed here overnight. Nina spent a minute digging through the pile to collect the bottles. Alison glanced over and opened her mouth to say something, then seemed to think better of it and looked away.

At the river's edge, Nina couldn't hear the argument clearly. She listened with half an ear while she worked anyway, trying to judge who was winning. *Mark and Sarah, so far,* she thought.

After she returned the bottles to their owners' packs, she looked around again for something else to do. Paul, catching her eye, made a vague *come here* gesture. Nina crossed the sandy ground to his tree stump and crouched beside him. "What is it?"

"Do you know," he asked, "if Aaron knows how to swim? I don't want to ask him, because if he don't, he might say he does just so I don't make him stop playin' down there."

"Yeah, he does," Nina answered. "There was another time we camped by a river like this, before you joined us. He and John and Mark all went for a swim to get cleaned up. Aaron wasn't doing laps or anything, but he seemed pretty confident."

"So that's them," he said. "What about you? And Alison and Sarah?"

"I can swim fine," Nina told him. "I don't know about them. Why do you ask?"

The ghost of a smile crossed his face. "So I know who needs rescuin' if we all fall into the river," he said.

"Let me guess, you were on the swim team in school?" she teased.

He chuckled. "Most people guess basketball! But no, I wasn't. Just wanted to know, in case. Best to be prepared."

A hawk flew by, low to the water, and Aaron stopped splashing to watch as it passed, heading downriver. Then he pointed at something in the distance and let out a whoop.

Paul pushed himself to standing, and Nina did the same as he called, "What is it, Aaron?"

The boy looked up the slope at them, his face alight. "A tire swing!"

"Not a chance," Paul said immediately, his tone faintly stern. "Do you want to be soakin' wet all afternoon? You don't have any other clothes."

"I could take them off!"

Nina went to the water's edge to stand by Aaron. "There's really a tire swing out here? We're not all that close to town yet, there can't be any houses nearby." But there it was, not even a quarter-mile downriver.

She heard Paul's voice from just over her shoulder—he'd come down to the water to see for himself. "The kids probably rode their bikes. I know I would've gone miles for a good tire swing when I was ten."

"Yeah, I guess," Nina said. A sudden idea seized her, but she wasn't sure if it was a good one. "Aaron, you go stay with your dad. Paul and I are going to take a look at the swing."

Paul took a quick breath, possibly getting ready to object, but Aaron was quicker. "You are? To see if it's safe for me to play on?"

"I'm sorry, Aaron," Nina replied, shaking her head at him. "I don't think that's a good idea. I know it sounds like fun, but it would be too easy to get hurt."

Aaron looked downcast, but he nodded. "Okay. Dad would have said no, anyway." He plodded off to join his father, still going over the map with Mark and Sarah.

"So why *are* we doin' this?" Paul asked as soon as Aaron was out of earshot.

Nina turned to face his puzzled expression. "Because no one has any rope."

That got a smile from him. "Good thinkin'."

There were some trees along the water's edge, but not much brush, so their hike to the swing was easy. It hung from a sturdy branch of a massive old oak. Nina guessed the rope was at least twenty feet long, which would be great, if they could figure out a way to get it down.

She circled around the trunk twice, studying the layout of the branches, before she let out a sigh. "I don't think I can get up there."

"I ain't the tree-climbing expert you are, apparently," he said. "Why not?"

"Whoever hung the swing climbed up, tied it on the highest sturdy branch he could find, then cut down the lower branches that were in the way. See the scars on the trunk?"

"Yeah, mostly covered over with bark. Must be an old swing."

"The rope looks good, though, no fraying. But with those lower branches gone, I don't see a way to get to it. The branches on the other side are still there, but badly spaced—even if I got high enough, I'm not sure I could get around the trunk."

Paul stepped closer to the tree, looking up at the branch with the swing and the branches nearest to it, like Nina had. "The ground slopes away from the tree pretty sharp, but at the trunk, the branches don't seem so far up. Think you could you reach that one, there, if you stood on my shoulders?"

She looked up at the tree again, trying to judge, but also to hide a sudden spasm of panic. Out of the corner of her eye, she could see Paul watching her, so she fought to keep her breathing under control.

"Nina, I'm serious," he went on when she didn't answer. "You want the rope, right? I think if I can get you to this branch," he said, pointing, "then you can pull yourself up and make it over to the one with the swing. Those two branches between them are close enough, right?"

She didn't want to do this. She wanted to turn around and go back to the others, to shake her head and say *No, it won't work.*

But she also wanted the rope.

"Yeah," she said, almost choking on the word. She cleared her throat and tried again. "Yeah, I think I can make it."

Without giving herself too much time to think, or a chance to change her mind, Nina bent down to take off her boots and socks. When she straightened, Paul was looking at her with a quizzical expression. "Better grip," she told him.

Then she checked her knife, to make sure it was secure in its sheath on her belt. Getting the knot undone without cutting was better—there would be more rope if she could. But she also didn't want to lose her knife during the climb, only to end up needing it when she got up there.

Next, Nina pulled off her canvas button-down. She didn't want the long sleeves getting in her way. She was left with the snug t-shirt she wore underneath, which wasn't immodest, but clung to her more than she was comfortable with Paul seeing.

It was a stupid time to be having that thought, but she couldn't help feeling a little self-conscious. It was just the two of them out here, so there was no one else for him to be looking at. She spared a moment for silent thanks that the holes in her shirt weren't in places that would embarrass her any further. Taking a deep breath, she blew it out through pursed lips and said, "All right, let's get on with it."

Paul went to the tree and Nina followed. "How'd you get to be such a champion climber, anyway?"

She waited as he crouched below the right branch and braced his hands against the trunk. "It's a good thing to know how to do when you're always the shortest kid in class. Most bullies won't chase you up a tree." He let out a short laugh, and then she asked, "Ready?"

"Yep."

She took another deep breath before she reached out to put her hands on his shoulders. It was the first time either one of them had touched the other since that first morning. Nina couldn't be sure if he flinched, just a little, under her hand. She wasn't worried that he wasn't strong enough, or that he'd let her fall—but maybe, she thought, he was.

Nina got her left knee up onto his left shoulder, moving her hand to brace herself on the tree trunk, then did the same with her right knee. Paul grunted, but he didn't tell her to stop. One foot at a time, she went from kneeling on his shoulders to standing, then said, "Okay, I'm good. Stand up."

He rose to his feet slowly, both of them walking their hands up the trunk. After a moment, he said, "Done. Can you reach it, or should I try to lift you?"

"No, I got it," she answered. The branch was just above her shoulder, so she stretched to wrap both arms around it and pull herself up.

From there she had to cross three small gaps between branches to get to the one with the swing. By the time she settled on it, clinging to the top and ready to crawl outward, Paul had stepped back from the trunk to follow her progress.

"You don't need to do that," Nina insisted, struggling with a sudden tightness in her chest. The height didn't bother her, but the obvious concern plastered all over Paul's face did. It was a more honest and open expression than she was used to seeing from him. He was friendly enough, but usually more guarded. It struck Nina then how worried he must be if he let so much of it show. "I'm not going to fall."

"Just let me make sure, okay?" he called up. "I'm not a big fan of broken bones."

Keeping him talking might distract him from his anxiety, which would ease hers. "You ever break any?" she asked as she started to inch toward the swing.

"My arm, when I was seven, and my nose in high school."

That made Nina pause and glance down at his face again. "Really? It was set well, then. There's no bump and you're not all crooked."

He smiled suddenly, a wide, bright grin, and there was a faint sinking feeling in Nina's chest she didn't like one bit. "Yeah, I guess I was lucky."

She looked back at the branch, at her hands, trying to focus, and started moving forward again. "You get in a fight?"

"Something like that, yeah." His tone was wry.

"Did you win?" she teased.

"Nope. Wasn't fightin' back."

"Why not?"

"My girlfriend's the one who punched me."

"Huh." Nina pulled herself forward another few inches. He sounded more like himself now—her plan seemed to be working. "Did you deserve it?"

"She seemed to think so."

Nina felt laughter bubble up unexpectedly and gave in to it. "That's not an answer!"

"No, I didn't," he replied, turning serious. "But I wasn't gonna defend myself, 'cause to someone watchin', it might have looked like I was the one hurtin' her. That's way more trouble than I wanted to be in. One of the problems with bein' a skyscraper is that people tend to think you're more of a threat than a littler guy."

Nina couldn't help but laugh again. "Tall person problems," she observed. "Not my area of expertise."

"No, that seems to be tree climbin'."

More than halfway there now. "So why'd she swing at you?"

"She thought I was cheatin' on her."

That made Nina pause again and look down to meet his eyes. She hadn't expected the plan to distract her, just him, but maybe he was easier to talk to when she was sure she was out of reach. "Were you?"

"No!" Paul's face creased in a frown. "One of my friends lied to her, tried to break us up 'cause he wanted her himself."

"Oh," she said, resuming her progress. "Not a good friend, then."

"Nope. Once it all came out, she apologized for breakin' my nose, but we stayed split up. As for the other guy, well, I never spoke to him again."

"Ah, high school. I don't miss it one bit."

"Me neither," he agreed.

Nina reached the swing and looked down, realizing Paul was no longer below her. She had to crane her neck to see him, standing at the water's edge and watching her, his arms crossed over his chest.

But staring at him wasn't going to get anything done. She turned her attention back to the rope and spent a minute working at the knot with her fingers. It didn't cooperate, being pulled tight from years of bearing the weight of the swing and the children who had used it. She tried to get some slack by pulling the swing upward with one hand, but the combined weight of the tire and the rope was too heavy for her. "I think you're going to have to get in the water," she said, frustration edging her tone. "I can't budge this thing. I was hoping I could cut it down and toss it your way, but I've got no leverage. We'll have to let it drop and fish it out."

"Okay, hold on." Just as Aaron had done to play in the river, Paul took off his boots and socks, then rolled up his jeans. He grabbed a fallen branch to test the depth of the water. A few feet from the edge, there seemed to be a sudden drop off, because the branch went all the way in, all at once. "It's deep here."

"Probably why they chose this spot, whoever put it up."

"All right, gimme a minute," Paul said as he went back to dry land. "Don't want my clothes soaked." He tossed the branch aside and undid the top button of his shirt.

Nina turned her face away, resting her cheek on her hand where she gripped the branch. Her breathing quickened as she realized she wanted to watch, even though she knew she shouldn't. Even though she'd hate him for doing the same. She waited, listening to the soft rustling sounds his clothes made as he discarded them, then to the sounds of the water as he waded in. He let out a hiss, and she swallowed a giggle, because she could guess what caused it. The river had been cold when she'd washed the bottles earlier, and that was in full afternoon sun. It wouldn't be any warmer under the shade of the tree.

"Okay, I'm ready," he called, and Nina finally looked down at him. The water came halfway up his ribs, so all she saw was the smooth, pale skin of his chest and shoulders. For a moment, she wondered if he was one of those people who couldn't tan at all and was always so fair. Or maybe he could lie out in the sun for an afternoon or two and get bronzed enough to look like her.

Not that the lean muscles of Paul's arms and shoulders were any less enticing for being pale.

She hoped he couldn't tell she was blushing.

Belatedly, Nina realized she was staring again and started sawing through the rope. It took a while to give, but with some work, the tire fell free.

Paul caught it just before it hit the water, so he didn't get splashed. He couldn't help letting some of the rope get wet, but all things considered, Nina thought it went pretty well. She watched as he coiled the rope on top of the floating tire before starting to push it back to shore. She looked away before he got out, and waited as he did his best to dry himself before getting back into his clothes.

"All right, Nina, I'm decent again."

Disappointment swooped through her like the hawk that had flown by, and for a moment she was disgusted by her reaction. There was no harm in thinking he was attractive, but there was in following those thoughts to their potential conclusion. The last thing she wanted was to develop a crush on Paul.

Nina inched backwards a foot or so before she realized they hadn't thought this all the way through. She didn't want to admit she'd missed it. "So . . ." she began, embarrassed.

"What is it?"

"We didn't stop to consider how I was going to get down."

He didn't answer right away. Nina still wasn't looking at him, so she couldn't read his expression. There were a lot of things he might have been thinking, but she was afraid she knew how this was going to end. "We can't just do the whole thing in reverse?"

"I don't think so."

"Well, the water's deep enough there to drop into. You wouldn't get hurt, but you would get soaked." He hesitated, and when he spoke again, his voice was noticeably less steady. "Or you could shimmy back a ways and drop down. I'd catch you."

Nina closed her eyes and rested her forehead on the branch. She felt a strong desire to kick herself for getting into this ridiculous situation, but if she did, she'd fall out of the tree. While it might solve the problem of how to get down, it wasn't her first choice. "I am such an idiot," she muttered, then began working her way backwards along the branch.

Paul stayed underneath her as she moved, but he didn't say anything. Maybe he could tell how mortified she was, or maybe he didn't want to startle her.

About halfway back, Nina looked down and tried to judge the distance. She didn't want to be too close, because Paul wouldn't have time to react properly when she dropped down. But she didn't want to be too far, either, because the farther she fell, the worse things could go wrong. She had no idea where the best spot would be, but her nervousness was escalating toward panic again and she just wanted it over with. "Okay," she said.

"Here?"

"Here," she confirmed. Without stopping to think much about it, she let herself tip to the side. She rotated around the branch until she was clinging to the underside with all four limbs instead of hugging it from the top. She let her legs go and straightened out until she was hanging by her hands. "Ready?" she asked, more breath than voice.

"Yeah," he answered. She didn't look down, because she didn't want to see his expression. She just let go.

It happened so fast she couldn't remember falling, just coming to rest in Paul's arms. He held her tightly, her face only a few inches from his, her arms wrapped partway around his neck. If Nina thought his worried look before had been open and honest, then what she saw while he held her was like looking straight into his heart. She saw fear, replaced by relief, then a quick rush of desire.

Nina had a moment to wonder if he was going to kiss her, and to wonder what she would do if he did. His arms shifted around her back, drawing her closer to him, but just as quickly his grip loosened. He let her slide down until her feet touched the ground, then stepped back immediately.

But he'd held on long enough for Nina to feel his body shaking like a tree in high winds. He turned away, and she thought maybe he still was.

She lifted her hand and watched it. So was she.

Neither of them said anything. Nina went to the tire and busied herself cutting the other end of the rope free. Paul got his socks and boots back on. She handed him the rope and he settled the coil over his shoulder, then she retrieved her discarded shirt and her own socks and boots. He waited while she got herself back in order, and then they headed back to the others, all without a single word.

Nina wanted to speak, but she couldn't think of a thing to say. At least, something not completely idiotic. She couldn't say to Paul, *You caught me, now I trust you.* And that wasn't even the worst. *You didn't kiss me, so now I trust you.*

But she did, sharp and sudden as a light switch being flipped. All the energy she had spent convincing herself not to had been a waste. She felt lighter, like her distrust had been chains dragging at her every step.

But she couldn't say it. Her thoughts scattered, flitting from the fall to the catch to the almost-kiss and back again in a fevered loop.

When they made it back to the camp, Paul lifted the rope over his shoulder and held it out to her. She remembered the long, lean muscles of his arms when he stood in the water, and the image spliced itself into her thoughts. She took the rope from him, and this time, her fingers brushed his. Those gold-green eyes widened, and Nina managed a weak smile before turning away.

She couldn't say it. But she had a feeling it wouldn't take him long to figure out.

CHAPTER TEN
TOOTHBRUSHES

September 10th, 8:23 am – Downtown, Mount Vernon, Ohio

Paul had seen places in worse shape than this, but still, it wasn't a pretty sight.

The outer edge of town was mostly residential, and before the plague hit, it had probably been well-maintained. But no one remained to repair the damage done by summer storms. Fences leaned out of true like drunks weaving their way home from the bar. Gardens teemed with weeds. The flower boxes hung empty on their windows, or lay tumbled on the ground below. Some houses had lost pieces of their siding, others were suffering from peeling paint.

Everyone was silent as they passed a tree which had probably been as old as the town itself, before lightning had split it in half. One side of the tree was still upright, but the other had fallen over, taking the nearest power lines out with it. Paul gave the ends of the snapped cables wide berth, even though they were obviously dead. There hadn't been power anywhere for months now.

John didn't want to forage in the houses, so they kept moving. He'd lost the argument to go around town, but he insisted they pass through as quickly as possible.

Mark had filled Paul in on the argument earlier, while John was fetching water. "He wanted to go around, and we didn't," Mark explained. He paused, looking away, and Paul followed his gaze. Nina was watching them, and Mark motioned her over.

"He doesn't think we need more food?" Paul asked when she had joined them. "I don't know how careful the rest of you are, but I only have enough for another two or three days."

"Well, that's the thing," Mark replied. "You knew we were headed to John's sister's, right? It's the next town down the road. He thinks we can make it without foraging for more. He doesn't want to get into trouble with anyone we might come across if we go into town."

"How far is it?" Nina asked.

"We stick to 36, a little less than forty miles to the town limit, then however far we have to go to find her place."

"Huh," Paul grunted. "On my own, I could cover twenty-five miles on a good day, but we don't usually do better than fifteen—Aaron just can't walk that fast, for that long. So John figured a day to get around this town, then three days to his sister's house?"

Mark nodded.

"I'm with you and Sarah, then," Paul said. "We need supplies." Though it hardly mattered now, since they'd won the argument already. But Mark smiled at him.

John may have lost the argument, but if he was angry, he hadn't shown it when he laid out the plan. "We stay on 36, it's the main road that runs right through the center of town, but we keep an eye out at all the cross streets. If anything within a few blocks seems worth investigating, we take a look, then head back to 36. I want to be through here as quick as we can manage."

So they split into two groups, though neither one was ever far from the other. Paul found himself with John, Alison, and Aaron as they scouted the south side of the street. Nina was with the others on the north side. While there was probably usable food left in some of the houses, John insisted they concentrate on the stores downtown. Everyone agreed, especially since any house might be home to another band of survivors.

No power meant no lights, which made it hard to tell which held people, and which held only the dead. Neither was an appealing prospect.

When the neighborhoods gave way to businesses, though, they slowed down and started checking the cross streets more carefully. Most of the buildings weren't in any better shape than the gas station where Paul had met them—broken windows, doors swinging open or missing entirely.

Someone who had passed through ahead of them had been busy with a can of red spray paint, writing "EMPTY" on the walls of some places. The first one Paul's group saw was a Mexican restaurant. They had a quick talk about checking it out anyway, but then a family of raccoons came trotting out the door, three little ones trailing behind their mother. Aaron laughed, and the sound startled the creatures, who scampered away. "If the human scavengers left anything behind," John said, "I'm sure the animals have gotten it by now." Alison laughed, though Paul didn't think John had meant it to be funny.

The next place with any promise was a small grocery, but it was marked empty, too. After a few blocks of nothing, Mark called them over to his side of the street.

"There's a gas station two blocks south, you see it?" he said, pointing. "No broken windows, and I don't see any spray paint."

"Worth a look, I guess," John answered.

They all went together—safer that way—but it didn't end up being worth the trip. Whoever looted this place hadn't done as much damage as they'd seen done elsewhere, but the emptiness left behind was just as thorough. Aaron found a chocolate bar fallen underneath one of the shelves, but nothing else.

The rest of the morning passed following the same pattern. Every few blocks someone would get their hopes up, only to find little or nothing. Both groups stopped together to have lunch in an accountant's office which was in decent shape. Paul supposed a place that didn't have food, drugs, or cash wouldn't be interesting to looters in the earliest days, or survivors in the months since.

John and Alison were making a rough search of the place for anything useful, while Mark and Sarah sat with Aaron and watched him do tricks with his yo-yo. Paul debated for a moment about joining them, but he decided he would rather be alone and ducked outside.

He would have felt better if he could pretend that he was putting himself on guard duty. But the truth was he didn't want the others to see he wasn't going to eat. He didn't have high hopes for finding more food in town, judging how things had gone so far. If it was going to take them three more days to get where they were going, he needed to start tightening his belt.

And that was assuming there would be food when they reached their destination. If there wasn't, they were going to be in real trouble. Paul sat down on the single step leading up to the entryway alcove, shaded by an awning stretching overhead. He folded his hands together, his elbows resting on his knees as he hunched over, trying not to worry, and failing.

If this goes badly, I could leave.

The thought struck him with unexpected force. He hadn't once considered leaving since Sarah asked him to stay. At the end of the day, if they hadn't found enough food, Paul could simply turn back, let the others go on without him, and keep looking. There was bound to be something in all these houses they were skipping over. He could forage for a few days, build his supplies back up, and when he was satisfied, pick a direction and start walking again, alone.

The door opened behind him. Nina came out and sat down beside him, close, but not touching. Once she had her pack off, she fished through it and came up with a protein bar, which she held out to him. Paul held up his hand in a polite but wordless refusal.

"Take it," she insisted. "I have enough for another week, at least. John always has us divide the food evenly, but I'm so small, I need less than anyone else but Aaron. And the way he's growing, not even him for much longer. It won't be long before he's taller than me."

It was the first time she'd spoken to him since the day before. With the confusion of hope and disbelief Paul felt about what had passed between them, he didn't want to talk about food with her. He wanted to find a way to ask her what she'd meant, without meeting a wall of defensiveness.

But he couldn't deny she had a point, though it went against all the rules he'd created for himself since the plague to take something without a trade. He couldn't take something from someone he wanted to help and to protect, someone he cared about. Even if it never went any further than this, sitting close, but not too close.

He wasn't the type to give anyone the silent treatment, and she was right. He took the offered food and said, softly, "Thanks."

While he ate, Nina pulled out half a packet of peanut butter crackers for herself. They sat together in a silence that, on Paul's part, felt tense. It was unusual for him not to know what to say.

And then Nina choked on a mouthful of cracker and began to cough violently. Paul turned, reaching out to her in the instinct everyone has to pound a coughing person on the back, whether or not it would actually help. Nina waved him off as tears leaked from her eyes. The fit was already dying down. A few moments later she was taking deep, raspy breaths and sniffling. Paul watched, concerned, as she drained half her water bottle trying to recover. Then he remembered something and rummaged in his pack, producing a tiny travel packet of tissues.

Nina took one from the packet and dried her eyes, but Paul continued to hold the whole thing out to her. "I have two," he said.

It wasn't a great trade for food, but after a long moment's hesitation, she took it. Paul felt better then, like his world was starting to shift back into balance after getting knocked askew the day before. He'd gotten used to dealing with cautious, suspicious Nina. It was the touch of her fingers, paired with tentative smile, that had sent his heart lurching and spinning like a kid on a carnival ride.

Paul hoped she wouldn't see the guilt in his eyes. He wouldn't leave, not for something as minor as a few days of short rations. He felt a rush of shame for considering it, even if it was only for a few minutes. It would take a lot more to drive him away.

The sound of the door opening caught his attention and put a halt to anything Paul was tempted to say. He and Nina turned to see Sarah pop her head out. "You okay?" she asked Nina. "It took us a minute to figure out what that noise was."

"Yeah, fine," she answered. "It's a bad idea to try to breathe stale crackers."

"Okay," Sarah said, a faint smile appearing at Nina's wry tone. "I think we'll get moving again in a few minutes. John and Alison are nearly done."

"Anything good?" Paul asked.

"Paper and pens, mostly, but some of those would be useful to have around. There's enough for everyone."

They followed her inside to collect them. Paul was as glad of the excuse to avoid any more awkwardness with Nina as he was to get the supplies themselves, a brand-new yellow legal pad and two black ballpoint pens.

"Better luck this afternoon, I hope," John said as everyone shouldered their packs again. "Let's get back out there."

They split up the same as before. There was no call from either group to the other for the first five blocks, which didn't seem to bode well for the rest of the day. But then Mark hailed Paul's group.

"Drugstore," he said when they joined up on his side of the street. "Not the best for food, but more meds would be worth the look, right? Cross your fingers."

This time, the inside looked promising—the shelves in the main area were only half empty, though the security door leading to the pharmacy proper swung open, its lock broken. Mark ducked in and came back out right away, reporting the section completely cleaned out. "Looks like they only wanted to bother with the good stuff," he said. "You guys get started, I'll keep watch here at the door. It's funny how I didn't feel like anyone was out there with us, until we found something. Now I'm getting goosebumps."

Alison laughed, but John gave him a firm nod. "Everybody else, pick a section and start stuffing your bags."

Paul headed for the center of the store and set to work. He ended up in front of the toothpaste and started pulling tubes out of their boxes to make them easier to pack. When he'd gotten a tube for each of them, he started on the toothbrushes. For a moment, he considered leaving those in their packaging, but space concerns won out over keeping them intact. He remembered that Nina had plastic bags, though, and looked around for her. He figured she'd be willing to lend him one to keep the toothbrushes in until he could parcel them out.

He didn't see her—in fact, he hardly saw anyone. The shelves weren't tall, but when his companions were bending or crouching down to get at items on the lowest shelves, they were out of sight. Mark was at the door, idly picking at his fingernails. Aaron sat on the floor looking through a magazine.

Paul had a moment to wonder why he wasn't with his father, learning which items were good to take and which were worthless, before he heard the door chime.

CHAPTER ELEVEN
A KNIFE

September 10th, 12:45 pm – The drugstore

Nina was inspecting a row of cold medicine boxes. The door chime sounded, bright, cheerful, and completely out of place.

As the ringing faded, there was a sharp crack and a loud cry. Nina dropped to a crouch, taking cover behind a shelf, her heart slamming against her ribs. She was in the far corner of the store, not facing the door—she didn't know what had happened. She turned and inched toward the edge of the shelf blocking her view.

A dark-haired woman brandished a rifle. She stood near Mark, who was curled up on the floor with his head in his hands. Nina hid behind the shelf again when two men came inside, each aiming a handgun. "Drop your stuff, everybody," the woman ordered. "Do that, and you can walk away."

Nina kept still. She didn't think any of the intruders had seen her, but without a better view of the store, she didn't know who they *could* see. They might not know they were outnumbered, but Nina knew they weren't outgunned. John had the group's only firearm, and Nina's little knife wouldn't help much in a standoff like this.

Her mind whirled with possibilities and plans. Her first option was to stay hidden, but she discarded it. If the others gave themselves up, they'd get to leave, but she'd be found when the intruders searched the store.

Giving herself up without a fight and losing all her supplies wasn't any better. She'd lost everything once before, and rebuilding her gear was something she didn't want to do twice. So she waited for somebody to say something, to do something, to give her any kind of cue.

Someone was moving—she heard the scuff of boots against the floor, the shivery plastic sound of vinyl straps moving against fabric, then a thud. A pack hitting the floor. There was a pause, then the woman spoke again. "Paul?" she asked, disbelieving.

Nina's heart was already racing, but now, it felt ready to burst.

Paul's voice, though, was steady. "Hello, Christine."

Paul *knew* her?

A long silence followed his greeting. Nina quivered with the effort required to keep still, to stop herself from screaming with frustration because she couldn't see what was happening. She pictured Paul facing the barrel of the woman's rifle. The image sent prickles of cold dancing over her skin, even as her heart burned with a liquid, searing fury.

"Down, boys," came the woman's voice—Christine's voice—again. "I know this guy. He's cool. Sorry about your friend, though, Paul. He should be all right, I didn't hit him that hard." She chuckled. "So, what brings you to this neck of the woods, with this fine family of people? Though they can't really be one, though, right? Not looking the way they do."

Family. The word jumped out at Nina—most people would have said *group*. Christine had seen Mark, she'd seen Paul—but family made Nina think Aaron and maybe Sarah were in sight too, and Aaron was the odd one out to her. Which potentially left John and Alison hidden somewhere.

"I could ask you the same thing," Paul answered. "I thought you were headed west. This is definitely not west of where you left me."

Without knowing where the others might be, though, Nina had to find them before they could come up with any kind of plan. She peeked past the shelf again. Crossing the aisle was risky—Paul stood there, but even with his body blocking it, Nina might be seen by their attackers if she tried.

"Oh, I did," Christine said, her tone deliberately casual. "I don't know how it happened, exactly—maybe somebody just got careless and flicked his cigarette too far from the side of the road. But it's been a real dry summer over there, and now a good chunk of Indiana has gone up in flames. You ever see a wildfire spreading across miles of untented farmland? Quite a sight. So I had to turn back. But you didn't answer my question. When we met, you were alone."

Nina turned to her right, crawling as soundlessly as she could toward the corner. The shelves turned there to run parallel to the outer wall of the building. Taking a deep breath, she leaned out for a quick look down the aisle.

"So were you," Paul retorted.

John crouched a few yards away, hidden behind a shelf just as Nina had been, only with his gun drawn. She waved one hand wildly, trying to get his attention without making any noise. Any odd sounds would invite one of those door guards to come investigate.

"Yeah, but I'm a people person," Christine said. "You struck me more as a lone-wolf type. And now here you are, all cozy with a kid! Did you take him in, or did they? Because this is all just too precious. Never would have thought it of you."

Nina thought she would dislike Christine even if the woman weren't threatening them—her condescending tone was at least as irritating as Alison's worst comments.

John turned his head and saw Nina, waving her forward. She crawled the distance to him. "Seen Alison?" he whispered. Nina shook her head.

"And I never thought I'd see you again at all, Christine," Paul was saying. "Especially at gunpoint."

"If we can get that rifle away from the woman somehow," John went on, "I can cover the men at the door. Just haven't figured out how yet."

Christine laughed, an unpleasant sound with an edge of malice to it. "Oh, we're not going to hurt you. Well, not more than we did. Daddy here should have been more careful. And armed."

"She's pretty focused on Paul," Nina whispered back. "If we create some kind of distraction? Maybe kick over one of the shelves?" But she didn't have anything more solid to offer.

John shook his head. "Bolted down, I already checked. If we found something heavy to throw, maybe . . ."

"Then what's the plan, Christine?" Paul asked. "Plenty here for all of us. I'm sure we can work something out."

The sly, inviting undertone in Paul's voice set Nina's teeth grinding. But she pushed her annoyance aside and cast about for something worth throwing. She'd been standing in front of the cold medicines . . .

Cough syrup bottles. "Be right back," she whispered to John.

"I missed you, sometimes," Christine said, her voice turning soft and coy. "I haven't found anyone since who was so . . . understanding."

Nina unclenched her fists, grabbed two bottles from the lowest shelf, and crawled back to John.

"I missed you, too," Paul replied. "Especially when I woke up and realized you'd left without saying goodbye."

"That's perfect, Nina," John whispered. "I'm going to go a little farther down the aisle toward those men. Watch me, and when I give you the signal, stand up, chuck those bottles at the woman's head, then get back down. They'll all turn to face you, but I can cover those two."

"What about her?" she whispered.

He let out a brief sigh. "Have to trust Paul to take care of her when she's distracted."

"I'm sorry about that," Christine was saying. There was a clicking sound which sent tiny echoes bouncing through the shelves—boot heels?—and when she spoke again, her voice sounded closer. Nina hoped she wasn't too close to Paul, she didn't want to hit him if her aim was bad. "Things were so hard in the first days. I didn't know if I was better off on my own, or with you. I left like that because I was afraid you'd be able to convince me to stay."

Nina watched John crawl away, then kept watching, waiting for the signal.

"I can be pretty persuasive," Paul said. His voice was suddenly so low and husky than Nina almost didn't recognize it. He didn't sound like the Paul she knew at all, but a complete stranger again, flirtatious, smooth, even seductive.

She waited.

When she heard soft moans and faintly wet sounds, her gut churned as she realized what was happening. She had to swallow another urge to scream, listening to it, but she watched John, worried now she would hit Paul instead of his paramour. Part of her felt like he'd deserve it, for having the bad taste to have ever been involved with this woman.

But getting kissed was an effective distraction.

John held up three fingers, then folded one back, counting down. Two. One.

Nina stood up, took half a second to orient herself, then hurled one of the bottles as hard as she could at Christine's head. She missed—it sailed past her to hit one of the shelves on the other side of the store, scattering a handful of boxes. On Nina's right, John had the surprised gunmen at the door covered. They waffled between looking at Nina, John, and Paul and Christine as the kiss continued.

But it was over as soon as Christine heard the noise and pulled away. The second bottle hit her squarely in the temple, sending her reeling back.

Alison darted out from behind the shelf where Paul stood and made a grab for Christine's rifle. In her dazed state, her grip wasn't solid, but she recovered enough to get her hand on the shoulder strap. A vicious tug-of-war began between the two women.

Nina dropped back down behind her shelf as instructed. But she'd seen where Aaron was, huddled in fright a few feet away from Paul. She hoped

John was right about Paul helping Alison subdue Christine, because there was nothing she could do to help.

But she was afraid the struggle might spook the two men into shooting, and Aaron was in sight.

Crawling was too slow—Nina made her best attempt at a crouching run behind the cover of the shelves. When she reached him, she pulled him out of sight of the gunmen and wrapped him in her arms.

She couldn't follow the sounds of what was happening clearly anymore. Aaron was sobbing. She held him and smoothed her hand over his dark curls, trying to soothe him. The sounds of the struggle continued—Alison's grunts against Christine's curses. Mark was groaning near the door. If Sarah was doing anything, she couldn't be heard over a sudden cry of pain followed by the sound of someone hitting the shelves and falling hard.

Alison let out a loud and strident laugh, then everything went quiet.

"So here's what's gonna happen," Paul said. His voice was hard and flat, but sharp breath sounds snuck in between his words. "Sarah, get Mark on his feet. The gentlemen with the guns will hand them over to you two, and then they're gonna leave. If all goes well, then, Christine, Alison won't shoot you with your own gun, and you'll follow them out. You can go on your way so long as you don't give us any more trouble."

"Shit," Christine spat out. "Fine, you win."

John spoke up from the far side of the room. "You heard her, gentlemen. Hand your weapons over."

Nina wanted to get up and see what was going on instead of trying to figure it out from listening, but Aaron was still shaking with sobs. She held him tighter and kissed the top of his head.

"Out you go," John said. The door opened, its chime ringing out again, then shut.

"Be smart about this, Christine," Paul said, his voice stern, all traces of his earlier interest gone. "Give me my knife back, and walk away."

Nina's heart squeezed down into a hard little knot of anxiety, listening to the silence stretching out and filling every corner of the drugstore. Then there was the receding click of boot heels and the friendly chime of the door.

John appeared at the edge of the shelf where Nina and Aaron were hiding, holstering his gun. "C'mere, son, everything's fine now, you're safe," he said as he crouched down nearby. Aaron let go of Nina to throw his arms around his father's neck, and John pulled him up and carried him toward the door. "Let's get out of here."

The door chime sounded as they went out, then again a moment later.

Sarah asked, "Where's Nina? I didn't see, did she get hurt? Nina!"

"I'll find her," Paul said.

Nina could have stood up and saved them the trouble, but she was frozen in place. The fear she'd pushed aside in order to act had come washing back over her, leaving her trembling and mute. Even the idea she might somehow get left behind—which part of her knew was absolutely ridiculous—couldn't get her to speak up.

"But you're hurt, Paul," Sarah protested. "Go on outside and rest a bit while we get reorganized. John's going to have his hands full getting Aaron calm again, but I'm sure he's going to want to get out of town as quick as we can after this."

"No, you've got Mark to look after," Paul insisted. "Nasty bump he's got, there. Don't fret about me, I'll find her."

It wasn't so much a matter of finding, as it turned out. The moment the door closed behind Mark and Sarah, Paul appeared from the same aisle John had when he'd come for Aaron. Paul crouched down just as John had, but didn't reach out. "You didn't get hurt, somehow, did you? You seemed okay when you got Aaron out of the way."

She hadn't realized he'd seen that, but then, he did always seem to know where she was. "I'm not hurt," she said. Turning to face him was hard, because she was afraid to look, but she made herself do it. "You are, though."

The right side of Paul's shirt was dark with blood, spreading downward from a rip that followed his collarbone across. "Looks worse than it is," he said, the softness of his voice not doing much to mask the pain in it. "I'll be fine."

"What happened?" Nina whispered.

"She snatched my knife once Alison got the gun away from her. I was trying to get her under control, but I didn't think she'd be that fast. And I ain't much of a fighter, anyway."

"Better than I did, hiding over here," Nina muttered.

"Come on, Nina, give yourself a little credit," he said with a hint of his lopsided smile. "You hit her right in the head." When Nina didn't reply, he sighed, and stretched out one hand. "Can we get outta here now?"

She took his hand and allowed him to pull her up. "Not yet," she said, going to retrieve her pack. It was still open, and the little bit of medicine she'd gathered lay on top. She picked it up and turned back to Paul. "At least if you had to get sliced open, it happened in a drugstore," she said. Her voice shook, her hands shook, and all she wanted was to curl up and cry, as Aaron had. But there was too much to do. "Do you see where the bandages are?"

CHAPTER TWELVE
A NEEDLE AND THREAD

September 10th, 6:34 pm – A farm, east of Mount Vernon, Ohio

No one spoke as they clustered together outside, waiting for John and Mark to check the farmhouse. Tonight, Nina wanted real shelter, and beds, and maybe even food, since they hadn't managed to get any in town.

But after a few minutes, the men came back out. Mark had his hand over his nose and stopped to take a few huge gulps of air before he joined them. John shook his head, his shoulders sagging.

"I guess it's the barn, then," Sarah said.

The barn proved to be empty, whatever animals it once housed long gone. Nina took a deep breath as she stepped inside, and all she could smell was hay.

"It's better than nothing," Alison said.

Paul moved past Nina, but she caught at his sleeve, and he stopped. "Back outside," she said. "So I can take care of your shoulder while there's still daylight."

He dropped his pack inside the door before following her out. He settled cross-legged with his back against the side of the barn, and she knelt in front of him, pulling the supplies she'd gathered out of her pack. Gauze pads, tape, antibiotic ointment, her water bottle, and Sarah's travel sewing kit. Nina had asked her for it outside the drugstore, thinking they'd be there long enough to patch Paul up, but John had wanted to move on right away. Paul hadn't objected, but Nina suspected he was in more pain than he let on, after going all afternoon without being treated.

"You ever stitched anyone up before?" he asked as Nina checked the points of the needles, choosing the sharpest one and sticking it through the sleeve of her shirt.

"No," she answered honestly. "But I've gotten them before, so I know what to do. Sort of. And I think you're going to need it. Though this isn't the right kind of needle, but we wouldn't find any hook needles unless we scrounged them up in a doctor's office or hospital. People don't usually have those lying around."

Paul nodded as he started to unbutton his shirt, but Nina pushed his hands away. "Don't move more than you have to," she told him. "You don't want to start bleeding again."

She tried not to think much about what she was actually doing. She fumbled at the buttons—it was awkward to come at them from the wrong side—and she hoped he wouldn't read anything into her clumsiness, good or bad.

She stole a glance at his face, but his eyes were closed as he leaned his head back against the wall of the barn. She relaxed, knowing he wasn't going to be watching her every move when she was only inches away from him.

When Nina had all the buttons undone, she pushed the left side of the shirt back over his shoulder. Where the blue flannel had gone dark with the blood stains, his thin white undershirt was bright red. "Good thing you have a spare," she said as he leaned forward and worked the shirt over his head, finally exposing the wound.

A narrow slash, maybe four or five inches long, ran just below his collarbone. She managed to hold in a curse, but a strangled noise escaped instead. Paul bent his head, trying to see the wound. "That bad?" he asked. "All I can really see is the blood."

"You'll be fine," Nina said in her firmest tone. He leaned back again as she tore open a gauze pad and wet it with her water bottle. "I'm sorry, Paul, but there's no help for it. This is going to hurt."

"No need to apologize," he replied. "Do what you have to."

She worked as quickly as she could, but even with the ointment, she was afraid of infection, so she tried to be thorough. The blood seeping down his chest, she ignored—there would be more before she was done, so she'd have to clean it up twice if she did it now.

She tossed aside the bloody gauze and retrieved the needle she'd chosen from her shirt sleeve. There were six tiny spools of thread in the sewing kit in different colors. Black would be the easiest to see against Paul's pale skin, so she unwound a length and cut it off with the tiny pair of scissors from the kit. She was trying to thread the needle when Paul's voice startled her.

"I met her on the road just north of Louisville, the day after I left. She was walkin', so I picked her up, gave her a ride."

Nina wasn't sure what to say in response, but she found herself feeling defensive. "I didn't ask."

"You didn't have to," he replied.

"It's not my business."

"Nina, look at me." She ignored him and kept trying the needle. "I'm serious, look at me," he insisted. She met his eyes, green and gold and intense. "I'm not ashamed, Nina. I didn't do anything wrong. I was alone and grievin'. I'd just lost all the family I had in the world. She offered me comfort, and I accepted it. If you're not the type to do that, fine, but I will not apologize for the fact that I am."

His voice was soft, but he was still reprimanding her. Nina felt like a coward for doing it, but she had to look away. She tried to thread the needle again, but with the way her hands were shaking it didn't seem possible. "You're right," she said. "I'm not like that. I wouldn't—I can't—" She broke off and needed a deep breath before she could go on. "You're right, though. I shouldn't judge."

"Well, maybe you can judge a little," he said, his tone turning wry. "She stole my car when she left."

Startled into a weak laugh, Nina caught herself ending it with a sniffle. She shook her head. Paul could not see her cry.

But he noticed she was about to, because he reached up to fold her hands in his, careful of the needle. "Nina. Take a deep breath, and then another one. I'm gonna be okay, 'cause you can do this."

She knew he meant to be kind. But his soothing gesture, to her, wasn't soothing at all. She couldn't calm her breathing, not with her hands trapped between his. She pulled them free, stood up, and walked away. He didn't call out after her, and no one else was outside to see it. Crossing her arms, hugging herself, she stood in the late sunshine, trying not to think about Paul or Christine or anything at all.

Five minutes later, maybe ten, her nerves settled and her breathing was back under control. She thought maybe she should try to find a watch, like Paul had. It seemed like a useful thing to have. She went back to Paul, knelt beside him, and threaded the needle on the first try.

He watched her do it and said, "Go on, then. I'm ready."

Nina held the edges of the wound together with her left hand and set the needle against his skin with her right. "I'll try to be quick."

It might have been the worst thing Nina had ever had to do. Her stomach churned the whole time. Pushing the needle into his skin over and over again was awful. She had trouble finding the right amount of force to use—too much and she'd stab too deep, too little and she'd just scratch the surface and not accomplish anything. And tugging the thread through flesh was nothing like sewing through cloth. It felt heavy and wet, like dragging something clean through mud.

Before long, Paul was holding his breath in anticipation of the next stitch. Beads of sweat broke out on his forehead. As Nina ran the thread through him again, he bit his lip, then let out a whimper when she tied off the stitch.

The sound, so unlike him, startled Nina. She pulled too hard, ripping the stitch free. He balled his right hand into a fist and beat the ground beside him a few times.

Nina flinched, struggling against a new wave of threatening tears. "Shit, Paul, I'm sorry, I'm so sorry. My hands are shaking again."

"How much more?" he asked, his voice thready and weak.

"Just past half done," she answered. "You need a break?"

"Yeah," he breathed.

Nina ripped open another gauze pad and used it to wipe as much blood off her hands as she could before rooting through her pack again. She found the bottle of aspirin he'd traded her and opened it, shaking a few pills out and offering them to him.

"No," he said. "Blood thinner. Last thing I need."

"Oh, right." She went to put them back, then thought better of it and downed them herself with a swallow of water. All of the odd twists and turns the day had taken had given her a headache. "Maybe one of the others got something better when we hit the store," she said, starting to get up, intending to ask around.

Paul reached out for her hand and pulled her back, though he didn't hold on long. "Later," he said. "Better finish up first."

Swallowing past a lump in her throat, Nina willed her stomach to stay down. "You ready?"

He nodded.

Nina started stitching again, slower, more carefully. Paul closed his eyes and took deep breaths, steady, rhythmic. She found herself counting in her head as he did. *In, two, three, four, out, two, three, four.* Neither of them spoke.

Eventually, she was done. Nina knotted the last stitch and set the scissors against his skin to snip off the last trailing bit of thread. "There," she said. She still had tears in her eyes. If she looked into his, they would spill over, so she busied herself washing the needle off and repacking the sewing kit.

"It's okay, Nina," he said. "You did good."

She swallowed hard and took a deep, shuddering breath, trying to choke back the tears. "The bandage," she said. "We need to get you cleaned up."

She wet yet another gauze pad and started to wipe the blood off his skin. When she was satisfied she couldn't get him any cleaner without throwing him in a river, she got the roll of tape and another piece of gauze.

They were going to have to find more of these if she kept running through them so fast.

Getting the bandage in place and taped down was easy, compared to stitching him up. When she finished, before she could change her mind, she sat back, unbuttoning her oversized canvas shirt and handing it to him. She hoped it would fit. She'd look awfully foolish giving it to him only to find out it didn't.

"You'll be cold," he said, trying to return it.

"Not as cold as you'd be in just your undershirt." Though he was right, her thin tee wasn't going to keep her warm. She hoped they'd find more clothes soon. If nothing else, she could search for something in the farmhouse, but the smell . . .

He held the shirt in his hands, staring at her without moving, without putting it on.

"You don't really want to wear this bloody mess again, do you?" she asked, holding up his torn, stained shirt for inspection before balling it up and tossing it aside. "Besides," she added, her voice low, "Alison's already tossing you enough inviting glances when you're fully clothed. It would only get worse if you're walking around in a shirt thinner than paper. Those things don't leave much to the imagination."

She was teasing him to try to hold off the waterworks. But she was also wondering what he'd say, if she could get any idea what was going on between him and Alison. She remembered her turn on watch, when she had found the barrette and jumped to uncomfortable conclusions.

When he didn't answer right away, Nina risked a glance at his expression, and he looked stunned. "What, hadn't you noticed?" she asked.

"Yeah," Paul said. "But honestly, I didn't think much of it. I'm kinda used to those looks, so when I'm not interested, I just ignore 'em."

"Right." Nina snorted. "Handsome guy like you must get them all the time."

"Well . . . yeah. I guess I did." He chuckled at her raised eyebrow. "Before you go thinkin' I'm full of myself, you should know that most of the time, the women givin' me those looks turned tail when I started talkin'. Kentucky accents aren't exactly appealin' to the New York crowd. No matter how good I looked, if I opened my mouth I became a backwoods hick."

"That's awful," Nina said, any hint of teasing gone.

Paul shrugged, then winced at the movement. "I got used to that, too," he replied, fishing his spare undershirt out of his pack. Once he got it on, he stood up carefully and tried to pull on Nina's shirt. He grunted when that tugged at the stitches too, so Nina sprang up to help, guiding the sleeves over his arms.

He shooed her hands away when she tried to do up the buttons, though. She backed up a step, relieved, because her hands were still shaking. But she was glad to see the shirt fit him well enough, though the sleeves were an inch or two short in the wrist. "There," he said. "All patched up. But I'm feeling kinda dizzy. I think I need to lie down awhile."

"Yeah," Nina agreed. "The others have probably all claimed piles of hay by now, but I'm sure there's still plenty of room. Go get some sleep."

He headed inside, but turned back just at the open door. "You coming in, too?"

She shook her head. "I thought I might circle the house, see if there's anything useful. John and Mark only checked inside."

He nodded, and she thought they were done, but then he gave her a tired smile and said, "Thank you, Nina."

She felt the tears coming back. "I'd say, anytime, but then you might go and get yourself hurt again. So don't."

Her teasing didn't sound nearly as lighthearted as she meant it to, but he nodded again and went inside.

She trudged over to the farmhouse. There was a deck out back, with a weathered kettle grill, a table, a few chairs. She sat down in one of them, folded her arms on the table, and put her head down. For a moment, she was a child in elementary school again, not feeling well enough to go out to recess, but not sick enough to go home. Alone in the classroom except for the teacher, who sat at her desk grading papers, the room had felt echoing and empty, much bigger than when her classmates were there.

Now, that's what the whole world felt like. Nina cried until she felt empty herself, until she was so exhausted she wasn't sure she would ever be able to lift her head again.

But she did, eventually.

She had to go back. She had to find out if she'd been assigned a watch, then curl up to sleep on a pile of hay, the softest bed she'd had in weeks.

Yesterday, it would have been something to look forward to. Tonight, she feared her dreams would run with blood.

CHAPTER THIRTEEN
GRAVE MARKERS

September 15th, 11:45 am – 1880 Cambridge Road, Coshocton, Ohio

The last leg of their journey, which John had estimated would take three days, actually took four and a half. For the first two, Paul suffered from dizzy spells and intermittently numb fingers, so John called more rest breaks than usual.

Paul didn't think he'd lost enough blood to put him in any danger. But when his injury was stacked on top of eating mostly junk food and not enough of it anyway, his ongoing weakness and exhaustion wasn't surprising.

Sleeping poorly wasn't helping, either. He and Mark weren't given watches those nights—Mark was still having headaches from the blow he'd taken—so the four other adults took over. Posting a watch every night might have been an overreaction to the confrontation at the drugstore. But John insisted, Sarah agreed, Alison only grumbled when she thought no one would notice, and Nina never said a word of complaint in Paul's hearing. The extra chance to rest was welcome, but the slow ache in his shoulder kept him from deep sleep. He woke and tossed and turned with every sound in the night.

While everyone was patient with Paul slowing them down, their tempers started to run high with each other. As the days passed and everyone got hungrier, snapping remarks became arguments which flared over nothing, then subsided into uneasy silence. Mark and Sarah fought over tiny things which wouldn't have bothered them at all the week before. Sarah would storm off to walk with John, or on her own, and Alison was usually close by, ready to soothe Mark's hurt feelings or wounded pride. Seeing the cycle forming, Paul couldn't help but remember the two of them sneaking back into camp while they thought everyone slept. He wondered if their affair was still going on—he hadn't seen any evidence since, but Alison had plenty of opportunity during her watches to spirit Mark away from the camp.

Aaron acted sullen with his father, and sometimes Paul couldn't blame him for it. John's temper was fraying around the edges, and he snapped at everyone over any little thing he wasn't pleased with. He said more harsh words in those four and a half days than Paul could remember him saying in the whole three weeks since he'd joined them.

Paul wondered if, the closer they got to John's goal of reaching his sister's house, the more afraid he was of what they would find. Even though Paul had lost his whole family, there was some comfort, at least, in the certainty. If he'd had to go searching for them, he wasn't sure he'd be holding himself together as well as John was, even then, near the end of the road.

Nina, though, wasn't losing her temper with anyone. She had boundless energy and patience. Every day, she slipped Paul extra food from her own supply when no one was looking, saying he needed it more to regain his strength. She ate little herself, without complaint. He tried to object once or twice, but he knew, deep down, she was right, so he let himself be overruled.

The first morning after leaving the barn behind, Nina took up her old, customary spot at the back of the line. Paul suspected she was keeping an eye on him, though he would have preferred having her close.

As the group became angrier and tempers surged more often, though, he realized she was keeping out of harm's way, too. But she was never far from him when he needed something—pain killers, or help getting his pack on and off, or a shoulder to lean on when he got tired. He only had to turn around enough to see her behind him, and her steps would quicken while his slowed, and then she'd be beside him. The first time she ducked under his arm, settling it over her shoulders, he thought it was almost worth getting attacked just for that moment. Then her arm slid neatly around his waist like it belonged there, and he felt better than he had all day.

Every evening as the others set up the camp around them, Nina checked his wound for fresh bleeding, spread it with more ointment, and put on a fresh bandage. Ten days, she told him the first time, before the stitches could come out. He'd given her a tired smile, and she'd smiled back and then sent him off to get some sleep.

At night, when the pain kept Paul wakeful, trying to get comfortable on the hard ground, he'd roll over and see Nina sitting nearby, if she was on watch. He didn't speak, and neither did she, but Paul watched her gazing into the firelight until he fell back asleep.

If what he had felt for her before hadn't been love, it certainly was now.

But they didn't talk about that—they didn't talk about much of anything. The words they traded were distilled to the bare necessities. Everything else, they said with fleeting looks and subtle gestures.

For one thing, the group was too tense, so near to their destination. No one said it, but everyone knew they wouldn't find John's sister there, safe and well with her family. They also knew John had to find out, to make certain. No one dared mention anything about what would happen after they got there, or tried to make any plans about what to do next.

The second thing was, even if they'd wanted to talk—and Paul had so much he wanted to say to Nina he thought he might burst, holding it all in— there was no privacy. The others were willing to turn a deaf ear to low-voiced conversations, but this wasn't something Paul wanted to discuss next to a fitful campfire with five other people nearby. Trying to talk on the move was difficult, when he needed all his energy to keep putting one foot in front of the other. And he doubted he'd have Nina to himself for any stretch of time, any time soon.

On top of all that, Paul grew more certain of his own feelings with every passing hour, but he had no way to know if Nina felt the same. Or if she might, given enough time. While his heart may have reveled silently whenever she touched him, when she did, it was assistance, not invitation. Sometimes, the way she'd smile, he thought she must feel something for him, too.

But other times, she was distant. Even when she stood inches away, her eyes had an unfocused, faraway look, and she didn't smile. The last thing he wanted to do was push her inside the defensive shell she'd had when they met, the one she was finally setting aside with him. So he was quiet and biddable and restrained, following her murmured instructions as she tended to his shoulder by firelight. Even though he wanted nothing more than to take her face in his hands and kiss her, he didn't.

She was so strong in some ways, and so fragile in others. This whole courtship he'd embarked on had become a slow series of tiny steps they'd taken toward each other. He wasn't about to risk it with a foolishly large one.

All of those thoughts ran through Paul's mind for the hundredth time as Nina helped him stay steady on the rough gravel of the long driveway. Despite her best efforts to counteract them, the lack of good food and solid sleep were taking a serious toll on him, and he felt almost too tired to move. He stopped for a moment to assess their destination.

The house was a two-story white Colonial, columns spaced along the front, screening a porch on the first floor and supporting the roof over a balcony on the second. It stood about twenty yards from the road, surrounded on all sides by wide stretches of lawn. A ring of pine trees marked the edges of the property, and a big maple stood in the side yard. The grass was overgrown and starting to brown, but the house itself seemed untouched.

He stood with Nina and watched the others go inside. "The front door's not locked," he said when John turned the knob and went straight in. It wasn't like him to be anything less than cautious. "I don't think that's a good sign."

"No," Nina agreed.

Once she got him up the steps, he took a seat on the bench on the front porch, dropping his pack beside it and his head into his hands. Nina shed her own pack and sat beside him without a word. But her anxiety showed in her left leg, which drummed up and down incessantly, though the rest of her body was still.

"I'm scared," she blurted out after a few minutes of silence. "After all this time, I don't know what it's going to do to John if they're not here. Even though we all know they're not. But when he finds out . . ."

Paul moved one hand away from his face and laid it on Nina's knee, palm up, inviting her to hold it. She hesitated, and Paul could picture her expression, uncertainty mixed with the faintest trace of surprise. He'd seen it enough by now. But he didn't take back his hand.

She held it. Her fingers were small and warm in his, and he resisted the temptation to squeeze them.

"How you holding up today?" she asked.

"Just tired," he answered. "Lookin' forward to sleeping in a real bed, hopefully."

"Yeah. Outside's not so bad in the summer, but it's getting much colder at night, and the ground ain't getting any softer."

Paul wondered if he'd heard her right. Then he laughed, a true, unrestrained laugh like he hadn't let loose for days, at least. Maybe not since the tire swing.

"What?" Nina demanded, withdrawing her hand.

Paul might have minded more if he weren't still laughing. "You just said *ain't*," he told her when he finally settled down enough to speak clearly.

Her face went blank, as if she were replaying her words in her head. "I did not," she protested.

"You did! You're pickin' up my accent."

She crossed her arms over her chest, and for a second, Paul worried he'd upset her. But then she quirked an eyebrow at him. "I don't know where you'd get such a crazy idea," she said in a near-perfect imitation of his slow drawl.

Paul burst out laughing again, and a heartbeat later Nina gave up on keeping a straight face and was laughing with him. He didn't stop until he was completely out of breath. "That was priceless," he said. "Spring that on the others sometime, I want to see their jaws drop."

"Was it good? Did I sound right?" Nina asked, still in his accent, starting him going again.

"Stop, Nina, please," he managed to squeeze out in between laughs. "I can't take much more."

"Oh, all right," she said in her own voice. "I suppose you do need to breathe."

"Thank you," he said, still wheezing.

The front door opened, and Mark stuck his head out. They both turned to him, and Nina's smile faded at the look on his face. "You'd better come," he said.

"Are they here?" Paul asked.

Mark shook his head.

"Oh, no," Nina whispered.

"But the house wasn't empty, either. We're, uh, kind of having a conference in the back yard."

They followed him inside. As Mark led them through to the back door, Paul glanced around at each room, noting the complete lack of destruction or disturbance. The inside looked as untouched as the outside. Being so far from the highway had protected this neighborhood—no one just passing through was going to stray too far from the main thoroughfare.

The backyard, though, was a different story. Sarah and Alison hung back, near the door, but John and Aaron stood together, facing a row of three graves marked with crosses made from broken branches. The first two were older, already starting to flatten, with a short growth of new grass over them. The third was brand new, a fresh pile of dark earth.

A thin teenage boy with dark red hair and a million freckles stood a few feet away, shoulders hunched and head bowed.

When John heard the door close behind them, he turned, and there were tears running down his face. "They're gone."

"I'm sorry, John," Paul said. "Truly I am."

John fell to his knees, giving into his grief with heaving sobs. Aaron sat down next to him, silent and dry-eyed, and took one of his father's hands.

Paul moved forward to rest a hand on John's shoulder, studying the markers. The left cross had a silver chain looped around the top, hung with a heart pendant carved from amber. The other two crosses had nails driven into them. The middle one was hung with a diamond ring, the new grave on the right with a plain golden band.

After a few minutes of silent vigil, Paul stepped back, then glanced around at everyone else and gestured his head at the back door, telling them to head inside. He was the last one to the door, except for the teenager, who didn't follow. Paul paused in the doorway and waved at him, and when his eyes widened, beckoned him over. He followed Paul in, his steps slow and heavy.

Everyone gathered in the kitchen. "What's your name?" Paul asked.

"Owen," he answered.

"How'd you end up here, Owen?" Mark asked him.

"I used to live a mile or so from here, closer to town," he began. His voice was hoarse, and his eyes bounced back and forth between everyone else, never focusing on any one person for long. "When my family . . . when they died, I didn't know what to do. It seemed like everyone in town was dead, but I didn't have anywhere else to go. So I buried them. And then I buried my neighbors, and took whatever food they had left. When I ran out, I went to the next neighborhood and buried them, too." He sniffled, trying not to cry. "I stayed in whichever house smelled the least awful, and when I had finished an area, I went to a new one and started over."

"Are we the first people, living people, you've seen all this time?" Sarah asked, horror in her voice.

"Yes, ma'am."

She reached out and embraced him. He flinched at first, but she held on, and his tears started flowing. "You poor thing," she murmured, petting the back of his head. When she let go and stepped back, he cleared his throat, visibly trying to compose himself.

"Only one of those graves is new, though." Alison's tone was surprisingly gentle, but the underlying question was obvious.

"Yeah," Owen said, wiping his nose with the back of his hand. "The other two were already there when I found this place. I've seen the pictures around the house—the girl who lived here was in my little sister's class, though I don't think they were friends. She and her mother were already buried, with their jewelry on the crosses. I only buried her father, so I made a cross for him and put his wedding band on it, like I think he would have wanted. He was already outside, too, near the graves. I think that was probably the last thing he did before he died."

"Oh, God," Sarah said, before she dashed from the room. Mark followed.

Nina sniffled, and Paul shot her a worried glance, but she smiled tightly at him, as if trying to tell him she was okay. He turned back to Owen.

"I don't know what John's gonna say when he comes back in," Paul told him. "He's our leader, and we came here to find his family. I don't think any of us had much hope, but still, knowin' the truth hurts." He paused, considering his words carefully. "I don't think you did anything wrong, though. None of us do." Alison and Nina both shook their heads in confirmation as Owen glanced at them. "I can't imagine what this has been like for you. But John might not want you to stay, now that we're here. I think it might be best if you pick a different house, for now."

Owen nodded. "I understand."

"I can already tell Sarah is going to want to take you in—the woman who hugged you," he went on. "She's the one who first asked me to stay, and I have a feeling she's going to argue against leaving you behind."

"No, she wouldn't stand for that, she takes in all the strays." Alison flicked a glance at Nina, which Paul noticed but hoped Nina didn't. "But we can't promise you anything."

"I understand," Owen repeated. "I wouldn't blame him if he doesn't want me around. But I don't . . . I don't want to be alone anymore."

"We'll do what we can," Paul said, extending his hand.

Owen took it with a firm shake, then drew his shoulders back and took a deep breath. "I haven't taken any of the food from here, and I won't. It's all yours, now, seeing how it's his family's place. I'll go back to the next house up the road, the brown brick one on the hill. If you need to find me." He cleared his throat again. "Thanks."

Paul turned to follow, meaning to see him out, but Nina caught his sleeve, pulling him back. "Leave it there," she whispered as Owen left the room. "In case we don't end up bringing him along."

"Yeah," he said, exhausted and heartsick at the thought. "I can't help but feel for him, though. I thought I had it bad on my own, but here he is, diggin' graves for his entire town. Makes me feel like an ass."

"Don't beat yourself up, Paul," Alison said. "We've all suffered. Whether you had it harder than him, or not, doesn't really matter, as long as we're all here for each other."

Kindness from Alison was unusual, but Paul didn't miss the edge of slyness to her tone which gave the words a different meaning. He thought she'd finally given up her subtle campaign for him, but with the prospect of a roof over their heads, maybe she saw a fresh opportunity. He ignored it, like he ignored all the rest. He had to say something, though, so he took the words at face value. "You're right," he said to her. "Guess I hadn't thought of it that way."

Alison seemed about to say something else, but Nina broke in. "I know it's early, Paul," she said, "but I might as well change your bandage now. We shouldn't do much until John comes back in—I don't think he'd like us poking around, like this is any other house we've scavenged."

"Don't imagine so."

He looked briefly at Alison, who nodded at him. "I'll stay here and keep an eye on John. You go get patched up."

"Let's go back out to the porch," Nina said. "The light's better, and we left our packs there."

CHAPTER FOURTEEN
BANDAGES

September 15th, 12:11 pm – 1880 Cambridge Road, Coshocton, Ohio

On her way to the front door, Nina saw Mark on the couch in the living room, holding Sarah curled up in his arms. She looked away before he could notice her watching.

Once she and Paul were out the door and out of earshot, she spoke. "Taking care of this now will give Sarah some time to pull herself together, too. That hit her really hard."

"Yeah." Paul sat on the bench, unbuttoned his shirt—she'd finally stopped thinking of it as hers, since it looked better on him anyway—and pulled the left side back in the familiar daily ritual. He'd stopped bothering with the undershirt after the second day. Nina had seen the grimace of pain on his face whenever he had to take it off.

"It's so nice that they still have each other," she went on, peeling back the tape on the edge of his bandage. Then she bit her lip at how foolish she sounded, and rushed to add, "Okay, *nice* isn't exactly the right word, but you know what I mean."

"Yeah," Paul repeated. He'd been talking a lot less since his injury, and Nina took it as a sign he was even more exhausted than he was willing to admit.

"To have someone to lean on when you need it, someone to take care of, someone to take care of you. Though . . ." she trailed off, her brows knotting together over her nose as she frowned. Everything she was saying about Mark and Sarah could apply to her and Paul right now, which was not a direction she wanted the conversation to take.

"Though?" Paul prompted.

She picked up her pack, set it on the bench, and rummaged through it for supplies. She didn't need to see the concern in his eyes when she heard it in his voice. "It's nothing. Never mind."

"I ain't so good at never mindin'. Something's botherin' you."

The roll of tape had managed to migrate all the way to the bottom of her pack, and she felt an irrational urge to swear at it. "A *lot* of things are bothering me."

"So what's this one?"

She looked up, straight into his eyes. So much for steering the conversation into safe waters. "I need to ask you something, Paul, and I want an honest answer. But I don't want you to read anything into it."

He frowned at her. "I ain't ever lied to you, Nina. What is it?"

"Okay." She took a deep breath, gathering her courage. "Are you sleeping with Alison?"

She expected Paul to be angry, to sputter a denial, but he surprised her. "No," he said, then hesitated. "Almost did," he amended. "The first night, when I meant to leave in the morning. But her idea of a good time, and mine, well, they don't seem to match up very well. So it didn't go far before I walked away."

Nina stared at him for a moment before she shoved her pack out of the way and sat down hard on the bench. "Shit," she muttered. "I'd almost rather it were you."

"You figured out she was sleepin' with someone, but not who it was?" Paul laughed weakly. "How did you manage that?"

"Wait—you knew about this already?" she asked, incredulous, and he nodded. She stared at him for a long time, but he waited, unconcerned by both her disbelief and the state of his bandages. His patience outlasted her stubbornness, and she drew a deep breath before telling him about the night she found the mysterious barrette.

"You and Mark had the watches before mine," she said at the end of the explanation. "So I knew it had to be one of you, and not John, if there was anything going on at all. I mean, the barrette could have belonged to someone else, which would make the whole thing was a coincidence." She paused. "So how did you know?"

"The alarm on my watch," he said, holding out his wrist. "I set it to wake me for my turn, in case Mark fell asleep. It was only the second night John trusted me to help out, and I didn't wanna mess up. Plus, since I didn't know y'all well yet, I wasn't sure how vigilant Mark was gonna be."

Admiration for Paul's practicality began to fight for space in Nina's thoughts with her uneasiness about the situation. "So your alarm woke you up, and Mark wasn't there?"

He nodded. "Alison neither. I thought it could be nothing, he could be up walkin' around, she could be answerin' the call of nature. Then I saw her blanket was gone. So I lay down and pretended to be asleep. He came back first, checked that we were all out, then she crept in, put her blanket down, and lay on it like she'd never been anywhere else. He only woke me up when she was settled."

Nina sighed. "Yeah, I don't see any other way to read that." She stood and got to work again, tearing open the gauze packet. "You didn't tell anyone?"

"Who was I gonna tell, and who'd have believed me, then? I wasn't sure what would happen if I did, so I kept quiet."

Nina laid the bandage in place, her fingers gentle. "Which is why you lied to me when we switched places that night. You said nothing happened." Paul went rigid under her hand, and she shook her head. "It's okay, Paul, I did the same thing when you woke up. I didn't tell you either, so I can't blame you for that."

"You didn't tell me because you thought it was me. Or at least that it could've been."

"But it's Mark." Nina sighed again. "I feel like I should tell Sarah, but imagining myself trying makes me feel sick. This could tear the group apart."

"I know."

Remembering the tape in her hand, Nina tore off a length and began securing the bandage. "What an awful day."

"Anything I can do to make it better, you just say," Paul offered.

The hesitant sweetness in his voice was disarming, and she smiled, though she didn't dare meet his eyes. "If I think of anything, I'll be sure to tell you," she whispered.

The sudden touch on her arm surprised her into taking a half-step back. Paul dropped his hand immediately, and Nina tried to pretend her reaction hadn't happened as she finished patching him up.

"I answered your question," Paul said as he buttoned his shirt. "Do I get to ask one, too?"

If Nina could have crawled inside her pack and disappeared, she would have. All she could do was focus on stowing her supplies so she didn't have to look at him. "That's fair," she said.

"So I guess I only lied to you the once, and it seems like you forgive me for that." He paused, and Nina felt the intensity of his gaze like heat on her skin. "Now that we've settled the question of Alison, I can't see that I've ever given you any other reason not to trust me. So what I wanna know is . . . why don't you?"

"I do," she answered, zipping her pack closed.

"Not as much as I want you to."

Anger flared to life in her chest, an animal breaking out of a cage which could only hold it for so long. "I'm not blind, Paul," she snapped, finally turning to face him. "And I'm not naïve. I know what you *want*, and it's not trust."

"But that is the first step," he replied. If her sudden emotional shift disturbed him, he gave no sign. "And I ain't ashamed of wantin' more than that, either. Why would I be?"

"You've said that before," Nina told him, her voice low and intense as she clenched her hands around the straps of her backpack. "That you're not ashamed of what you want, what you've done. But if that's true . . ."

"Yeah?" he prompted when she didn't go on.

"Why did you *almost* sleep with Alison, then, when it was me you wanted?"

Paul looked away then, something he almost never did. "When she woke me up, she was just . . . a whisper in the darkness. When she kissed me, I didn't know who it was. It could have been you. I hoped it was, even though I didn't really believe it."

Nina folded her arms across her body, resisting the urge to stop her ears with her fingers like a child. If she'd been stupid enough to ask the question, she had to suffer through the answer. "And when it wasn't me?"

"I was lonely," he said with simple honesty, turning back to her. "I thought I'd be on my way in the morning and never see either of you again. Alison knew that, and didn't expect anything else. I didn't think it would do any harm, not to her, not to you, not to anyone."

After a long silence where Nina tried to hold on to her anger, she whispered, "I'm sorry." Paul shook his head, trying to head off her apology, but she cleared her throat and soldiered on in a stronger voice. "I know I don't have a right to be angry. It's not my business, and I shouldn't have asked. You didn't owe me anything then."

"Do I owe you something now?"

That was the real question, and Nina didn't know how to answer. She threw her pack over her shoulder and turned for the door without speaking. Before she could move, Paul took her arm. His grip was loose enough that she could break it with a quick twist, but she didn't. She looked down at him, and her heart quivered, seeing the faint trace of hope in his expression that cut through the exhaustion.

She didn't know the answer, but she had to say something. "Whatever else you were going to say, Paul, don't. Part of me wants to kiss you, but the rest wants to slap you, so I don't think this is doing us any good right now."

Paul bowed his head and let her go.

CHAPTER FIFTEEN
BED SHEETS

September 15th, 1:05 pm – 1880 Cambridge Road, Coshocton, Ohio

Paul was surprised when Sarah found him outside, both by her red-rimmed-but-dry eyes, and the news she shared with him.

"John came in a few minutes ago, and he thinks we should stay here a few days to rest."

He followed her to the kitchen, where everyone was gathering.

"We're all hungry and tired," she said as they chose seats at the table, which was almost big enough to fit everyone without crowding. Paul waited until Nina sat down, then picked a chair on the other side. It seemed best to keep his distance again. "So that's what we're going to tackle first. John, you and Alison go through the food here, see what we have, and get rid of anything spoiled. Aaron, dear, you can help them with that if you like, or if you're too tired you can take a nap on the couch. Mark, I'd like you to go get Owen, and the two of you bring all the food you can manage from that house too. If there's more than you can take, we can go back for it later. Nina, you and Paul will be in charge of the beds. See if there's enough clean sheets, then strip all the beds and remake them. It's a big house, so hopefully there's enough room for everyone."

"Four bedrooms upstairs and a guest room on the first floor," John said. His voice was hoarse, but he seemed to have weathered the first storm in one piece. "One for you and Mark, one for me and Aaron, then three to split between everyone else." He glanced around the table. "Either the gentlemen or the ladies will have to share."

Paul spoke up before Nina or Alison could. "I don't mind, as long as it turns out Owen don't snore—if he does, he can sleep on the couch," he said, making a joke of it.

"Perfect," Sarah said with a bright smile. "I'll stay here and sort out lunch as the food comes in. Once we've eaten and cleaned up, I think everyone could do with a nap."

"Sounds good, honey," Mark said as he stood. "I'll be back in no time."

Paul found the guest room on the first floor without any trouble, while Nina lingered a moment in the living room, studying the pictures on the mantel above the fireplace.

Trying to strip the bed with only one arm was awkward, even his dominant one. He was so tired he'd almost objected to his given chore, on top of being paired with Nina. Most days he was happy to be anywhere near her, but at the moment, he doubted she felt the same. Sarah had made the right call, though. He wouldn't be able to carry as much food back from the other house as Mark could. Sarah would do a better job organizing the food and putting some kind of meal together. And complaining to John about anything was out of the question.

He managed to get the quilt off the bed and the pillows out of their cases without much trouble. When Nina came in and saw him struggling with the bed itself, she moved to the other side and pulled everything loose at once, rolling it into a messy bundle. "I can handle the other rooms on my own," she said. "If we make up this bed first, you can stay here and rest."

Which was being kind to them both. "All right."

She nodded. "I'll get sheets. I'm sure the linen closet won't be hard to find."

When she returned a minute later with a small stack of bedding, he held out his hands to take something and help, but she shook her head. "I got it," she told him. "Sit down."

There was a plush stuffed chair in the corner, and he sank into it. He studied the room, but there wasn't much to see. John had called it a guest room, which explained the basic furniture and lack of any personal touches—no bookshelves, no decorations on the walls, no clothes hanging in the dark space beyond the open closet door. There was nothing to distract him as he tried not to watch Nina putting the bed together, not wanting to bother her.

"It's worse than John told us," she said. Paul glanced over to find her looking at him. When she was sure she had his attention, she went back to making up the bed. "I thought it was odd, when he said there were four bedrooms, with only one child in the family. So I checked the pictures. His sister had three kids. The girl was the youngest. There were two boys, too, but they're not in the newest pictures." She paused, tucking the sheets under the corners. "And they don't have graves in the yard."

Paul let out a sigh. "I wonder what happened."

"I doubt John will ever tell us," she replied, stuffing first one pillow, then the other, into their pillowcases. "But I thought I should mention it, so the pictures wouldn't surprise you. I wonder if we should take them down."

"Maybe," Paul said. "I'm not sure."

"I'll ask Sarah what she thinks. She's pretty sensitive to that kind of thing." She flung the quilt back over the bed, tugging the edges even first on one side, then the other. She smoothed out the last wrinkle with one hand and said, "There. Ready for your nap."

"Thank you."

"I'll come get you when lunch is ready."

She left, and Paul lay on top of the covers and closed his eyes. As exhausted as he was, sleep still seemed far away, and his shoulder throbbed with every heartbeat. Between the discomfort and the sounds of the others moving around the house at their tasks, he doubted he'd get any real rest. Instead, he concentrated on taking deep, even breaths, trying to relax, even if he didn't sleep.

Why had he said any of that nonsense to Nina? He'd managed, in the space of a single conversation, to do exactly what he'd been trying not to since the moment she started talking to him by her own choice. He'd put her back on her guard, pushed her back toward the Nina he'd met three weeks ago, who was suspicious and angry and coldly civil. Even worse, he hadn't said anything he would take back. He couldn't rewrite the conversation in his head to make it end differently. Only afterward could he see the problem didn't lie in what he had said, but having said it at all. Her sweet little smile had gone straight to his heart, bypassing his brain completely when he opened his mouth and said things which should have waited. She hadn't been ready to hear them.

Everything she had said played in an endless loop in his brain, a counterpoint to his own thoughts chasing themselves in circles. But as he lay there and felt discouraged, he didn't abandon all hope.

Part of me wants to kiss you.

Even though she was furious with him—and Paul didn't harbor a single doubt she was—she still hadn't rejected him entirely. He would just have to be careful again. Patient. And penitent.

Half an hour later, the door opened a crack. "Paul?"

He sat up as Nina poked her head in, rubbing his eyes and faking a yawn. "Hungry?" she asked, smiling tentatively.

Since he doubted he was suddenly back in her good graces, he guessed there was promising news on the food front. "They find something good?"

"Canned pears and peaches," she said. "It's been weeks since I had any fruit that wasn't dried, and barely any of that. Lots of other stuff, too, but I love peaches."

"Sounds great," Paul replied. She started to leave, but he called her name, and she turned back, one hand gripping the edge of the door. "Thanks again."

She shrugged. "Sarah didn't realize how bad you were hurting or she would've had you do something else. Or maybe nothing at all. I don't mind."

"Well, I'm still grateful," he insisted.

She shrugged again, and left without another word.

Lunch proved to be even better than Paul expected. "It was a challenge," Sarah said as she presided over the table, getting things passed around. "Spaghetti sauce with no way to cook the pasta for it, ten different kinds of soup we can't heat up, four types of canned beans. Three kinds of homemade jam, but no bread. I thought I wasn't going to be able to manage anything. But then Mark and Owen came back with these blocks of cheese, all unopened and perfectly unspoiled. Cheese and crackers and fruit is a wonderful summer lunch."

"It's September, honey," Mark said around a mouthful of pear.

She gave him a light smack on the arm. "Close enough," she said with a smile.

As tempted as Paul was to eat until he was bursting, he'd only be making himself sick. He cleaned his plate once, resisted any second helpings, and then took his dishes to the sink. He reached halfway to the faucet before he stopped and chuckled at himself. "Don't s'pose the water's still running. For a minute there, I forgot."

"Actually, it is," Owen said. "You'd think this far out from town, you'd be on well water, not the city system, but the tower isn't even half a mile from here. We'll have water as long as it does. Or until something breaks and no one's there to fix it, anyway."

Paul turned the handle on the faucet, and water came out. Everyone listened to it running. It took a few moments for the implications to sink in, and Nina was the first to say it. "You mean, we can take showers?"

Owen laughed. Since he wasn't worried about his reception by the group anymore, he was less nervous and more cheerful. Paul remembered the feeling, the sudden sense of acceptance—he'd had it when he joined the group, with everyone but Nina. "Well, without power there's no water heater, but, yeah. If you don't mind cold, you can take showers." He looked at everyone around the table. "You are all kind of... grimy."

"We've been roughing it," Alison said. "Scrubbing your face in a river's not the same as getting properly clean."

"Okay, then," Sarah said. "New chore on the to-do list. Find enough soap and towels for everyone."

There was a bottle of dish soap sitting on the edge of the sink, so Paul set the plug in the drain and let the basin fill. "I got the dishes covered, just bring me your plate when you finish."

"If we're getting cleaned up," John said, "then I suppose we should see about new clothes. We might not find things for everyone here, but my sister was close to your size, Alison, and Sarah's not too far off, either. Some of Rachel's things might fit Nina. I can't promise they'll be your style," he said to her, "since she was so much younger."

"It's okay, John. I'm sure they'll be fine."

"I'm not sure about the rest of us. Owen and Will might have some luck with Bob's closet, but Paul, you're a lot taller, and I'm a lot, uh..."

"Beefier?" Alison suggested, and John gave a weak laugh.

"It's fine," Paul said over his shoulder while he worked. "Maybe we'll turn up something in one of the other houses, if nothing here works."

"Yeah. I suppose we should search them too."

"One thing at a time, John," Sarah said. "This is the safest place we've seen since this whole mess started, and there's plenty of food. We can take our time, and rest, and not have to rush through everything."

There wasn't much more conversation as people finished up their meals and brought Paul their dishes. He resisted the urge to edge away when Nina approached with hers—she glanced up at him for half a second before focusing squarely on her plate. Her message couldn't have been clearer if she'd shouted at him. But he stood his ground, because the last thing he wanted was to telegraph his argument with Nina to everyone. He washed each dish methodically, setting them on the rack to dry. He was nearly done when he heard John's voice behind him. "Let me finish, Paul. You look dead on your feet."

Paul turned and saw he and John were the last ones left in the kitchen. "Nina wouldn't let me help with the beds," he confessed. "I feel like I ought to be doing something needful."

"I get it. But you should rest up, I'm sure Sarah will put you to work tomorrow."

"She seems real comfortable ordering us around," Paul observed.

"You're too tired to be subtle," John said, but he didn't sound angry, just worn out. "It's fine. Sarah can run the show for a while. It's easier for her to look at this house and see it as a resource, instead of someone's home."

"Oh, hell, John, I'm sorry."

"I know we have to be practical. I know it's the right thing to do. But it's hard."

"Yeah. I didn't know I was leaving my place for good when I headed out, and I couldn't bring myself to take much when I left my dad's house. After a few days I wished I had, but I get what you're saying. I have no problem taking from random empty houses, but it's different when you knew who lived there."

"I'm glad you understand," John said. "I want this place treated with respect, not gutted like some of the other places we've seen."

"I get it." Paul hesitated. "Nina mentioned taking the pictures down, but she wasn't sure if that would make it better for you, or worse."

"I'll take them down. I want to keep one or two, and that way, they're not making the rest of you jumpy. I'll be okay, Paul. I knew this was what we were going to find, even if I let myself hope we wouldn't."

"How's Aaron doing?" Paul finished the last plate and pulled the stopper out of the drain. There was a towel hanging on the stove, so he used it to dry his hands. It wasn't until he put it back that he was struck by how reassuringly normal it seemed, and how he'd known it would be there without thinking.

"Pretty well. The last time we came here to visit, he was only four—he barely remembers them. I think he understands that it makes me sad, but it doesn't seem to bother him that much."

"You and your sister weren't close?"

"As kids, not really. Wendy and I weren't much alike. We got along better as teenagers, but once we were both out of the house, we grew apart again. Honestly, it sounds petty now, but one of the reasons I made excuses not to visit more was that I didn't like her husband, Bob. Not that he mistreated her, or anything like that—if I'd ever thought he was hurting my little sister, things would have gotten ugly. We just didn't get along. It was easier for everyone if we weren't butting heads over stupid shit, so the visits just sort of stopped." He sighed. "Anyway, now you're all finished, and I'm still talking.

I'll let you go get some sleep."

Paul let out a short laugh, more breath than sound. "It's funny, everyone keeps saying that to me. I think I've gone past sleep now. I know I'm running on fumes, but when Nina insisted I rest, I lay down and nothing happened. I pretended, when she came back, so she didn't worry. But sleep seems miles away."

"Something's on your mind."

It was a statement, not a question, but Paul answered anyway. "Yeah."

"I'm guessing that something is Nina?" John said with a trace of humor. When Paul started, he actually laughed. "I did say you were too tired to be subtle, and it's not like it was much of a secret anyway. We all know you've got a thing for her."

"Oh, hell," Paul muttered under his breath.

"We're all friends, here, Paul. No one's laughing at you behind your back. If you want the truth, no one's talked about it much, but Mark and I are rooting for you from the sidelines. Sarah gave us both a piece of her mind when we were wondering how to give Nina a push in your direction, but she's doing it too. She'll try to stick the two of you together whenever she can, while she's ordering us around."

"Well, see if you could wave her off, would you?" Paul asked. "Things between us are a little . . . strained, I guess, right now. I kinda stuck my foot in my mouth."

John clapped him on his uninjured shoulder. "Sorry to hear that, but you might want to reconsider. If I tell Sarah what you just told me, she's going to make sure you spend as much time with Nina as possible, to give you a chance to make it up to her."

Paul sighed. "Good point. Forget I said anything."

John used the hand on Paul's shoulder to steer him out of the kitchen. "Go get in bed, Paul. Sleep will find you eventually."

CHAPTER SIXTEEN
TWEEZERS

September 15th, 2:15 pm – 1880 Cambridge Road, Coshocton, Ohio

Nina marveled at how completely normal the house looked.

After lunch, everyone scattered to their new bedrooms to nap. Everyone but Owen, who hadn't been traveling on short rations for days and didn't feel particularly tired. Since the weather was fine, he volunteered to start sorting through the shed in the backyard. Sarah smiled and nodded at him, and off he went.

Nina tried to rest, but she found herself wide awake, focused on the details of her new room with a surprising clarity. She hadn't been eating any better or sleeping any more than anyone else had the past few days. But she lay on her bed and stared at the glow-in-the-dark plastic stars stuck to the ceiling. Without light pollution, Nina had seen more stars in the clear night sky than she had ever seen before the plague. She didn't want to see them inside, too. She doubted she could reach them standing on the bed, but maybe someone would turn up a ladder, once they started going through the house for supplies.

Or maybe Paul would take them down for her.

Or maybe Paul would never speak to her again.

Nina flushed, even though there was no one to see her embarrassment. He'd never do that. No matter how hostile she was, whether she meant to be or not, he would give her distance for long enough to cool down. He'd find small ways to be nearby again, and then he would find reasons to talk to her, to pull her gently out of her self-imposed silence. She'd been right about him, when she'd let him stay—he was the one who wouldn't leave her to herself, who wouldn't let her hide away in peace. At least, not for long.

The stars had to go, though.

She closed her eyes and tried again to relax her body into sleep. But her mind wouldn't settle. Everything felt unreal. When she changed all the bedding earlier, she discovered the house was eerily clean. The master bedroom, except for a thin layer of dust, might have been straightened up earlier in the day, instead of months ago. No clothes off their hangers, no socks balled up under the bed, not even a book out of place on the shelves or sitting face-down on the nightstand.

The next two bedrooms on the upstairs hall had both been nearly empty. The only furniture they had were the beds, plus one nightstand and dresser a piece. Out of curiosity she'd checked the drawers, but they were empty too. Whatever posters or photos used to hang on the walls were gone, leaving slightly brighter patches of paint on the walls.

Those must have been the boys' rooms. Nina could imagine them with school books and clothes strewn everywhere, sports equipment, comics, toys. But now they were as bare and uninviting as cheap hotel rooms. She hadn't lingered long in either one after she finished making the beds.

Only the last bedroom at the end of the hall, the girl's room—*Rachel, John said her name was Rachel*—showed any signs of the person who had lived there. A sweater lay crumpled in the corner, and a backpack sat unzipped and half-open at the foot of the bed. On the desk, an open sketchbook lay beside a box of colored pencils. A few of the pencils were out, though the paper was blank. Nina had turned back the pages to see what the girl had drawn. Sketches of birds, trees, abstract designs based on repeating hearts or flowers, all heavily featuring pink and purple.

Rolling onto her side with a sigh, Nina idly traced over the pattern on the sheets with her finger. The ones she'd found for this bed were pale pink with tiny rainbows arcing between pairs of tiny clouds. A good match, she thought, for her cartoon pony blanket. A shelf above the bed held stuffed animals, and she wanted to take one down and hold it, for the small amount of comfort it might give her.

But then she might cry, and the last thing she wanted to do was cry.

Most of her anger at Paul had already faded. As much as she hated the thought of him and Alison together and pushed it repeatedly out of her mind, he hadn't actually done anything wrong. And if she hadn't wanted to know, she shouldn't have asked. No, the anger keeping her from sleeping was directed at herself.

The last few days had been so easy. Not physically—the lack of food, the nights of uneasy sleep broken by her turn at watch, or sometimes, by nightmares—but emotionally. Everything came down to a single directive. *Paul is hurt, so take care of him.* She hadn't suffered, those days, the constant anxiety which came with his presence, his attention, and the certainty of his desire for her. No matter how low he kept that fire banked, it always remained between them. Knowing that, even his gentlest, most undemanding touch could be alarming.

But not when she was the one to reach out to him, to support him, to care for him. He'd been surprised the first time she'd insisted he lean on her as he walked, near the end of the day after the confrontation with Christine. She'd felt it, the way he tensed at first, then relaxed against her. But she'd reached out for him without thinking. His exhaustion had been obvious, the way he was barely keeping himself upright. She'd been afraid he would pass out right there in the middle of the road.

And it had only gotten easier as the days passed.

Why can't the rest of it be so simple?

She gave up trying to sleep and got out of bed. As long as she was quiet enough not to wake the others, she could explore the house. All the other bedroom doors upstairs were shut, so she crept past them, then down the stairs. None of the steps creaked, which was a relief—the last few months had turned her into a light sleeper.

The living room took up most of the first floor. She'd noticed the fireplace already, when she stopped to examine the family photos. A cluster of two couches and a handful of plush, comfortable chairs made a cozy conversation area around it. A long, low coffee table stood in the center. In the corner past the fireplace was the door to the guest bedroom—to Paul and Owen's bedroom, now. In the opposite corner was the open kitchen entry. The wall stretching between them held a piano, a curio cabinet, and another door, which turned out to be to a tiny bathroom.

Rifling through the medicine cabinet behind the mirror turned up a small assortment of pretty common drugs—antacids, pain killers, and the like—but Nina did find something she'd been hoping to see. Tweezers. It had been five days since she stitched Paul up, and in five more, she'd need to take those stitches out. She didn't think anyone would begrudge her claiming them.

She left off searching the cabinets, figuring someone would be going to go through them soon anyway. If they didn't turn up enough soap here, one of the other houses would have some. Nina felt odd not worrying about resources, about where she could find what she needed and how to make it last. She didn't intend to squander what she took away from this place, but it was a relief to know she would have shelter and safety. For a few days, at least.

Back in the living room, she trailed one finger through the dust on the piano. She missed music. She'd never been good at it herself—she didn't sing or play any instruments. Well, she used to sing when she was driving alone, following along with the radio as best she could, because it was fun. But no one could hear her, there. She'd sung in the shower, too, but she wasn't about to start that habit up again.

Maybe Paul would, though. That was a thought too tempting to let herself consider for long. But she wanted to hear him sing again.

She shook her head, trying to stop that train of thought. Even if she couldn't sleep, she could scrounge up the necessary items for a shower. Her own sliver of soap was gone, her bottle of shampoo nearly empty, but there was plenty to be had here. And real towels, too, not her ragged little dish towel.

But Nina stood there and stared at the door of Paul's room, one hand resting on the piano. Now that there was a semblance of privacy again, closed doors to separate rooms, she wanted to go in and check on him, to see if he was sleeping well or not at all. Though she only stood a few yards away, this was the farthest she'd been from him while he slept in days.

She heard footsteps in the upstairs hall, and shook herself out of her reverie, not wanting someone to catch her doing something so foolish. The footsteps didn't come downstairs—whoever it was used the bathroom, then crossed the hall back to a bedroom.

But the spell was broken, and Nina strode away from the piano. There were too many things to do to stand around daydreaming and feeling oddly lonely.

CHAPTER SEVENTEEN
A SWEATER

September 16th, 8:35 am - 1880 Cambridge Road, Coshocton, Ohio

Paul woke to the sound of curtains being drawn and a flood of sunshine. He threw a hand over his face, squinting past his fingers to see who was waking him up.

"Sarah? What time is it?"

"It's tomorrow morning, Paul," she told him, tying back the curtains. "I let you sleep through dinner last night when Mark couldn't wake you, and Owen said this morning you never even noticed when he came in last night. But you need food as much as rest, so I wasn't about to let you skip another meal."

He sat up with a wide yawn. "Thanks. What did I miss last night?"

"Not too much," she replied. "The shower works, so a few of us took advantage of that before dinner, but no one stayed awake too long after we'd eaten."

"And what's the plan this morning?" He yawned again. "After breakfast, I mean?"

"A thorough search of the house," she answered. "Clothes, food, tools, anything useful. The garage too, and the shed out back, though Owen started there yesterday."

"Sounds good," he said, standing and stretching, rolling his shoulder to work out the stiffness.

Sarah watched him with a critical eye. "How's that cut?"

"Hurts some," he admitted. "It's not infected, though, Nina's been keepin' an eye on that. She don't seem too worried, so I'm tryin' not to be."

"That's good, then. Come get some breakfast. And eat more than you did yesterday at lunch, please. You were skinny enough when we met you, but now, there can't be an ounce of extra weight left on you. You lose any more and somebody will mistake you for a scarecrow and hang you in a field."

Over the meal, the conversation was mostly yawns and sleepy-sounding greetings. Sarah seemed to be the only one ready to face the day—everyone else looked as though an hour of extra sleep would have been welcome.

When Nina joined them, though, Paul wasn't too groggy to notice how she'd changed overnight. Her clean skin glowed in the sunlight, and her hair looked so soft Paul wanted to bury his face in it. She'd found new clothes. Her blouse was a bright pink floral print more appropriate to a thirteen-year-old than a twenty-something, but it was clean and it fit. Over it she wore a lightweight purple cardigan, left hanging open in the front. The new pair of jeans she wore was definitely smaller than her old pair, but Paul thought that was a good thing. He'd never had a taste for baggy clothing on women. He realized he was staring and looked away, hoping she hadn't noticed. He didn't want to give her any new reasons to be uncomfortable around him.

At the end of the meal, Alison started doing the dishes while Sarah laid out the morning's work. Before she could assign Paul anything, he decided he might as well ask. "Whatever you were plannin' on givin' me, can it wait til this afternoon? Now that other people are turnin' up clean, I feel even filthier. I'm hopin' I can hunt up some new clothes and then take my turn in the shower."

"That's fine, Paul. If you end up going to one of the other houses, make sure you take someone else with you—I don't want anyone going out alone unless absolutely necessary. Whoever you take along can bring back food or whatever other useful things you find."

He nodded. "Got it."

Mark had found clothes in the master bedroom closet the night before, but John was right—nothing would fit Paul, being too short in the arm and leg. Figuring that out didn't even take a whole minute. He went in search of Owen, figuring if they were going to be roommates, he should get to know the guy. Owen might find new clothes for himself, too.

"Sure, I'll go," Owen answered when Paul found him and asked. "We can skip the house where I was yesterday, I already checked for clothes. The man who lived there was a pretty big guy."

They tried the neighboring house to the other side. "I already buried them," Owen said as he pushed open the front door. "You don't need to worry about finding them inside."

"Good to know." Paul followed him in and up the stairs. "How are you getting along with everyone so far?" he asked to change the subject. "I've slept through most of you being here."

"I like them," he said in an offhand tone. "Everybody's been nice." He opened the first door at the top of the stairs. "Right, the little girl's bedroom, don't need to bother with that right now."

Paul tried the next door. "Bathroom. Seems like a good place for you to start while I'm checking the closets. I'll let you know if I find something that might work for you."

"Yeah, okay," Owen said. "If you turn up a decent-sized box in a closet or something, let me know. Easier to carry."

"Right." The next door Paul tried was another girl's bedroom. The one at the end of the hall was the master, so Paul opened the curtains to let in some light and started pulling clothes out of the closet.

He skipped the suits, which wouldn't wear well for travel even if they fit. Same for the crisp button-down shirts. He'd be happy with another flannel shirt like the one that had gotten ruined, but that didn't seem to be an option here. Finally he turned up a few t-shirts, all printed with the names and dates of marathons. *He was a runner.*

Paul shucked off Nina's shirt—he still didn't think of it as his, which amused him sometimes and worried him others—and pulled one of the t-shirts on. It fit well enough, a little broader in the shoulder and shorter in the torso than he liked, but passable. He pulled it off and chose two more for spares.

Next he tried the dresser on the wall opposite the bed. The top drawer held socks and boxers. The socks were the basic white one-size-fits-all type, so he took two pairs. He wrinkled his nose at the idea of wearing another man's underdrawers, but checked the size on the band anyway. Too big. Which meant whatever pants he found probably would be too, but some progress was better than none.

The next drawer down contained white undershirts, thin as tissue. Paul sorted through to find the ones in the best condition and added two of those to his pile.

The third drawer held jeans. Paul held the first pair up to himself and immediately knew he could skip the rest. Too short, too big in the waist. And since Owen was nearly as much of a beanpole as he was, Paul knew they wouldn't fit him, either.

The bottom drawer held the best find. Sweaters. If he couldn't have another flannel shirt, he'd happily take a nice, soft sweater. He pawed through them, testing how they felt when he rubbed them between his fingers. Since there were enough to be choosy, he spent some time deciding, discarding the scratchy ones and the colors he didn't like. He finally settled on a deep green wool sweater, thick enough to be warm, but thin enough not to feel bulky. It fit well, too, long enough in the sleeves. He found it near the bottom of the drawer, and it looked newer than the others, so Paul guessed it had never been worn because it was the wrong size.

"Owen!" he called. "You want any sweaters?"

While Owen checked them over, Paul turned up a sturdy cardboard box from the depths of the closet. It held a few pairs of shoes, their laces all tangled together, but they didn't turn out to be the right size for either Paul or Owen. "Too dressy, anyway," Owen said. "I can't imagine walking any real distance in those."

"Yeah," Paul agreed. "I didn't think to ask John and Mark their sizes. We don't need to bother with these, but I suppose if we come across any good boots, we should bring them along, in case."

Twenty minutes later, they returned to their house, each with a box filled to the top. Paul piled the new clothes on his bed, while Owen distributed the rest wherever it needed to go—food to the kitchen, soap to the bathroom, and one pair of boots to the mat by the front door so Mark and John could test them later. "Let's bring these with us to the next house," Owen said, hefting his empty box. "It's pretty far down the road, and I'd hate to not find a good one there."

That house, pale blue with a gray slate roof, turned out to be better. Owen got himself an entirely new set of clothes—black jeans and some rock band t-shirt—from what was obviously another teenage boy's bedroom. "I know my own clothes are right where I left them," he said when Paul saw him wearing the new things, "but I'd really rather not go back there unless I have to."

Paul managed to get spare boxers, but still had no luck with anything else. "It's going to be hard to find you pants, I think," Owen said, giving him a once-over glance. "I mean, you're what, ninety feet tall?"

"Six-four."

"Close enough. I thought I was tall before I met you, I'm five-eleven. Though it helped that no one else in my family was over five-seven."

Paul smiled. "Yeah, that would do it."

"Well, we didn't fill our boxes, so let's try one more house before we go back."

"Sure."

Paul had better luck there. The first pair of jeans he found looked right, so he tried them on. "Perfect." He grabbed another pair and went to find Owen in the kitchen. They filled the rest of the space in their boxes with canned vegetables and set off for home.

Sarah was in the kitchen when they delivered their latest haul, and the smile on her face as she sorted through it brightened the room like sunshine. "Corn, green beans, cut carrots, oh, bless you boys. And little canned potatoes! Thank goodness that someone around here was too lazy to peel their own potatoes! Go on, then, Paul, you've more than earned your shower. Owen, would you help me put all this away?"

In his room, Paul sorted through his new things, deciding what to wear and what to stash in his pack. He gathered what he needed in a pile and went to find Nina.

She turned out to be in a bedroom upstairs, searching through desk drawers. By the décor, Paul guessed this had been Rachel's room. It looked feminine, though not the sort of over-the-top girly he would have pictured for a girl of twelve or thirteen, boy-band pictures on every wall and a pink bedspread. Instead, the room was painted a soft gray, with furniture in some type of dark wood. The curtains and the bedspread were both white and trimmed with narrow bands of lace. There was a shelf above the bed with an assortment of stuffed animals and some glow-in-the-dark stars stuck to the ceiling, but that was about as girly as it got.

He spotted Nina's pack on the floor next to the bed, so this was her room, now. It suited her, though he couldn't figure out exactly why he thought so.

The door was open, but Paul tapped his knuckles lightly on the frame. "Hey."

"Do you need something?" she asked without looking up from her work.

So many things he could say which he shouldn't. Sticking to the practical was safest. "Time for a shower." She looked over, quirking her eyebrow at him. "I'll have to take off the bandage, I know that, but how careful do I need to be with the stitches? Getting them wet won't matter, right?"

"It shouldn't," Nina answered. "Don't scrub too hard at them and they should be fine. When you're done I'll get you bandaged back up."

With access to a mirror, he'd be perfectly capable of doing it himself—but he wasn't about to turn down any attention he could get from her. "Thanks."

"Yeah." She started rooting through the drawers again, which he took as his cue to leave.

The upstairs bathroom was spacious, unlike its tiny downstairs counterpart. Sunlight from the single high window bounced cheerfully off the white walls and white tile floor. Paul stripped down, then faced the mirror so he could see what he was doing while he took off the bandage over his collarbone.

He did a double take at his own face. Getting used to how he looked with a beard had taken him a while, when he caught his reflection in a storefront window, or on the wavering surface of a stream. But this man was nearly a stranger, with his dark-circled, sunken eyes and hollow cheeks. His cheekbones stood out sharp enough to cut glass. *I look . . . older. Years older.*

It wasn't a comforting thought.

As he peeled back the tape holding the bandage in place, Paul got his first real look at the knife slash on his skin. Underneath the line of stitches, the wound wasn't as bloody and scabbed as he'd expected it to be. He studied Nina's handiwork, looking for the spot where the stitches changed. Toward the right side, where she'd started, the stitches were crooked and unevenly spaced. To the left, after she'd begun again, they were smaller, straighter, more even.

A wave of nausea gripped him as he remembered what it had felt like to be sewn together. But seeing the wound clearly for the first time, he felt worse for Nina, for having to do it. Paul wasn't sure he'd have been able to manage it, if someone else had been the one hurt.

Once he got in the shower, it took forever to get clean, scrubbing off layer after layer of sweat and grime and no small amount of dried blood. By the time he washed his hair and rinsed off, the cold water had him shivering. He rubbed himself vigorously with the towel, everywhere but the stitches, trying to get warm. Those, he patted gently, glad to see the towel came away clean.

He dressed in everything but the t-shirt, which he threw over his good shoulder, and headed back to Nina's room, still drying his hair with the towel. "Your patient has returned," he said from the doorway.

"Okay," Nina said, dropping a few small items into a box on the floor beside the desk. "I guess the doctor is in, then."

He sat down on the bed, retrieving her pack from the floor and handing it to her as she approached. "I got a good look at it, finally, in the mirror. You stitched it well."

She snorted. "No, I didn't, but it's nice of you to pretend. I guess I'll do better next time someone gets cut open." She leaned in to examine the wound. "It looks good, though. Now that it's clean, it's easier to see it's healing well."

"Good." Paul flexed his fingers against the bedspread and tried not to think too much about how close her face was to his.

It only took a few minutes for Nina to get the new gauze taped in place. When she was done, he pulled his shirt on. "I like your new clothes," he told her. "They look nice on you."

"Paul . . ." she said, a warning in her tone. He gave her an innocent look, and she sighed. "Thank you."

He didn't have any reason to stay, except that he wanted to. "I spent most of the morning with Owen," he said, just to have something to talk about. "He seems like a good guy. Level-headed, even pretty cheerful, sometimes. I wouldn't have thought someone could bounce back so fast from being alone for so long."

She started tidying up her supplies, discarding the empty gauze wrapper, repacking the tape and tiny scissors. "Yeah. I don't think we met him at his best."

"Well, he didn't really meet us at ours, either. I'm glad John wanted him to join us. I felt awful sending him away, even for a little while."

"You did what you thought best," Nina said, stowing her pack in the bottom of the closet. "Owen understood."

"Another reason to like him," Paul replied. "Not everyone would have."

"Sarah's already mothering him," she said, sitting down at the desk. She couldn't weigh much more than a child, but she sank into the chair like she carried mountains on her back. "You saw her when we met him. Sometimes, the way she looks at Aaron, I think she pretends he's hers. I think in her head she's already adopting Owen, too." She paused, glancing at the open door. When she went on, her voice was much lower, and Paul leaned forward to catch what she said. "I can't bring myself to ask, but I think Mark and Sarah never had kids. They both dote on Aaron, though they're careful never to step on John's toes about parenting him. I wondered for a while if they lost kids in the plague, but they don't seem *sad* enough for that to be true."

"You're probably right," Paul said. "When I talked to Sarah, that first day on the road, she didn't say anything directly, but I got the impression it's always been just her and Mark."

"You can tell, though, that she wanted them," she said, staring out the door with blank eyes. "Mark, too, maybe, but it doesn't seem to be as intense with him. If I'd just lost my parents in the plague, instead of years ago, it might have been harder to accept the way they . . . they became attached to me so quickly. I guess I needed a little mothering. Mark's more distant, but Sarah has no problem treating me like a daughter."

They were both silent for a time. Paul got the sense Nina was edging around something she didn't want to say, and he struggled to find a way to draw it out of her. Before he could, John called out from downstairs. "Lunch time!"

Paul stood and headed for the door, holding his hand out to Nina. She stared at it for a moment. When she didn't take it, Paul nodded, and left. He heard Nina coming down the stairs behind him, but he didn't look back.

CHAPTER EIGHTEEN
A FIREPLACE

September 16th, 12:15 pm - 1880 Cambridge Road, Coshocton, Ohio

If the mood at the kitchen table at breakfast had been sleepy and grumbling, at lunch, it was eager. As Paul sat down with his plate of food, Mark shared a discovery he'd made during his search. "I found lot of camping gear in the shed," he told them. "Two tents, one big and one smaller."

"Yeah," John said. "I remember Wendy mentioning camping trips. She and Bob would go on their own sometimes, leave the kids with friends."

"One tent for everyone, one for just them." Mark nodded. "It makes sense. There was some fishing gear too, nothing fancy, but I used to fish sometimes, so we could give it a try."

"It would be nice to eat something fresh," Alison said. "I guess we could cook it over the fire in the living room, if we can get one going—that would be an interesting challenge."

"Well, see, that's the thing, Allie," Mark said with a smile. "I also found a camp stove. Two burners, uses those little tanks of propane. There's one partial and one full."

"Did you test it?" Paul asked at the same time as Alison asking, "Does it work?"

"Yep," Mark answered, nodding to them both. "We're going to have hot food for dinner tonight."

"Hooray!" Aaron cried, prompting a fond ruffling of his hair from his father, and laughs from everyone else. Even from Nina, who'd hardly spoken a word since stepping into the kitchen. Hearing her soft laughter warmed

Paul from the top of his head straight down to his fingertips and toes, banishing the last chill of his cold shower.

"We should also try to get the fireplace up and running," John said. "It's still plenty warm during the day, but last night got chilly. It's not as good as regular heating, but it should help."

"That, and more blankets," Sarah added. "If I can get a clothesline set up, I might air some out this afternoon."

"So," Paul said. "Who needs help with what?"

The afternoon passed pleasantly enough for Paul in a series of easy chores. Sarah sent him to find cord to use as a clothesline. He remembered the rope in Nina's pack, but he decided not to ask for it unless he couldn't find anything else. When he turned up a hank of woven cotton cord in the garage, he returned to Sarah. She didn't take advantage of his height to hang it, not wanting him to strain his shoulder, so she sent him to find Mark. He was in the living room with John, setting up the fireplace. Paul volunteered to take his place so he could help his wife instead.

"I think I remember how this goes," John said. They'd already removed the grate and the split logs which had rested there, so John could peer up the chimney and figure out the mechanics. "Bob showed me years ago. I think just open the damper, here, so the smoke goes up instead of back into the room . . . yeah, I think I got it." He pulled himself back out and set the grate and the wood back in place before turning to Paul. "Would you find me some newspaper or something, to use for kindling? I'm just going to test this with a small fire, to make sure we're not going to choke ourselves on the smoke later."

Paul had seen a recycling bin in the garage while he looked for the cord, which gave him the needed newspapers. The one on top of the pile was dated April 2nd—the first day reports had run about the mysterious illness popping up around the country. The illness which had gone almost unnoticed for weeks, appearing only as isolated cases, before rapidly escalating into an epidemic.

The day before Paul had left New York City, driving home to see his dying father, only to find out he was too late.

He shoved the thought aside. He'd thought he'd made peace with it. But seeing the headline was an uncomfortable reminder that as long ago as that mad dash home to his family seemed, barely five months had passed. Hardly any time at all.

Rolling the papers in his hand so he wouldn't be distracted by the text, he ducked into his room to get one of his spare lighters from his pack. Then

John wouldn't have to go upstairs to get his own. John nodded his thanks as Paul handed them over. "There's a fire extinguisher in the kitchen," he said. "Maybe I should get that too?"

John chuckled. "Yeah. And open a few of these windows a crack, just in case."

Once everything was in place, it only took John about five minutes to get the kindling to start and the tiny fire to light. Paul couldn't help much. Standing back seemed like a good idea, so he went to the piano, which he'd noticed the day before. Though it hadn't had such a deliberate streak in the dust on the top then, nor the imprint of fingertips on the arm. He smiled before folding back the cover. Softly, he pressed a few keys—first middle C, then its first high and low octaves, checking to see if the instrument was out of tune.

"Do you play?" John asked.

For a moment, Paul saw flashes of his old life, the thousands of hours he'd spent sitting at one piano or another, in all those bars and clubs. Some nights he was pounding out tired old chestnuts for a crowd three times his age, just to make ends meet. Other nights were better, like when he had a run at a nice jazz place, backing up a singer who made come-hither eyes at him for two months before he finally gave in. Paul chose to remember her that way, standing at the microphone in one of those gorgeous slinky dresses. Those memories didn't hurt as much as the guilt and shame on her face when he'd caught her cheating, or the fear and anger when he'd left her behind as she was dying.

But the best nights were the ones he'd been playing his own songs. Each of them was painstakingly crafted during the day on the piano he had barely had enough to buy, at home in the tiny apartment he had barely had enough to rent. That's why he'd gone to New York in the first place.

"Yeah," he said. "I play. Did your sister?"

"Some. She took lessons as a kid, but she didn't have much patience for it. That was our mother's piano. Since I didn't really want it when she passed away, Wendy took it, hoping one of the kids would want to learn. I think Rachel tried but didn't really stick with it."

Paul quietly ran through a simple warm up and didn't hear any wrong notes. "Your sister kept it tuned, though. It sounds fine."

"Maybe you can play for us, later."

Paul pulled the cover back over the keys. "Maybe."

"What do you think of the fire?" John asked, and Paul turned to look. The flames were small, leaping from the center of the two split logs, but they were steady.

"Looks good. Should we let it die, or keep it going and just build it up later, after dinner?"

"Keep it going," John said, setting the screen across the front. "So I don't have to bother lighting it again."

Mark came back in. "Hey, you're done already! That was fast."

John smiled. "It turns out I remembered how the thing worked, so it didn't take long."

"Great," Mark said. "Paul, you want to come help me in the garage? I was going to check the cars, see if they run."

"Sure," he answered, though he knew he wouldn't actually be much help. This was just the first opportunity he'd had to talk to Mark in private.

Mark popped open the hood of one of the cars, an unremarkable blue sedan. Paul had no idea what he was looking for, but he let Mark mutter to himself while he thought of how to approach the subject.

"You planning on helping?" Mark asked after a few moments.

"Don't know a thing about cars. I always bought cheap clunkers and just drove them til they wore out."

Mark glanced up at him with frown darkening his face. "Then why'd you come out here?"

"Because I do know about you and Alison," Paul answered, relieved, almost glad Mark forced the issue before he could chicken out. "Thought it was time I did something about it."

To his credit, Mark didn't sputter any denials. He backed out from under the hood, stood up straight, and looked Paul in the eye. "What exactly do you intend to do?"

"Ask you to end it, today. You do that, and my lips are sealed. No one hears a word from me."

"Nobody else knows? Just you?"

Paul found himself tempted to lie, to keep Nina out of it. But if this ever came out in the open, everyone needed to be on the same page. "Nina does. She figured out Alison was sleepin' with somebody, but she didn't know if it was you, or me. So she asked. And I told her."

The faintest ghost of a smile appeared on Mark's face. "That must have been a fun conversation."

"Not in the slightest," Paul replied with a hint of venom in his tone, enough to make Mark flinch.

"She's not going to tell?"

Paul shook his head. "She don't seem inclined to, though her heart's breakin' for Sarah. But if she sees somehow that it's still goin' on, I wouldn't put it past her to speak up."

Mark crossed his arms over his chest. "And you? Why do you care?"

"Because I like you, Mark, and I like your wife. I don't much like your mistress, but even so, I don't wanna see any of you hurt when Sarah eventually finds out for herself. I've been down that road, and it don't lead anywhere good."

Mark's brow furrowed. "You've cheated before? You don't seem like the type."

"No," Paul spat out. "She cheated on me. I was gonna marry her, and she cheated on me."

"I'm sorry to hear that," Mark replied, his tone solemn. "And I understand if you think less of me because of it. What I don't understand is how that makes any of this your business, or gives you the right to tell me what to do."

"Okay, then, how about this—what do you think is gonna happen to the group when this comes out?" Mark flinched again, and Paul pressed his advantage. "Sarah's gonna feel betrayed, and rightfully so. She won't be able to trust you anymore, Alison neither. You know your wife better than I do—will she wanna keep dependin' on you for her survival after that? Would she turn you and Alison out? I don't know that she would, but if she does, then I'll stand by her. I'm gonna bet John and Nina will, too. Owen just wants people to belong to, so he'll stay with us, because at that point the only person you'll have left on your side is Alison herself. Who would want to choose the two cheaters over everybody else?" He stopped and took a deep breath. "I don't wanna see us splinter apart. I don't wanna lose anyone. So I'm asking you to break it off with Alison, for good. If you don't, sooner or later things are going to get ugly."

Mark glared at him through the whole speech, his mouth set in a hard line. "You done now?"

"Yeah."

"No ultimatum to throw at me? You're not planning to tell Sarah if I don't do as you say?"

"I don't know," Paul answered honestly. "Do you think she'd believe me if I did?"

"Shit," Mark muttered. "She might. Things between us haven't been that great since we've been on the road."

"Then chuck Alison," Paul insisted, "and fix your damn marriage already."

He stalked out, not wanting to spend another moment with Mark. He went outside and sat on the front porch, hoping to calm down some. If anyone saw him right now, they would know something was wrong, and start digging at him to find out what. No one had seen him angry yet, since his fuse was long and slow to light, but there would be no mistaking the signs. He closed his eyes, took deep breaths, and imagined the breeze carrying his anger away, like a bad smell vanishing from his clothes and hair and skin. When he felt like he could smile again and not grit his teeth doing it, he went in search of Sarah so she could give him something else to do.

Paul found her in the kitchen, where she and Owen and Alison were taking inventory. Drawers and cupboard doors were open all across the kitchen, pots and pans and utensils sat on the table and most of the open counter space. "Wow," Paul said as he walked in. "Tearin' everything down to the floorboards?"

"Now that I can cook," Sarah explained, "I need to know what I have to work with."

Alison pulled a crock pot from the cupboard under the sink. "Useless," she said, handing it to Owen, who took it to a different cupboard they were beginning to fill back up.

"Everything electric is going over there," Sarah told Paul. "The kitchen was organized for a more normal lifestyle, but there's so many things now we can't use. Crock pot, toaster, ice cream maker—"

"Not that we don't all miss ice cream," Owen cut in. "Or even just plain old milk."

"—and the electric tea kettle, so far. I'm hoping we find a stove-top kettle squirreled away somewhere, though. There's quite a bit of tea here, and I suppose we could use a pan to boil the water, but a kettle would be so much easier."

"Any coffee?" Paul asked.

"There's a coffee pot," Alison replied. "But it's electric, too, of course."

"Well, it only needs to heat up the water, which we could do on the camp stove, then pour it in to brew it. Wouldn't that work well enough?"

Sarah gave him a curious look. "Miss it that much, do you?"

Paul couldn't help but grin. "I'm pretty well detoxed by now, but I used to live on the stuff."

"Leave the coffee pot out then," Sarah said to Owen. "We'll give it a try."

"Thanks," Paul said. "Anyway, I came to ask what else needs to be done. It don't look like you need any more help in here, though, you already got a system worked out. I'd just be in the way."

"You could . . ." Sarah said, her tone hesitant. Paul waited, wondering what she wanted that she couldn't just tell him to do. "You could spend the rest of the afternoon with Aaron," she went on. "I was trying to keep him busy helping out this morning, but there isn't much to do right now I can trust to a ten-year-old. Nina gave him paper and colored pencils that she found, but I don't think coloring will keep him occupied for long."

"Sure," Paul said. "Happy to."

Before he went to find the boy, though, he headed for the garage, where John had joined Mark, inspecting the cars. "Decided to help us after all?" Mark asked him, managing to keep any hint of their previous conversation out of his tone.

Paul shook his head. "I'm looking for a way to keep Aaron entertained for a while. Found any sports stuff? Catcher's mitts, a football, anything like that?"

John looked stunned for a moment, and Paul wondered if he was thinking he should be spending some time with his son instead of Paul. Then Paul remembered the two boys in the pictures, too, and felt like an ass. "Sarah thinks he's going to get bored with coloring pretty quick," he explained to fill the sudden, awkward silence. "So I thought runnin' him around a little outside would do him good. Now that we're not walkin' all day, anyway."

"Yeah," John said. "There's some stuff here," he said, pulling a sturdy cardboard box off a shelf and handing it to him. "Thanks."

"Come join us when you get done here," Paul told him. "It'll do you good, too."

Aaron was thrilled when Paul showed him the box. "Let's play catch!" he cried, pulling on one of the mitts.

"Not inside," Paul told him as he reached back in for the baseball. "How about the driveway?"

"Okay!" Aaron agreed, his gap-toothed smile wide. "Baseball and hot food! This is the best day!"

Paul followed him outside, wishing that was all it would take to be happy again.

CHAPTER NINETEEN
WHISKEY

September 16th, 7:03 pm – 1880 Cambridge Road, Coshocton, Ohio

Trying to cook food for eight people on a two-burner camp stove wasn't an easy task, but Nina thought Sarah managed it well. She lined up all the cans of soup and told everyone to choose, then heated two at a time, rinsing the pots in between. There was some argument over who got what, with the can of chicken noodle being the most sought-after. Eventually Owen let Aaron have it. Nina picked the minestrone and didn't have to fight anyone.

Paul volunteered to wash the dishes again, and when the others went to the living room, Nina lagged behind to help him, drying each dish and putting it away. They said little, but Nina was constantly aware of how close they stood, the movement of his arms as he reached for a dirty dish or handed her a clean one, the moments when their hands brushed. The silence between them quivered with possibility, but when Nina tried to find the right words to say, she came up with nothing.

When they joined the others before the fire, Paul took an empty space on the one of the couches, next to Owen. There was enough room on his other side for Nina. For a moment, she considered settling beside him, tucked under his arm. She already knew how well she fit there, and part of her hoped it would be a simple, silent way to break the tension between them. The rest of her resisted, arguing that supporting him as he walked was one thing, but casual affection, in front of everyone, was another matter entirely. She wasn't ready for it.

Instead she settled on the floor between the fireplace and the other couch, where Mark and Sarah sat together. John, Aaron, and Alison all sat on mismatched armchairs borrowed from other rooms—the living room furniture hadn't had enough seats for everyone. The silence out here was much more comfortable, with everyone relaxing in the light of the crackling fire.

"This seems like the kind of time we'd want a little music," Mark said. "And some whiskey."

Sarah laughed. "The whiskey we have. There's a bottle in the cupboard above the fridge."

"I think I'd better go get it!" Mark declared, which drew laughter from everyone else.

"As for the music," Sarah said as her husband headed to the kitchen, "there's a stereo, but without electricity it's no good, of course. I don't think anyone turned up any musical instruments while we were looking around, except that piano over there."

Owen snorted. "I played the tuba in the band at school, but I doubt we'll ever run into one of those."

"I played the flute for a year or two," Alison added with an offhand, dismissive gesture, "but I was never very good."

"I had to learn the recorder in school last year, but I hated it," Aaron said, scowling.

John reached over to squeeze his son's shoulder. "I didn't like it much when I had to learn, either. If we find a guitar somewhere, I'll teach you to play that instead."

"That would be nice," Nina remarked. "I miss music."

Paul turned to her. "Do you play anything?"

The reflection of the fire in his eyes was distracting enough she almost forgot to answer. "I wanted to, but I didn't want to be in band in school—everyone hated the director, he was a nightmare. Private lessons were too expensive, though, so I never picked anything up." She paused, twisting her fingers together in her lap. "Do you?"

"Piano. My mom insisted. She kept all the books she learned from as a kid and started me on the first one when I was six."

"Did you like it?" Aaron asked. "Were you any good?"

Paul smiled, seeming undisturbed by the bluntness of the question. "Yes, and yes. For a while I wanted to study music after high school instead of going to a regular college, but my dad didn't approve."

"Didn't your mom want you to go, if she was the one who taught you in the first place?" Aaron asked.

"No, it was just my dad, then. My mom passed away when I was thirteen."

"Oh," Aaron said, his voice small. "Sorry."

Mark returned from the kitchen with the bottle of whiskey and a tray of empty glasses, saving everyone the need to fill the awkward moment with conversation.

"Excellent," John said. Mark opened the bottle and poured him the first glass, which he took gladly.

The other glasses were poured and passed around, even one for Aaron, though it barely had anything in it. John gave Mark a piercing look when he held it out to the boy, but Mark only winked and said, "It's just a sip, John. Let him try it."

John considered a moment, then nodded. Aaron took the glass and gave his father a bright smile.

When everyone had been served, Mark held his up and said, "Cheers!"

Everyone echoed him and clinked glasses with whoever sat closest, which left Nina and Alison out, being across the room from each other. Though Nina didn't want to share a salute with Alison anyway. Instead she watched Paul touch his glass briefly to Owen's. "You ever had it before?" Paul asked him.

"No. I've snuck a few beers," he admitted, "but never anything stronger."

"Well, it's got a lot more kick, so go slow."

Owen took a sip and seemed to like it, but Aaron reacted by coughing violently the moment the alcohol hit his tongue. John glowered at Mark, who just laughed. "That's pretty much what I thought of it, too, the first time." John's expression didn't change. "Okay, okay," Mark capitulated. "I'll go get him a glass of water."

"It tastes the way gasoline smells," Aaron said, sticking his tongue out. "Why would anybody drink it?"

"Because adults are crazy," Alison told him. She curled up in her big armchair, the drink in her hand already half-finished. "Sometimes they do things that make no sense at all."

Aaron nodded vigorously, which prompted another round of laughter. Mark returned with the water for him and took a seat next to Sarah again.

Nina took a sip of her whiskey, gazing over the glass at Paul. "Will you play something for us?" she asked. In the pause between her question and his answer, she vacillated between hope he would, and embarrassment she had asked. But she couldn't ask him to sing, because he didn't know she knew he could. Hearing him play would be the next best thing.

And maybe he would sing anyway, without her having to ask.

"Sure," he said, setting his glass down. "Happy to."

It only took him a few strides of those long legs to cross the room. Nina might have felt odd watching him as he settled on the bench and folded back the cover, except everyone else was too. Even Alison twisted dramatically in her chair to keep him in sight. Paul pressed his hands together, stretching his fingers, then laid them lightly on the keys.

Nina didn't recognize the song he played. Slow and wistful, the simple melody wrapped all her thoughts into it, bending them to the music, slowing her heartbeat to match the rhythm of the song. Halfway through, she thought she might be able to sing it, if there had been words. She wouldn't be surprised if she heard it in her dreams at night.

No one spoke while Paul played—the only other sounds came from the fire, a crackling counterpoint to the notes his hands drew out of the piano. When the song came to an end, the silence lasted a few moments.

"Paul, that was beautiful," Sarah breathed.

He turned on the bench to look over his audience. Nina quickly looked away, studying the others so Paul wouldn't see something in her expression she didn't mean him to. Mark had his arm around his wife, who was brushing a tear from the corner of her eye. Aaron looked sleepy and content, just starting to nod off. John sat back in his chair with his eyes closed and a faint smile on his face. Owen was staring at the fire with an absent, dreamy look.

Alison, on the other hand, watched Paul with a smile of her own, a predatory sort of expression that made Nina's fingers itch to slap it off her face. Nina had noticed Alison's attraction to Paul long before he had confessed their failed encounter—but she had never been so blatant in her interest before, not in front of everyone. Nina hoped the whiskey wouldn't make her brave, or reckless. She didn't think she could stomach Alison falling all over herself chasing Paul tonight. Not knowing that he'd chosen to walk away, and she was still chasing him.

Wasn't Paul doing the same to her?

No, Nina answered her own question instantly. *It's not the same, because I haven't walked away. I haven't been able to.*

Nina looked back at Paul just in time to see his face go blank as he turned back to the piano. Laying his hands on the keys, he played another song, an old, familiar tune Nina thought she would know if she heard the words, but couldn't place without them. When the song was over, he transitioned smoothly into a classic lullaby without any pause.

Which clearly signaled the end of this little concert. So Nina wasn't surprised when Paul swung his legs around the bench to sit facing the room instead of the piano. Though one tiny corner of her heart felt disappointed he hadn't sung for them.

Aaron had gone from nodding off to snoring softly, so John nudged his shoulder and got him awake enough to be led off to bed.

"Sweet dreams," Nina told them, and Aaron gave her a sleepy smile.

Mark stood up and stretched. "That was wonderful, Paul, thank you. But I'm going to turn in, too. I could do with some extra sleep."

He kissed Sarah on the cheek before heading upstairs to a chorus of goodnights, but Sarah didn't join in. Nina watched her watch her husband climb the stairs. After a moment, she stood up as well. "Sounds good to me, too," she said, setting her unfinished drink down.

At the top of the stairs, Mark waited for her to catch up, taking her hand. Nina looked away as they crossed the balcony to their bedroom door. She felt flushed and uncomfortable, and she was tempted to blame it on the whiskey, but she suspected her embarrassment was because she had just witnessed something private.

When she looked away, she found herself locking gazes with Paul. His expression held relief and worry in equal parts, which Nina didn't understand, and didn't have much hope of untangling without talking to him.

With the firelight reflecting in his eyes as he looked at her and the alcohol turning her thoughts fizzy and disconnected, talking didn't seem like such a bad idea. She wondered if she could manage to be the last one in the room with him again, like she had earlier in the kitchen.

Owen leaned forward, elbows on his knees, cradling his empty glass in both hands. "Anybody want to go fishing tomorrow? I asked Mark earlier, and he said he'd teach us."

"Yeah, maybe," Paul answered. "If my shoulder feels any better."

"I guess I should," Alison said, "but I can't say I'm excited about it. I always thought fishing would be boring, but that was when it was just a hobby. For food, though . . ." She trailed off, maybe expecting Nina to volunteer in her place. Nina kept silent.

"Well, maybe John will want to," Owen said, adding his glass to the growing collection on the table. "I'll ask him in the morning." He yawned widely as he got up from the couch. "I didn't know that stuff will knock you right out. I'm off, too."

"'Night, Owen," Paul said. Nina echoed him first, then Alison.

Paul stood up from the bench and started back for the couch where he'd sat earlier, but Alison snagged his arm as he passed. "You're not going to bed already, are you?" she asked in a tone of exaggerated innocence.

"Haven't finished my drink yet," he said, pulling his arm free with more force than strictly necessary. As he sat down, Alison got up, and Nina was afraid she was going to cuddle up next to him. The thought made her stomach turn over. It would ruin Nina's hope to get Paul alone without asking him directly.

But Alison only laid a hand on his shoulder as she went by, trailing it up his neck and through his hair before heading up the stairs. "Sweet dreams," she called down, echoing Nina's words from before, but in a low, husky voice which left no doubt about whether her caress had been an invitation.

At the sound of her bedroom door clicking shut, Paul shuddered. He grabbed his glass and downed the whole thing in one swallow. "Mark left the bottle," he said to Nina without looking at her, pouring himself another. "You want more?"

"No," Nina said. "I'm not aiming for drunk, just relaxed."

"Relaxed is good. Drunk always sounds like fun, until you get there."

"I thought . . ." she began, then stopped, swallowing what she'd wanted to say. Paul looked over at her and raised his eyebrows in an unspoken question. "I thought she wasn't after you anymore," she managed, making a vague gesture at the staircase. "But that was pretty obvious, even before the others left."

"Won't happen," Paul declared. "She's just windin' me up because she's pissed. I'm guessin' that Mark broke it off with her this afternoon."

Nina frowned. "Why do you say that?" But then she remembered the way Mark waited at the top of the stairs for Sarah and taken her hand.

"Because I told him to. Seems like he told her why, too."

"Paul . . ."

He threw back his second drink just as fast as his first, then reached for the bottle again.

Nina moved forward, reaching out her hand to his, stopping him before he could pour. She knelt on the opposite side of the table and studied his face with concern. "Are you aiming for drunk?"

"No," he answered. "But I don't want to feel like this anymore either."

Nina couldn't tell if he meant it as a rebuke or not, so she let go of his hand, but he let go of the bottle. "She doesn't want *me*," he went on in a low, pained voice. "Or, hell, maybe she does, but really, she just wants somebody to choose her over somebody else. Mark did, for a while, but now that it's come down to it, he picked his wife."

"And now she wants you to choose her over me," Nina said. She almost couldn't believe she had, but it seemed foolish to keep dancing around Paul's attraction to her, since he'd admitted it.

Paul didn't even blink. "Won't happen. I almost made that mistake once. This whole bottle of whiskey wouldn't be enough to get me to make it again. Even if you never . . ." Paul didn't finish the thought, though, breaking off and running a hand over his face.

"Even if I never choose you, instead of being alone," she finished for him.

He sloshed some more whiskey into his glass, but didn't pick it up. "Sometimes I wonder why you won't say yes," he said, his tone deliberate and careful, as if he were already drunk and worried the words would come out garbled. "And I'm afraid I won't like the answer if you ever tell me. But what I don't understand is why you won't say no, either."

"Paul . . ."

"It doesn't matter," he snapped, cutting her off. "I'm not going up there. Three bottles of whiskey wouldn't be enough. And she knew that."

Nina said nothing, and he wouldn't look at her. That, more than anything, told her how much he was hurting, because there was hardly a time when he wasn't watching her. The sudden absence of his gaze felt as strange to her as his constant attention had before.

Her heart pounded painfully against her ribs as she considered what to say. She knew she had to say something. She hadn't realized the indecision paralyzing her was torturing him, patient as he always was.

But why did it matter if he were patient, if he was only waiting for her to say no?

I have to walk away.

"I . . . I can't be with you, Paul," she said, her voice hardly more than a whisper. "I'm sorry, because I know that will hurt you, but . . . but I can't. It won't work."

"I'd say I disagree," he answered, still staring at his glass on the table, "but clearly you know something I don't. Will you tell me why?"

She nodded, then took the bottle of whiskey and poured herself another. Paul reached forward to take the glass from her hand before she could drink any. "Not if you have to get drunk first," he told her, finally meeting her gaze. "You'll be angry at yourself tomorrow about it. And at me. I don't want either."

Closing her eyes, Nina took a deep breath and let it out slowly before she spoke. When she felt brave enough to look at him again, she was almost undone by the mix of tenderness and worry she saw written across his face.

"You said before you're not ashamed of what you've done. We can't be together because... because I am. I've done things I'm ashamed of."

Paul's brow furrowed. "I can't imagine you doing anything that would make me feel any different about you."

"I know." A single tear leaked from the corner of one eye, and she wiped it away impatiently. "But you're wrong."

"Why don't you tell me, and let me decide what I think?"

Though his voice was soft, the thought of telling him sent her into a panic, and her words tumbled out in a disjointed frenzy. "No, Paul, please—I can't—I don't—please don't make me." The glasses rattled together on the table as she pushed herself up, intending to dash from the room before one tear became a flood.

Paul stood too, catching her in his outstretched arms when she stumbled around the table to get past him. She should have fought him. She should have broken free. He would have let her go if she had struggled. He always let go, when that was what she wanted.

But it wasn't what she wanted. It wasn't fair to him to send such mixed messages, telling him she didn't want to be with him, then falling into his arms not two minutes later.

I have to walk away.

But I can't.

She clung to him with all of the strength in her small frame, tears welling up as she pressed her cheek to his chest. With the ridiculous difference in their heights, skyscraper that he was, her ear was right against his heart. She heard its steady beat quicken as he folded her in his arms.

After a moment, Paul sat down on the couch again, settling Nina across his lap with her head on his shoulder. One hand lay still against her back while he smoothed her hair with the other. "You don't have to be so strong all the time, Nina," he whispered. "You've been holding me together for days now, don't think I don't see how hard that's been on you. So it's your turn now. I've got you this time. It's okay to let go." He paused and cleared his throat softly. "And I'm not going to make you do anything. You tell me, or you don't. I'm here for you either way."

Her shoulders shook as her tears turned to wracking sobs, and she lost all track of time as she wept. No more words passed between them—there was only the crackling of the fire, the steady motion of his hand over her hair, the warmth of his body against her own. It might have been twenty minutes or two hours later when her weeping slowed, then stopped.

"Better now?" Paul asked.

"Yeah, a little." She unwound herself from him, shifting back so that she had enough distance to think clearly. "But—"

"Shh, Nina, not now. I'm sorry I pushed you. I mean, I still wanna know, but we've both been drinkin', and that's not a good time for talk. 'Least not about the important things. But I meant it. I won't ever make you tell me anything."

His kindness threatened to make her cry again. She stood up to go before that could happen, put a hand to her head, and immediately sat back down. Next to him, this time, instead of draped all over him. "Whoa. Light-headed."

"Not surprised," Paul said with a slight smile, standing. "It's kinda been a rough night. Here, lemme help."

She took his offered hands and pulled herself up while he steadied her. "I'm glad you stopped me from having that second whiskey," she told him. "One was plenty."

He led her to the bottom of the staircase. "Yeah, well, you're a tiny thing. One for you is probably two or three for me. And I'm startin' to feel it, too."

Halfway up the stairs, Nina stopped and looked down. He was still there at the bottom.

"You don't need to do that," she said. "I'm not going to fall."

"Just lemme make sure, okay? I'm not a big fan of broken bones."

She remembered him saying those same words before, standing beneath her in the shadow of the oak tree. Her heart stuttered for a moment, and she nodded at him before trudging up the rest of the stairs and down the hall to her bedroom. Only when she lay in bed, under the faint light of the glowing stars on the ceiling, did she allow herself to smile at the memory.

CHAPTER TWENTY
A DECK OF CARDS

September 19th, 2:15 pm – 1880 Cambridge Road, Coshocton, Ohio

Nina closed her eyes and listened to the rain. Her book lay half-forgotten on her stomach, one thumb stuck between the pages as a bookmark. She hadn't meant to doze, but reading on a rainy afternoon always put her into a trance of hazy daydreams and sleepiness. She was laughing, being chased through the downpour, darting down garden paths under flowering trees. But it wasn't frightening at all, no, it was sweet and exciting and she wanted to be caught...

The tentative knock on her door startled her. She'd left it open a crack— Mark and Sarah had started stealing away together at all hours of the day, so closed doors took on new meaning. But whoever knocked wouldn't push the door farther open until she answered. She sat up, smoothed her hair into some semblance of order, and set the book aside.

"Come in," she called softly.

The timid knock made her think Paul was there, wanting to talk, finally, but not wanting to seem forceful about it, or wake her if she were sleeping. But Aaron stuck his curly head through the opening. "Nina?"

"Hi, Aaron," she said, smiling at him. "What's up?"

"I got bored of coloring, and I want to play cards. Do you want to? Dad's asleep, Alison always says no, and I couldn't find Paul."

She felt a pang of guilty concern, wondering where he could have hid himself, but she tried not to let it show on her face. "Sure. How about downstairs? I don't think we'd both fit at that little desk very well. And you'd be able to see my hand."

Aaron raced out of the room so fast Nina was afraid he'd tumble down the stairs. She followed at a more reasonable pace and sat down on the carpet next to the coffee table, across from Aaron, who was already shuffling the deck of cards. "Go Fish?" she asked.

The boy shook his head. "War?"

Nina laughed. "That can take hours, we wouldn't finish before dinner! How about Crazy Eights?"

"Okay." Aaron shuffled one last time and offered Nina the deck to cut. She waved her hand over it and hid a smile as he dealt their hands out. The serious expression on his face and business-like efficiency of his movements amused her.

The jack of hearts came up first, and Nina immediately played her two of hearts on top of it. Aaron played out of his hand, and then Nina did. They traded turns until they were both almost out. Nina had one card left while Aaron had two. She wondered if this would be the shortest game of Crazy Eights she'd ever played—though she hadn't played many—when Aaron played a three of clubs. Nina saw she would have to draw.

And draw, and draw, and draw again, as it turned out.

"I don't like the rain," Aaron complained. "It makes everybody sad."

"I don't think that's true," Nina said as she added another useless card to her hand. "I like the rain, I always have. Except when I'm out walking in it. But the sound is soothing." She finally drew an eight and set it down on the three. "Hearts. And I'm not sad, either."

Aaron scowled at his last card, which apparently wasn't a heart, and started to draw new ones. "Dad is. And Sarah, and Paul, too. They're sad."

Nina looked up from her hand swiftly, but Aaron was too busy organizing his growing collection of cards to notice. "What makes you think that?" she asked, trying to keep her voice light.

"Dad is sad because Aunt Wendy is gone. I think Sarah's sad because Dad is—she's real nice and never wants anybody to feel bad about anything."

Aaron finally played a card, and Nina took her turn, saying, "I think you're right. Sarah's one of the nicest people I've ever known." She didn't prompt him for anything else, but waited to see what he would say next.

"And Paul, he's sad because you're not talking to him." He played from his hand, and looked up at Nina. "Are you mad at him? What did he do?"

She wanted to protest, to insist he must be wrong, but deep down she knew he wasn't. The chill in the air between her and Paul must have been obvious to everyone, but Aaron was the only one innocent enough to comment on it. She sighed instead, and started drawing cards. "He didn't do anything wrong, Aaron, and I'm not mad at him." How could she explain this to a ten-year-old? "But we did have a disagreement about something, and now I don't think either of us knows what to say."

"Can't you just say sorry?"

"That would be a good place to start," Nina agreed, finally drawing a card she could play. "But it's not always that easy. If I were wrong, I would go tell Paul so and apologize. And if he were wrong, I'm sure he would too. But we're having one of those really complicated grown-up problems where neither of us is right, and neither of us is wrong. The answer is somewhere in the middle, and we haven't found it yet."

Aaron played a card, then held onto his last one tightly with both hands. "How hard are you looking?"

The question pierced her brain like the one ray of sunlight stabbing her eyes when she wanted to sleep in. She wasn't looking at all. She was avoiding trying to find a solution because pushing Paul away was easier. "It's going to be fine, Aaron. I know it can hurt to see your friends not getting along, but I don't want you to worry." She played one of her cards, and tried to smile. "We'll figure it out."

"I won!" Aaron cried happily, placing his last card on the pile. "Play again?"

She almost said no. She wanted to find Paul, wherever he had tucked himself away to avoid her. Talking with Aaron was nothing like chatting with her friends back in high school, but she was seized by the same feeling she always got then—the urge to act immediately, while she was still feeling brave. Whenever a friend told her a guy had a crush on her—*oh, hey, hadn't you noticed?*—she was filled with the desire to investigate, to go careening through the halls like a pinball to find him, to flirt and be flirted with.

Nina wasn't looking for that with Paul, but when she'd tried to tell him so, she messed it up. He still had reason to hope she returned his feelings—or she might, given time. And then she'd done her best to avoid him for three days. She hadn't even checked on his injury. Whenever she thought of that, guilt swamped her, even though by now Paul knew what to do on his own. And he was healing fine. He wouldn't need her help for much longer.

But that thought hurt, too. Because a tiny voice in her heart told her he did need her, and she needed him, too. Maybe, with him, things could be different. Maybe he would understand.

Or maybe he wouldn't. Either way, she should find out.

She had to tell him what had happened to her after the plague had struck, and how she had ended up here, with John's little band of survivors. The idea made her hands shake and her heart quiver, but he needed to know, and she couldn't put it off much longer.

"Yeah," she said instead, snapping out of her own tangled emotions. "I'll play again."

She gathered the cards and began to shuffle. Giving in to her impulsiveness wasn't a good idea. Going to find Paul now, when she knew what she had to do, but didn't have the words yet . . . it wouldn't end well. She didn't want to make things worse. And as uncomfortable as this tension was, it could still get worse.

Nina hoped Paul wouldn't hate her for what she'd done.

Aaron picked up the hand she dealt him and smiled when she turned the first card over, playing on it immediately. Nina had to draw more cards, which didn't bode well for her chances at winning this rematch, but playing with Aaron was a pleasant enough way to spend the afternoon. If she tried to read again, she'd only spend the time agonizing over what she knew she had to do. There would be plenty of racing thoughts when she tried to fall asleep later. For the moment, she kept drawing cards.

So she smiled and laid an eight down on the pile. "Hearts."

CHAPTER TWENTY-ONE
A PAIR OF SCISSORS

September 20th, 9:36 am – 1880 Cambridge Road, Coshocton, Ohio

Paul looked out the front window and frowned. The sun was almost halfway up the sky. Each morning, breakfast had been later than the day before. He glanced at his watch and saw the morning wasn't as far gone as he'd thought, but on the road Paul was used to getting up with the sun. He'd been awake for over an hour, but as near as he could tell, he was the only one in the house who was.

The first few days, he hadn't begrudged anyone a late morning. Mark and Sarah needed the time to themselves, and Paul was glad to see they both seemed happier for it. Nina, too, had slept in on the second morning in the house, after she'd cried herself to pieces the night before. Paul himself hadn't been the first to show his face on any given day, at least until now. There was an itch between his shoulder blades, and he felt a sudden craving for the wind in his hair.

The realization struck him as he turned away from the window and saw a half-full water glass on an end table. They were getting comfortable here. After only five days, this place was starting to feel more like home than shelter.

"We've been here too long," he said to the empty room.

John had lost direction here under the weight of his grief. Sarah had taken charge, but she was nesting, not looking ahead. Until coming here, Paul hadn't spent more than two days in the same place. The chance to recover from his injury had been welcome at first, and the steady supply of food had certainly helped him get his strength back. Now, Paul fought the urge to shoulder his pack, pick a direction, and start walking.

Because that was ridiculous. No matter how strong the pull was, he couldn't leave. Not without warning, not without a plan, not without saying his goodbyes.

Not without Nina.

Leaving her behind was out of the question. If he hadn't been able to bring himself to go before she'd devoted all her energy to caring for him, he certainly couldn't after. He owed her too much.

Even if she was currently devoting all her energy to ignoring him. Her prickly moods didn't change how he felt.

So he was stuck in place with nervous energy to burn. He decided to channel it into cleaning up and making breakfast. He'd never been much of a cook, but there was nothing to eat anymore which would need him to be. When the others got up, the meal would be ready, and he'd have worked out what to say to shake them up and get them thinking about moving on.

Owen came into the kitchen first, yawning and trying to flatten his unruly hair. "'Morning. Where is everybody?"

"Still in bed," Paul said. "I wouldn't wait for them, go on and eat."

"Okay." He filled a plate with food, wrinkling his nose at the pears. "I miss bacon," he said, then glanced at Paul and looked sheepish. "No offense to your cooking."

"If you can call this cooking at all," Paul answered with a smile. "Two weeks ago I'd have gone miles to get canned fruit. Now, I'm getting tired of it. I miss bacon, too. And eggs."

"I miss bananas," John said from the doorway. Aaron trailed in behind him. "Can't get those in a can."

"Pancakes!" Aaron said as he sat down. "With whipped cream and chocolate chips and strawberry syrup."

Paul stole a glance at John, who smiled. "Birthday breakfast, every year since he was eating solid food."

"Dad!" Aaron whined. "Don't tell them about me as a baby!"

John smirked. "Sorry, little man."

"When is your birthday, Aaron?" Owen asked.

"October ninth," he answered. "I'll be eleven."

"That's pretty soon," Paul said, checking the date on his watch.

"I used to have a watch like that," John remarked. "I stopped wearing it when I got a smartphone. Didn't need it any more."

Paul nodded. "I never wore one, before. But I picked one up pretty early on when I was out lookin' for supplies. Figured it would be a good thing to have. And I wanted to get it set while I still knew the date. I'm sure the time ain't right, because I just called the sunrise six in the morning. But it's close enough."

"It's a good idea," John told him. "I'll keep an eye out for one myself."

"The battery will go eventually," Paul said. "But not for at least a few years."

Silence spread over the table, the last word sinking like a stone dropped into a well. Paul regretted it the instant he said it. No one talked about the next few years. No one talked about anything more than the next few days.

Alison turned up next. "Who died?" she quipped as she strode in, looking at their somber faces.

"That's not funny," Owen snapped. She only shrugged in reply and sat down to fill her plate. "I think I'm done," he went on, taking his dishes to the sink. "Thanks for making breakfast today, Paul."

Owen was in such a rush to get out of the kitchen he nearly knocked Nina over as she came in. He muttered an apology and bolted. Nina's gaze traveled from him to the rest of the room, asking a silent question. No one answered, but when she caught Paul's eye, he shot a glance at Alison. Nina straightened her shoulders and headed for the table, choosing the seat on Paul's right, where Owen had just been sitting.

"How have you been sleeping, Nina?" Alison asked the question in a sweet voice with an undertone of malice.

"Just fine, thank you," Nina replied as she started filling her plate.

"No nightmares? It seemed like you were having a lot of them, for a while."

Paul drew in a breath to chide Alison, but bit back the words when he felt Nina's dainty foot press down on his toes. "No, I actually had a good dream last night. I don't think I've had any nightmares for weeks."

"I dreamed about dinosaurs!" Aaron chimed in, oblivious to the tension.

"That's darling," Alison said. "What about you, Paul? Are you getting enough rest? Having trouble relaxing?"

"Not a bit," he answered. "Now that my shoulder's mostly stopped hurtin', I sleep like a log."

Nina turned to him and took advantage of his change of subject. "Those stitches need to come out today. If they're in much longer, they might be trouble."

"Sounds good."

"You'll have to show me your scar sometime," Alison said. "So I can see how well Nina's taking care of you."

Paul caught the stormy look John sent at Alison, but if she saw it, she gave no sign.

"I have a scar from falling off my bike," Aaron said, pulling back his sleeve and shoving his arm in front of Alison. She gave him a weak smile and a pat on the head. Paul began to wonder if he had better instincts than the adults gave him credit for. He certainly seemed to know when to be a distraction, and Paul used the opportunity to take his plate to the sink and leave the room, casting one last glance at Nina, who gave him the slightest nod.

Since Owen had probably retreated to their shared room, Paul headed outside to the bench on the front porch. He didn't have a way to tell Nina where he was headed, but he didn't think he'd be hard to find. He'd spent most of his free time there over the past three days, thinking and trying to stay out of Nina's way. He didn't want to avoid her for his own sake—if he thought he could, he'd spend every minute with her. But she'd hardly spoken to him since she broke down in his arms. She hadn't been hostile, which was a relief. But the distance was obvious in her refusal to be drawn out by anything he said.

The hint of chill in the air made him glad he'd put on his sweater. The grass was turning brown, and though he couldn't see the maple tree in the side yard from here, the breeze rustled its drying leaves. He'd always heard fall in the Midwest was pretty, and he wondered if the leaves were starting to change color, and when they would start to fall.

Paul wondered if he'd still be here to see it.

Nina came outside and gave him a half-smile from the doorway, breaking through his building anxiety. "You want to do this out here? It's too chilly. I was thinking of the first floor bathroom."

"Yeah, that's fine," he said, getting up. "I just like to come out here to think."

"Silly Paul," she teased, and his heart leaped. This was the side of Nina he liked best, the side he hadn't seen for days. "I can think anywhere."

The temptation to tease back was strong, but he resisted. Everything that sprang to mind was, if he was being perfectly honest with himself, far too intimate. He was about to be half-naked in front of her in a confined space. If her guard was down today, for whatever reason, the last thing he wanted to do was put it back up by saying something crude.

The downstairs bathroom was hardly bigger than a closet, a narrow box with a toilet, sink, and mirror, one tiny window letting in the sunlight. Paul went in first, closing the toilet lid and sitting on it. Nina followed him in, bumping into his knees as she shut the door behind her. When he took off his sweater and shirt, he had to be careful not to elbow her. She had to step between his feet to reach his injured side, and ended up with her back to the wall, even as small as she was. Paul kept his arms relaxed, hands resting on his knees, even though she was so close he hardly had to move if he wanted to touch her.

Supplies sat on the counter around the sink in a neat row: a clean cloth, small scissors, tweezers, a fresh bandage, the roll of tape. Nina must have laid them out before she came to find him. She reached for the scissors first and began to snip each stitch open. "I hope I didn't leave this too long," she said. "When I got my stitches, the doctor insisted they stay in ten days. But those were done with proper sutures, nylon, or whatever they were made of. Sewing thread might not be as easy to get out."

Paul watched her face as she concentrated on her task. He liked the way she pursed her lips slightly, and the way she tilted her head to the side, emphasizing the line of her neck. He wanted to ask how she'd ended up needing stitches, like when she'd asked about his broken bones, but decided against it. "If you're tryin' to tell me this might hurt, I kinda figured that," he said instead. "Can't leave 'em in, right?"

"I'm hoping it won't be much more than uncomfortable," she said. "Your skin looks like it's healed pretty well. I'm not really worried that it's going to reopen once the stitches are out."

"That's good," he replied. "I'd hate to ruin another shirt."

She glanced at his face before turning to exchange the scissors for the tweezers. "Okay, here goes."

The process was slow, even slower than stitching him up to begin with, but more unpleasant than painful. Nina pulled on each thread gently, working them free from his healing skin, pausing to blot the wound with the clean cloth. When she set it back on the sink he could see tiny dots of blood forming neat rows on the fabric.

After a few minutes of silent work, Nina asked, "So what set off Alison this morning?"

"I don't know," Paul answered. "She was like that the moment she showed up in the kitchen, before anyone said a thing to her."

"Probably wasn't pleased that Mark and Sarah hadn't come down yet," she said. "Not that I'm not happy for them. And not that I don't think Alison got herself into this mess, because she did. But it's bound to make her lash out."

"I'd rather she didn't turn it on you, though. Drives me mad, the way she picks on you."

Nina met his eyes for a moment, in between removing one stitch and the next. Her expression softened, and Paul gazed unblinking back at her. She didn't say anything, and he held his breath, waiting for her to react to his admission.

The moment passed, though, and Nina began tugging on the next stitch. Paul let out his breath in a soft hiss. "Sorry," she whispered.

"So . . ." Paul began. When Nina didn't give him a warning look, he pressed on. "How've you been, the last few days?"

Nina paused, resting both of her hands on his shoulder as if she needed the support. "If you were anyone else, I'd say that was a passive-aggressive way to bring up the fact that I've barely been speaking to you."

Paul cringed inwardly. "And since it's me?"

She went back to work on the stitches before she answered. "It's hard to forget the last time we did talk, I nearly cried myself to sleep in your arms. I'm sorry I worried you."

"About that—"

"Yeah, about that. Thank you. For being there." She tugged another stitch free and dropped it onto the tiny pile accumulating on the counter. "You've done a lot for me, and I realized I don't thank you enough. It's not easy for me to accept help."

Paul licked his lips, which had gone suddenly dry. "Don't worry about it. After everything you've done for me, all of this, I ain't gonna be upset if you don't say it all the time. If anything, I gotta say it to you more. I owe you a lot too."

Nina frowned, but not at his words—she tugged hard at a stubborn stitch. "I don't think you do. I don't want things between us to be like that. You know, trading favors, and food, and figuring out who owes what. I'm tired of it."

"Nina, are you saying . . ." But he couldn't finish the question. He was afraid to ask.

"I'm saying," she answered softly, "that there are things we should talk about. I have a lot I should tell you, and you're not going to like some of it. But whatever happens, good or bad, when we cross that bridge, I don't want to deal with any of that nonsense. We haven't just been traveling companions for a while now, we've been friends. You never said it, because you want to be more, and I never said it because I can be incredibly stubborn and defensive. But we are. And friends help each other."

Clearly, Nina had been doing plenty of thinking during their time apart, too. Paul wondered what he wasn't going to like, then shoved the thought aside. "Yeah, they do. And we are."

She took a deep breath and went to work on the next stitch, silent until she dropped it on the counter. When she spoke again, her tone was faintly bitter. "You're not disappointed, are you?"

"You said we should talk, so we'll talk," he answered, choosing his words carefully. "But until then . . . no. I won't deny I want more from you, but why would I turn down friendship?"

One corner of her mouth turned up in a quick, lopsided smile. "I doubt you even could. You make people like you as easily as most people breathe."

"Nina—"

"Not now," she interrupted. "I'm almost done, and this tiny bathroom isn't exactly the best place for a heart-to-heart."

"Yeah."

"Before dinner?" she asked, then answered herself. "No, after. In case things go badly, that way we won't have to face anyone for a while, and they won't all be staring at the two of us not talking again."

"I didn't like that much," Paul told her in a low voice. "I tried to be kind and make myself scarce, since you didn't seem to want me around. But it was hard. If we're gonna fight about something, let's fight and have done with it, not avoid each other for days. We won't even be able to do that, once we're on the road again."

Nina gave him a blank, unreadable look. "Has anybody said when we're leaving? Or where we're going? I hadn't heard anything."

Paul shook his head. "I was gonna bring it up at breakfast, but when Alison showed up with her claws out, I didn't wanna stick around waitin' for Mark and Sarah. I think we need to move on soon."

Nina went back to working on his stitches. "We have been here almost a week now. We're all rested, and you're nearly healed."

"And it's getting colder," Paul added. "We've gotta start heading south or we're gonna get snowed on."

She blotted his skin again. "There. All done."

He stood and studied the injury in the mirror. Nina hovered close behind him as he ran a finger over the thin red line of his new scar. Every stitch had left two tiny holes behind, pinpricks of red on his skin which were already darkening toward black as they clotted.

"I'm not even sure you need a bandage any more," Nina said. "Unless you think your clothes might irritate it."

"I'll try goin' without for a few hours," he said. "If it's bothering me, we'll put one back on."

"Okay." She edged around him to reach the sink and tidy up the supplies. He pulled her into his arms instead. Her body tensed, but after a moment, she hugged him back tentatively.

Probably should have put my shirt on first. He resisted the laugh building in his stomach and said, "Thank you."

"You're welcome," she whispered before pulling away. She started to clean up again. This time, he let her, moving back so he had enough room to pull his shirt and sweater on without knocking her in the head.

In the living room, Mark and Sarah sat with John, deep in conversation. Mark glanced up at Paul and gave a nod of greeting, followed by a furrowed brow. Paul glanced behind him to see Nina exiting the bathroom. "Just got my stitches out," Paul explained.

"Wonderful," Sarah said. "How are you feeling?"

"Fine. Ready to face the world again."

John frowned. "About that," he began, and Paul felt a rush of relief. He wasn't going to have to broach the subject himself. "The last day or two, the three of us have talked about the idea of us staying here. At least for the winter."

"What?" Paul nearly choked on the word. A thousand objections flew through his mind at once, so tangled together he didn't know where to start. "Are you crazy?"

Sarah flinched at his disbelieving tone. "It's not crazy, Paul. We haven't got it all worked out yet, but we think it's doable."

He strode across the room and flung himself down on the empty couch. "Well then, convince me it's not as ridiculous as I think it is."

John opened his mouth to speak, but Nina got there first. "Shouldn't we all be here for this?"

Sarah nodded. "I'll go find Alison, if you want to look for Owen."

None of the men said anything to each other while they were gone. Paul switched between watching John pointedly not meet his eyes and intercepting nervous glances from Mark. There was a silent argument brewing between them, and Paul hoped things wouldn't turn sour when they started throwing words at each other instead.

CHAPTER TWENTY-TWO
AN OUTHOUSE

September 20th, 10:13 am – 1880 Cambridge Road, Coshocton, Ohio

Nina returned to the living room with Owen to find everyone assembled. "I checked on Aaron," Sarah said to John. "He's reading in his room."

A half-smile appeared on John's face, but he turned sober again instantly. "I guess it's time for our first group meeting."

Everyone had taken their usual spots on the chairs and couches, but Nina didn't think sitting on the floor in front of the fireplace was appropriate for a discussion this serious. She glanced at Paul, who moved an inch or two closer to Owen to make more room for her. She perched on the edge of the couch, her spine straight, her hands folded in her lap.

"We've never really had one before," John went on, "but Nina rightly pointed out that everyone needed to hear this. Mark and Sarah and I have been discussing the idea of staying here for the winter."

"And I think that's gonna go badly if we try it," Paul objected. "We need to get movin' again. If we head south now, we might still be able to skip winter entirely."

"You afraid of a little snow?" Alison scoffed.

"A little, no," Paul answered in a flat tone. "A lot, yes. Things might go fine at first. But on toward spring, you wanna be snowed in, stuck here with food runnin' low and no way to get more? Because I don't. Stayin' in one place for a bit ain't bad, but you always gotta be ready to leave."

Alison glared at him, but said nothing in response. Nina wasn't sure what there was to say—the scenario Paul outlined was dire enough to be a deterrent. But the idea of having a roof over her head for more than just a few nights exerted a strong pull on her thoughts. No endless days of walking, no nights out in the open, no wondering what lay around the next bend in the road...

"So there's the choice: stay here, or head out." John looked around the room, making brief eye contact with each of them in turn. "I'd like to know what everyone thinks."

"Most of us have spent plenty of time on the road, so we know what Paul's plan involves," Sarah said. "Well, not you, Owen, but you're a bright young man, I'm sure you would adapt. If it comes to that, we'll make sure you have what you need."

Owen gave her a small smile.

"But staying here would be a lot more complicated than that," Alison countered. "We should hear your plan, too, before we have to decide."

Beside her, Nina noticed Paul's small flinch of surprise. He probably hadn't thought Alison would support his plan. Nina was willing to bet she wasn't looking forward to an entire winter cooped up in a house with her former lover and his happy wife.

"We spend the next few weeks while the weather is good stockpiling supplies," John began. "Food, toiletries, candles and lanterns and batteries. Medicine and vitamins, warmer clothes and winter gear—hats, coats, mittens, that sort of thing."

"One of the cars is in good shape," Mark added. "We can't travel in it because we won't all fit, but we can use it to go farther when we forage, maybe check the towns around us, too."

"We have the fireplace for heat," John continued. "In the worst cold, we might all be in sleeping bags down here on the floor instead of our bedrooms. But it's still better shelter than we'd have any given night on the road."

"We have water," Sarah said. "Cold water, true, but it's still running."

"You can't know it will be all winter," Paul broke in. "There's no one out there maintainin' the system. We could lose the water tomorrow, for all we know. Either the tower will run dry, or a valve or something will break somewhere and no one will fix it. Even if we still have it when winter comes, without real heat through the whole house, the pipes will freeze."

"So we find barrels and collect rainwater through the fall, and store it," Mark countered. "And if that's not enough, we'll melt snow."

"If we lose the water," Owen said, grimacing, "we lose the toilets."

"Then we build an outhouse." Mark smiled. "That's good, though, Owen, we hadn't thought of that."

"And what do we do with ourselves all winter, sit on our asses and whistle while we wait for spring?" Alison asked. "It's not like there's much good on television anymore."

"Books," Sarah said, her abrupt tone betraying a hint of anger that her friend wasn't supporting her plan. "Cards. Board games. Maybe Paul can teach us all to play piano."

"If he's still here," Alison replied with a sudden venomous sweetness and a glance at Nina, who returned her look with a calm expression.

She refused to break down again where anyone could see her. Even Paul.

He glanced over at her as well, guilt flashing across his face. And something else, too. Anger? Nina had never seen Paul angry, so she couldn't be sure what his look meant.

"No one's decided anything yet," he said, facing the group again. "We have to talk all this through first."

"But that's worth discussing, too," John said. "This doesn't have to be unanimous either way. Anyone who wants to is free to go their own way. We've stuck together, some of us since the beginning, because we needed each other to survive. But if we don't all agree on the best way to do that, then no one should feel obligated to abide by something they feel is the wrong decision."

Everyone was silent a few moments as that sunk in. Nina clenched her fingers together until her knuckles turned white, considering how a vote, taken right then, would fall out. John, Mark and Sarah all definitely wanted to stay, which meant Aaron would too. Owen, she thought, would choose to stay, with his lack of traveling experience, and with more people staying than going.

Which left Alison, who seemed to be against staying, at least, if not exactly in favor of leaving. And Paul, whose restless energy practically had him vibrating in his seat. He was ready to move on.

Nina bent her head to hide the sudden wave of loneliness which swept over her, threatening her with tears. She could pretend she didn't understand him when Sarah teased her or Aaron questioned her. But in her heart, she knew Paul had stayed for her. She hadn't lied to him, less than an hour ago, while taking his stitches out. They were friends. She'd come to depend on him more than she'd ever expected to. She didn't want him to go. She would miss him.

But she had told him they couldn't be together, and now he was leaving. His stated reasons were solid—she didn't doubt he was telling the truth about not wanting to be at winter's mercy—but the timing argued for more.

Christine had said it—Paul was the lone-wolf type. He had turned up at their camp with more valuable supplies than the rest of them put together, and he obviously knew how to take care of himself. He didn't need them—he had never needed them. Paul had stayed for Nina.

And now, he didn't have to.

Would he stay if she changed her mind? And did she even want that?

"Does anyone have anything else to add?" John asked. Nina caught his glance at her, but she ignored it. Nothing she had to say was appropriate for such a public forum. "All right, then," he went on. "We should all take some more time to think about this. Let's let it go for the rest of the day, and talk more tomorrow. No sense in rehashing it over lunch or dinner."

As the meeting broke up, Paul turned to Nina before she was half out of her seat, but John came up to him. "It's not that I want you to leave, Paul, I hope you know that. But you won't convince me to go."

Nina caught Paul's brief look of worry as she slipped away. "I understand, John," he said as she climbed the stairs. "Really, it's hard either way. I think you're makin' the wrong choice, but I do understand why..."

She shut her bedroom door behind her, blocking the sound of his voice. Would he leave tomorrow, or the day after? Could all this confusion between them be over so quickly? The stuffed animals on the shelves above the bed caught her eye again, and this time she pulled one down, a snow leopard with a faintly sad expression. Hugging it to her, she curled up on top of the covers.

Footsteps sounded from the hallway, coming right up to her door. But there was no knock. Nina waited, her face tucked against the stuffed cat, but there was no knock. And then there were more footsteps, retreating.

Nina rolled over and told herself she wasn't going to cry. And she didn't. But keeping her tears under control did nothing to ease the ever-tightening pain in her chest.

CHAPTER TWENTY-THREE
CANNED PEACHES

September 20th, 6:15 pm – 1880 Cambridge Road, Coshocton, Ohio

"She says she's not feeling well," Aaron announced as he returned to the kitchen.

"She skipped lunch, too," Sarah fretted. "I'll take her up a plate when we're done here."

Paul stared at his own plate and ate silently, feeling the weight of several pairs of eyes on him. No one was talking about the argument, but everyone was thinking about it. Nina's absence didn't help. Paul could almost hear everyone asking themselves, *will he leave?*

As soon as he thought he could while still being reasonably polite, he stood up from the table. After taking his plate to the sink, he returned for the clean one in front of Nina's empty chair. "I've got it, Sarah," he said. The hot dish for dinner was beans and potatoes, which wasn't Nina's favorite, so he went light on it in favor of a large side of canned peaches.

"Paul . . ." she said uneasily.

"I don't mind." Though he knew his willingness to help wasn't her objection. Before she could say anything else, he grabbed the fork from the place setting and left the kitchen.

Upstairs, he tapped on her door. "Nina? You awake? I brought you some dinner."

He'd expected she might not answer right away, and worried she might not answer at all. So he was surprised when the door opened after only a few moments. She stared up at him from behind the door, half her face hidden.

She didn't look like she'd been crying, which Paul thought was a good sign, but she didn't reach out to take the plate, either. "You feeling any better? Aaron said—"

"What I told him to say," Nina finished for him. "I didn't want to be down there with everyone staring at the two of us. I couldn't."

"Yeah, it was . . . uncomfortable. I left as soon as I could." Her mouth flattened into a thin line, and he realized what he'd said. "Oh, hell, Nina, if you're so pissed about it, at least let me in so we can have this fight in private."

She took the food from him, pushed the door open wider, and waved him in. He shut the door as she put the plate on her desk. She turned to him with her arms folded. "Are you leaving?"

Paul wondered if her bluntness was a symptom of her anger. She didn't seem to have problems asking piercing questions when she was mad. "I ain't sure," he answered honestly. "It depends on who else wants to go. What about you? You never said a thing."

"I want the group to stick together. Either we all stay, or we all go. I didn't say so because it's obvious that's not going to happen. They're dead set on staying, and you on leaving."

"I'm not," Paul corrected her. "I think it's the better plan, that's all. I didn't say I was goin' no matter what." He hesitated, then decided if they were going to fight, it might as well all come out at once. "Besides, you didn't seem to object to us movin' on when I mentioned it earlier. I thought you'd be on my side."

"That was before there were sides," she retorted. "I'd never thought staying here was an option."

"But you want to." It was half question and half accusation.

"I want the group to stick together," she repeated.

"You already said you think that can't happen, so don't hide behind it." Usually at this point in an argument, Paul would lean in, towering over his opponent—he knew his height could be intimidating and was willing to use it as an advantage. But not with Nina. He kept his distance. "Do you want to stay here?"

"Yes," she said, the anger in her voice turning the word into a hiss. "Do you want to leave?"

"Yes."

"You came with us," Nina said, "because of me. Right?" He took a breath to answer, but she didn't wait for him to reply before going on. "So if you leave . . . will that be because of me, too?"

"No. Don't think it, not for a second. That ain't what this is about, I swear. I don't want to be trapped here, waiting for something to go wrong. Because it will, Nina. Something will go wrong."

She nodded. "I get it, Paul, I do."

"Then come with me," he pleaded. Her eyes widened as she gasped, but he didn't let the reaction stop him. "This ain't about us bein' together. Even if the door on that ends up staying shut, I still want you with me. Havin' a friend to watch my back is better than bein' alone."

"You're impossible, you know that?" Nina asked with a slight shake of her head and an even slighter smile. "I almost believe you."

"Believe me?" Paul sank into the armchair in the corner, confused. "What does that mean? I ain't lyin' about anything."

"Could you really box up all the mess between us and stick it on a shelf and forget about it?"

Paul held Nina's stare without flinching. "If I had to. If you say so. Wouldn't be easy, but I'd do it." There was a lump in his throat the size of a cannonball, and as he swallowed past it, Paul wondered how much was pride and how much was fear. "So will you come with me? Lover, or friend, your choice."

She hesitated, then shook her head. "I'm sorry. I know that isn't the answer you want, but . . ." Her face crumpled, as if a mask fell away, leaving her near tears. "You're afraid of being trapped. But I'm afraid of being alone."

"Nina, you'd have me," Paul said, fighting the urge to stand up and take her in his arms. "That's the whole point, we wouldn't be alone."

She came forward slowly, uncrossing her arms and extending one hand to trace the scar on his shoulder through his clothes. Paul held his breath at her touch. She couldn't see it, but she knew exactly where it was. "What if it's worse, next time?"

All the air came out of him in a rush, and he hung his head.

"I'm sorry," she repeated. "I just can't face that again."

That last word made him look back up. "Again?"

Nina backed away to sit on her bed, drawing her knees up and hugging them. "I was going to tell you. I'd made up my mind to, finally. Tonight, even. This just isn't how I imagined it starting."

Paul clasped his hands tightly together to keep from reaching across the space between them. "Then tell me."

"Before the plague," she began, her eyes focused on her knees and her voice soft, "I had a boring office job I hated. I was trying to figure out what to do with myself, how to get a job I really wanted, and all that. I wasn't close to any of my coworkers, because I always felt like I had one foot out the door already. Or at least, I wanted to. But . . ."

"It's okay, Nina," Paul said when she hesitated. "Go on."

"There was a guy. Darren. I guess I had a crush on him, but I'd seen enough drama over office romances, and I never intended to do anything about it. He was just this fantasy I had. The first day the sickness hit—before anyone knew how bad it was, before anyone used the word *plague*—about a third of the office called in. It was such a strange day, trying to get everything done without everyone there. The next morning, only ten people came in. We didn't even try to work, we just sat in one of the empty conference rooms and talked about how weird things were getting, how worried we all were." Her voice dropped lower, so Paul had to lean forward to make sure he caught the words. "The day after that, the only two people to show up were Darren, and me."

"So the two of you ended up on the road together?"

She nodded. "He came decked out in hiking gear—I hadn't known that was one of his hobbies. I mean, I didn't know him very well at all. He was just the cute coworker I daydreamed about sometimes. But he said he was leaving town, and he'd only come to the office to see if anyone was still alive. That was the first time . . ." She paused and licked her lips. "That was the first time I understood that the world wasn't going to go back to normal. I thought everyone was getting sick, but they'd recover, and that would be the end of it. But by then, people were already dying."

"So what happened once you left with him?" Paul asked. "Where did you go?"

"South," she said with a faint grin. "The two of you had that in common. It was spring then, but northern Michigan springs are still pretty cold. And he thought we'd find more people, the farther we got. Maybe even a community of survivors trying to rebuild—he was always asking the people we traded with if they'd heard about anything like that. No one had." She hugged her legs tighter, so tight Paul worried for the strain on her knees. But telling her to relax would get him a nasty look at best, and he'd forfeit the rest of the story at worst. Now that he'd heard the beginning, he needed to hear the end.

"As for being on the road with him," Nina went on, "I learned a lot from him about survival." She let out a soft snort. "I guess being a hardcore wilderness hiker is pretty good preparation for enduring the complete collapse of modern society," she said with a trace of her usual humor. Then she sighed. "He was patient with me, and I learned. But before long, things changed."

She paused, and Paul waited. She looked at him directly for the first time since she'd begun her tale. "From the things you've said, you've seen a lot of people, traded with them. Did you ever run into any groups where the men all seemed happy, but the women seemed . . . numb? Blank faces, hardly talked?"

Paul's skin went cold all over. "Yeah, a few times."

"Darren was teaching me to survive, and after the first few days, it became clear that I didn't have much to offer in return. Except myself. So . . . so we made a deal. A trade. Sex for protection."

"Oh, hell."

She looked away, staring at a spot on the wall past his shoulder. "In a way, it wasn't so bad. He never hurt me, and I never got the feeling he'd turn violent if I said no, one night. He wasn't even a bad lover. But . . ." She stopped and sighed. "But there's a difference between being willing, and being obligated, and it was hard to forget that. I . . . I retreated into myself. Stopped talking, stopped caring."

"Nina . . ." Paul began, then fell silent when she shook her head quickly.

"Things went on that way for a while. Most of the summer—I wasn't keeping track of the days. I didn't even know what date it was until you showed up with that watch of yours. Anyway, we ran into people, some, but not many. We traded, shared shelter for a night, and went on our way. Most of the time it was just us. But then . . ."

A tear escaped the corner of her eye, and Paul couldn't sit still any longer. He shifted to the bed, settling beside her and wrapping one arm gently around her shoulders. She didn't pull away, but she didn't relax, either. "Nina, you can stop, we don't have to do this now. I'm sorry."

"No!" she protested, even as more tears started to fall. "You need to know. You need to understand." She sniffled loudly and wiped her eyes with the sleeve of her sweater. "We ran into a man, alone on the road, going the same direction. In his forties, maybe, scruffy, dirty like we were by then, but polite. He introduced himself as Louie. Darren invited him to travel with us almost on the spot—I can't say what made him do that. I'll never understand it, because I had a bad feeling about Louie from the moment we met him. Something about the way he looked at me made me shiver."

Paul sensed where the story was going, and his heart beat painfully, thumping against his ribs.

"Three nights later, Louie tried to rape me." The flat, even tone of Nina's voice didn't match her trembling, and Paul longed to wrap his other arm around her, to hold her and let her cry again. But the last thing he wanted was for his offer of comfort to undermine her control, when she was trying so hard to be strong. "But I wasn't so far gone that I didn't fight back, and Darren wasn't that deep a sleeper. He woke up, and . . . and he fought for me. He told me to run, but I didn't. I stayed, and tried to help. So I was still there when . . . when Louie killed him. Darren was murdered defending me. That's when I ran."

"Nina . . ." Paul breathed. But he didn't know what else to say.

"Louie chased me, and I was terrified. I kept tripping and falling, but I could hear him crashing along behind me, shouting and swearing when he ran into branches. I kept going, and the sounds got farther and farther away. After a while, I knew he wouldn't catch me, but I couldn't stop. Eventually I saw a fire, and I headed for it. Right then, I never wanted to see another person again, ever. But I knew I needed to find people to survive, because I'd left my pack behind when I ran. I had nothing left but the clothes I was wearing. So that's how I met Sarah, who was on watch when I burst into the camp."

"And so you got taken in," Paul said. "By good people, this time."

"Yeah," she answered. "I was lucky."

"How long was that before we met?"

Nina closed her eyes. "Ten days."

"Shit. No wonder you were . . ." But he didn't finish the sentence.

"Yeah," she repeated. "I was."

Nina fell silent, and Paul waited for a handful of heartbeats, considering what to say. So much of Nina's behavior fell into place—her early mistrust and anxiety, and the slow unfurling of their friendship she had seemed to fight against, until his injury. It didn't explain her unwavering support afterwards—but that could be the way she was, underneath all the fears which buried her. When she decided someone was worth her time and loyalty, she gave it unstintingly.

If her trust was so precious, Paul was even more determined not to lose it.

"I can see why that made you skittish with me," he began. He felt like he was walking into a minefield. "And me being so . . . open, I guess, about my interest in you, that didn't help any. But that's how I am—I've always been pretty straightforward with women. I didn't mean any harm by it."

Nina leaned her head against his shoulder. "I know," she whispered. "That's why I tried to be cold to you at first. Because I thought it would make you dislike me, and leave me alone."

"Didn't work," he replied. "But . . . well, I still don't really understand, I guess. I get why you didn't trust me, and I get why I made you uncomfortable. But, Nina, aren't we past that now? You wouldn't be cuddled up to me like this if you didn't want me around."

"I do," she whispered. "That's what scares me so much."

"But why? Why don't you want to be with me?" Paul heard the frustration in his voice and took a deep breath to calm himself before he went on. "I ain't tryin' to play dumb, I really just don't see the problem. If you said no, Paul, I don't give a shit about you, get lost—well that I'd understand. It's all this, this—gettin' close to me, then retreatin' when I make the wrong move, or say the wrong thing—that's what I don't get. You do want me, Nina. You won't say so, but I've seen that look before, and I know what it means. And you know how I feel. So what's stopping you?"

"Paul . . . Darren *died*. Protecting me. I have to live with that guilt, and after all those silly little daydreams, it turned out I didn't even *like* him. But you . . ."

When she looked up at him, his hand rose, without conscious thought, to touch her cheek.

She turned her face away from the caress. "You want me to go off alone with you," she said, her voice low and intense, "travel with you and *sleep* with you, just like he did. I don't want it to end the same way!"

"First of all, no, I do not want those things 'just like he did'." Paul felt the first stirrings of anger, though he made an effort to keep it out of his voice. "He used you, Nina, and you used him right back. Now, I ain't judgin'—if the two of you thought that was a fair deal, then that's your business. Though you didn't sound happy with your end of the bargain. But that is not what I want."

She shifted against him, curling more tightly into herself.

"Second," Paul went on, "I would *never* ask you to trade sex for anything, certainly not my protection. I'd look after you anyway. You think I wouldn't defend you if an attacker burst into this room, right now, even though we ain't sleepin' together? Because that's bullshit and you know it. I'd do it tonight. I'd have done it a week ago, or two weeks ago, hell, even that first day when I wasn't sure if you'd ever speak more than ten words to me. You said yourself you don't want us keepin' score, and I don't either, so don't tell me what I'm askin' for is the same thing."

"What exactly are you asking for, then?"

Nina's eyes were wider and bluer and more beautiful then than he'd ever seen them before. "I want you to love me," he said before he had a chance to second-guess the words. Nina pulled back, just far enough for his arm to fall away from her, but he didn't stop there. "I want you with me, here or on the road, because you're smart, and resourceful, and a lot tougher than I think you realize. I want you to watch my back because I trust you. And I want you to love me," he repeated, "because I spend far more time than I should imaginin' what it would be like to kiss you."

Nina stared at him without speaking while he waited, tense and hopeful, for her reaction. Then one corner of her mouth quirked up in a half-smile, and she began to snicker. Paul felt a heartbeat's relief that she'd stopped crying, followed by a stab of hurt because she was laughing at him. "What?" he asked, bewildered. "What did I say that was so funny?"

She laid a hand on his uninjured shoulder and gave it a squeeze. "I'm sorry, Paul, really I am," she managed to say in between giggles. "But I couldn't help but think that was probably the closest thing to a marriage proposal that anyone's had since this whole mess started. Since the world doesn't have much in the way of government or laws or churches anymore. That's what made me laugh, not what you said."

Heat washed over Paul's face, and he turned away, knowing she would see the blush staining his cheeks even in just the candlelight. "Hadn't thought of it that way." He braced himself for the inevitable. He'd said too much again, and Nina would withdraw from him, like she always did when he came too close. If his heart was as honest and uncomplicated as sunshine, then hers was the tide, advancing and retreating in waves.

The sudden sense of weight shifting on the bed was the only warning Paul got before Nina laid a hand on his cheek, turning his face back to hers. Her other hand tightened on his shoulder to hold herself steady as she kissed him.

Whatever he had imagined before, as sweet as those fantasies had been, the reality of Nina's lips against his was something else entirely. He thought she might be shy, hesitant, finally lured in by his patient determination. He pictured taking her in his arms gently, his fingers sliding lightly up her back, or twining through her hair as he cupped the back of her head.

He had never expected her tongue to dart between his lips almost instantly, as if he were the one who had to be coaxed and convinced. But he needed no more encouragement to open his mouth under hers, to press one hand to her back and wind the other in her hair. When she drew his lower lip into her mouth and sucked hard on it, all the nerves in his body flared with simultaneous arousal.

His desire became less of a distant, romantic notion to turn over in his mind while he fell asleep, and more of an insistent tugging in his blood. He needed to pull her closer, to find out what the skin of her throat tasted like, to nibble on her ear and slide his hands along the length of her body.

"Nina," he said, hearing the huskiness in his own voice and knowing she couldn't possibly miss it. "Where did that come from?"

"You wanted to know what kissing me would be like," she whispered against his mouth. "I was wondering the same thing about you."

Paul let out a weak huff of laughter as she planted a line of soft kisses from the corner of his mouth back to his ear. "I didn't realize we were done talkin'."

"We're not. I still need to ask you something."

Paul got his hands on her shoulders and pushed her back far enough to see her face, though his body protested the sudden lack of her kissing him. "What is it?"

She met his eyes squarely, something she had hardly managed to do all night. "I still don't want to leave here, Paul, and I know you do. But I want to find out if this will work. If we can be good for each other. Will you stay?"

"Yes," he answered without a trace of hesitation. "But what changed your mind? This morning I thought—"

"You hadn't said you loved me, then," she interrupted, brushing his hair back from his eyes with one hand.

"And I still haven't," he corrected. "I'm sure I didn't, because I was afraid to. Seemed like the kind of thing that would push you away when I didn't mean it to."

She smiled at him, a small, sweet smile. His favorite smile in the world. "You may not have said those words exactly, but that's what you meant. How else was I supposed to interpret 'I want you to love me'?"

"I love you, Nina," he said, framing her face with his hands. "And I'll stay."

CHAPTER TWENTY-FOUR
KITCHEN CHAIRS

September 21st, 7:14 am – 1880 Cambridge Road, Coshocton, Ohio

A light breeze made the long stalks of grass bend and wave in the yard. Nina sat on the front porch bench, wrapped snugly in a blanket to ward off the chill morning air, and watched the ripples.

Sleep eluded her the night before. She thought she may have dozed off for a while, but most of the dark hours she'd spent tossing and turning. When the first rays of the sun set the glass of her window glowing, she gave up, and got up. Unsurprisingly, no one else was awake yet.

Her usual early-morning rituals for dealing with a sleepless night were impractical now. Curling up with a mug of tea and a book wasn't as easy as before—it seemed wasteful to turn on the camp stove to heat water for only herself. Yoga, a pastime she had flirted with, was out of the question. There was no room in the house with both the necessary floor space and privacy, and she did not want anyone to walk in on her contorted like a pretzel. If she could even achieve pretzel-form anymore, which she doubted.

Thinking about why she might want to stay flexible, though, only led her down the path she had been trying not to tread all morning.

If she thought about Paul, and that kiss, and what it could have led to, she would lose all capacity to think about anything else for at least an hour. Possibly the rest of the day.

Her tossing and turning was a direct result of that kiss. Every time she thought she was falling asleep, she recalled it so vividly she could feel Paul's arms around her again and breathe in the scent of his skin. She was never sure if she was dreaming or only fantasizing as she lay half-awake in the dark. Then the feeling of his hands on her was gone, and she squirmed in frustration, rolled over to try to get comfortable, and took a few deep breaths to relax.

Then the process would start all over again.

She'd almost stopped him from leaving. If he had any idea how close she'd been to calling his name as he shut the door behind him on his way out . . .

But even with the air cleared between them, and a few things decided, Nina knew asking him to stay was moving too fast.

That thought made her giggle unexpectedly. She had asked him to stay. Asking him to stay in the house, to stay with the group, had been sensible. He had proved his worth a dozen times over since Sarah had invited him along. Paul was a friend, now, someone valued and trusted. Someone no one wanted to leave.

Asking him to stay the night was a different matter completely. There was no mistaking the fire in him, the depths of passion waiting to be explored. But Nina feared what would happen if she dove in headfirst.

If she was wrong, if being with Paul was a mistake . . . then they couldn't go back.

So as much as she wanted him to slide into bed beside her, she kept their kisses light. As much as she wanted to know if his hands were as clever with her body as they were with a piano, she didn't let them wander far. When he had looked at her by the light of her flickering candle with an unmistakable question in his eyes, she had answered with the tiniest shake of her head.

He had smoothed a hand across her hair, kissed her on the forehead, and left without a word. The tenderness of his silent reply turned her heart over and brought his name to her lips. But she held back, as she was always holding back from him.

Despite the uncertainty still between them, her heart felt lighter as she sat in the hazy morning sunlight. Even though she was tired from lack of sleep and light-headed from missing two meals, since she'd forgotten about the plate of food Paul had brought her until she got up in the morning. By then it wasn't worth eating. But sharing her secret lessened its weight and allowed her to set aside some of the anxiety she hadn't realized was crushing her.

The hinge on the front door squeaked as it opened. Nina turned to see Paul standing half-in, half-out. "'Morning," he greeted her.

"I take my mockery back," she said. "This is a great place to think."

He grinned and joined her on the bench, sitting close enough for their legs to touch. "How'd you sleep?"

"Terrible," she said pleasantly. "You?"

"Not much better," he admitted. "What are you thinkin' about?"

"You get one guess."

He looked at her sidelong. "Right. Me, too. About that . . ."

"Yeah. About that."

Paul folded his hands together and stared out over the waving grass. "I'm not gonna push," he said. "If I don't keep askin', then you don't need to keep sayin' no. You just . . . you just tell me when." He broke off suddenly and laughed. "Was that as awkward as it sounded? I feel like a teenager again, tryin' to be a gentleman to his first sweetheart. It's so . . ." He trailed off, mouth open, like he was reaching for a word he couldn't find.

"Sappy? Clichéd?" Nina prompted, and Paul ducked his head. "It is, a little. But I know you mean it. And . . ."

"And?" Paul turned to her, scratching the back of his head with one hand. Nina was amazed he wasn't blushing. The Paul who'd pursued her had an easy confidence she admired, even when she'd wished he'd leave her alone—but the Paul who'd caught her was turning out to be slightly bashful.

"I've never been good at letting someone get close to me. Most of my relationships have been short-lived and pretty casual." Nina chose her words carefully, but she knew they'd sound awkward anyway. "But this, with us? This isn't. We've gotten this far so slowly, it . . . it doesn't feel right to leap the rest of the way all at once."

"No," Paul replied. "Much as I think we'd enjoy it, I also think you're probably right." He cleared his throat and wouldn't meet Nina's eyes. "I will say, though, I hope you're done shyin' away from me. Because I think I might go a little bit mad if I can't touch you."

"You can touch me," Nina whispered. "But we'll have to be careful. I don't want everybody knowing right away. Or interfering."

Paul leaned forward, his hands forming fists. "Alison," he said. "She'll make your life hell."

Nina reached out from under her blanket and wrapped her hand around one of Paul's, working her fingers in, forcing him to uncurl his. "Yours, too. I don't want to keep this a secret forever, Paul. If we even could—someone's always watching. The two of us know that better than anyone. But I want a little time to ourselves, to get this right before we let everyone else see."

"Sarah's gonna know," Paul replied, turning to face her. "Soon as I say I'm stayin'. Hell, maybe even soon as she sees me. She's got eyes like a hawk about romantic stuff."

Nina grinned. "Sometime I'll have to tell you about the things she's said to me. She was pushing me toward you almost from the first day you turned up."

"I'd thank her," Paul said, squeezing Nina's hand, "except that I have a feeling that when she pushed, you pushed right back. You can be awfully stubborn."

"She'll be so happy to see that she ended up being right, she'll play along," Nina predicted, which made Paul chuckle. "We should go in, though, before someone comes looking for us."

"Right," Paul answered, standing up and heading for the door. Because he hadn't let go of her hand, Nina had to follow. Just before they went inside, Paul leaned down to give her a brief kiss. "Time to get used to stealing these when I can."

Nina stretched up on her tiptoes to get a more satisfying kiss from him. "We'll find time," she said as she settled back to her usual height. "We'll make time. And I suspect sneaking around for a while is going to be its own kind of fun."

Paul's mouth dropped open. "Nina," he breathed, his eyes alight with desire. "Are you wicked, underneath? You gonna enjoy teasin' me?"

"Maybe a little," she answered with her best innocent look. She batted her eyelashes, and Paul let out a sound halfway between a growl and a groan, which made her giggle.

He stepped back and made a visible effort to control himself, closing his eyes while he took a few deep breaths. "This conversation is not over," he said as Nina opened the door.

"I hope not," she answered as she stepped through.

Paul followed her inside, and they found Sarah and Mark in the kitchen, starting breakfast. "Morning, you two," Sarah said.

"Need help with anything?" Paul asked, which earned him a smile from Sarah.

"No, I think we can manage. There's not much left of what we gathered to start with, so it's going to be a bit of a strange meal. But since we're staying, we can start stockpiling more food."

Nina slid into a chair at the table. Paul hadn't followed her across the room and leaned with exaggerated casualness against the counter near the doorway. She couldn't resist giving Paul one last glimpse of the wickedness he'd seemed to enjoy, so she yawned and stretched, the movement just as overdone as his pose. As she unfolded her arm to reach up, she trailed her hand with a deliberate slowness up her neck and through her hair.

When she looked back at him, she was rewarded by the sight of him gripping the edge of the counter with white knuckles. Since Mark and Sarah had their backs turned, she crooked her finger at Paul, then used one foot to push out the chair across the table from her. Him sitting next to her might look unusual, with just the two of them at the table, but standing across the room and looking tense wasn't any better. When he sat down, she mouthed the word *relax*, and he nodded.

Nina opened her mouth to say something to Sarah, and realized she had no idea what to talk about. She didn't particularly want to discuss the business of staying in the house until she had to—though Sarah had mentioned it. But there wasn't much else to say. She could hardly ask the two of them how they were enjoying all the time they'd gotten to spend together.

Though they had, and it showed. Sarah hummed to herself, and as Mark moved around the kitchen, he touched her in passing. A hand on her shoulder, a kiss on her cheek, a one-armed hug around her waist while she was busy scooping the last beans out of a can. If they'd been alone, Nina imagined there could've been a slap or two on the bottom, but Mark showed some restraint.

It hit her then, a feeling like a hand squeezing her heart. This was what Paul wanted. It wasn't about the sex for him, though he obviously desired her. What he wanted were the small gestures of affection, the comfortable sense of belonging together, of belonging to each other. Snippets of memory flashed before her, of all the times he had lifted his hand to reach out to her, only to stop halfway. He'd held back those little gestures, or she'd denied them, because she'd seen them as a prelude to something more, something she hadn't wanted to pursue.

She turned to Paul to find him watching her. He narrowed his eyes at her stunned expression, but there was nothing she could say, not when they weren't alone. She couldn't even reach out to touch his hand where it rested on the table, because over his shoulder, she could see Owen coming into the kitchen.

The others weren't far behind, and within a few minutes, Mark and Sarah brought platters of food to the table, and breakfast began. There wasn't much conversation. For her own sake Nina kept her eyes on her plate for most of the meal. She couldn't risk looking at Paul too much—maybe sitting beside him would have been better, after all. She didn't dare glance at Alison, who had come in last and greeted everyone with sleepy grumbling which was hardly intelligible. The last thing she wanted was to draw Alison's attention to her, not when what she and Paul were building was so new and fragile.

While Mark cleared the table and started doing the dishes, John cleared his throat ominously. "I think it's time we heard from everyone about what they plan to do," he began. "For those of us who stay, our break's over. There's plenty to do, and we need to get started today." He started working his way around the table. "Sarah, Mark, either of you change your minds?"

"No, John," Sarah answered for them both. "We're staying."

"Nina?"

"Staying," she answered.

"Owen, how about you?" John gave the teenager a smile. "I hope you are, because this is your town, you know where everything is. That'd be a big help."

"I'll stay." He smiled back and sat straighter in his chair at the kind words.

John nodded. "Paul?" he asked next. "Still want to go?"

"If I could convince you all to come with me, yes. But I'd be a fool to leave on my own. I'll stay."

Nina watched Paul as he answered—they all did, except for Mark at the sink with his hands in the dishwater—but out of the corner of her eye, she thought she saw Alison flinch.

"Alison?"

She hesitated a long moment, staring down at the table like it might tell her what to say. "Looks like we're all sticking together," she said, then shoved back from the table and stalked out of the room. Sarah watched her leave with a faintly confused expression, but said nothing. Nina shifted in her chair, glancing at Paul again, who returned her look with a grim expression.

"That's settled, then," John said. He began to lay out the plan.

CHAPTER TWENTY-FIVE
A SILK NIGHTGOWN

September 21st, 9:30 am – 1910 Cambridge Road, Coshocton, Ohio

Paul checked the size on a pair of winter boots and tossed them back onto the floor of the closet. Tens, so no good. John and Mark wore size eleven, Owen twelve, and Paul himself, fourteen. *Tall people problems*, he thought, recalling Nina's dry humor. It didn't seem as funny now, but this was only the first house, so he tried not to worry about finding a pair big enough to fit.

For an hour after breakfast, John fired off questions and compiled a list of everyone's clothing and shoe sizes. Then he copied it over several times so everyone could have one, tearing off sheet after sheet of lemon-yellow paper from his legal pad. Then came a personalized list for each one of them, so they could cross items off when things got brought back and parceled out. Hat, scarf, mittens or gloves, winter coat, hiking boots, snow boots, sweaters and thermals if possible. Backup sets of regular clothing, since doing laundry wasn't realistic. Extra sheets, extra blankets, extra towels. Within the next few days, John explained, he was hoping everyone would have a complete personal stockpile of clothing, bedding, and outdoor gear. They were going to sweep the neighborhood for those first, then again for tools, toiletries, and food—they'd done some foraging for the last, but only haphazardly. John meant to gather everything.

Alison didn't return to the kitchen until near the end of the discussion, taking her seat again sullenly. John interrupted himself to ask for her sizes, add them to the list, and assign her a partner, since no one was going out alone. John glanced at Paul just as he said it, so Paul had gotten a moment's warning to school his face to stillness before John said his name. Alison flicked him a glance and said nothing.

Her silence had stretched out, unbroken, as they walked to the first house. John gave them the north side of the street heading east from their place, all of which were untouched—he and Owen had gone west when they'd looked for Paul's clothing. Paul had been concerned about what they'd find in these homes, but a few quick words with Owen before leaving eased his mind. The teenager told Paul he'd nearly finished this neighborhood when they'd run across him. He'd chosen John's sister's place to stay because it was empty, so it didn't have the same stink as the others.

The first thing he and Alison did when they arrived was open all the windows to let fresh air in. Even though it had been at least a week since Owen had cleared the house, the rooms still smelled of decay.

Paul heard Alison coming down the stairs and ducked back into the coat closet near the front door to check the next pair of shoes. Women's running shoes, white and blue, size eight. He tossed them onto the pile of items in the center of the living room rug. Chances are the green hiking boots were size eights, too, which meant they'd both be for Sarah.

"That the good stuff?" Alison asked, jerking her chin at the shoes. She carried a large cardboard box filled with fluffy white towels, neatly folded and arranged sideways like folders in a filing cabinet.

"Yeah," he answered.

She set her burden on the floor next to his pile. "I'll see if I can find you a box too."

"Thanks," he called as she headed back up the stairs.

Paul didn't mind the silent treatment from her and wasn't bothered by curt civility while they worked. But there was something in her tone, in the stiff angle of her head as she looked at him, which made him think she was seething inside. If Alison had wanted to leave the group, she could have left, but she hadn't. From there, it wasn't a huge leap to assume she didn't want to go alone, and had been counting on Paul to go. When he announced his decision, he'd ruined her plan.

But he had a hard time believing she had honestly expected things to go her way—for the two of them to leave and travel together. He hadn't made any real effort to hide his attraction to Nina. He couldn't understand why Alison seemed so shocked he'd decided to stay.

If she was angry at him for spoiling her hopes, it was only icing on the cake. She was already furious with him for splitting up her and Mark. Which made it even stranger to think she'd been counting on him leaving, so she could tag along.

He turned the problem over and over in his head while he systematically checked everything in the coat closet. It yielded two sets of gloves, one gray wool scarf, and two adult-size coats in good condition. One was clearly a woman's coat, but Paul tried on the other, a red anorak with a drawstring hood. He almost laughed at the three inches of his wrists sticking out beyond the cuffs.

Alison kicked an empty box down the stairs, then followed it down with another loaded one in her hands. Sheets, this time, Paul saw as he hurried to retrieve the empty box before she reached the bottom. He packed the shoes first, then folded everything else and laid it on top.

"All done here," he said. "Have you started on the bedrooms?"

"Just about to," she answered. He followed her up, then through the first door on the left, which proved to be the master bedroom. The walk-in closet was too small for the two of them to share comfortably, though if Nina had been there instead, Paul wouldn't have minded. He let Alison step inside to sort and select, while he took the items from her, discarded the hangers, and folded the clothing into neat stacks on the bed.

The dressers came next, a his-and-hers pair against the wall on the far side of the room. Paul took one and Alison the other, hunting for warm socks and clean underwear. Out of the corner of his eye he saw Alison inspecting a series of brightly colored bras, checking the bands for size. Their lists didn't include that information. Either John hadn't thought of it and none of the women had bothered to mention it, or he had, and decided he'd let the ladies fend for themselves. Though Paul surrendered to a brief daydream of looking for something appropriately pretty for Nina—

Alison gave a low, appreciate whistle, which put those thoughts on hold. He turned to look at whatever she found so interesting, only to have them all come rushing right back. She was holding up a long nightgown, black lace on top and slinky crimson silk below. She draped it against her body, checking the fit. "Someone here had good taste," she remarked. "Seems a shame to give it to Sarah, but then, I don't have anyone to wear it for."

Paul gritted his teeth and said nothing. He knew a trap when he heard one, especially when she gave him a wink before he turned his attention back to the sock drawer.

"Unless you're finally getting tired of waiting for Nina," she said in a tone dripping equal parts playfulness and malice. "I could slip into this right now, see how it fits for a few minutes before you tear it off me."

"Won't happen." He'd gotten plenty of practice at ignoring her passing shots, but this felt different. They were alone together, but not just for a few moments while the others were somewhere in another room. Ignoring her didn't seem as effective without them nearby.

"You think I don't see how lonely you are, how frustrated? You think I don't feel it too?" She let the nightgown drop to the floor and sidled over to him. "Why did you break up me and Mark if you didn't want me yourself?"

That was an angle Paul had never once considered, and he wanted to kick himself for missing it. "One cheating woman in my life was enough, thank you. Don't need another."

"Oh, come on, pretty boy," she chided him. "I've known Mark and Sarah for years, so I know quite a few of their secrets. I wasn't the first woman to take Sarah's place, and she's not so perfect herself."

"Don't care," he said. "I could only deal with what was in front of me, and that was Mark bein' with you when he should have been with his wife. If you want me to apologize for that, you'll be waitin' a long time. Yeah, it hurt you, but a lot less than findin' out the truth would have hurt Sarah. So I can live with what I did. Can you?"

"Easily," she answered, leaning in close. "If you want me to apologize for that, then you'll have a long wait, too. I'm not ashamed."

"That ain't true. If it were, you would've kept on no matter what I said, or even told Sarah yourself instead of lettin' Mark go. You knew you were wrong."

"Fine, so what?" she exclaimed, pulling back and throwing her hands in the air. "It's over now, and I've been a good girl and kept my distance. Does that get me any credit, or are you going to hate me forever because of it?"

He turned and met her eyes. "I don't hate you, Alison," he told her, his voice soft but serious. "I don't like you much, but that's not the same as hate. I think you're a spiteful woman who don't give much thought to anyone's feelings but her own. I think you lash out and hurt others 'cause it makes you feel better. Now, I can put that aside to work with you, to live under the same roof. We're a family of sorts, even if it's plenty dysfunctional. If you were in trouble, I'd help. If you got hurt, I'd help. But you can't ask more from me than that. Not with what you've done, and how you've treated me, and how you treat the people I care about."

Her lips thinned in a grim expression. "Nina."

"Yeah," he replied. "Nina. Don't think I ain't noticed how you've been aimin' to come between us."

She brushed her fingers down his arm, and his hands clenched into fists around two rolled-up pairs of socks. "She's a sweet girl when she's not spooking like a skittish horse," Alison said, her voice sad, as if she actually meant it. Paul couldn't be sure. "But she'll never be what you need, Paul. She's a broken doll that you can't put back together."

All Paul wanted in that moment was to strike Alison, to slap the false concern right off her face. He'd never hit anyone in anger before, and he never thought he'd feel the need. It terrified him. His body shook with the effort of keeping still. "Get your hand off me," he forced out through gritted teeth. To his surprise, she did, backing away. He turned to face her, and her eyes widened. Something in his expression frightened her. "No more of this, Alison. Unless you're tryin' to save my life, don't ever touch me again, understand? You do, and I'll defend myself. Don't think for a second that I won't." He took a step closer, towering over her as she found herself backed against a wall. "I ain't yours, and I won't ever be. So stop all this nonsense before someone really does get hurt."

"Paul—"

"I love Nina," he said, cutting her off. "Your opinion of her don't matter to me one bit. The way you treat her, though, that does. And it stops now. No more loaded questions, no more backhanded compliments, no more spite."

"Her knight in shining armor," Alison said, disdain tinting her voice.

"You better fuckin' believe it," Paul grated out. "There ain't much in this world I can protect her from, so what I can, I will. And that includes you. We both been turnin' the other cheek to you to keep the peace. That's over. My first loyalty is to her, now, not the group. You do something to hurt her, and I will hurt you back."

Paul felt a wave of relief at being able to say what was in his heart without worrying how it would be heard. Strange that he could tell Alison how he felt about Nina more clearly than he could tell Nina herself. But his anger, and his fear of what Alison might do if left to her own devices, made it easy to find the words.

Alison crossed her arms, defensive, but less obviously afraid. "That won't win you many points with the others."

"Don't care," he repeated. "She means more to me than the rest of you put together. I'll stick around for this crazy plan and pull my weight, and if all goes well, none of them ever need to know we had this chat."

Sudden understanding came to Alison's eyes. "I thought—I thought you chickened out, didn't want to leave on your own after all. But you didn't. Nina asked you to stay."

Paul nodded silently. What had passed between them was far more complicated, but no one, least of all Alison, needed to know the details.

"I didn't think she had it in her," Alison muttered. "So I guess that's the line in the sand." She looked up at him, uneasy, but no longer defiant. "I'll keep to my side of it. Truce?"

"Truce," Paul confirmed. She didn't offer her hand, which was fine, because Paul didn't think he could have taken it. "Let's get back to work."

CHAPTER TWENTY-SIX
HIKING BOOTS

September 21st, 2:02 pm – 1955 Cambridge Road, Coshocton, Ohio

Sarah managed to hold in her curiosity for almost an hour, which impressed Nina. She'd expected to hear a comment about Paul's change of heart in the first five minutes.

"So he's staying," Sarah said as they sorted clothes into piles in the master bedroom. The woman who had lived here must have been close to Sarah's size—everything seemed to fit her well. Nina wasn't having as much luck, but this was only the first house. "I suppose you had something to do with that."

"We talked, yeah," Nina said, as noncommittal as she could be without dodging the question entirely.

Sarah paused halfway through folding a shirt. "And this 'talk' lasted from dinner time until well past dark? I was still downstairs reading by the fire when Paul finally went to his room. And he looked pleased."

Nina sighed and reached for another sweater to fold. "If you're implying what I think you are, then the answer is no. And I would think you're pleased enough with your sex life right now that you don't need to go prying into mine."

Sarah's laughter rang through the room. "I guess I deserved that," she said. "I suppose I'm so happy today that I want everyone else to be just as happy. So you'll just have to forgive me for wishing you and Paul might be happy together."

A brief memory of the night before flashed through her mind—when Paul's fingers tangled in her hair as they kissed. Nina bent her head, focusing on the clothing she needed to box up. She was thankful her skin was dark enough to hide a blush from all but the most determined observer. "I did ask him to stay," she admitted, certain Sarah would get at least that much out of her eventually. Nina needed to choose her battles. "But if you were hoping for fireworks, you're going to be disappointed."

"If he's staying, then there's still time for fireworks. If I were twenty years younger and didn't have Mark . . ."

"Sarah!" Nina exclaimed, throwing a wide-eyed glance at her.

"Don't give me that look!" Sarah said with another laugh. "I had a friend in college who insisted musicians made the best lovers, because they were better with their hands."

Hearing something so closely echoing her own thoughts coming from Sarah's mouth made Nina uncomfortable. But then, the whole conversation made her uncomfortable and she wanted to be done with it as soon as she could manage. Maybe teasing back would ease her out of this. "If you didn't have Mark, then there'd still be John, right? He said he played guitar."

Sarah finished folding a shirt and laid it in her box. "Did he?" she said in a polite, restrained tone which was miles away from the playfulness of her words just a few moments before.

"Yeah, he offered to teach Aaron if we find one. That night Paul played for us, remember?"

"Right, now I do." She placed one last piece of clothing in the box before picking it up. "I'm going to add this to the stack downstairs. Do you think we're about done with this house? We did pretty well here."

Watching Sarah go was like looking in a mirror to Nina. She recognized avoidance when she saw it. Especially when a few minutes passed and Sarah didn't return. Nina's box wasn't full, so she cast about for other useful things to take. They had all the sheets and towels, and all the usable clothing, but the bathroom was sure to yield something worthwhile. Nina gathered the partial bottles of shampoo and conditioner from the shower, and the spare bars of soap from the cabinet under the sink.

While they were shuttling the boxes back home, Paul and Owen did the same on the other side of the street, with one notable difference—they had found a child's wagon. Owen pulled it behind him loaded with two boxes, while Paul carried another, and they all met in the middle of the road.

"It will save us a little time, at least," Owen said. "It's not big enough to haul much, but it's more than I can carry myself."

"You couldn't stack two more boxes on top?" Sarah asked. "Or was that too heavy?"

"Not to pull," Paul answered. "But it did make it tip over, which don't save any time when you have to put everything back to rights."

"Looks like you found a lot," Nina said as they got moving again. "Is this your first trip back?"

"Second," Paul answered, falling in beside her and shortening his stride to match hers. "You find anything good?"

"Lots of clothing for Sarah, nothing really for anyone else. Some sheets and towels and toiletries."

Paul smiled down at her. "I found something for you. No luck on the clothes, but there's a pair of hiking boots that should fit you, and a pair of bedroom slippers too. Well," he amended, "you might have to wear a pair of socks with the slippers. Or two pairs. But if it gets real cold, you'd do that anyway, right?"

"Yeah, I would. That's great, thank you." She felt the urge to link arms with him while they walked together, but she couldn't when they were both carrying boxes. She settled for giving him her brightest smile instead, and a thrill traveled down her spine at the grin she got in return. He was an absolute fool for her, and seeing it sent sparks shooting across her nerves.

Back at the house, they brought their haul to the living room and took a few minutes to unpack it. There was a designated spot for items for each person—things for Mark and Sarah were at either end of one of the couches, Paul and Owen had chairs near the door to their room, and so on. The shared items like bedding and toiletries had their own corner, away from the fireplace. After helping Sarah unload most of the things they'd gathered onto her couch, Nina checked her own chair.

The pile on the seat was small. There was a matched set of winter accessories, all child-sized but not especially childish-looking: a hat, scarf, and pair of mittens in bright red fleece patterned with white snowflakes. Under those, there were two sweaters which looked big for her, but certainly too small for anyone else. She didn't mind, because she'd be wearing them with other layers. Possibly a lot of layers.

Despite the warmth of the autumn day, she shivered, thinking of how cold winter might be.

Paul appeared at her side holding the promised boots in one hand and the bedroom slippers in the other. She shoved the items on the chair back to perch on the edge while she stripped her worn boots off to try the new pair on.

"They're almost perfect," she said after tying the laces and standing up. "Maybe a little big, but extra socks, right? And they're practically brand new.

There's almost no wear on the soles, and I can't feel the shape of someone's foot on the inside. I never liked that feeling."

Paul chuckled. "Me neither. Never quite goes away, even when they're so old they look like this," he said, gesturing at his own ragged boots.

"How many pairs have you been through so far?"

"This is number four. None of 'em started new, though. You should get plenty of miles out of those."

"They'll be my third. But not yet," Nina said, sitting back down to tug them off. "Not till pair number two are completely worn out."

The slippers were light blue and fuzzy, and they warmed her toes instantly. "Thank you," she said, stretching out her legs and wiggling her feet. "This feels like Christmas morning. I got a new pair of slippers from my parents every year."

She bent down to put her old boots back on, but looked up when Paul made a strangled sort of sound.

"Hadn't thought about Christmas in a while," he said. "I think I kinda forgot."

There was a long pause while Nina got herself back in order and added the new footwear to her pile. Paul hovered nearby, but she glanced around the room and saw no signs of Sarah or Owen.

"When's your birthday?" Paul asked.

"Not till March. The twenty-seventh."

"Mine's in July, the seventeenth." Another pause, and she turned to face him, pushing aside the hint of unease she felt when she saw the intensity of his expression. "And how old are you?" he asked.

Nina forced a grin and teased to try to lighten the mood. "I thought a gentleman never asked a lady her age."

"I wouldn't think you're old enough to be offended by it, yet," he retorted, but at least she'd gotten him to smile. "If it makes you feel better tellin' me, I turned twenty-six over the summer."

"I'm older than you?" Nina asked as she sat back down, hard, squashing the slippers beneath her. "Huh."

"Are you? I would've guessed you weren't more than twenty-three or twenty-four."

"Yeah, but I'm actually twenty-eight. Between the big blue eyes and the fact that I don't break five feet, people always think I'm younger. A bartender once told me to expect to get carded until I was at least thirty-five. Not much of a problem anymore, which is good, because I lost my ID months ago."

"I like your big blue eyes," Paul said, the last traces of his brief dark mood gone. "And I don't think it occurred to Mark to card any of us. I've still got my license, though."

"Do you really?"

He nodded and went to his room. Nina stood and followed, staying at the door until he waved her in.

Paul dug through one of the outer pockets on his pack and produced a worn leather wallet. "Didn't seem needful to keep it in my pocket like I used to," he said as he passed it to her, "since money ain't much of a thing anymore. But it don't seem right to throw it away, either. Might come in handy for something."

Nina opened it and flipped up the windowed flap on one side to read his driver's license. "Paul Matthew Ingersson." She paused. "I'm not sure I've ever heard that last name before."

"Unless you grew up somewhere a lot of Swedish immigrants settled, then, no, you probably wouldn't. Same type of name as Andersen, Sorenson, all that. Just not as common."

"There a big Swedish community in Kentucky?"

He laughed. "No, but there was in Minnesota, where my grandpa was from originally. Moved to Louisville as a kid."

"Family histories," she mused, studying the card again as she sat down on the bed. "They do end up strange sometimes. You lived in Brooklyn?"

"The last place, yeah. I started out years ago sharing a two-bedroom in Tribeca with three other guys and still barely making rent—even the cheapest places in Manhattan were crazy expensive. As the jobs got better, so did where I lived. By the time the plague hit, I had a cozy little studio all to myself in Flatbush. It was small, but it was mine."

"I've always lived on my own," Nina said absently as she refolded the wallet. "Since college, I mean, I lived with my parents before that. But then, people weren't clamoring to live in rural Michigan."

"Don't imagine so, though I've never been up that way." The mattress shifted as Paul sat down beside her. "Lots of snow, right?"

"More than you've probably ever seen. If the wind was bad, the drifts would pile up taller than me. When that happened, there wasn't much to do but stay inside with blankets and books and tea."

"That's something you can teach me, then." Paul slid his arm around Nina's waist and leaned over to whisper in her ear. "How to keep warm in the winter."

Nina dropped the wallet on the bed as Paul kissed her. But the difference in their heights proved to be awkward when they were both sitting, so she broke away with a laugh. "How about this?" she whispered as she straddled him, raising herself on her knees until she could look him in the eye.

"Much better." But when he tried to kiss her again, she backed a few inches away.

"Just a few minutes," she told him. "We can't stay in here long like this. Sarah and Owen could already be waiting on us to head back out, and this is Owen's room, too. He wouldn't have any reason not to walk right in."

Paul glanced over her shoulder. "And we didn't even shut the door all the way. Damn." He gave her one quick peck on the cheek before lifting her up with firm hands on her ribs. Her heartbeat quickened with an odd mix of shock and desire as he stood and set her on her feet. She wasn't used to being handled so easily. "Another time. And maybe I can get a little of your family history, too." He grinned. "And your last name."

"Summerfield."

Paul just blinked.

"Yeah. Nina Charlotte Summerfield. Each of my parents picked a name from somewhere in their family tree. So I'm named for my abuela on one side, and my great-aunt on the other." She put her hands on her hips and tried to look stern, but she was also trying not to laugh. "What, were you expecting something more Hispanic? Martinez? Rodriguez?"

"I wasn't expectin' anything!" Paul protested.

"My mother's maiden name was Moreno, actually, and my great-grandfather was born down in Oaxaca. But I grew up in small-town Michigan, which is one of the least Hispanic places there was. Mom taught me Spanish growing up and insisted I take it in high school. And she taught me to make tamales, but that was about it as far as my cultural heritage goes." She dropped her hands and shrugged. "I do really like tamales, though. And posole."

Paul groaned. "And now I want tamales. There was this great little Mexican place a few blocks away from me, I ate there all the time."

"Sorry, didn't mean to make you hungry. We should get back. More work to do." She smiled up at him. "Find me something else nice?"

He kissed the top of her head. "Always lookin'."

CHAPTER TWENTY-SEVEN
A PIANO

September 21st, 6:39 pm – 1880 Cambridge Road, Coshocton, Ohio

When Paul suggested at dinner that he'd be up for another night of music and whiskey, the idea met with hearty approval. Spirits were high already, with the big decision made and the preparations begun. It wouldn't take much for the mood to shift from relieved to relaxed, and Paul was hoping to help things along.

He had a surprise planned, too, and he had to stop himself from smiling whenever he thought of it.

His ridiculous grin wouldn't have mattered, though, judging by the expressions the others wore as they settled in the living room. John was uncharacteristically buoyant, smiling and laughing, acting much more like Aaron than he ever had before. Paul had never doubted John's love for his son, but he'd never thought they were much alike, either. But tonight, John's wide grin was the same as Aaron's.

Owen joked with them both as if they were old friends, not people he'd known for six days. He was overjoyed to have people to stay with for the winter—he'd told Paul so earlier, as they searched more houses together. "I'm not saying I won't go, when the time comes to leave," the teenager had said. "But if you hadn't taken me in, I would have been alone here anyway, and I might not have made it on my own." Owen had thrown himself at their task with a kind of determined efficiency which Paul admired. During his own teenage years he'd been driven to excel at music, which led him to think less of his peers who hadn't had the same drive. Owen did, though. He was as hard a worker and helpful a partner as anyone could ask for, and Paul liked him better every day.

Sarah was practically glowing, though some of it might have been the firelight. She snuggled next to Mark on one of the couches, fitting herself beneath his arm and laying her head on his shoulder. For a moment, Paul wanted that for himself, sitting in front of the fire with Nina tucked under his arm. It hit him like a kick straight to his chest that he still couldn't be open about his feelings for her in front of the others. He understood her reasons and even agreed, to a point—but the picture was so perfect it made him ache with wanting to hold her, right then, with everyone watching.

The worst of it was already over—or so he hoped—though he hadn't had a chance to tell Nina about his confrontation with Alison. He'd forgotten about it when he'd stolen those few minutes with Nina in the afternoon, only remembering when he saw Alison at dinner. He didn't think it mattered much, though. Everyone else would be happy for them. She'd been the only one to make their budding relationship difficult.

He hoped Nina would agree with what he'd done. Once his anger faded back to a manageable level, he started to second-guess himself, wondering if he'd overreacted to Alison's taunts, if he'd gone too far in threatening her.

At dinner, though, she'd been mostly silent, and blessedly civil when she did speak, so Paul felt more certain he'd done the right thing.

And Nina herself. If she wasn't as exuberant as Aaron or as blissfully content as Mark and Sarah, at least she seemed relaxed, happy in her own restrained way. It had taken him time, but Paul was beginning to understand her. If he wore his heart on his sleeve, she kept hers hidden in a pretty little box, only to be shown like a treasure to someone who deserved it. She was intensely private, and he was trying to respect that. He would only get to know her in bits and pieces. The time hadn't come yet to cuddle with her on the couch in front of everyone, much as he wanted to.

Paul settled on the piano bench and flexed his hands together. As he wondered what to play first, Mark plunked a glass of whiskey down on top of the piano for him.

Starting with a love song seemed too obvious, so he warmed up with an old Broadway standard he could play in his sleep if he needed to. Afterward, without waiting to gauge his audience's reaction, he did instrumental versions of a few popular songs, some recent, some older than he was. At one point, Sarah murmured, "Oh, I love this song." But no one else spoke.

Between finishing one song and starting the next, he kept wondering if he was brave enough. He let his fingers drift over the keys, improvising, leading him to the right decision.

Paul played the opening measures of one of the last songs he wrote before the world went wrong. At the fifth bar, he opened his mouth to sing.

He hadn't practiced. There hadn't been a chance. His first verse was shaky, but on the second verse, he felt his voice grow stronger. He had never had the clear, perfectly balanced voice his high school choir teacher had tried to draw from him. Paul's tenor wasn't operatic and was never going to be. His voice had always been a little raspy, without sounding like he dragged the notes ten yards over gravel before they came out of him. Now, after months of disuse, his singing had an almost smoky quality, like a jazz singer.

Like Jessica's. The thought blindsided him during the bridge, and his fingers fumbled on the keys, striking one note out of tune with the rest of its chord. He'd fallen in love with her voice during those weeks he'd played backup for her, while she tempted him with those smoldering glances. They'd never sung together on any stage, but they'd done plenty of duets together for fun, laughing together over the piano which dominated the space of his small apartment.

He pushed those memories aside to come back in for the last verse. *Always finish strong, because that's what the audience will remember.*

In the silence at the end of the song, he drew a deep breath. Remembering Jessica when he sang made sense. Music was a huge part of the life they'd shared. With all the emotions Nina was churning up—and the desire—he should have expected to think of the last woman he'd loved. But he hadn't, and he didn't want thoughts of her clouding his mind tonight. He didn't want to be singing to the ghost of the woman he'd lost. He wanted to be singing to Nina.

"I haven't sung in ages," he said as he brought the cover down over the keys. "Don't sound quite right, but it'll do for now, I guess. Maybe I'll have time to practice some." But he didn't turn around, afraid of what he might see. Stage fright never seemed to hit him before a performance, but uncertainty sometimes caught him after. And whatever the others thought, he had played his song for an audience of exactly one person.

"That was beautiful, Paul," Sarah said.

Paul swung his legs around the bench and smiled at her. "Thanks."

"We won't ask you to play every night," John said, "but I hope you won't mind doing this sometimes. It's wonderful to hear music again."

"Of course," Paul replied.

Aaron stood up and joined Paul at the piano, studying the keys in the firelight and reaching out to press one gently. "Would you teach me?" he asked.

"Yeah. Not tonight, but yeah, I will." Paul cleared his throat around an unexpected lump. "Used to teach, sometimes, to fill in the gaps between jobs. I'd be happy to."

"Cool." Aaron played a few more random keys, smiling. "It'll be fun."

"Might not be for the rest of us, while he's learning," Alison grumbled.

John's face was stormy, but Mark beat him to it. "Don't be like that, Allie," he chided. "What's the harm in listening to him pound on the thing for a while, if it makes him happy?"

Alison finished the rest of her drink in one swallow and didn't answer.

An awkward silence followed as Aaron sat back down. Paul risked a glance at Nina. He hoped she would be looking at him. He hoped he could find her reaction in her eyes, since he knew she wouldn't say it out loud.

She rested her head on the crook of her elbow where it lay on the arm of the couch. Her eyes were closed, and she might have been sleeping. But her lips curved in a small, dreamy smile. The dancing light of the fire painted streaks of red and orange in her hair, which made Paul wild to run his fingers through it.

Instead he twisted to retrieve his whiskey from the top of the piano. There was space on the couch beside Nina, but he stayed where he was on the bench, sipping his drink, letting the conversation revive around him without contributing. They spoke of the things they'd found. They spoke of plans for tomorrow's gathering, making room in the closets to store what they brought back, and what they still hoped to find.

Paul and Nina became islands of silence, and their companions seemed content to let them be.

As the evening crawled on, the talk slowed. Paul hoped he and Nina would be last to bed again, so they could have some time together, but she was the first to leave. The fire popped loudly and she stirred, startled out of her dozing. Paul offered a good night along with everyone else as she headed to her room.

Not long after, the rest of them headed to their beds as well, and Paul found himself alone in the living room. He set down his empty glass and crept up the stairs, thankful none of them creaked. At Nina's door, he tapped so softly he could barely hear it himself.

He waited five minutes, repeating the soft knock twice more. Either she couldn't hear it, she was already asleep, or she wasn't going to answer.

But he didn't open the door himself. As much as his heart raced at the thought of stepping inside, he hadn't been invited.

In his own room, Owen was snoring lightly, lying as close to the far edge of the bed as possible. Paul wondered sometimes how he managed not to fall off, but never asked, not wanting to draw any attention to how uncomfortable Owen was sharing a bed. He couldn't be much older than sixteen or seventeen—he probably never had before.

Paul shucked off his boots and slid into his side of the bed clothed, since he hadn't found pajamas yet. He expected to lay awake a long time, aching for Nina, but if he did, he couldn't remember any of it in the morning.

CHAPTER TWENTY-EIGHT
A PAIR OF SOCKS

September 24th, 8:33 am – 1880 Cambridge Road, Coshocton, Ohio

The system Sarah used to figure out who partnered together for any assigned task was incomprehensible to Nina. She couldn't complain about hardly ever working with Alison, but somehow she hadn't been paired with Paul once in the past three days. Yes, the men did the heavier physical work: digging the trash pits at the far end of the backyard and another closer one for the outhouse, once they got it built. Nina had no desire to help with that particular chore, which had left Paul, John, and Mark all dirt-covered and exhausted. But she got sent out with Owen plenty of times when they were stockpiling food and toiletries, and John or Mark on occasion. Just not Paul.

Which led to her nearly jumping out of her skin when she heard her name and his in the same breath. She shifted in her chair so violently she banged her knee on the underside of the kitchen table.

"You okay?" Mark asked, his face shaded with a mix of amusement and concern.

"Fine," she grated out. "I didn't realize my foot had fallen asleep until I tried to move it." She scooped the last few bites of food into her mouth and took her plate to the sink to avoid returning the stares of everyone at the table. She didn't need to fake a limp for her cover story as she left, because her knee throbbed with every step.

Once she was out of the kitchen, though, Nina realized she hadn't been listening. She had no idea what she and Paul had been assigned. She wasn't about to go back to ask and compound her embarrassment. Instead she plodded up the stairs to her room to strip off her jeans and check on the bruise she was sure was forming.

There was a knock on her door before she had them back on.

"Just a second!" she cried, struggling with the zipper, which had chosen the worst possible moment to get stuck. She blew out a sharp sigh of frustration, buttoned the waistband, and opened the door.

Paul stood on the other side. "Rough morning?"

"My knee is already turning purple," she answered. "I'm such a klutz."

"No, you're not. But you do seem pretty flustered. Spending a few hours with me got you all tied up in knots?"

Nina thought he deserved a solid punch to the arm in reply, but settled for making a face at him. "We've hardly had a chance to talk for three days, let alone anything else. I was surprised, that's all."

Paul lifted his hands like he was going to grip her arms, but halfway there, he dropped them again. "Don't mind, though, do you?"

"I am annoyed at Sarah," she said, each word deliberate and clear, "because I suspect she may have been keeping us apart on purpose."

A hint of confusion showed in Paul's expression. "Why would she do that? And if she was, then why did she stop?"

"Absence makes the heart grow fonder, I think," Nina answered. "The day we all decided to stay, she asked me . . . oh, never mind that. She implied a lot, and the word 'fireworks' got thrown around. So now I think she's trying to start some."

Paul threw back his head and laughed. "On the one hand, that's a little sweet. On the other, it's kinda mean, too. That she thinks I'd need any help getting a spark."

Nina crossed her arms and stared at him without speaking, which made him laugh harder. "The only reason I ain't touchin' you already," he explained, "is I'm not sure I could stop if I started. We got work to do, so let's get that done first, okay? Maybe we can sneak in some kissin' before lunch."

His smile didn't falter as she stared him down, trying to figure out if he was serious. She wouldn't have bet against it. "So . . . I wasn't paying much attention," she admitted. "I have no idea what Sarah gave us to do."

"We're emptyin' the closets in here today, takin' the stuff we don't need out as trash. Pretty easy. Seein' as how you just roughed up your knee, though, I guess you can sort and stuff everything into the bags, then I'll take 'em out and dump 'em. No need for you to do all that walkin'."

Nina didn't move. "There's no way that's going to take us all morning."

"I know."

"And I'm guessing she sent everyone else out of the house."

"She did. Mark was waitin' for her to finish the dishes before they left, but that won't be more than a few minutes. They might be gone already."

"I don't like feeling cornered."

Paul held up his hands, palms out. "Wasn't my idea."

"Oh, I know, I just . . ." She sighed again. "I just don't like it."

"It'd be silly not to take advantage of Sarah's thoughtfulness, though," he said. "Even if we just talk. There's still a thousand things I wanna know about you."

An involuntary smile spread over Nina's face. "Like what?"

"Like what your favorite color is. And what you like to do for fun." He paused, and his voice changed, growing softer and deeper at the same time. "And how you get your hair to smell so good."

"Do you have the trash bags with you?"

Paul shook his head. "Be right back."

"I'll get started." Nina turned and slid open her closet doors. She'd already sorted through Rachel's clothes and decided what to keep, hanging them on the left side with the few things found for her elsewhere. There wasn't as much as she would have liked, but as their food supplies had run low, clothes had gotten moved down the priority list.

Everything hanging on the right side was too small, worn, or flimsy to be worth keeping. Nina liked a few of the floral-print sundresses, but they weren't warm or practical, so they were going with the rest. She started to pull the items off the hangers and toss them on the bed behind her.

Paul came back in, shook out a trash bag to open it, and began filling it with the discarded clothes. "Still don't have much for yourself yet, looks like."

"More than I've had for a while, so I'll manage. But I'm hoping I can still find a few things."

"Like what?" Paul asked, bringing the bag over and holding it open so Nina could drop things into it.

"Flannel pajamas, mostly," she answered. "There weren't any here, and I haven't run across any that wouldn't be falling off me if I wore them."

Nina half-expected Paul to smirk at her, but he considered her words with a thoughtful expression. "You might have better luck trying boys' rooms than girls'," he said after a moment. "Plaid is plaid, right? I never had sisters, but I always got the impression girls that age wore frilly things to bed."

"The winters get plenty cold here, so I'd have thought she'd have something practical to sleep in. But I guess not. Boys' pajamas it'll be then, if I can find any. You're right, plaid is plaid." She dropped the last bit of clothing into the bag. "Next room?"

Paul nodded. They skipped the rooms which belonged to John and Aaron, and Alison. "There wasn't anything in them to start with," Nina told him, remembering the day she'd made up the beds.

In the master bedroom, it turned out Sarah had set aside the clothes she and Mark were keeping, stacked neatly in piles to hang later when the closet was emptied. "She really didn't want to make this hard for us," Paul said. "Especially since there's nothing to get rid of from my room, either."

Ten minutes later, they'd filled two more trash bags with clothing. Paul lifted them all easily and headed downstairs. Nina followed him, still favoring her bruised knee. Halfway down, Paul turned and frowned. "You sure you don't wanna stay in your room? I got this."

Nina was certain she didn't want to stay in her room, since Paul would return there if she did. "I'll just stretch out on one of the couches. That way I won't have to go far for lunch." He nodded and headed toward the kitchen to go out the back door.

She had hardly gotten settled before he was back. Without asking, he lifted her legs so he could slide underneath them, sitting with her calves resting across his thighs. The whole maneuver took so little time she only opened her mouth to object when he was already done. He'd been careful not to touch her knee, so she sighed instead and dropped her head back on the pillow.

"So . . . d'you wanna talk?" Paul asked. "Or I could go grab whatever you're readin' right now, if you don't. Though I s'pose I should've asked before I sat down, but it wouldn't take long."

"What would you do if I were reading? Watch me read?"

He gave her a sheepish smile. "Well, no, not exactly. I was thinkin' you might want a foot massage. Do you like 'em? I've been told I'm pretty good."

Nina caught her bottom lip between her teeth for a moment before she spoke. "I don't know. No one's ever offered before."

"That's a shame," he said in a soft voice, reaching for the laces of one of her boots. "Can I try?"

She nodded, and he set about getting her feet bare. He placed her boots on the floor at the end of the couch, and her socks, he draped over the armrest. Nina watched the whole process with trepidation, but Paul's movements were calm and purposeful, and his touch gentle. He didn't grin or tease or mock the terrible state of her toenails.

When he took her left foot between his hands and pressed the sole lightly with his thumbs, Nina's whole body tensed in response to the unfamiliar sensation. But when he rubbed the arch of her foot in little circles, her spine went loose, a string of knots untying themselves all at once. She was disintegrating under the motion of his hands, melting, sinking into the couch cushions.

"Good, then?" he asked. She only nodded. "Okay."

"So . . . what do you want to talk about?" Nina asked, closing her eyes. "Anything in particular?"

"What's your favorite color?"

"Really? I thought you were kidding."

"It's as good a place to start as any," Paul answered, kneading the spaces in between the knuckles of her toes.

"Blue," Nina told him. "Lots of shades of blue. Sky blue's my favorite. Like those slippers you found. What about you?"

"Red. Fire-engine red. Don't have any red lipstick stashed in your pack, do you?"

She could hear the smile in his voice. "Not a one."

"I knew that'd be a long shot. Oh, well." He dug one thumb into a particularly stubborn spot on the ball of her foot, and Nina let out a moan. Her eyes popped open and she clapped one hand over her mouth to hold in a fit of embarrassed giggling.

Paul stopped massaging and shot Nina a concerned glance. "You all right? I ain't ticklin' you, am I?"

"No," she answered, trying not to sound too breathless. "I'm fine."

And then he started on her right foot.

Nina had never felt this kind of sensual pleasure before without it being attached to actual sex. As Paul's hands continued their work, though, her body began to respond as if it were. She felt the slow uncoiling of heat inside of her, starting between her legs but spreading everywhere, like her skin was lit from within by candle flame. She never considered her feet to be erogenous zones, but feeling Paul's fingers there made her imagine his fingers elsewhere.

Which made it increasingly difficult to hold up her end of the conversation. Paul asked a steady stream of questions; her favorite food, books, music. Did she like coffee or tea better? Dogs or cats? Chocolate ice cream, or vanilla?

Every question was ridiculous. She couldn't get her favorite food anymore or listen to her favorite music. If she ever found a copy of her favorite book, she'd make room in her pack for it, but she wasn't holding out much hope. And ice cream? They were never going to see ice cream again.

But when Nina opened her mouth to say so, before he could ask about some other pointless thing, she caught his glance at her face. His expression held a mixture of relaxation and satisfaction, and she realized the questions didn't matter. They were just an excuse for Paul to talk to her. To be near her.

Though she was sure he would remember all of her answers anyway.

"There was something else I wanted to ask," Paul said, switching back to her left foot. "Something I'm a little embarrassed to."

Lying completely prone made Nina feel more helpless than she liked, so she pushed herself up on her elbows to gain some height. "What is it?"

"You never said anything the other night, about the song I sang. Did you like it?"

His voice was hardly more than a whisper, and the hesitation in his tone was startling. Nina had never once heard Paul sound so vulnerable. "I did." She waited a moment, but his expression didn't change, and he didn't reply. "I didn't know it, though, like the other ones you played. I recognized all of those."

"That's 'cause I wrote it."

"You did? That's amazing." Something in the tone of her voice made Paul look over at her, and whatever showed in her expression made his eyes widen.

"Oh," he breathed. "Good." He looked away, picking up one of her socks and slipping it back on her foot. "I wasn't sure I should ask, 'cause it wasn't you I wrote it for, but I ain't had much time lately to be writing new songs—"

"Paul, stop," she interrupted, pushing herself the rest of the way up. "You don't have to apologize for that. We both had lives before the plague, before we met each other. Honestly, I'd be surprised if you hadn't had any love in your life, back then."

Paul paused in the middle of putting on her other sock. "Hadn't thought of it that way." He gave her a long, level look. "There's something, maybe, I should tell you, then."

Nina folded her knees to sit cross-legged facing him, pulling her sock on the rest of the way before taking one of his hands in both of hers. "What is it?"

"I was . . ." He let out a heavy sigh. "I was engaged. I hadn't thought about it much for a while. I try not to. But that night I remembered, because I wrote that song for her. And our wedding date was supposed to be next week. Kinda snuck up on me."

Nina's heart tried to swallow itself inside her chest. "Paul, I'm so sorry. We all lost people in the plague, but . . ." She broke off, shaking her head. "I can't imagine."

Paul let out a bitter laugh. "It's actually worse than that."

"How could it be worse?"

"We'd already split by then, a couple of months before. 'Cause she was cheating on me. I caught her at it, and it broke my heart."

Nina squeezed his hand. "No wonder you were lonely."

"Yeah, well, before I left the city, I did something real stupid. I was goin' back home, to see my dad after my brother called to tell me he'd gotten sick. But . . . but I had to see her, one more time. I guess I still loved her that much." He paused, picking at a loose thread on arm of the couch. "It took her forever to get to the door when I knocked. I almost left, thinkin' she wasn't home. But she answered, and it was plain as day that she was dyin'." His voice dropped to a whisper. "And when I saw her, I hated her all over again for what she'd done to me. She begged me to forgive her, to stay with her until the end—she knew she didn't have long. But I couldn't. I walked away, and she stood there in the doorway and screamed at me as I left. I was probably the last person she ever saw, and I couldn't lie to her, to give her peace for her last few hours. I didn't have it in me, and that, I regret. Either I should've lied, or I never should've gone to see her in the first place."

Nina shifted on the couch, settling close beside Paul. She let go of his hand so he could loop his arm around her as she nestled her head against his shoulder. "I don't know what to say," Nina told him. "I mean, I want to comfort you, I want you to feel better . . . but everyone handles grief differently. And some part of you is still grieving for her. There's no way to make that better with just words."

"Tell me you're not angry," he whispered.

Nina turned her face up to look into his eyes. "Why would I be?"

He rewarded her with a smile. "That was the right thing to say. I wasn't sure how to tell you," he said as she got her head settled back against him. "You ain't s'posed to talk about your exes, right? But it don't seem right to keep it from you, either. I wanted you to know."

"Paul, nobody starts a new relationship without some kind of baggage." She laid her hand on his chest. "Yours is a canceled wedding and a broken heart that seems like it's pretty well put back together, considering all that's happened. I wish you hadn't had to go through it, but I'm glad you told me."

They sat together awhile in silence. Nina closed her eyes and concentrated on the steady pulse beneath her fingers.

"Sometimes," Paul began, folding his free hand over hers where it lay over his heart, "sometimes I worry that I fell in love with you so fast 'cause I wanted back what I had with her."

So that's what lay underneath his sudden attack of nerves. "It makes a kind of sense," Nina replied, her voice steady. "You're certainly the snuggliest man I ever met. You need that closeness."

"And that don't make you mad, either?"

"Should it? Am I anything like her? Have you ever once thought of me as her replacement?"

"No!" Paul cried, flinching away from her. "Never," he went on in a calmer tone of voice, getting comfortable again and pulling Nina closer than before. "You're . . . you. Not like her at all. It feels wrong to say so, but I think if she had lived through the plague, she wouldn't have survived long after. I never saw the same kind of strength in her that you have."

Nina tilted her head to kiss Paul's neck, since she couldn't reach his lips. "And what kind of strength is that?"

"You never let bein' afraid stop you from doin' what needs to be done," he said, looking down at her with a serious expression.

Nina opened her mouth to object, then shut it with a snap. He was right. When Christine and her goons had threatened them, Nina had been terrified, but much more for Paul and the others than for herself. And she had formed a plan on her own, even if it had only been to find the others so they could form a better plan. She'd followed John's instructions without freezing. She'd taken it upon herself to get Aaron to safety. And finally, she had sutured Paul's wound, even though she was terrified she would do it badly, because she'd been more afraid of what could happen if she didn't.

Maybe all of those thoughts passed over her face, because Paul watched her with a half-smile. "Not used to thinkin' of yourself as tough?"

"No," Nina answered. "I'm not. But I can see why you do."

"Yeah," he said, kissing the top of her head. "Strong enough to keep me at arm's length even when I was makin' eyes at you all the time."

Nina giggled. "But smart enough to admit I was wrong, and let you get closer."

"Yeah," he said again. "I like smart, too. I like smart a lot."

"Let me guess," Nina said with another giggle. "You've got a nerdy girl fantasy, with the glasses and pigtails and all that? Don't tell me, the schoolgirl uniform, too, those pleated skirts and white button-downs."

Paul groaned and lifted her onto his lap. "If we're gonna talk about fantasies, then I'll have to admit all of mine are about you these days, and no, they don't involve any uniforms. But if I ain't mistaken, I do believe you owe me some kissin' from the other day. I had no idea you'd turn out to be such a tease."

CHAPTER TWENTY-NINE
BOOKS

September 27th, 10:35 am – 655 Main Street, Coshocton, OH

"Right up here," Owen said, pointing. "That one's the library."

Abandoned cars dotted the street, but Mark had no problem finding an empty parking space. He cut the engine of the blue sedan, and the four men studied the outside of the building.

"It doesn't look like it's been broken into," John said. "Not like the hunting supply yesterday."

Paul shifted in his seat in the back, uncomfortably aware of the gun attached to his belt by a brand new holster. He hadn't gone with them the day before, but after they'd returned, John had given him both items, and a five-minute rundown on how to shoot. The gun was one of the ones they'd taken from the men at the drugstore. Mark had the other, and John had the rifle.

"Big windows," Paul observed. "Won't be so dark inside, since it's a bright day."

Mark grunted. "We'll still probably need a lantern or two. The shelves will block a lot of the sunlight."

"Right," John agreed. "We ready?"

Once he got nods from all three of them, they got out of the car and headed to the trunk for supplies. As John parceled them out, Paul scanned the street for any movement. When they'd met Owen, he'd said he hadn't seen anyone alive since the last plague deaths, and Paul believed him. But it didn't mean someone couldn't be passing through. Paul thought the others were getting complacent, taking the car out across town two days in a row, making themselves so visible. But the trip to the hunting supply had been for weapons, and Paul couldn't argue the necessity. And the trip to the library today was just as vital if they wanted to stay at the house all winter.

John snagged Paul's sleeve to get his attention, then handed him a camping lantern. Owen got one too, while John and Mark took empty tote bags.

The front door wasn't locked, which was odd. The reason became clear when they saw the remains of a body slumped over the front desk.

"I didn't think of checking here for anyone," Owen said, his thin shoulders trembling. "Poor Mrs. Arthur."

"She came to work sick, and didn't leave," Mark guessed. "Never locked up."

"You knew her?" Paul asked.

"A little," Owen replied. "I didn't come here much. But she'd been the head librarian forever, and she was friends with my grandma." He sighed.

"Let's find what we came here for," John said, steering Owen away from the desk.

Paul joined Mark in scanning the ends of the shelving units for the section they wanted. "The good old Dewey Decimal System," Mark said sarcastically. "We had to memorize it in school, so I knew it once, but then I didn't need it for forty years, so I forgot it all."

"I learned how to look things up, but we never needed more than that," Paul said. "Most of the time in high school I did research for papers on the Internet, anyway."

"So neither of us knows where to look. Great. But the place isn't that big, we'll find it eventually." He moved to the next shelf, farther from the windows. "Time for the lantern, I can't read this one clearly."

Paul and Mark systematically checked one row of shelves while John and Owen did the same to another. After a few minutes, Owen called out, "Over here!"

The four of them gathered in the stacks, the light of the two lanterns throwing strange and conflicting shadows over the books. Paul squinted to make out titles. *The Rose-Grower's Companion. 50 Native Plants to Enhance Your Garden. Landscaping Made Easy.*

On his right, Mark and John were choosing books from the next section. Each one got leafed through, then either stowed in a bag or reshelved. Paul couldn't see the titles of the ones they kept, but he doubted any of them were called *How To Build An Outhouse.* General do-it-yourself building and carpentry books would have to serve, since it turned out no one in their group had any knowledge or experience with construction.

After ten minutes, Paul cleared his throat awkwardly. He had been hoping there would be a chance to slip away, but none had presented itself, and soon they'd have finished combing the shelves for what they needed. "There's something else I want to grab, while we're here," he said. "Shouldn't take more than a minute or two."

Three faces turned up to his, each looking sickly in the lantern light, as if they stared at him from underwater. He wondered if he should explain, but before he could, John gave a sharp nod.

Paul wove his way through the stacks again. He'd seen the section he wanted while he and Mark searched. It didn't take him long to find it again. With the lantern held high, he started scanning the authors' names. *Ayers.* He skipped down to the next shelf, then each one in turn down to the floor. *Barstow, Billingsley, Boyce, Carlton. Too far.* Paul knelt and ran his fingers along the second-to-last shelf, tapping each book lightly while he searched for the right author. In a childish gesture he was glad no one would see, he crossed his fingers as he read the titles, hoping to find the right book.

"Gotcha," he said, pulling a slim orange paperback from the shelf. The spine was cracked, and the corners of the front cover were worn down to ragged curves from age and handling. But he'd found Nina's favorite book, so as long as there were no pages missing, the rest didn't matter.

With one mission accomplished, he crossed the building to the kids' section and grabbed a few things for Aaron, who'd been reading steadily through what the house had to offer. He was going to need more soon, so Paul pulled a few titles he recognized from his own school days off the shelves, loading the stack under one arm.

He met up with the others as they headed for the front door. "These are for Aaron," he said to John, setting his lantern down on the floor and passing him all but one of the books. "Got room in the bags?"

John nodded. "Find everything you wanted? We're probably not coming back."

"This'll do." Paul hefted his lantern again, ready to leave.

"Good," John replied as he stowed the extra books. "Let's go home, then."

On the drive back, Paul listened to Mark and John discuss drawing up the outhouse plans, but only with half an ear. He turned the book over in his hands and read the back cover, and, when it sounded interesting, opened to the first page. The distinct queasiness of motion sickness overtook him about five pages in, forcing him to close the book and look out the window to quiet his rebellious stomach. But he was already hooked. He'd intended to give the book to Nina the first chance he had, but instead he decided he would read it before he did. It would be strange to give it to her as a gift, then ask immediately to borrow it.

When they reached the house, Paul held the book in one hand at his side, shielding it from view with his body as he came through the door. There was no way of knowing where Nina would be in the house, and he didn't want to spoil the surprise. But she wasn't in sight, so Paul headed for his room and buried the book in his pack, promising himself to make time for it soon. Nina knew they'd gone to the library today. If he waited too long to give it to her, she'd wonder why he'd taken the trouble to find it but not to pass it along.

It wasn't a terribly long book, so if he stayed up late, reading by the fire, he might be able to finish it in a night or two . . .

Paul smiled to himself and went to find out what Nina was up to. He didn't think there was any sense in wasting his good mood on being alone, when he could share it with her.

CHAPTER THIRTY
GLASSES

September 30th, 6:21 pm – 1880 Cambridge Road, Coshocton, OH

Nina ran water to start washing the dishes. Behind her, at the table, John cleared his throat. "How is everyone doing on their personal inventories? Anyone still missing anything vital?"

There was a silence which was probably filled with shaking heads Nina couldn't see. She almost spoke up about wanting a better winter coat, but decided against it. The one John had found for her was down-filled, puffy as a marshmallow, and about three sizes too big. But Rachel's coat had turned out to be uncomfortably tight across the shoulders when worn over anything more than a tee shirt, and nothing else had turned up.

She decided to mention it to Paul. He'd keep looking whenever he had the chance, so there was no need to bother everyone with it. He was already keeping an eye out for pajamas for her, just as she was still trying to find him a new pair of boots.

"All right, then," John continued. "We've gotten pretty much everything we can get from the neighborhood now, and we've laid in a good supply of food and toiletries on top of the gear we need. But now we're going to have to start going farther afield, and that means we need transportation. There's only the one working car right now, and what we really need are pickup trucks."

"We do?" Owen asked.

"We don't want to waste time or gas making multiple trips to bring things home," Mark explained. "And we'll need something with plenty of space when we go to get the materials for the outhouse."

"You finished the plan for it?" Paul asked.

"Yep," Mark answered. "It's going to be a heck of a trip to get the lumber. But Owen knows where the building supply is, and we figure if everyone goes, there'll be plenty of hands to hold the lanterns while we cut everything to size."

"With handsaws, unfortunately," John added. "It will probably take us all day since we won't be able to use any power tools."

"So tomorrow we start looking for the trucks?" Paul asked. The concern in his voice was so mild Nina doubted anyone else heard it, but she did. They'd managed to steal some time together a few nights ago, curled up together on one of the couches in front of the fire. Instead of making out like horny teenagers, though, he'd just wanted to talk. And admitting how jumpy going into town had made him, how exposed he'd felt, had been one of the things on his mind.

Given what had happened at the drugstore, and the healing scar on his shoulder he had to show for it, Nina couldn't blame him. She was starting to get anxious herself, knowing she'd be going along to the building supply. Looking for the trucks didn't bother her much—they were so far from the highway, she felt safe from anyone randomly stumbling across them in the house, or while they scavenged nearby. But she trusted Paul's instincts, and his worry colored her reactions.

Shoving those thoughts aside as best she could, Nina set the last plate on the drying rack, pulled the drain stopper, and reached for the towel to dry her hands. They ached from the cold water. She folded her arms as she turned around, tucking her fingers into the crease of her elbows to warm them up. Leaning against the counter, she listened to John relay their instructions.

"If you remember seeing any trucks while you were out getting supplies, start there. Otherwise, go house to house like before. If you find one, look for the keys. If you manage to find them, open the garage door and give the truck a try. If it works, back it out into the driveway and leave it there, then put the keys in the mailbox. That way we won't lose track of them, but they won't get mixed up, either."

Alison clucked her tongue. "That's a lot of *ifs*."

Nina spoke up for the first time. "Whenever I found keys in a house, I left them by the front door. On a hook, if they had one, or on a table, sometimes on the floor if there was nothing else."

Paul sent a quick smile her way, not quite beaming with pride, but she got the message. *He likes smart.*

"Good thinking," John said. "That could save us some trouble. I suggest everyone else do the same when we start foraging in new neighborhoods."

"And we should probably be testing out the cars and trucks there, too," Mark added. "The more we have, the less we'll have to worry about siphoning gas from the ones that don't run."

"And there's something I should have asked before, and didn't," John said. "Is there anyone who can't drive?" Then he smiled. "Aside from Aaron, at least. I was thinking of teaching him before sixteen anyway, so he'd have plenty of time to learn before his driving test. For now I have to wait until he's tall enough to reach the pedals and still be able to see over the wheel."

Alison flicked a glance at Nina, maybe intending to say something biting about her height, but she only pursed her lips and looked back at John instead. Nina's shoulders sagged, relieved she'd dodged one of Alison's snappy bullets.

"I can't drive," Sarah said, staring down at her interlaced fingers where they rested on the table. "I mean, I know how to drive, but I'm not supposed to without my glasses. And I know that doesn't really matter anymore, but still, I wouldn't feel safe doing it."

Mark reached over to wrap an arm over his wife's shoulders. "It's okay, honey, it looks like the rest of us can, so you don't need to."

Nina watched the others' reactions. Alison had clearly known, too, that Sarah needed glasses, having been her friend and neighbor. Paul and Owen seemed stunned and faintly worried, echoing Nina's own feelings.

But John reached out to lay his hand over Sarah's. "You said you didn't need them," he said, his voice soft with concern. "We could have tried to find you new ones."

"All we'd have found were cheap reading glasses," she replied. "Those wouldn't help me, I'm near-sighted. Everything more than a few yards away starts to get a little blurry. And I couldn't stomach trying on glasses taken from . . ." She trailed off, unwilling to say it.

"We get it, Sarah," Nina said, surprising herself. "I wouldn't, either. But I've seen plenty of glasses cases in the houses I've been through. I could have taken them, if I'd known someone needed them. You should have told us."

She waved Nina's concern off with a vague gesture, causing John to let go of her hand. "It doesn't bother me much," she explained. "It's been long enough that I'm used to it now. And someone's always with me."

That was true enough, though Nina had never thought to wonder why before. It did explain Sarah tagging along whenever Nina went to wash up. Nina always assumed Sarah didn't want her out on her own. Now she knew it was for Sarah's benefit, not hers.

She wanted to say something more, but Sarah had clearly closed the subject. John laid out a few final details, and then the after-dinner meeting broke up, everyone saying their goodnights. No one seemed in the mood for an evening around the fire.

But Nina caught Paul's eye as he stood up, and he gave a tiny nod. As the others filtered out of the kitchen, he lingered. When they were alone, he joined her at the counter, leaning against it in a mirror of her pose.

"Want to go out before breakfast tomorrow and look for some glasses?" Nina asked, staring out into the living room through the doorway.

"Absolutely," he replied, and she could hear the smile in his voice. "You remember where any were?"

"I think so. But it won't take long to check each house, all the ones I saw were either on bedside tables, or in bathrooms. We should be able to get through the whole neighborhood and be back in time for food. Leave around sunrise?"

"Yeah," Paul answered, then paused. "You think John will be pissed at us for going out unscheduled? I mean, we're not going out alone, but . . ."

Nina thought of the way John laid his hand over Sarah's. "I think there's a very real possibility we'll find him up and about just as early as we are, and that he's going to want to come with us. He can't get mad at us then, right?"

Paul turned, taking her in his arms. She pulled away from the counter to lean into his embrace. "You're not keeping anything like that from me, right? Leaving anything off your list?"

She shook her head against his sweater. "Nothing that serious. My winter coat's too big, so I'm still hoping to find a better one. I think that's the only thing I hadn't told you yet."

"Good." He settled his hands at her waist and lifted her to sit on the counter, bringing her face much closer to his height. There was heat in his eyes, but his kiss was slow and sweet. True to his word, Paul wasn't pushing. "I think everyone's headed to their rooms for the night," he whispered against her lips. "Grab a book and cuddle with me in front of the fire while I try to write?"

Nina couldn't help but giggle. "*Try* to write? Are you sure I won't be a distraction?"

"No," he breathed. "No, I need you there with me, for this. Please?"

Paul never let her see inside his dog-eared notebook, so she knew better than to ask what he was working on. "Okay. I'll go get ready for bed and meet you back down there in a bit. Last time, I fell asleep without brushing my teeth," she finished, scrunching her nose in disgust.

The tension around Paul's eyes faded as his expression softened. She hadn't meant to doze off snuggled up to him, but he'd looked at her the same way when he'd woken her up so she could get herself to bed. She suspected he'd watched her sleep for a long time before he had. She just hoped she hadn't drooled on him.

A smile crossed her face at the memory, which invited Paul to kiss her again. And he did, much more thoroughly the second time. Eventually, though, she pulled away. "If you want me to come back, you have to let me go first."

"Don't want to," he whispered, tucking her hair behind her ear. He never missed a chance to touch her hair.

"Five minutes. Promise."

He stepped back and glanced at his watch. "Fine. But I'm timing you."

Nina made a face at him as she hopped down from the counter. The sound of his laughter chased her upstairs.

CHAPTER THIRTY-ONE
CURTAINS

October 2nd, 8:45 am – River Run Plaza, Coshocton, OH

Navigating the building supply by the light of three camping lanterns proved to be difficult, but not impossible. Paul kept to the end of the line, not wanting his height to block any light for the others. Nina walked ahead of him, a small form mostly made of shadow, with her lifted lantern casting a strange green-tinted glow over her dark hair.

The smell of decay here was faint, almost nonexistent. Paul didn't know if it was because few people had died here, because the space was vast, or because enough time had passed for the stink to fade. Whatever the reason, he was grateful. And glad that if there were any bodies, John would steer the group around them as best he could.

He was also glad that Aaron had stayed behind with Sarah to look after him. There was too much trouble the boy could get into here, and no small amount of fuel for nightmares. Paul always thought his nerves were steady, but the absolute blackness here was barely dented by the lights they carried. He wanted to reach out a hand to Nina, to be reassured by the solid presence of someone near him in the dark. But he didn't want to startle her, so he settled for staying as close as he could. Falling behind, out of the pools of light they carried with them, was a prospect he didn't care to face.

He couldn't shake the feeling someone was behind him. There was no sound but their own footsteps, scuffing and slapping on the concrete floor. On the way here, he and Nina had almost managed to forget their anxiety about making the trip in their new fleet of three pickup trucks—almost.

They'd joked and laughed until Nina, on the passenger side, thought she saw someone walking down a side street.

She insisted she'd only seen them for a second, and she couldn't be sure. They didn't stop to investigate. Even if there had been someone, better to let them be, and get on with what needed doing.

But Paul felt the sheer size of the darkness behind him like firm hands on his back, pressing him forward. Anything could be hidden in it, and anything could be swallowed up by it.

This place was going to give him nightmares. Nina, too, probably, though he hoped she was holding up better than he was.

They reached the section of the store with the uncut lumber, which leaned in bundles against the wall. Paul hadn't bothered looking at the books they'd taken from the library, and he'd never built anything in his life. So he could only guess at the meaning of the colored bindings holding the bundles together. Maybe they indicated different types of wood, or different widths or thicknesses of board. He couldn't tell by looking. Maybe it would have been obvious in normal light.

John walked up and down the aisle, Alison trailing with her lantern held close when he needed to check a label. "We need this one," he said, standing at the fourth stack after checking everything and doubling back.

"All right, then," Mark said. "Anybody seen one of those wheeled staircase things? I guess if we don't find one, they'd at least have ladders for sale somewhere."

Owen followed Mark away. They returned a few minutes later with a regular step ladder, eight feet high. They set it in front of the correct lumber, and Mark climbed up. Standing on the second-to-last rung, he pulled the knife from his belt. "Ready below?"

"Not quite," John said with a mild laugh. "Owen, set your lantern down on the floor. You and Paul and I are going to be handling the wood after Mark opens up the bundle, so get your gloves on, okay? Nina, Alison, you might want to stand a little farther back. We'll be pivoting the boards and laying them down along the aisle until we can cut them."

Everyone took up their positions, the women holding their lanterns high, the men donning their work gloves. "Ready," John told Mark, who sliced the plastic wrapping along its length.

John separated three boards from the bundle and started to ease them down. Paul, being taller, had the next job, grabbing them above John's head to support their weight. He walked his hands along their edges as he backpedaled toward Owen, who stood farthest away, ready to grab the ends and help lower them to the ground. Dropping the boards could damage them. Worse, they could hurt someone.

They wouldn't need the entire bundle, but John wanted to take it all down, so no loose boards would fall while they were cutting the ones they needed. So the slow, methodical process was repeated for another set, and another.

At first, the work soothed Paul's nerves by giving him something to focus on besides his fears. But by the fourth time through, he was concerned about something else. His arms were starting to tremble. He knew his job wasn't the hardest—John was handling the full weight of the lumber before Paul got his hands on it. But on the fifth set, his shoulder started to throb. There hadn't seemed to be any muscle damage from his injury, but then, he'd been favoring his left side ever since . . .

Something went wrong the sixth time. Five boards remained, and instead of dividing them into sets of three and two, Mark put all five into John's hands. Strong as he was, he fumbled with the extra weight. Paul rushed forward as the boards tipped the wrong way, hoping to redirect them. But he wasn't fast enough. John staggered into Paul, and they both crashed into the ladder.

In the confusion of sounds, it was impossible to catalog what happened in the second it took Paul to fall. The sharp scrape of metal, the hollow smack of wood, the dull thump his own body made when he landed. The overlapping shouts of those around him.

The cement floor was hard, and the cold seeped into Paul as he lay on his back, the wind knocked out of him. His arm was pinned under something heavy, but he could tell it wasn't broken. He remembered that pain distinctly from when he'd broken it as a kid. After a moment, he heard a groan and the weight lifted.

"Everybody okay?" John asked, his voice weak and shaky. "I'm bruised, I think, but no real harm done."

Paul groaned too as he got to his feet and stretched, checking for twinges or aches. "Same here. Managed not to hit my head, so I'll be okay. Sore, but okay."

They all waited for Mark to say something along those lines.

Silence.

"Mark?" Alison said, stepping forward with her lantern held out.

The lumber was much longer than the width of the aisle, so it had landed on the highest shelf, forming a slanted roof over their heads. Mark lay beneath it, tangled in the fallen ladder. One foot bent upward at a grotesque angle, still hooked in the rungs. But he hadn't cried out. A small pool of blood glistened beneath his head, more black than red in the dim light, and he lay completely still.

John went to his side, feeling for a pulse. Then he dropped his hand and shook his head.

Paul heard the scream but didn't understand what it meant. Not until someone slammed into him, propelling him backwards against the shelves. His ribs struck metal and he grunted in pain, but his head hit cardboard. He had a moment to appreciate his luck before Alison's hands, curled into claws, tore at his face and throat.

A sharp spike of panic gripped him as he raised his arms to protect himself. He had both his knife and the gun on his belt—if she grabbed either one he was in real trouble. Christine had managed to wound him, but if Alison got the gun he was in for a lot worse. He had to get her hands under control, but the shadows kept shifting, and he couldn't see her attacks coming clearly enough.

She was still screaming at him, the words so shrill and frenzied he couldn't make out what she was saying. He wasn't even sure she knew. He managed to get a solid grip on one of her arms, which slowed her down, but her other hand was going for his throat.

An image of Nina grappling with John flashed through his mind, from the first time he watched her learning self-defense.

Paul dodged to the side so Alison's reaching hand went past him, punching a box on the shelf instead. He braced his free hand on the shelf for balance and explored the floor around him with one foot. When he brushed up against Alison's foot, he hooked his ankle behind Alison's and pulled, letting go of her arm at the same time.

She staggered back but managed not to fall. Shadows darted in from either side. John was behind her, wrapping his arms around her, pinning hers to her sides. She struggled against his hold, but she had nowhere to go, because Nina was doing the same to her legs.

"Alison!" John growled in her ear. "Get a hold of yourself!" She continued to struggle, not hearing him, or not caring. "I don't want to hurt you, but if you don't stop this, I will tie you up to keep you from hurting someone else."

"He killed Mark!" she wailed, slumping in his hold as the frenzy turned into tears. "He ruins everything!"

Paul swallowed hard against a wave of guilt. "It was an accident."

Alison broke down, her unintelligible words mixed with harsh, labored sobbing. Nina let go and backed away, but Alison didn't lash out with her feet. John loosened his hold then, lowering her gently to the floor when it became clear she couldn't hold herself upright.

"Owen," he said. The stunned teenager moved forward. "Look after her. Get her back outside to the trucks and wait for us. We'll take care of Mark."

Owen grabbed one of the discarded lanterns and coaxed Alison to her feet. She clung to him, weeping with a child's utter abandonment, and allowed him to lead her away.

Nina took up her dropped lantern as well. Tear tracks on her cheeks caught its light. "I'll find something to wrap him in," she said before heading off to a cross aisle, her bobbing light disappearing.

"Are you all right?" John asked Paul, taking the third lantern and holding up to get a better look at the damage. "How bad did she hurt you?"

"Some scratches," he answered. "And my side ain't right where I hit the shelf. Never broken a rib before, so I don't know what it feels like."

"Let's hope it's not that serious." John looked him straight in the eye. "Alison's wrong, you know. This isn't your fault."

"I know." Paul took an experimental deep breath, waiting for any sharp pain to tell him he was broken inside. Nothing happened but a dull tug in his muscles. "Hurts to hear her say it, though."

"If you're to blame, then so am I," John said, lowering the lantern. "And so is Mark, for that matter. He gave me the extra boards, I couldn't handle them, and you didn't get them under control so that I didn't fall."

"We might not want to tell Sarah that part, though. Saying Mark screwed up is gonna make it look like we're shifting blame off us."

"Sarah won't blame anyone," John said, the sadness heavy in his voice. "She'll be heartbroken, but she'll never hold it against us. Somehow, that almost makes it worse. Even if either of us were to blame, she'd forgive us."

"Yeah," Paul agreed, then took another deep breath to steady himself. "We should get the ladder off Mark. Nina might be back soon, and we need to get him home."

John nodded.

With the lantern set on the floor nearby, John eased the ladder off of Mark, while Paul disentangled his broken foot from it. He shivered with disgust, feeling the bones scrape together as he straightened it.

A light appeared at the end of the aisle, moving toward them. Nina returned with a flat plastic package about the size of a dinner plate. "Curtains," she explained, setting her lantern down and slitting the top of the package with her knife. The wad of fabric she pulled out hardly looked big enough to be a shirt, but then she shook it out, revealing yards of thin material. "There's two. I figured, wrap him in one, then carry him on the other?"

"That's good, Nina," John said as he took one from her. "We'll handle this. You spread out the other one off to the side, okay?"

The tone of voice he used, gentle and reassuring, struck a note of jealousy in Paul, as fierce as it was unexpected. That's how Paul spoke to Nina, when she needed it. He should be doing it right now, but the words weren't coming. All he wanted was to wrap his arms around her and forget all of this had happened.

John led Paul through the unpleasant task with the grim efficiency of a soldier. Five minutes later, they were ready to leave. Nina went first with both lanterns, one held at her side, the other held high to guide them out. John was next, holding onto the end of the curtain at Mark's feet, while Paul followed behind with the other end. All of Paul's aches screamed in protest, carrying that weight, but he grit his teeth and let the tears fall silently.

CHAPTER THIRTY-TWO
A BENCH

October 2nd, 11:36 am – 1880 Cambridge Road, Coshocton, OH

The three trucks pulled into the driveway slowly, one after the other. John led, driving the truck with Mark laid out in the back. Owen followed with Alison, and finally, Nina pulled in behind them.

Paul was silent the entire drive back. He hadn't even argued when she said she was driving. He'd driven on the way out, but now he seemed numb, saying nothing. Nina had no way of knowing what was going through his mind, so she had no idea what to say. A feeling she was uncomfortably acquainted with.

So she was silent too.

They sat in the parked truck, watching the others head inside. "I can't go in there," Paul whispered.

"What?" Nina asked, not sure if she'd heard him right.

"I can't go in there," he repeated, his voice stronger.

"It wasn't your fault," she told him. "Sarah's not going to blame you."

"It's not that," he said, staring at the house and not meeting her eyes. "Not sure I can live under the same roof as Alison anymore. I knew she hated me before, but now there's fury behind it. She might attack me again, if I go in there."

"You're not afraid of her, are you?" Nina asked. Then she winced, because it had come out wrong, harsher than she meant it to sound.

Paul didn't seem bothered. "I am," he admitted. "After what just happened, yeah, I am."

"Paul . . ." Nina began hesitantly. "I'm not trying to be dismissive. But I don't think you need to worry." She reached over to take his hand. "Alison went a little insane with grief, in the moment, and I'm not excusing that. But I don't think she'll do it again."

He sighed and squeezed her fingers. "You're probably right. I'm gonna be a little jumpy 'round her, though."

Nina was almost pathetically grateful to see him moving, reacting, finally looking at her. The blankness in his eyes had been terrifying. She had never had to be anyone's comfort before, not like this, and she didn't think she was making a great job of it so far. "I imagine that's going to be true for most of us," she said. "I don't think she's going to be happy with me for trying to tackle her. I'd have knocked her right over if John hadn't gotten hold of her first."

"Thanks, by the way," Paul said with a weak smile, glancing away. "For comin' to my rescue."

Nina snorted. "I'm only sorry I didn't do it quicker. She tore you up pretty badly. But she was so wild I was afraid I'd get knocked out by one of her flying elbows before I got close enough to do anything. That's why I decided to go for her legs." She reached for the door handle. "You ready to go in?"

"I don't know."

"Paul." She said his name firmly, and he turned to face her. "You're hurt, and we haven't even figured out how badly yet, so you can't just leave. You're in no shape for it. If you want, I will go get your pack, and some food, and we can set you up in a different house for a few days until things settle down. If we take the truck, a different neighborhood, even. I won't tell anyone where you are, so Alison won't find you. If you want," she said again, "I will get my pack and come with you. And when you feel better, when you're stronger, when Alison's gotten her shit together, we'll come back."

"You'd come with me?" Behind the tear tracks and the bloody scratches, hope lit in his eyes, so strong Nina's pulse raced faster seeing it. She nodded, not trusting her voice just then. There was a long silence between them. "I ain't gonna put you through that, if I don't have to," he finally said. "Let's go in and see how things stand first." He reached out to tuck a loose strand of her hair behind her ear. "But thank you. For offerin'."

Nina nodded, and they went inside together.

Sarah was sitting on one of the couches with John, crying in his arms. But she looked up when the door shut behind them, and she gasped. "Oh, Paul," she said, getting up. "Look at what she's done to you!"

Even without touching him, Nina could sense some of the tension vanish from Paul. "I'm all right," he said. "Nina and John got her off me before she did too much damage."

Crossing the room, she took Paul in an embrace which seemed to comfort them both. "I don't see why she went mad like that," Sarah said as she drew away, wiping her eyes delicately with one hand. "But then, I wasn't there. John told me what happened, all of it, Paul, and I want you to know I don't blame you, or anyone."

Paul's shoulders sagged, and Nina slipped underneath one of his arms, wrapping one of hers around his back. Then she looked to Sarah, who had turned to study her.

"How are you holding up, dear?"

"Shouldn't I be asking you that?" Nina responded. "You seem . . . calmer than I thought you'd be. I wasn't expecting anything like Alison, but . . ."

"It hurts, Nina," Sarah answered. "More than I can say. But at the same time, I've always known something like this was coming. We're all just living on borrowed time, now. I've been . . ." She broke off on a swallowed sob. "I've been preparing for this, I think, since the day we left home with John. I won't fall apart. Or, I don't know, maybe I will, later, when I'm alone."

Nina stepped forward, letting go of Paul to hug Sarah. When they separated, Sarah was smiling at her. "Thank you."

Nina nodded, at a loss for anything else to say.

Across the room, John cleared his throat. "He's still in the truck. We should take him out back."

Sarah turned, shooting him a surprised look. "You're going to bury him beside your family?"

"He was family," John murmured.

Shaking her head, Sarah said, "I appreciate that, John, truly I do. But it doesn't feel right. He never knew them. Maybe . . . maybe under the maple tree in the side yard? That's a pretty spot, now that the leaves are changing. I think I'd like sitting out there, with him."

Nina wept fresh tears then, turning away so Sarah wouldn't see. But Paul must have, because he laid a hand on her shoulder.

"All right," John said. "If that's what you want." The two of them went outside together. Nina watched them through the window as they headed toward the side of the house.

"I should go with them," Paul said, wrapping both arms around her shoulders from behind. "Help John with the grave."

Nina roused herself when she saw the state of Paul's hands and forearms, marked with scratches. "Let Owen do it," she protested. "You're a mess. We need to get you cleaned up."

"Owen's buried enough people already, don't you think?"

She heard the steel in his voice, so she didn't argue. "Go on, then," she said, choking back more tears. "Just let me look after you when it's done, okay?"

He kissed her briefly on the cheek, and she relaxed against him. She'd been worried she'd wounded his pride. "Countin' on it," he whispered.

The afternoon dragged on forever. Lunchtime passed without a meal. Nina fixed a small plate of food and ate alone before checking in with everyone to see if she could bring them anything. John and Paul refused, in the midst of their digging, and so did Sarah, sitting quietly next to Mark's body and watching the wind rustle the reddening leaves. Alison had locked herself in her room and wouldn't answer Nina's knocking or her offer of food. Owen turned out to be in Aaron's room, playing cards with the boy. There were signs of tears on both their faces. Aaron took Nina up on lunch, but Owen only shook his head. She returned with a plate of cheese and crackers, gave Aaron a kiss on the top of his head, and told them to call for her if they needed anything.

Then Nina was at a loss for what to do. It seemed crass to hide in her room and sulk like Alison. Owen was already taking care of Aaron, so she wasn't needed there. She couldn't help with the grave, and she couldn't bear the idea of sitting with Sarah and trying to offer comfort, only to have Sarah be the one comforting her. After wandering through each room, searching for anything to keep herself occupied, Nina found herself standing in the master bedroom, which was just Sarah's now, looking out the window.

They had moved the front-porch bench to the side yard for Sarah to sit on. John was resting for a moment, standing beside the grave and leaning hard on his shovel. Paul was still digging, the ground level with his waist.

When the grave was as deep as he was tall, they'd be done.

Nina shook herself out of her dark thoughts. They'd been digging a while now, so they'd be thirsty. She would take them water, and she doubted they would refuse it as they had the food.

They didn't. They thanked her, and she was glad she'd done it. Until Sarah snagged her arm as she tried to go back inside. "Sit with me a while, dear? It's a lovely day out."

Something inside Nina quailed at Sarah's tone, peaceful, almost cheerful. "I can't, Sarah, I'm sorry," she blurted out. "I need to stay busy."

Sarah nodded and went back to watching the men work without a word.

Back inside, Nina threw herself into any activity she could come up with. She washed the few dirty dishes from her halfhearted attempt at lunch. She gathered all the used towels from the bathroom and took them outside, draping them over the front porch railing. If she couldn't wash them properly, at least she could air them out. Then she got a few new ones from their stockpile and set them in the linen closet to use next.

Then she tackled organizing the closet itself. It didn't need to be done, but by the time she'd finished, she'd made more room for extra sheets, which she retrieved from their boxes as well. The satisfaction she felt looking at the shelves, with their neat arrangements of bedding, held back her feelings of unreality.

She considered stripping the beds and remaking them, but they'd only been used for two weeks. With access to proper laundry, she would have, but since she couldn't wash the old sheets, they'd need to last a while longer before she could switch them for new. She settled for making everyone's beds. Except Alison's, of course. And Aaron's, since he and Owen were sitting on it while they played cards.

In Paul's room, though, she stood next to the bed, staring at the nightstand, her attention captured by a book. *The Martian Chronicles.* Her favorite book.

She picked it up, running a finger down the spine. At the bottom she found the sticker printed with the call number. Paul had taken this from the library earlier in the week. There was a bookmark sticking out of the top, about three-quarters of the way through. She opened the book and saw it was a flattened granola-bar wrapper, which made her laugh out loud.

He'd told them, the first night in the gas station, that he wasn't much of a reader. He spent his free time—at least, what he didn't spend with her—playing cards, playing piano, or scribbling in his notebook. But Paul was reading her favorite book in secret. That, more than anything else he had ever done, any time he had touched her, any word he had said, convinced Nina he was truly in love with her.

Her heart puffed up inside her chest like a blowfish, complete with spines that pierced her lungs and stifled her breathing. As she clutched the book to her chest, she promised herself she would find a way to make it up to him for doubting it. Because she had. Even just a few hours before, when she had offered to go with him to another house, she still hadn't been completely sure.

Even when he had said, "I love you." Though she knew he wasn't lying, she hadn't managed to accept it. And he hadn't said it again.

Maybe because she hadn't said it at all.

She set the book back, trying to leave it in exactly the same spot. If Paul knew he'd been discovered, he might be embarrassed, or feel guilty he hadn't told her. She didn't want either. If he was going to tell her, she wanted him to do it without prompting. And if he never did, well, she would tell him someday. When he wanted to know exactly when she was sure she had fallen in love with him.

The pinball feeling of impulsiveness gripped her again, making her want to rush outside and shout her love at the top of her lungs. Which she knew was a terrible idea. She wasn't wrong to feel such happiness surrounded by grief, but she would be wrong to flaunt it. She sat down on the bed, wondering, thinking, planning how to approach this. After everything she'd gotten wrong, the last thing she wanted was to make another mistake.

A few minutes later, she headed upstairs to collect supplies from her pack and from the bathroom. Paul's body had taken a lot of punishment, between the fall, the fight with Alison, and now the toil of digging Mark's grave. He was going to hurt like hell when he finally stopped moving. She needed to be ready. She laid out everything she thought she might need in neat rows on her desk. She started practicing things to say in her head, the words she wanted to use to tell Paul how she felt.

She suspected she'd forget all of them the second she saw him again, and she'd be just as awkward as ever. But it kept her occupied while she waited.

CHAPTER THIRTY-THREE
PILLOWS

October 2nd, 8:05 pm – 1880 Cambridge Road, Coshocton, OH

Paul ran the flat of his shovel over the mound, smoothing out the last bit of dirt. The sun had just slipped below the horizon. Dusk seemed like the right time to finish this task.

"We'll bring everyone out tomorrow, then, and say a few words?" John asked, holding his hand out to Sarah, who sat silent and motionless on the bench. When Paul asked earlier, before they started filling the grave back in, she shook her head.

This time, she nodded. "In the morning. Before breakfast, I think, so it's not hanging over everyone's head all day." She took John's hand and pulled herself up. "I don't think I could stand everyone tiptoeing around me."

Paul smiled at her insistent tone. "Well, I can promise not to tiptoe, but you won't mind some extra sweetness, right? I'd give you a hug if I weren't so filthy."

Sarah laughed, which surprised Paul, but then he remembered Nina's words. *Everyone handles grief differently.* So he tried not to show any signs of surprise. Sarah being able to laugh was a good thing.

"Both of you, go get cleaned up," she ordered. "I'll put together something simple for dinner when you're ready. The others may very well have eaten by now. Poor Nina, trying so hard to fill in for me . . . I feel awful about earlier. She looked ready to shake herself apart from worry."

Paul agreed, feeling a twinge of guilt that he hadn't been there to help her this afternoon. But his sense of duty had pulled him in two directions, and proper respect for the dead had won. Nina wasn't selfish. She'd let him go, so she understood he'd needed to do it.

Or so he hoped.

John let Paul have the shower first, so he left his dirty boots at the door. It might be time to switch to the new pair Nina had found for him. He'd been careful at the building supply, but he may have gotten blood on them. If he had, he didn't care to wear them again.

He gathered a set of new clothes from his spares and trudged upstairs to the bathroom. When he saw how little the trailing end of sunset illuminated the room, he went back down for a candle and his lighter. Nina would have lent him one if he'd asked—he'd seen light coming from her open door—but he didn't want to go her covered in grave dirt.

The candle went on the corner of the sink counter, where it gave him decent light in the shower if he left the curtain open just right. He was careful and thorough scrubbing himself down. The scratches from Alison's nails hadn't drawn much blood, and the soap made them sting like a thousand hot needles, but he scrubbed anyway. Any one of them could get infected. He hadn't been smart to ignore them all day, but leaving John to dig alone while he got patched up was something he couldn't bring himself to do.

And he would have had to go through it all twice, then, because he'd have gotten his bandages filthy, too.

He was shivering by the time he was done, so much he had to brace himself against the wall to keep from falling as he stepped out. The pulsing ache in his back had grown steadily worse over the past few hours, and the muscles of shoulders burned whenever he moved his arms.

Dried off and half-dressed, he threw his shirt over his shoulder and stepped into the hall, intending to knock on Nina's door and get her help bandaging up.

She was leaning against the wall next to the bathroom door. Paul nearly jumped out of his skin. "What are you doin'?"

"Waiting for you, of course," she answered with mild exasperation. "You ignored your injuries all day. I need to make sure you weren't going to do it indefinitely."

"And you knew it was me in there, and not John, how exactly?" he asked as she led him into her room, shutting the door behind him.

"Pffft," she scoffed. "You think I don't know your footsteps from his by now? Besides, I could hear him downstairs talking to Aaron and Sarah. You were in there so long, they started dinner without you."

"Have you eaten?" Paul asked.

She nodded. "So we're getting you patched up, then fed. Don't worry about me."

"I'm not," he said, getting a raised eyebrow in response. "Not much, anyway."

"But I'm worried about you," she fired back. "I have been all day. So turn around. There's some bruising here on your side, and I want to see how bad the rest of it is."

Paul obeyed. Her stern tone brought back his guilt about neglecting her, even as her concern tugged on his heart.

"Holy shit," Nina murmured. "You're ten different shades of purple. If you just spent all day exhausting yourself when you've got a broken rib . . . does it hurt to breathe?"

"No," he answered, then hissed when she laid her hand right in the middle of the sore spot. "Nina . . ."

"I know, I'm sorry, but I'm trying to feel for a break." She circled him, pressing her hand firmly against him as she traced the path of his bones. "I think you're clear. And since we don't have any ice to make a cold pack for that bruise, there's not much we can do about it. Sit down and we'll start working on those scratches. I don't think any of them are serious, but they're all getting cleaned anyway. Who knows how nasty Alison's damn fingernails are," she finished off in a mutter.

He sat down on the end of the bed, so Nina could stand in front of him and reach the supplies on her desk. "You got all this ready earlier?" he asked.

She nodded. Then she picked up a bottle of hydrogen peroxide and pressed a cotton ball against its mouth, turning it over and back with a practiced hand. She noticed him watching and smiled. "Same thing I used to do with nail polish remover. You think I don't know how to take care of you by now?"

Paul answered with a slight shake of his head. But he couldn't help flinching when she swabbed at a scratch on his cheek. "Hold still," she said, taking his chin in her other hand. She tried again with more success, but the stinging made his eyes water, and he trembled.

Nina's expression softened. "I'm sorry," she whispered. "I'll try to be quick. But I am not losing you to a damn infected scratch, okay?"

The anger and fear simmering underneath her words pulled at him. He yearned to kiss her, to take her in his arms and pitch them both backwards onto her bed, injured or not. The effort it took to stop himself, to keep still, made his whole body quiver.

Nina had to see the state he was in, but she ignored it while she methodically cleaned all the narrow rents in his skin. His face came first, then his throat and upper chest—she had to feel the pulse racing under her careful fingers—then one arm, then the other.

"I don't think any of these need bandaging," she said as she finished the last scratch. "I'd like to put some antibiotic ointment on them, but without bandages you'll be sticky until it dries. And I know you're cold. Can you manage a while longer?"

Could he manage to keep being half-naked while she kept touching him? He wasn't about to admit the cold wasn't why he was shivering. "Yeah," he breathed.

She started with his arms this time, maybe so he could get his shirt on sooner. He closed his eyes and let her handle him when she repositioned his limbs with gentle touches. While she tended to the scratches on his chest and neck, her hand resting on his shoulder for support made his breathing quicken. When she held his chin in her dainty fingers again, he opened his eyes, needing to see her face inches from his. "Patience," she whispered. "Almost done."

"Nina..."

"I know, Paul. I know." Her breathing was getting faster, too. He focused on the ridge of her collarbone where it peeked out from the collar of her shirt, watching it rise and fall almost as fast as his heartbeat. "Just let me finish this."

Paul kept himself under control while she turned away to tidy up the medical supplies. When she turned back, he grabbed her head in his hands and pulled her in for a kiss, fierce and hungry and desperate.

She broke away, laughing. "Slow down."

"I don't know if I can." Paul wound his fingers through her hair, trying to keep his grip gentle. "I need you, Nina. Please. I know I said I wasn't gonna push—"

"Shh," she interrupted with a finger against his lips. "I may be a tease sometimes, and you even like it. But I knew what I was getting into when I brought you in here. I knew tonight was different."

Paul groaned and tried to pull her against him, but she squirmed in his arms. He didn't let go—he didn't think he could—but he gave her some space to move.

"But I need you to understand me, Paul," she went on. "I am not about to let you pull a muscle or dislocate that rib trying to impress me with your lovemaking abilities. Because I'm sure you would. So you are going to lie back, and let me impress you instead. I'm going to take care of you, and you're going to have to remember to be quiet, because I am very, very good at it."

She held his eyes captive with hers, they were so blue and wide and filled with desire. "Okay?"

Paul nodded, not sure his voice would work if he tried to speak.

"Good," she said, laying a soft hand on his shoulder and giving him a light push.

It was a very unusual form of torture, Paul decided, to rest motionless on the bed while Nina knelt beside it, undoing his belt buckle and the fly of his jeans. It was worse when she wiggled them down his thighs, along with his boxers. He lifted his hips to make it easier for her, and she didn't scold him for it, but the temptation to do more was maddening. He was on fire with wanting to touch her.

When one of her tiny hands wrapped around him, he thought he might come undone on the spot. He gritted his teeth and held on, not wanting to embarrass them both. His whole body coiled with tension.

And Nina could sense it, because she said, "Look at me, Paul. Relax. Breathe."

He lifted his head high enough to meet her gaze. Seeing the flickering candle flame reflected in her eyes gave him something to focus on besides the agony of his pent-up need. He took one deep breath, then another and another. Nina smiled up at him. "That's better."

Then, without breaking eye contact, she took him into her mouth.

Paul threw his head back against the bed and let out a long moan. It had been almost a year since any woman had done this for him, and he hadn't realized how much he had missed it. Nina's tongue moved against him as she bobbed her head up and down, slowly at first, then faster as he began to rock his hips to meet her. It went on and on and on . . .

He gasped as she let go. "Why'd you stop?" he asked, his voice hoarse.

She giggled. "You're getting a little loud," she answered. "We're not alone, remember? If you're a screamer, you'd better grab my pillow to muffle it. And try and hold back anyway, these walls are pretty thin."

"Oh, hell, Nina," he said as he reached for the pillow, "I didn't know I was makin' noise at all."

"I will take that as a compliment," she said. "Ready?"

"Please," he whispered, gripping the pillow in both hands.

She'd been holding back herself, Paul realized as she descended on him again. She worked every part of him with her lips, her tongue, or, toward the end, her hands. Her gentle, stroking fingers nearly sent him over the edge, but he held on, not wanting the pleasure to stop, not even for the intensity of its conclusion. If he could have had this go on forever, he might have.

Until he thought of how much he wanted to touch Nina, to see her beautiful bronzed skin glowing in the candlelight, all of it, not just her face and hands and her adorable little feet.

Paul's entire body jerked with the force of his orgasm, lifting him off the bed then crashing him back onto it, the pillow pressed to his face to muffle his cries. Nina didn't ease up, leading him through it, taking everything he gave until there was nothing more left.

As the high retreated, leaving him shaky and breathless, he felt the mattress shift. Nina climbed onto the bed beside him and pulled the pillow away. "Feel better now?" she asked with an impish grin.

"Holy hell, Nina," he whispered. "I feel like you turned me inside-out."

She licked her swollen bottom lip. "Good."

Moving was a struggle, but Paul managed to lever himself up on his elbows. "And do I get to return the favor?"

"Absolutely," she said with a smile. "But not right now. You're going to crash any minute. You're injured, you're exhausted, you missed two meals, and now this. If I thought you'd be awake when I got back, I could go get you some food, but..."

"Nina, I ain't sleepy. Promise."

"You say that now, but you're going to be when you get your clothes back on and curl up in bed with me."

That statement made him sit up completely. "You want me to stay?"

She raised an eyebrow at him. "Do you want to leave?"

"No," he breathed, and she smiled again. "No," he repeated, reaching out to frame her face in his hands for another kiss, long and thorough.

Getting up, Nina retrieved her candle from the desk and set it on the nightstand. Paul got his boxers and jeans set back to rights and started hunting for his discarded shirt. "Sure I need this?" he asked before he put it back on.

Nina reached out to lay a hand on his chest. Her fingers felt almost fevered against his skin. "Tonight you do. You're warmer now than you were, but you're still colder than I am. So we're sleeping in clothes, under plenty of blankets. I'm not big enough to keep you warm all night on my own."

They cuddled together, close as puppies, in her narrow bed. As much as he wanted to be there, Paul had a hard time getting comfortable. He had to lie on his uninjured side, one arm and leg folded over Nina. Her head fit neatly beneath his chin as she lay on her back beside him. "I'm gonna be sore as hell in the morning," he predicted.

"You were going to be anyway," Nina replied. "If it gets too bad, though, you can go stretch out in your own bed. I won't be mad. I just thought you'd want to stay."

"I do," he said, his eyelids drooping. "I do want to stay."

"Good." Her voice seemed faint and far away as she turned her head to blow out the candle. "So just go to sleep."

CHAPTER THIRTY-FOUR
A BED

October 3rd, 7:01 am – 1880 Cambridge Road, Coshocton, OH

Nina woke up first, warm and content and surprisingly well-rested, considering the events of the day and night before. She lay still, not wanting to wake Paul yet. Sometime during the night he had shifted to lie with his head on her shoulder. One of his feet stuck out beyond the blanket at the end of the bed. She noticed a hole in his sock and felt a wave of tenderness wash over her. He was as beaten-down and ragged as she was.

Why had she ever distrusted him?

Listening to his quiet, even breathing, she couldn't remember how it had felt. She couldn't summon any memory of the bone-deep anxiety, though it had lived inside her for weeks. The weight of Paul's head on her shoulder and his arm across her body, the way his hand was tucked between her back and the bed, the scent of his skin . . . they eased the ever-present knot in her chest, loosening its stranglehold on her heart.

She offered me comfort, and I accepted it. Paul's words echoed through her mind. On the surface, he was so lighthearted, with his ready charm and easy way of talking to anyone. But underneath, something in him craved comfort and warmth and the small gestures of affection which, with her, he had worked so hard to rein in.

Paul just needed to be touched.

She cradled his head closer, one hand gripping the back of his neck. With the other, she idly finger-combed his hair, wondering if he'd enjoy it when he was awake. She hoped so, because she found it soothing.

For a few minutes, she wrestled with the decision to wake him up or not. She was happy to stay in bed until he woke up on his own, and possibly longer—but this wasn't the best day to laze away the morning. At least a few of their companions probably knew Paul was up here with her. Owen would have noticed him missing from their room last night. John or Sarah might have figured it out when he didn't turn up for dinner after his shower.

Showing up to breakfast late with silly smiles seemed rude, under the circumstances. And disrespectful. She sighed. "Time to wake up, Paul," she whispered.

He stirred, and his lips curved in a sleepy, contented smile. Without opening his eyes, he settled his head deeper into the hollow of her neck. She kept running her fingers through his hair, but then his eyes snapped open. He pushed himself half-upright, bracing himself with one hand on the bed while he ran the other over his face. "Nina? What . . ."

Free from the weight of his embrace, she propped herself up on her elbows so he wasn't looking down at her. "Forgot already?"

A swift look of embarrassment crossed his face, replacing the confusion. "No. But I—I dreamt about you. And I wasn't sure for a second if I still was."

"Oh. Good dream?"

"Yeah," he said, the word drawn-out and satisfied, like it had to encompass all the wonderful things he had seen in the night.

"So tell me about it," she teased, reaching for him.

"Oh, no, or we'll never get out of bed," he said, untangling his legs from hers and sliding free from the covers. He stood, stretched, and grimaced. "That hurts more than I'd like."

"Poor Paul," Nina said, sitting up. "Just when you were almost healed, you get attacked by a crazy woman again."

"I do seem to have a knack for it," he joked, rolling his shoulders to work out the stiffness.

Nina got out of bed and wrapped her arms around his waist, looking up at him. "Will you at least try to take it easy today?"

"Don't know if I can," he said, returning her embrace. "We've got to go back for the lumber."

"It just needs to be cut, now, right? John and Owen can do that. And I can go too, to hold the light. So you don't have to go."

"We'll see," he said, promising nothing.

She frowned at him, narrowing her eyes.

"Okay, okay!" he capitulated. "If John thinks the three of you can manage, I'll stay here and rest." When she rewarded him with a wide grin, he laughed. "Do you always get your way? Am I just gonna have to get used to doin' what you say?"

"When it comes to taking care of yourself, I plan to be incredibly stubborn and get my way as often as I can. Everything else can be up for discussion."

"And there's lots of discussion left to have, about all sorts of important things," he said. "But not right now. Sarah wants to have Mark's . . . well, his funeral, I guess, before breakfast. Said she didn't want it hanging over everybody's head all day."

"I wondered about that yesterday, when no one came to get me. I didn't want to assume anything." She pulled away from him. "You want to go first? I don't think we want to advertise, today."

"Can't keep it a secret much longer, though. Owen's bound to wonder where I was last night. Or, not to wonder, anyway. He may not have been with us long, but it's no secret how I feel about you."

"I'll talk to him," Nina said. "I need to ask him a favor anyway." Paul's eyes widened, but he didn't ask the question. "What? That bed isn't big enough for both of us."

"Tonight?" He squeezed so much hope into only one word.

Nina nodded. "Yeah, tonight." She meant to say more, but Paul interrupted her with a deep, powerful kiss, drawing her into his arms again. When he released her, she lifted a hand to run her fingers down his cheek, careful of the scratches. "Let's just get through today first, okay? I don't think it's going to be easy."

After Paul left, she found things to do to keep herself occupied while she waited to follow. She picked out a change of clothes for the day. Though the things she wore were reasonably clean and far from wearing out, she had been living in them for two weeks now, so they were rumpled. It seemed wrong to show up to a funeral looking like she'd just rolled out of bed. Even if she had.

One of the sweaters she'd acquired was black, and one of the pairs of jeans a deep, inky blue. It looked like the best she could manage.

After she changed, she combed out her hair carefully. Leaving it loose all the time meant tangles, but at the slow rate it was growing, she didn't have enough length yet to braid back. She had three hair ties in her pack saved for the day she could. She might be able to manage tiny pigtails, but she'd always avoided anything which made her look even younger than she already did.

Neat and tidy and soberly dressed, she went downstairs to find out who else was awake. No one was in the living room or the kitchen, but as she headed for the front door, Owen came out of his room.

Figuring this was as good a chance as she was likely to get, she approached him and said, "'Morning."

"Hi, Nina," he answered, a faintly worried look on his face. "How are you doing?"

"I'm okay. How about you, holding up all right?"

He shook his head. "Not really. Aaron woke me up last night. He had a nightmare and didn't want to bother his dad, so he came looking for Paul." He cleared his throat and looked away. "I let him stay with me, but I didn't know what to tell him."

"Oh, hell," Nina said, only realizing after she did she had borrowed one of Paul's casual curses. "I'm sorry, Owen. We didn't think—I mean, it wasn't planned—and then, we knew you'd figure it out, and you wouldn't worry. But it never occurred to me something like that might happen." She took a deep breath, trying to collect herself. "That's something I wanted to talk to you about, actually. Well, the favor I wanted to ask, to be honest."

Owen nodded. "Switch rooms?"

Nina sighed with relief. "Yeah. Do you mind?"

"No, it's fine," he answered. "I had a feeling that I might need to sooner or later."

"Has everyone just been sitting around watching me make a fool of myself?" Nina asked with a sheepish grin. "Because I feel like there's a conspiracy around here."

"Paul's the one who's been acting like a fool," Owen said. "You make him a little crazy, but he adores you. If I—" He broke off, shaking his head. "Never mind."

"If you what?" Nina prompted.

"I wasn't exactly popular in school," he said. "I didn't date a lot. But if I had ever known anyone felt about me the way Paul does about you, I'd never have let him go."

On impulse, she stretched up to kiss his cheek. He ducked his head and mumbled something she didn't catch before brushing past her to go into the kitchen. She turned to watch, amused when he came right back out, as she had. "Where is everybody?"

"I was about to go check outside."

As Nina expected, Sarah was awake and sitting on the bench under the maple tree. Paul was with her, an arm wrapped companionably around her shoulders. When Nina approached them, Paul gave her a slight smile, but Sarah turned and gave her a huge grin.

Nina stopped a few feet away and planted her hands on her hips. "You told her," she accused Paul.

"Didn't have to," he answered. "Told you she'd know."

"I'm thrilled for you both," Sarah declared.

Paul's eyes went past Nina to Owen. "She tell you?"

"I'm on board," Owen replied. "We'll move our stuff sometime later today."

"Thanks," Paul said with a nod.

Sarah fidgeted. "Is there any sign of Alison? She never came out of her room yesterday."

Nina shook her head. "Owen, maybe you better go get her." Since Alison wasn't going to open her door for Paul or Nina herself. Owen nodded and went inside.

"I'll get John and Aaron," Paul volunteered, standing. As he passed Nina on his way to the door, he paused to kiss her forehead.

Taking Paul's spot on the bench, Nina regarded Sarah carefully. "It really doesn't bother you?"

"That you and Paul are going to be walking around for days with ridiculous smiles on your faces? No, it doesn't."

"I guess . . ." Nina began, glancing at the leaves that had fallen on the grave, bright splashes of red on the dirt. "I guess it seems like bad timing."

"It's terrible timing. The two of you should have gotten together weeks ago."

"I meant—"

"I know what you meant," Sarah cut her off. "But it doesn't bother me because I also know you couldn't help it. Death always makes you turn to the ones you love and hold them a little closer. Besides, Mark was fond of both of you and he would want you to be happy, whether or not he's here."

"Thank you," Nina said. "I've been trying not to feel guilty, and it hasn't been working very well."

Sarah looked back at her husband's grave. "Life's too short now for guilt."

CHAPTER THIRTY-FIVE
DIRT

October 3rd, 8:15 am – 1880 Cambridge Road, Coshocton, OH

Minutes passed without anyone saying a word.

Aaron shifted restlessly on Paul's left. He laid a hand on the boy's shoulder. Aaron responded by throwing his arms around Paul's waist.

On the boy's other side, John opened his mouth to say something to his son, then shut it abruptly. No one wanted to break the deep silence. Paul caught John's eye and nodded, trying to say he didn't mind.

To Paul's right, Nina stood straight-backed and solemn. She clasped her hands before her and didn't look away from the grave.

Beyond her, Owen hung his head, maybe to hide tears. Past him, Sarah had her arm around Alison. Anyone who didn't know better would think Alison was the grieving widow, not Sarah. The two women were near the same age, based on what they'd told Paul, but Alison looked a decade older. Her skin was tinged with gray, and her eyes were red and swollen from weeping. She seemed smaller, frailer, than she had the day before, her spine curved and shoulders hunched.

John cleared his throat. "I guess I'll go first. I can't thank Mark enough for all he did for me. And I didn't thank him enough while I still could. When we first met, it was kindness that made him, Sarah, and Alison take us in for the night. It was trust that grew on the road together, and friendship that kept us headed in the same direction. And in the end, he was just as much family as the people I grew up with. You all are," he said, casting his gaze over everyone. "I hope you know that."

"That was lovely, John," Sarah said. "Thank you. I know I speak for Mark when I say that we both depended on you to keep going, to keep everyone together. He thought highly of you, and he'd be glad to know you did the same."

After a few moments, Owen said, "I didn't know him long." When no one else spoke up, he took a deep breath, lifted his head, and continued. "But I've never been more happy to see anyone than when he came to get me, after I'd gone to the other house. He told me to come back. He told me you all would take me in. I broke down and cried like a little kid." He stopped and glanced at Aaron with half a smile. "No offense, Aaron."

"It's okay," the boy said, letting go of Paul to go hug Owen. "There's nothing bad about crying, unless you do it to get your way."

"That's true," Owen agreed. "After I calmed down, Mark brought me back here. He never mentioned it again. And he never talked down to me. He always treated me like an adult, like an equal."

"After what you've been through," Paul said, "you earned it. But you're right. Mark always dealt fairly with me, too, even when we disagreed. And I respected him for it. Maybe those disagreements stood in the way of me gettin' to know him better, and that I regret. But we're the poorer for havin' lost him."

He glanced around, seeing who might speak next, and caught a glare from Alison. The others might think Paul was referring to the argument about staying at the house, but she knew better—she knew he meant the affair, too. Tension screamed from every rigid angle of her posture, and for a heartbeat, Paul was afraid again. Afraid she'd make a scene, afraid she'd leap over the grave to try and tear him to pieces.

"Mark said something to me that I will never forget," Nina began. The sound of her voice cut through the strained connection stretching between Paul and Alison. By slow degrees, he let his body relax. "It's no secret to anyone who was there when I showed up that I came from a bad situation. No food, no gear, terrified half out of my wits. So I had nightmares for a while. The first time I woke up from one after I joined you, Mark was on watch. Once he'd made sure I wasn't being attacked, he sat with me. I was crying, but I wouldn't let him near me, so he just sat down a few feet away and said, 'Whatever happened, it's over now. You might never manage to forget, but every day, you'll start walking, and every night it will be a little farther behind you." She smiled. "Then he started telling me jokes to get me to laugh."

"Oh, of course he did!" Sarah exclaimed. "That sounds just like him. Did he tell the one about the bear and the bottle of wine? That was his favorite."

"Yeah, the very first one. It's terrible." Nina crossed her arms over her waist, like she was giving herself a hug. "He was disappointed I didn't laugh, but it did make me feel better."

"Get over here," Sarah demanded, letting go of Alison to hold out her arms to Nina, who ducked around Owen to slip into her embrace. Whatever Sarah said to her was too quiet for Paul to hear, but neither of them burst into tears, so he tried not to worry.

Until he noticed the look of open hostility on Alison's face. Apparently she wasn't so wracked by grief she couldn't spare the energy to be furious at Nina. Paul clenched his fists and rose to the balls of his feet, ready to launch himself at her if she tried anything. No matter how sore he might be from his injuries, he was not going to let her hurt Nina the way she'd hurt him.

But Alison took a few steps forward, away from the other two women, until she stood at the edge of the grave. She pulled the knife from her belt, and Paul's nerves tightened another notch. She raised it to her neck and took a small section of her hair in the other hand. With a sharp motion, she cut the hair loose, then dropped it on the grave and walked away without a word.

The gesture shocked Paul with its finality. It seemed melodramatic, especially compared to the quiet, accepting nature of Sarah's grief. As Alison retreated into the house, Sarah let go of Nina to follow her.

John was the first to break the new silence Alison's departure cast over them. "Come on, Aaron, let's get breakfast started."

Aaron joined his father as he headed inside, but not before crouching down to pat the dirt of Mark's grave. "'Bye, Mark. You were always nice to me."

The simple, childish gesture did what nothing else said that morning had done yet. Nina started to cry. Without thinking, Paul closed the distance between them with three long strides and swept her up in his arms.

She pulled herself together after only a few minutes, but they found themselves alone outside when she was done. Paul loosened his hold on her, moving one hand to run through her hair, pushing it back from her face. "I don't know many jokes," he whispered. "But if you ever have nightmares with me around, you can have all the lullabies you want."

"I know." Nina sniffled and smiled. "I heard you sing to Aaron that one night. At least, I'm guessing you only did it once. I never heard any others."

Paul's heart rate doubled, thinking about singing to just her. "And you liked it? You never said."

"What could I have said? I was hardly speaking to you. But yes, I liked it.

It was a really sweet thing to do."

"I'm good at sweet," he said, giving her a brief kiss. "But we should go in, when you're ready. The longer I have you alone, the more I want it to stay that way. I know it's selfish and I feel like hell for it, but all I want right now is to spend the whole day in bed with you. I'd do just about anything to make you feel better."

"As wonderful as that sounds . . ." Nina stopped herself with a sigh. "I was thinking, while I'm gone today, it might be a good time for you to start teaching Aaron to play piano. I don't think Sarah's going to have time to look after him, if she's spending it trying to comfort Alison."

"That was . . . strange," Paul said, having a hard time finding just the right word for what Alison had done.

"It was," Nina agreed. "But this has to be hard for her. The way she acted toward you, I sort of thought Mark was an affair of convenience. But maybe she did love him. And the only people who know why this hurts her so much are the two of us. She can't tell Sarah the truth, so she's got nowhere to turn."

"Hadn't thought of it that way," Paul said. "But she ain't gonna accept any sympathy from us."

"No, she won't. And I never thought I'd feel much for her. But I wouldn't wish that sort of heartache on anyone." She squared her shoulders. "Let's go in. I don't know that this gave everyone the closure Sarah was hoping for, but my stomach's growling. We've still got to eat."

CHAPTER THIRTY-SIX
CANDLES

October 3rd, 7:39 pm – 1880 Cambridge Road, Coshocton, OH

Nina took in the changes Paul had made to his room—their room, now—with parted lips and quickened breathing. "This is why you disappeared after dinner?"

Paul got up from the chair, setting his notebook aside. "Yeah. Do you like it?"

At least a dozen candles burned, perched in proper holders or set on saucers, scattered over every available surface but the bed. They were all shapes and sizes, some brand new, some already half-burnt, the upper edges curling down around the flickering wicks. Most of them were white, but one, on the nightstand, was purple. Nina went over to it and breathed in deeply. "Lavender," she murmured.

"I hope it's okay," Paul said. He'd made no move toward her since she came in. "Didn't have a lot to choose from."

Nina turned to him, noticing how stiffly he stood, the way he rubbed the knuckles of one of his hands with the fingers of the other one. "You're nervous," she blurted out in surprise.

"A little, yeah," he admitted.

After everything they'd been through to get them there, sharing a room and a bed, Nina didn't feel the slightest twinge of nerves. She was beyond it, with Paul, and she'd thought he would be too. "Why?" she asked simply.

"It's been a long time since I've been with anyone who mattered to me so much. Who I loved."

Nina raised one eyebrow at him. "Last night?"

"Was wonderful," he said immediately. "But I'm hopin' tonight is more."

The undercurrents of longing and need in his voice sent a spike of heat through Nina's body.

"And now that you're here," he went on, taking a single step forward, "I'm afraid I'm gonna mess it up somehow. There's still so much we ain't figured out yet."

Nina took a step forward, too. She was still out of arm's reach, but she was close enough to see the candlelight pick out all the gold in his eyes. "Like what?"

"Like, which side of the bed d'you like to sleep on?" he asked, reaching for his usual lighthearted tone, and not finding it. "Because that could be awkward, if we both want the same one."

"Do you think it's going to matter when we spend all night wrapped around each other?" Paul's expression didn't change, and she laughed. "The left side."

Her answer got him to crack a faint smile, but none of the tension left his posture as he took another step toward her. "Good, I've been sleepin' on the right."

"See, that wasn't so hard." Another step brought her close enough to offer him her hands, which he took. "What else?"

"I don't . . ." His voice faltered. "I don't know how you want to be loved," he went on, much softer. "Am I talkin' too much, should I be tearin' your clothes off instead? Or can I be slow and sweet and gentle?"

Nina bit back the joke which sprang to her lips about not ruining their clothes, since they had so few to spare. Her first try at humor hadn't done much to ease his nervousness, so more wouldn't help. "Urgency is good, and I don't mind rough, either, sometimes," she answered. "But it sounds like that's not what you need right now. We've got all night, Paul. Be sweet to me."

He pulled her close and did nothing more than hold her. Nina splayed her hands on his back, careful where she placed them, and felt some of the tension in his muscles drain away. Then he bent his head to whisper in her ear. "Can I undress you? I've been dyin' to see how beautiful you are."

Desire gave his voice a rough edge, which made her heart beat faster. She nodded, her cheek ruffling his hair.

Paul gripped the hem of her sweater and pulled it over her head, dropping it to the floor beside them. Underneath she wore a t-shirt, dark green and two sizes too big. Paul's hands skimmed under it, seeking her skin. When he found more fabric instead, he let out a faint sound of surprise. He peeled off the shirt to reveal a white camisole, so thin it bordered on transparent. "Didn't think I could get a bra undone?" he asked with the ghost of a smile as he stripped that away, too.

"I have no doubt you could, but I don't usually wear one. Since I don't really need to."

Paul opened his mouth, like he was about to say something else, but shut it with a snap and knelt before her. His fingers were nimble getting her jeans unfastened, and his hands firm as he slid them down her hips. "Blue polka dots?" he asked as he revealed her underwear. "That's perfect. That's exactly what I would've pictured you in if I'd thought about it."

Nina smiled down at him. "You didn't think about it?"

"You think I wasn't imaginin' you naked?" he retorted, finally allowing his sense of humor to show through his serious side again.

She laughed as he slid her panties down her legs and coaxed her to step out of them. The laughter turned into a startled gasp as he lifted her by the waist and set her on the edge of the bed. Nina was getting used to all of his casual affections, but she still hadn't adjusted to how easily he could handle her. She let him, trusting him as he spread her legs, settled one over his shoulder, and teased her with a long, slow lick along her inner thigh.

"Paul . . ." she said, and her voice shook on his name, breathy and weak.

"Remember, you gotta keep quiet," he said, looking up at her. "Last night you had your fun takin' control of me. Now I want you to let me do the same. Lie back and let me be sweet to you."

She nodded and let her spine sink into the layers of blankets. They were cool against her skin. The only places she was warm were the ones where Paul touched her. His sweater was soft against her leg, radiating the warmth of his skin. His mouth was gentle against her body, generating an entirely different kind of heat.

But there was no urgency or impatience. Paul took his time learning every bit of her, exploring with slow strokes of his tongue, pressing his lips to tender skin. The air seemed to grow colder as Paul turned up the flame inside her. She lifted one hand for a moment and stared at it, surprised the tips of her fingers weren't glowing—she felt as if she could light the candles by touch.

Her soft gasps and moans became frustrated mewling, though, when the sweet simmer wasn't growing to a full boil. When he heard the change, Paul stopped, laying his cheek against her leg. His voice rumbled through her body when he spoke. "What do you need, sweetheart?"

"More," she gasped. "Please."

"What do you want?"

She raised her head to meet his eyes as he gazed at her over the curves and hollows of her body. "You, inside me," she whispered. "I feel so empty, I need you."

She hoped he would stand up and shed his clothes and join her on the bed. He didn't. Instead, he teased her with his tongue again, drawing another whimper from her. When he slid a finger inside her, it was a complete surprise, and she squealed, her head falling back against the bed.

"Shh, Nina," Paul told her, and she could hear the smile in his voice. "Not what you had in mind?"

"No," she breathed. Not then, at least. She'd had plenty of thoughts about his long, skillful fingers since the night she'd kissed him, then turned him away. And a few even before that.

"Want me to stop?" he said, slowly sliding within her.

"No," she repeated, this time on a moan.

"Good," he said, adding a second finger.

Pressure built behind Nina's eyes and all throughout her veins. She could feel her heartbeat pulsing everywhere in her body. She rocked her hips against Paul's hand.

"Is that what you need, sweetheart?"

Nina meant to say yes, but it came out as a whimper as she trembled with the strain of hovering so close to the edge.

Paul pushed a third finger inside of her, never changing his steady pace. The candle flames swirled in her vision as she tossed her head from side to side, choking back the screams she couldn't let loose. The pleasure rushed through her all at once, her clenching muscles pulling at his hand, so hard she was afraid for a moment she'd crush his fingers.

It wasn't until Paul climbed onto the bed to lay beside her that she realized she had curled up into a ball. It wasn't until he gently brushed the tears from her face that she realized she was crying.

"You all right?" There was a whole world of meaning in his simple question.

"Yeah," she answered, scraping her tear-dampened hair back from her face. "I just—I'm sorry, I didn't expect to cry." She rolled onto her side, turning into his embrace. "It's been a long time since this was something I wanted," she whispered. "And I do want you, Paul. But that was . . . that was really intense. Which explains the tears, I guess. But I'm fine." She sniffled and wiped away the last traces of them from her face. "Promise."

Paul studied her for a moment and seemed about to say something, but lifted his hand to smooth her hair instead. Nina guessed he was having second thoughts about continuing, so she grabbed his other hand and sucked his forefinger into her mouth.

"Holy hell, Nina. You tryin' to make my heart burst?"

She smirked as she switched to the next finger, then the third, holding his gaze the whole time. "Maybe a little," she answered when she was done.

"Well, it's workin'," he replied, standing up and pulling off his sweater and undershirt together in one smooth motion.

Nina watched with an appraising eye. "How's your back feeling?"

"Took pain killers with dinner. Didn't wanna be complainin' tonight." He shed his pants and boxers too and knelt on the bed beside her. "Just don't be too rough with me."

"After all the time I've spent looking after you, you think I'd do something like that?" she asked, leaning forward to kiss him.

His lips still tasted like her. "No," he breathed in between kisses. "Never." He pressed forward, gradually bearing her down onto the bed. His hands drifted constantly up and down her body, caressing her neck, tracing the bones of her hip, gripping her ass to pull her closer against him.

Nina broke away with a giggle. "This might be a challenge," she observed, looking down the length of their bodies as they lay beside each other. "I don't think we fit together very well."

Paul followed her gaze and laughed softly. "So we'll get creative. Missionary's not my favorite anyway."

"What is?" she asked, running her fingers down his neck and over his chest, tracing the unbroken skin between the red lines of his scratches.

"I love it when a woman rides me. Nothing hotter in the world than that, watchin' her move, lookin' in her eyes, bein' able to touch her just about anywhere."

"Makin' her do all the work," Nina teased, mimicking Paul's accent.

He shook his head with a smile. "I'll prove you wrong, if you let me."

"Sounds good to me." She began to climb on top of him, but he lifted her right back off again with firm hands on her waist.

"Hang on a second," he said as he bent double to rummage in his pack, which sat on the floor beside the bed. Nina was patient as she waited, though a large portion of her patience came from admiring the muscles of his back and the curve of his ass, a fine view even with the angry bruise marring his skin. When he straightened, he had a condom in one hand. He tore it open with his teeth with a certain amount of relish, spitting the corner of the wrapper to the side. His enthusiasm made Nina laugh.

Her laughter faded, though, when Paul settled his back against the headboard and pulled her on top of him. She pressed her face into the join of his neck and shoulder to stifle the moan she made as he entered her. He wrapped his arms around her securely, one across her back and one around her bottom, and began to rock her up and down. "See?" he whispered in her ear as she bit her lip against a cry of pleasure. "I'm doin' plenty of the work."

"At least let me help, then," she said, adding little circles of her hips to the rhythm.

Paul groaned. "You were wrong about something else, too. I think we fit together just fine."

"Yeah," she said, stretching up to kiss the underside of his jaw. "Yeah, I think we do."

CHAPTER THIRTY-SEVEN
A BACKPACK

October 7th, 11:01 am – 1880 Cambridge Road, Coshocton, OH

Aaron struck a wrong note and Paul hid a wince. His last teaching session was months behind him, and apparently he'd lost some patience. Or some of his skill in pretending he hadn't.

When Aaron reached the end of the simple melody without another mistake, Paul encouraged him. "Almost got it," he said. "But remember to use your whole hand. You're moving it up the scale to get the high notes with just three fingers, when you could be using your pinkie. Do you want me to show you again?"

"No, I can do it," Aaron answered. "But I think I messed up a note. What's it supposed to be?"

Paul played a few measures for him, an octave lower. Aaron laid his fingers on the right keys, and Paul played them again, with Aaron following along. "I think I got it now."

"Okay, show me."

Aaron made it through the song without missing a note, though the tempo was halting as he tried harder to use all of his fingers. "That was better, right?"

"Sure was. Now play it again, but try to keep the rhythm steady."

Aaron ran through the tune three more times, improving with each rendition. During the last one, a door slammed upstairs. Alison appeared at the top of the staircase, leaning over the banister.

"Can't you teach him something good?" she complained. "Three days of this crap and I'm already going insane."

Paul resisted the urge to snap back at her. Much as he wanted to, he shouldn't in front of Aaron.

Unfortunately, Aaron beat him to it, setting both hands on the keys and pounding out several discordant combinations of notes. "Why are you so mean?" he cried. "Being sad all the time doesn't mean you can be nasty! And Mark said you should let me play. I want to learn, so you should let me play!"

Alison vanished from the stairs without another word, and her door slammed again. Paul let out a sigh. "Aaron, I know you're upset, but you didn't need to do that." The boy opened his mouth to object, but Paul kept going. "No, let me finish. I know, you're gonna say she started it. And she did. But part of growin' up is knowin' that sometimes you gotta act better than those around you. You gotta be stronger, and not give in when they make you angry. I bet it felt good to tell her off, but now she's madder than ever. So do you think what you said made things better?"

"But she's so awful and grumpy now!" Aaron wailed. "Why can she be mean to me if I can't be mean back?"

"You can, if you want," Paul told him. "But think about how bad you're hurtin' inside, missin' Mark. And Alison knew him for years and years before all this. Longer than you've been alive. So try to imagine how much she's hurtin' too. So much that she can't keep it all inside anymore, and what spills out is what makes her nasty."

Aaron's face screwed up into a frown. "But Sarah must miss him even more, and she's not like that. She's just as nice as before."

"Yeah, she is. But Sarah's lettin' her friends help. Me, and Nina, and your dad. You, too. We're all bein' kind to her, and rememberin' that she needs us. We talk to her when she wants us to, and tell her funny stories and give her a little distance from her sadness. When she wants to feel sad, so she can start to heal, we listen to her talk about Mark, or just sit with her and not talk at all. But we're there, and that's what counts."

Aaron's lower lip trembled. "So why can't we do that with Alison? Doesn't she need us, too?"

"We could try," Paul said. "But she's put a lot of effort into pushin' everybody away. We can't help her if she doesn't want us to." Paul tugged on the key cover, and Aaron moved his hands out of the way as Paul lowered it. "I know you want to keep practicin', but if we're botherin' Alison right now, we should take a break. I ain't sayin' it's fair that she's mean, or that you deserve it, 'cause you don't. But it's better to be kind than to keep on doin' whatever you want. You wanna play some cards instead?"

"I don't think so," Aaron said, downcast. "I might go see how they're doing on the outhouse. Dad's really hoping it gets done today."

Paul smiled. "Yeah, I think bein' cooped up in here for two days of solid rain was makin' him a little anxious. Good thing we already set up those rain barrels, though. Let's go see, and after that, maybe we can get Sarah and start lunch. All that hammerin' would make anybody hungry, right?"

As far as Paul could tell, the building project was going smoothly. Aaron dashed ahead of him to get close to the action, but Paul hung back, observing from a distance. Nina chose a new board from an organized layout of different sizes, then held it up to the framework. John crouched at her feet to secure it to the bottom, and Owen stretched upwards to attach it to the top. The little peaked roof was already in place, and the door hung on the front. They were only just starting to put up the walls, but it seemed like good progress for a single morning's work.

Nina saw him and smiled, giving him a tiny wave as soon as she could let go of the board. They hadn't found any smaller work gloves for her, so she borrowed Paul's. They looked ridiculous, the oversized fingers flapping loosely where they extended past her hand. He smiled and waved back.

Aaron gamboled around the construction site like a puppy, asking questions, darting in to examine something up close, ducking back when his father shooed him away. Something he said made Nina laugh, throwing her head back and dropping the board she picked up back to the ground. She stripped off her gloves, handed them to Aaron, and pointed at the board.

Aaron donned the gloves and dutifully strained to pick up the length of wood. He got it off the ground easily enough, but tipping it up to stand straight proved to be a challenge. The end of the board was easily three feet above his head, so he wobbled trying to hold it steady. John and Owen both stepped out of the way as Aaron made his way to the outhouse and slapped the board against the side. Nina had one arm around her waist and the other hand over her mouth, trying to hold in more laughter.

The two men stepped back in to hammer the nails into place. Aaron moved away gingerly, looking up at the outhouse like he was afraid it would fall down on top of him. When it didn't, he returned the gloves to Nina, who squeezed his shoulder. Then she turned back to Paul and beckoned him over.

"You feel up to taking my place for a while?" she asked. "My arms are starting to get tired."

John broke in before Paul could answer. "Nina, you should've said something. We can manage without you, we'll just be a little slower. Go on, take a break." Then he grinned. "I'm sure Paul would rub your shoulders if you ask nicely."

Paul laughed. "I'm sure I would, too." He held out his hand and waited while Nina hesitated to take it. She glared at him, but the effect was spoiled by the smile twitching the corners of her mouth. "Come on."

She grabbed his hand.

Inside, the house was quiet. As soon as the kitchen door closed behind them, they were all over each other, kissing and caressing. "You're going to do a lot more than rub my shoulders, right?" Nina asked as Paul lifted her off her feet. She wrapped her legs around his waist and let him carry her.

"Hell, yes," he answered.

Desire flared between them, sharp and insistent. When Paul could keep his distance, he could keep himself under control. But for the last two days, whenever he touched her, his need became an almost magnetic force, drawing them closer. The downpour which delayed the outhouse project had been an unexpected blessing for them. They hadn't gone so far as to stay in bed the whole time, only appearing for meals, but they had hidden themselves away as much as they could manage.

Every moment of it had been joy and wonder to Paul. There were all the different ways Nina could sigh with pleasure. He had thought of trying to count them, once, but he lost track when she kissed him. Then it didn't seem important anymore.

There was the wide-eyed look of delighted surprise the first time he pulled her hair. He loved to run his hands through it, to hold her head as he kissed her. What she'd said about being rough sometimes came back to him, and he made a fist in her hair, catching hold of a handful. Slowly, he pulled her head back, breaking the kiss and exposing her throat. She stared up at him and gave the tiniest nod of her head. He responded with a hundred kisses up and down her neck and over her breasts, tightening his grip on her hair whenever she squirmed.

So he discovered she liked to surrender control just as much as she liked to wield it. Because that he had already known. She pinned him to the bed once, holding him down with one hand on his throat and the other over his heart as she rode him. He could have easily thrown her off, and he might have, if she had been someone else. But she held his eyes with hers the whole time, and she wasn't choking him or cutting off his blood flow. She wasn't being violent. She was being possessive.

And surrendering to her desires was something he found he liked, more than he ever would have guessed.

Making his way across the living room while carrying and kissing Nina proved to be too much of a challenge. When he banged his knee against the piano bench, he grunted and set her down. She giggled and turned toward their door.

On the other side of it, though, she turned back to him, puzzled. "Did you need to borrow something?"

Paul stepped past her. "No," he answered, staring at the bed. Nina's pack lay open on it, some of the contents spilling out. "I would've asked first. And I wouldn't have left such a mess."

"But then . . ." she trailed off.

"Who did?"

Nina moved forward to start emptying the backpack. "And what did they take?"

Each item got removed and laid on the bed. "It had to be Sarah or Alison," Paul said as she worked. "I was either in this room, or sittin' right out there at the piano with Aaron, all morning. At least until—" He paused to check his watch. "Half an hour ago when we went outside to see how y'all were doin' on the outhouse. But they were both still inside."

"I know Sarah keeps pretty good track of what everyone's got," Nina said, unzipping a pocket and reaching in. "Alison's never seemed to care. So unless she just did this to mess with me—but that's ridiculous, if she bothered, I would think she would have taken something. And Sarah would have asked first, too. I was right outside."

Seeing everything spread out across the bed intrigued Paul, despite the circumstances. He knew a lot of what Nina carried—some of it, he'd traded to her—but there were a lot of unfamiliar items as well. The bottle of aspirin and packet of tissues had both been his once. The lighter was from the gas station, where they'd met. There were the medicines she'd gathered in the drugstore, and the last few remnants of her stash of bandages. She'd used most of them up on the trip here, and since then she'd been taking them from the common stock they'd all gathered from the neighborhood.

There was the sewing kit, which gave Paul a shiver to see. There was the half-full box of zip-top plastic bags, and the yellow legal pad and pens they'd gotten from the accountant's office. There was a spare change of clothes, which she'd added to her pack only the day before, at his insistence. It might not be soon, but they'd be on the move again eventually. Saving a set of clothing would spare them both traveling in tatters.

But the other items were a mix of common sense and surprises. A comb with hair ties wrapped around the handle. A stick of deodorant and a new bar of soap in a plastic bag. A compact travel umbrella, still it its plastic sleeve.

Either she'd never used it because they didn't travel much in the rain, preferring to find shelter, or because she'd found it since they settled at the house.

A silver locket, which she held tightly in her fist for a handful of heartbeats before setting it gently on the bed.

Paul had never seen any jewelry on Nina. He shifted closer to get a better look. He had his hand halfway out to touch it before he reconsidered. "You don't wear it?"

She looked up to meet his gaze. "I wore it every day for almost ten years. I took it off after a few days with Darren because I didn't want it to look like I had anything valuable." She huffed a weak, wry laugh. "That's old-world thinking, though. No one's out to steal money or jewelry. I didn't want to put it back on, though, so I kept it in my pocket. That's how I still have it, even after I had to leave all my stuff behind when I ran."

"May I?" Paul asked, stretching his hand out again. She nodded.

The locket was oval-shaped, embossed with a complicated design of curlicues. The catch was so small he could hardly get it open. On the left side was a picture of a woman with skin a few shades darker than Nina's but the same glossy black hair and bright smile. Facing it on the right was the image of a blond man with a neatly-trimmed beard, a sober expression, and piercing blue eyes. "Your parents," Paul said, handing it back. "I remember you said they were gone before the plague, but I didn't want to pry. Ten years ago? You lost them that young?"

"You were younger when your mother died," she said with a shrug.

"Yeah, but I still had my dad. Did until just a few months ago. And you've never mentioned any brothers or sisters. Were you all alone, then?"

She nodded. "I'll tell you some other time, I don't want to get into it now. I need to figure out what isn't here. This doesn't make any sense."

Paul studied the items on the bed again. "I've got an idea. Do you mind if I rearrange 'em a little?"

"Why?" She sounded curious, not angry.

"So I can lay 'em out in the order I saw 'em. It won't help if what's missing is something I ain't ever seen, but I got a pretty good memory for all the time I spent watchin' you."

"Okay," she said, stepping back.

The aspirin and lighter went to his left, the small pile of clothes to his right. The other objects he recognized went into the middle somewhere, and sometimes he shuffled them to one side or the other to make room for the next one. Before long, though, the same sense of wrongness Nina had expressed came over him. Something was definitely missing, though he couldn't figure out what.

Then Nina gasped. Paul met her eyes and saw cold horror. "The rope," she whispered.

CHAPTER THIRTY-EIGHT
A MAPLE TREE

October 7th, 12:13 pm – 1880 Cambridge Road, Coshocton, OH

Trivial things like doors and walls and furniture didn't matter as Nina sprinted for the front entrance. She heard Paul curse behind her and spared a second to hope she hadn't toppled something directly in his path.

But she kept running.

Sarah couldn't have killed herself. Sarah was upstairs. Sarah was fine. If Nina had only gone up and knocked on her door then she would see Sarah was fine.

But she hadn't. Because Nina knew, with a certainty born of terror, that Sarah was hanging from the tree above her husband's grave. No one could weather the storm of a loved one's passing so well. Sarah barely seemed to grieve at all.

Nina skipped the stairs down from the porch entirely, leaping over them and stumbling as she landed.

If she hadn't taken so long to figure out what was missing, they might have reached Sarah in time, they might have caught her while she was still setting up . . .

When Nina turned the corner into the side yard, she froze. Paul caught up to her a moment later and swung her around, pulling her into his arms. She hid her face against his chest, but she couldn't pretend she hadn't seen, and she couldn't forget.

There was no breeze, so Alison's body hung motionless. A chair taken from the living room lay on its side on the grave. There were deep indentations showing where she'd placed it, and grooves in the dirt from kicking it over. One bright red leaf clung to the deeper, dirtier tones of Alison's hair. Even right after she had washed it, it never looked completely clean.

"We . . . we should get her down," Paul said, his voice unsteady. "Before the others see."

Nina disentangled herself from his arms and went to the trunk of the tree, looking up and studying the branches.

"Need me to get you up there?"

"No, I got it," she said as she shed her boots and socks. The ground was cold against her bare feet, and her hands shook as she reached for lowest branch.

"I can't believe she did it," Paul said. "I knew she was unhappy, but . . ."

The soft, sad tone of his voice struck all the wrong notes in Nina's head. "Don't you dare feel guilty about this, Paul."

Paul looked up at her, near to tears, as she hauled herself up to the next branch, crouching against the trunk. "You don't? Not even a little? After what you said the other day about how we were the only ones who knew what kind of pain she was in?"

"No, I don't," Nina answered, trying to keep her voice from rising to a shout. Though she wanted to shout. But if the others were still around the back, they'd hear her and come investigate. "This was her choice and I won't take any responsibility." Reaching up again, she got her arms around the branch with the rope and pulled herself onto it.

"We could've helped her," Paul insisted. "We at least could've tried."

"She wouldn't have let us." Nina began to inch forward along the branch. "And she didn't deserve it. She was a selfish bitch who went out of her way to hurt us, both of us. All those times she harassed you, and all those awful things she said, needling me all the time. She may have finally stopped a while back, but she never apologized, so I'm not about to forgive her, whatever the reason."

"She stopped because I told her to." Nina's progress halted as she stared down at Paul, who paused and cleared his throat. "No, that's not the whole truth. She stopped because I threatened her."

"What?" Nina dug her fingertips into the bark of the tree as the blood rushed in her ears. She didn't want to fall because of the sudden wave of dizziness gripping her.

"When she and I were out getting supplies together," Paul began, "she came on to me. Real strong, not like the times you saw when I could just brush her off. When she pushed . . . well, she said some nasty things about you, and I snapped. Shouted at her. Told her I loved you, that my first loyalty was to you. And if she hurt you, I'd hurt her back. So . . ." He broke off with a sigh. "So she stopped."

"Paul . . ."

"When Mark died, Alison said, 'He ruins everything.' Me. I ruined everything. And to her, that was true. I wouldn't sleep with her, I convinced Mark to ditch her, I threatened her. And then she blamed me for Mark dying. From that very first night, everything I did was a thorn in her side."

"None of that makes you the bad guy," Nina insisted. "She wanted things she couldn't have. That's her fault, not yours."

"She didn't want to be alone. That's something I understand. I'd think you would, too." Standing beside the grave, he drew himself up straight and looked at her with eyes harder than she'd ever seen. "So yeah, I feel guilty. And while I understand you mean well, you don't get to tell me how to feel."

"Paul—"

He shook his head and cut her off. "Let's just get this done."

When Nina reached the spot where the rope wound around the branch, she took her knife from her belt. Paul stepped onto the grave and wrapped his arms around Alison's legs.

The rope took as long to cut through the second time as it had the first. When the last strands gave way, Paul grunted under the weight. Nina didn't keep to her perch to watch him handle it. She shuffled backwards on the branch and made her way back down on her own.

While she trusted Paul to catch her, just then she doubted he wanted to.

With her feet on the ground again, Nina said, "I'll go inside and get a sheet to cover her. Should we . . . should we tell Sarah first?"

Paul ran a hand over his face. "I don't even know. I'm tempted to tell John first and let him do it. But he already spared me that once. Don't seem right to make him do it again." He squared his shoulders. "Go get the sheet and . . . and check to see if she left a note. If she did, we should see what it says before we tell anyone."

Inside, the house was quiet. Nina glanced at Sarah's closed door as she came up the stairs and hoped it would stay shut. She hoped Sarah didn't look out the window. She hoped Sarah didn't feel the need to visit her husband's grave. They could only tiptoe around her for so long before she'd need to be told.

Nina crept down the hallway and opened the door to Alison's room.

It was spotless. Her bed was made, straight and neat, without a single wrinkle in the covers. Her pack was fastened and sitting beside the dresser. The closet door was closed. The room looked empty in a way almost as eerie as the day they'd reached the house. Even with her pack still there, it was clear no one lived here anymore.

Nina checked the top of the dresser for a note, then the bed, looking under the pillow. There was no desk, which would be the obvious place, so she tried to think of not-so-obvious ones. Then she stopped and almost laughed at herself. If Alison had written a note, she would have wanted it to be found. There was no sense tearing the room apart.

She did pull back the blanket and take the top sheet off the bed, though. There was also no sense in using a clean sheet to bury someone.

Paul was leaning against the wall of the house when she returned, arms crossed. He wasn't staring at the body, which she thought was a good sign. But he said nothing to her as she covered it up, which seemed like a bad one.

"No note," she said. "Do you want me to tell Sarah?"

He nodded sharply, then pushed off the wall and headed around to the back yard. His task of telling John would be far easier than hers, but after what she'd said to Paul, she didn't begrudge him. Her heart folded into itself, trying to disappear inside her chest. She'd never felt smaller or more stupid in her life.

The climb up the stairs seemed longer than it had been a few minutes ago, and her feet heavier. She tried to rehearse what to say, but nothing stuck in her head. Her thoughts fled from the racing emotions cycling through her: white-hot anger, then sickening shame, then oppressive dread.

Sarah's door was still closed, so Nina had the luxury of standing outside of it, thinking through how to handle the situation while she waited to knock. But she couldn't stall for long. Paul was outside telling John and Owen and Aaron.

Paul had told her she was tough. Which was close enough to brave. She did what needed to be done.

She knocked.

"Come in," Sarah called. She sat in bed reading, but she looked over at Nina and smiled. The expression faded almost before it finished forming. "What is it?"

"I have some bad news," Nina told her, sitting on the edge of the bed. "I don't know if there's any way to do this gently, so I'm just going to say it. Alison is dead."

"What?" Sarah cried, bolting up from the bed. "How?"

Nina reached for her hands and sat her back down. "She killed herself. We just found her a few minutes ago."

"Oh, God," Sarah choked out through the weeping that overtook her.

Nina pulled Sarah into a hug. She didn't fight it. Nina held her and let her cry. A faint shadow of the guilt that gutted Paul settled over her shoulders now, faced with Sarah's pain. She may not have cared for Alison, but Sarah had. And for her to lose both the people she knew from before the plague...

Maybe Paul was right. Maybe they could have done more, instead of being wrapped up in each other. Nina wanted to tell Sarah what had happened, about the missing rope and how she had never stopped to consider it might be Alison. But that was the guilt inside her, seeking forgiveness from her because she was the only one left to give it. Sarah didn't need the extra burden of absolving her.

And the forgiveness she really needed was from Paul. She cringed at the memory of what she'd said to him, and shame swept over her again.

The first storm of weeping was slowing down when there was a tap on the door frame. She looked up to see John, his face haggard, standing just inside the threshold. "I'll take over from here," he said, quiet but firm.

Nina withdrew her arms and stood.

Sarah sniffled and looked up at John. "She's gone," she whispered.

"I know," John answered. "I'm sorry."

Fresh tears came, and John took Nina's spot on the bed and folded Sarah in his arms. Nina fled the room, but not before she saw the tender expression on John's face. Though their features could hardly be more different, in that moment, Nina thought he looked an awful lot like Paul.

CHAPTER THIRTY-NINE
SHOVELS

October 7th, 2:23 pm – 1880 Cambridge Road, Coshocton, OH

Paul kept vigil on the bench beneath the maple tree.

Breaking the news to the others was hard, but this was worse, somehow. Waiting to bury her. Knowing what he did, Paul didn't think Alison's grave should be beside Mark's, but he didn't want to be the one to suggest otherwise.

And given how angry Nina was, he didn't know if she would. Paul hoped she'd keep the affair to herself when she spoke to Sarah, but if Sarah questioned why . . . well, it was hard to believe it hadn't been a factor. And Nina might tell her the truth.

The sound of the front door hinge squeaking was faint at this distance, but it let Paul know someone was coming outside. He stood up just as John and Sarah approached. His face was drawn with worry, and hers was red from weeping.

"I'm sorry, Sarah," Paul said. She nodded and moved past him. When she bent to lift up a corner of the sheet, Paul almost snapped at her not to. He and Nina had cut Alison down, but he realized they hadn't taken the rope off her neck. Too busy fighting each other.

After staring at her friend's face for a long time, Sarah let the sheet fall back into place. "I think I'd like to go lay down for a bit," she said in a weak, thready voice. "Should we put her here, next to Mark?"

John went to her side, giving her a brief hug. "Wherever you want," he answered. Over the top of Sarah's bent head, he met Paul's gaze with a level stare.

He knows, Paul thought suddenly. Maybe he always had. And he was telling Paul to keep his mouth shut.

Which meant Nina hadn't told Sarah. As John watched her head back inside, Paul sighed in relief.

There was no sense in putting off what needed to be done, as much as his back still ached. He crossed the side yard and headed around the corner toward the shed. Footsteps behind him meant John was following.

"Maybe Owen should be down here instead of you," John said when Paul handed him one of the shovels. "You sure you're up to this?"

Paul nodded wordlessly and backtracked to the maple tree. He set the point of his shovel to the ground a few feet away from the bare dirt of Mark's grave, put his foot on it, and pushed. Three more times he did it, to mark the other corners. Then he looked at John, who stood a few yards away, watching. "This is gonna take me an awful long time by myself."

He didn't say it sarcastically, and John didn't take it that way. "You should be with Nina right now."

"No, I shouldn't," Paul said, tossing the first spadeful of dirt to the side. "Not when I'm in a temper like this. I need to work it off some first."

John moved to the opposite end of the grave and found the corner to start digging out. "You don't strike me as having much of one. I think the only time I've seen you angry was when you were arguing for us to leave the house."

Paul didn't answer. The scattering of loose dirt became a knee-high pile before John spoke again.

"Did you fight?"

"Yeah," Paul answered. He flicked a glance at the house, but their room didn't have a window on this side—he wouldn't catch sight of her. "I know it'll happen. And I know we can fix it. But right now . . ."

John nodded when he trailed off. "You need a little distance."

Paul let out a hollow laugh. "No, I need to go curl up with my head in her lap and forget all of this is my fault."

"It's not your fault," John said. His voice was quiet, but it carried over the scrape of dirt on metal.

"Then whose is it?" Paul exclaimed suddenly, planting his shovel and spreading his arms in a gesture which took in the whole world. "Because it sure feels like mine. Alison didn't want to stay here, John. She thought I would leave, and she wanted to go with me. I don't think I'd have liked that much, but when I stayed, she didn't go on her own. She'd be alive if I'd gone."

John tossed more dirt on the pile. "You don't know that. You both might be dead by now if you'd left." Then he leaned heavily on his shovel. "And if that's the metric we're using, then her death and Mark's are both my fault. Because we stayed. If we'd all gone together . . . who knows what would have happened, who'd still be alive." He sighed. "It's easy to count the dead, Paul. But it's impossible to count the living."

They worked side by side in silence. When the grave was two feet deep, John climbed out and sat down on the bench for a break. "You're angry with Nina because you fought," he said, like the conversation hadn't stopped. "And you're angry at yourself because you think you made bad choices."

"I have," Paul said. "I should've left. I hate myself for sayin' so, because it would've meant walkin' away from Nina. She wasn't gonna come with me. But it's true. I should've left."

"Do you still want to?" John's question was quiet and sharp, like a knife sliding in between his ribs.

Paul threw another load of dirt to the side. "Yes." He plunged the shovel into the ground again. "But I can't leave her, John. I won't break her heart." More dirt flung at the pile. "Hell, it'd break mine too. It's too late to change that decision. Have to live with it, now."

"I think you were right to stay." John leaned forward, elbows on his knees, hands loose. "But then, I'm the one who was pushing for it. And you're not the only one with regrets."

Something in John's tone made Paul meet his eyes. "You feel guilty? Why?"

"You're right that Mark and Alison might have lived if we'd gone back on the road. You think that's your fault, but like I said, I'm the one who pushed for us to stay. That puts the biggest part of the burden on me. And then . . ." He sighed. "Alison saw me coming out of Sarah's room this morning."

For a heartbeat, Paul cracked a smile. It faded when John didn't smile back. "She was out of options," Paul said as he realized the implications. "Feels crass to say it, but at least she wasn't after Owen. You, though? I never saw her show any interest in you."

"Because it was before you were with us. Before Mark, even, back in the early days together. But I was so focused on keeping Aaron safe and learning how to live in this new world. I turned her down. I didn't want the distraction."

"Smart," Paul offered.

John managed a half-smile at the compliment. "And because of Aaron, if I were ever with a woman, she'd have to be someone who wanted both of us, not just me. Alison never had kids. According to Sarah, she never wanted them, never liked them." He paused and cleared his throat. "Sarah always wished she had them, but she couldn't."

"She's great with Aaron," Paul said. "Nothing to worry about there."

John nodded. "And I think, once I find the right way to tell him, he'll be happy, too. But Alison . . . I don't think she could face being cooped up all winter surrounded by people happier than she was, without anyone for herself." Then he chuckled, and there was a trace of genuine humor in the sound. "At least Aaron doesn't think it was his fault. He told me about the piano incident this morning. But he was only upset about it because he never got to tell her he was sorry."

Paul smiled briefly before setting back to work. John stood and said, "You take a break now, I'll keep going for a bit." They switched places. Paul stretched his long frame out on the bench, wincing at the hard wooden slats against his bruised back. But it felt better than being bent over the shovel.

The sky was cloudless, as blue as Nina's eyes. Paul wanted to go to her and sort everything out, but he was already filthy and didn't want to track it all inside. He waited for the faint squeak of the front door hinge. He waited for Nina to appear with their water bottles. He closed his eyes and waited for the touch of her hand to his face.

There was only the rhythmic sound of John's breathing, providing a steady beat overlaid by the rasp of dirt against the shovel and the patter when it fell onto the pile. Paul abandoned the bench when it started to sound too much like music to him, an odd kind which had lyrics about sorrow and loss spinning through his head. Anything could inspire music, but this wasn't something Paul ever wanted to write.

All afternoon they worked together, with no friendly hands bringing them water, and no friendly voices to speak a few words before they laid Alison's body in the ground.

"You can have the shower first," Paul said when they finished. The sun hung low in the sky, painting everything in oranges and pinks. "Go on and get back to Sarah quick. I think I'll stay out here a while." He slumped on the bench.

John laid a hand on his shoulder. "Thanks. I won't be long, though. And I'll ask Owen to fix dinner while we get cleaned up. I doubt anyone else is up for it."

Paul nodded. "I'll be in soon."

When John was gone, Paul stared for a long time at the fresh mound of dirt, unspoiled by the fallen leaves gathering on Mark's grave. "I'm sorry,

Alison," he whispered. "Sorry things weren't different, so that you didn't think this was the only answer. But Nina was right—I'm done lettin' you hurt me."

He turned away from the cold earth and went inside, seeking food and warmth and comfort.

CHAPTER FORTY
PENS AND PAPER

October 7th, 7:15 pm – 1880 Cambridge Road, Coshocton, OH

The sound of the shower upstairs stopped. Nina huddled on the bed and worried at one of her fingernails with her teeth.

John had been by a few minutes before to tell her dinner was ready, but she didn't want to miss Paul returning. He hadn't come in for new clothes before going to get cleaned up, so he had to get them after. She hadn't left their room all afternoon, waiting for them to be done. Waiting for Paul to come back.

Waiting to apologize, and to find out if she needed to find someplace else to sleep tonight.

She tasted blood. Surprised, she looked down at her hand. She'd managed to tear her nail down past the quick.

The door opened, and she clenched her hand into a fist so Paul wouldn't see.

He came in wearing only a towel. Another night, Nina would have taken advantage of the opportunities it presented. Instead she stared dumbly at him as he gathered fresh clothing and got dressed. "Dinner?" he asked when he was ready.

"Okay." Paul turned for the door, and she remembered what else she had to say. "I'm sorry," she blurted out.

With one hand on the knob, he looked back at her. "I know. I am too. And we'll talk, but food first? I'm awful hungry."

Nina nodded and followed him out.

The meal was strange and tense. Paul propped his head up with one hand while he ate, and John's hunched posture spoke of an equal exhaustion. Sarah picked at her food, only managing to eat half of it. Owen and Aaron sat close together and traded uncomfortable looks. Nina saw, and felt the same. None of them knew what to say.

The scrape of a chair against the floor seemed violent and loud in the silence. Sarah strode out of the kitchen, leaving her half-empty plate behind. John glanced around the table, uncertainty radiating from him like heat. When he met Nina's eyes, she nodded and said, "Go."

Paul gave her an odd look which she couldn't decode. Without a reply handy, she shrugged and rose from her place, taking her dishes to the sink. She set the plug in the bottom and started the water before collecting the unfinished plates John and Sarah had left behind.

In the next few minutes, Aaron and Owen finished their food and handed her their dishes, saying goodnight. She and Paul were the last ones in the room. She took her time washing up, waiting for him to say something.

She felt his presence at her shoulder just before he touched one hand to her back. "I'll help you finish," he said as she took his plate.

They worked side by side in silence. How many times, since they'd met, had they done that? Vivid memories paraded through Nina's mind, but she couldn't count them. There were too many of those moments, because Paul was always there for her when she needed him. Searching the shelves of a convenience store. Setting up the campfire. Washing and drying the dishes, standing so close, but not touching, at the kitchen sink, as they had once before. Paul had been silent, then, too.

Nina had taught him how to be.

But now, she needed to hear his voice. "Say something," she whispered.

She glanced up at him just as he smiled. "I love you."

With her arms in the cold dishwater halfway to her elbows, she burst into tears and laughed at the same time. She couldn't wipe her eyes because her hands were wet and it wouldn't help, and because they were soapy, which would sting. She laughed and cried and clenched her fingers around a plate to keep them still when Paul turned and wrapped her in his arms.

"Shh, sweetheart," he murmured. "Fightin' stinks, but we'll get past it. We already got the apologies out of the way, so the rest can't be that bad, right? So let's get the chores done and go snuggle up and start fixin' things."

One of his hands slid up to pet the back of her neck, and she melted closer to him. "I was afraid—" She broke off with a choked sniffle. "I was afraid I'd have to find somewhere else to sleep tonight."

"No, Nina, no." Paul brushed a soft kiss against her temple. "I always want you with me."

Once she got her stuttering breathing under control, Nina washed the last few dishes. Paul kept one arm around her, giving her enough space to work, but holding on tightly enough she could believe he wasn't willing to let her go. She was tired. Tired of fearing the worst, tired of doubting him. Tired of grieving for the way of life that had vanished, the people she had lost, and the pain of those left behind.

She was tired of standing still, being the same frightened woman she was when she walked out of her office with a man she hardly knew to face a world she didn't recognize. Sometimes the fear was a nightmare beast that hid in the shadows and waited to stalk her dreams. Other times it was another layer to her skin, a living part of her she couldn't seem to shed, and it prevented anyone from touching her.

Even Paul, who was trying so hard.

After she dried her shaking hands, Paul took one of them and led her to their bedroom. He lit a handful of the candles still scattered around the room, then stretched out on the bed and patted the empty space beside him. Curling into him was easy, and despite his stated desire to resolve their fight, he held her without a word spoken. She lay against him, her body still but her mind restless, teasing apart the meaning of her epiphany.

After a while, when he still hadn't said anything, Nina came to another realization—for him, this was fixing things. She'd said she was sorry, and all he needed now was the closeness he hungered for.

"Paul?" she said tentatively.

He shifted until he could see her face. "What is it?"

"I . . . I think I owe you another apology."

His brow furrowed. "For what?"

"For not leaving with you when you asked." Nina swallowed against another wave of tears, thinking about what might be different if she hadn't been so afraid. "I wish I had, but I was too scared."

"Sweetheart, you don't need to apologize for that. You never need to be sorry for bein' honest with me." He lifted one hand to caress her cheek. "But I wish you had, too."

Nina closed her eyes and tilted her head into his touch. "Is it too late?"

His hand fell away, and Nina opened her eyes. Shock was painted on every line of his face. "What?"

"Is it too late for us to go, like you wanted to?" Now that she had managed to broach the subject, the words came tumbling out. "It's still only early October. There's more rain coming, but the snow won't start for at least another month, maybe a month and a half. We could be a long way from here by then. Especially if we take one of the trucks, drive until the gas runs out, or until we hit a roadblock. That would give us a good head start on the bad weather."

"You've been thinkin', if you've already got that much of a plan," Paul said. "I was just gettin' used to you and me sharin' this room, and this nice soft bed. And now you wanna pack up and leave?"

Nina couldn't tell if he was angry, or sad, or sarcastic. But he valued honesty, and so she answered truthfully. "Yes. I don't think I could live here anymore, not after what's happened. Certainly not for the whole winter." She took a deep, steadying breath. "Even if it wasn't really our fault, it still feels wrong to stay."

Paul studied her intently, his eyes never leaving her face. "You sure about this?" She nodded. "Okay, then. We'll do it."

Relief washed over Nina. She sagged against Paul, giddy with the combination of exhaustion and release. "Good," she whispered. "I was worried you'd think we'd missed our chance."

"On foot? Maybe," he replied, pulling her closer. "But your idea about the truck is a good one. They still make me jumpy, but we'll want speed more than stealth for a while." His voice became stern. "But we're not walking out of here in the morning, Nina. We're both gonna be antsy to get moving, but there's plenty we need to get our hands on to be ready."

"Like what? My pack's all in order now, I'd just need food from the kitchen."

Paul paused. "A map, for starters. We can bring a tent, too, at least until we have to give up driving. We can ask John for the small one from the shed. That leaves the big one for the four of them, if they want it when they leave in the spring."

"Right. And better blankets, I guess. Or even real sleeping bags if we can find them."

"That'd be nice." Nina couldn't see it, but she could hear the smile in his voice.

"We're really going to do this," she said, wondering at her lack of fear.

"I'll miss the bed," Paul admitted. "But we've still got it for two more nights, at least. I don't think we could be ready to leave tomorrow, and I want to get an early start."

Exhaustion and the late hour pulled at them, but Nina roused herself enough to fetch her legal pad and pen. They sat close together, talking over what they wanted, making a list and figuring out the best places to look for each item.

The candle closest to the bed winked out. Nina tried to relight it, her fingers fumbling with the lighter, but her sleepy clumsiness wasn't the problem. The wick had burned so low it got extinguished by its own pool of melted wax.

Paul swiped his watch from the nightstand. "Oh, hell. We need to get to sleep now, or we won't be up before noon tomorrow." He replaced the watch, kissed her cheek, and stood up to pull off his sweater.

Nina watched him with a smile.

"Come on, now, you too," he said as he stripped. "Too risky to sleep skin-to-skin on the road, so we're not skipping any chance we have."

"I guess it's a good thing, then," Nina said, pausing to yawn widely, "that neither of us ever found pajamas."

Paul chuckled as Nina laid the notepad aside and started on her own clothing. He blew out all of the candles but one before slipping under the covers. Nina joined him, tucking her head into his chest and her arm around his waist. Between the blankets and the heat of his body, she was instantly, blissfully warm.

"I think we'll have most of the day to ourselves tomorrow," Paul said around a yawn of his own. "Because things are so off-kilter right now. We should be able to find everything before dinner, and we'll leave the tent for last. When we're ready to tell 'em we're leavin'."

"I'll miss them," Nina whispered. "But after making so many bad decisions, this feels right. This feels like a good one."

Paul pulled her closer and nuzzled her hair. "I know exactly what you mean, sweetheart."

CHAPTER FORTY-ONE
A TRUCK

October 9th, 7:05 am – 1880 Cambridge Road, Coshocton, OH

Paul waved out the window for the whole length of the driveway as Nina backed the truck out. He smiled to see John standing with one arm around Aaron and the other around Sarah. Owen stood apart, waving too, but with a sadness plain on his face the others didn't seem to share. Aaron had cried some, the night before, when Paul and Nina had shared their plan with the others. One last round of whiskey left in the bottle, one last night of music and songs in front of the fire.

They'd make a good family, the four of them. Paul knew Owen had been real fond of him, like a big brother, but he'd make a good big brother himself to Aaron. John had always been a father figure as their leader, and Sarah was mother enough for everyone.

Paul and Nina were the ones who didn't fit. Not anymore. Which is why it felt so good to be moving again. He twisted in his seat to keep waving at them as they drove away. He dropped his hand when they were out of sight, missing them already.

Still, turning to Nina, Paul didn't lose his smile. She perched on the edge of the seat so she could reach the pedals, and sat with her spine completely straight so she could see over the steering wheel. Pickup trucks generally weren't designed with petite female drivers in mind.

"So," Nina said, "there's no radio anymore. What do you want to do to keep me entertained on this road trip?"

Paul chuckled. "The pleasure of my company isn't enough?"

"Well, start talking, then. Tell me funny stories about things that happened to you in New York. Or what you were like in school as a kid. Or your family, whatever you like."

"Not sure how many funny stories I can think of right now."

"Okay, then. You could read to me."

Paul glanced down at their packs, both tucked around his feet on the floor of the cab. "You bring any books?" he asked.

"No," she said, smiling and risking a quick glance at him. The road was clear, for now, and she was only going half the speed limit. "But I know you did."

Paul held his tongue for a moment, wondering how she knew.

"You left it out accidentally, I didn't mean to find it. And I didn't want to spoil your surprise. But since you went to the trouble to get it from the library and still haven't given it to me, I figure you brought it along."

"I did," he confirmed. "But readin' on the road makes me queasy."

"Ugh, motion sickness," Nina said sympathetically. "Too bad we didn't think to bring anything for that."

"You get it at all?"

She shook her head. "Lucky that way."

They drove in silence for a mile, maybe two. Nina had studied the map the night before and memorized the easiest route out of town. At least as long as they didn't hit any roadblocks like fallen trees or abandoned cars.

"Really not in the mood to talk, then?" Nina asked.

"Mine's the only voice you're likely to hear for a while," Paul said. "Don't want you to get sick of it too soon."

"That won't happen. And driving makes me sleepy sometimes, if it's too quiet, so really it's your own safety at stake."

"I'll drive if you want."

"I know. But sitting like this for more than a few hours is going to make me sore, so your turns at the wheel are going to be longer than mine. Might as well start with me, in that case."

"Makes sense."

Nina glanced over at him again. When she looked back to the road, she was biting her lower lip. "You could sing."

Paul's heart flipped over in his chest. "I could."

"Not for hours or anything, I wouldn't ask you to strain your voice. But I'd like it if you did for a little while."

They turned onto the highway, and Nina risked more speed. Not as fast as anyone would have driven under normal circumstances, because they'd both seen plenty of places while they traveled on foot where roads had become impassable. They could be in the truck all day, or they could have to abandon it within an hour. The uncertainty should have bothered him. It should have made Nina crazy. But they were both smiling.

"What do you want to hear?"

"Anything. Just sing to me, please."

He started with something from one of the musicals he'd been in back in high school, then switched to songs from the last few years of radio hits. On the third one, Nina began to sing along.

Her voice was thin and thready, all breath and no power. Paul could tell she'd never had a single minute of training. But she followed the tune well enough, only missing the highest notes she didn't have the range to reach.

All the same, Paul felt his heart pounding. Not because her voice was beautiful, but simply because he had never expected to hear her sing.

At the end of the song, Paul faltered and didn't start another one quickly enough. Nina shot him a look which mixed concern and embarrassment. "You don't mind, do you?"

"No!" Paul protested. "Not a bit. I was just surprised."

"I know I don't sound anywhere near as good as you do, but I really like that song."

"It's fine, Nina, I promise. Sing along whenever you want. I don't mind."

"Okay," she said, then glanced over at him with a smirk. "Have you finished that song you've been writing for me yet?"

"You knew that, too?"

She laughed, rich and loud. "You *asked* me to sit with you while you were working on it! And no, I didn't sneak a look, but what else could it have been?" She laughed again, smaller and shorter but still beautiful. "If it's not finished, I won't ask about it again. That's not something I should tease about. But whenever it's ready . . ."

"You'll hear it," Paul finished for her. "Promise."

"I'm holding you to that."

Paul watched her as she focused on the road ahead. The necessary stiffness of her posture aside, she seemed happier and more relaxed than he had ever seen her, even when he had watched her sleep curled up beside him. "This is gonna be good," he said. "The two of us together on the road."

"Yeah, it is." She giggled. "Remember this feeling when we've abandoned the truck and your back aches from carrying the tent along with your pack."

Paul laughed. "So I'll add nightly back rubs to your list of responsibilities."

"Done," she said. "Any excuse to get your shirt off."

"Nina! Is that why you played nurse all that time? Just to get a peek at me?"

"No. Well, not at first," she admitted. "After we got to the house, you could have managed your own bandages, right? But you kept coming to me. So I kept helping." She shrugged. "If you hadn't wanted me to look..."

"Well, I am awful handsome," he joked.

"And you artist types always need to be petted and admired, or you waste away into nothing."

"I'd say I'm insulted by that, but I'm afraid then I won't get any more petting. If that's what you wanna call it."

Nina laughed. "I wouldn't worry too much about that. When is a back rub ever really just a back rub?"

Paul joined in her laughter. As it faded, they settled into a comfortable silence. After ten miles or so, Nina asked for her water bottle, which Paul passed to her. After a dozen more, she asked for another song, which he sang to her.

After forty miles, she pulled over and asked to switch places. Paul settled himself in the driver's seat, adjusted the mirrors to his liking, and pulled back onto the road. "What are you going to do to keep me entertained?" he teased.

"I was thinking," she said in a low voice, "that you probably have more questions. You can't exactly rub my feet this time while you ask, but that means I probably won't be so distracted while I answer."

"You sure? I think I covered all the basics already. That means I'd have to start asking you the personal stuff."

"Well, what do you want to know?"

Paul thought for a moment. "Anything. Everything. Tell me about your parents. Or your first kiss. Or what college was like, since I never went. I'd imagine you have a lot of funny stories from that."

"That's a lot of ground to cover," Nina said.

"That's okay," Paul replied. The trees on either side of the highway flew past in a colorful blur of red and brown and gold. The mile counter on the dashboard ticked steadily higher, and with every new number, his heart grew lighter. "We've got time."

ABOUT THE AUTHOR

Elena Johansen pursued a lot of interests in her life before she decided she really should have been a writer all along.

Now she is one. That whole rock-star thing probably wouldn't have worked out, anyway.

She lives in Michigan with her husband.

Want to know more? Visit her at elenajohansen.com.